Love M

By, Nick

Love Me Whole

Copyright © 2018 by Nicky James

This is a work of fiction. Names, characters, businesses, places, events, and incidents are either the products of the author's imagination or used in a fictitious manner. Any resemblance to actual persons, living or dead, or actual events is purely coincidental.

Cover Artist:

Nicky James

Editing:

Undivided Editing

All rights reserved.

No part of this book may be reproduced or transmitted in any form or by any means without written permission of the author.

Note to Readers

This book contains one short scene of self-harm. Self-harm will also be discussed in various other scenes which may be disturbing for some readers.
Most victims of dissociative identity disorder have undergone significant abuse as children.
Although there is underlying knowledge that one main character has undergone an abusive past, this topic will NEVER be discussed openly or in any detail in this book. This is not the focus of the story. However, the ramifications of how this past abuse has affected the main character could be trigger inducing.

Chapter One

"Tell me why I'm doing this again?"

Harbor View's campus grounds were surprisingly busy in the evening. Small groupings of students came and went from the main entrance, while others gathered around parked cars in the lot or smoked under nearby trees. The odd loner wandered blindly, nose buried in a book or a cellphone. Each carried a shoulder bag or backpack of one variety or another, packed to bursting with all the supplies necessary for their studies.

Observing them individually, I deduced one commonality; ninety percent of them were young—or younger than me.

"I swear there isn't a person my age here. Everyone is in their mid-twenties. What was I thinking?" I asked Evan again.

He was on speakerphone while I sat in my car and decided if my impromptu decision to take night classes was still sane. I really needed to learn to think before acting. School suddenly felt incredibly impulsive.

"Do you want a list? I'd say your excuse to tuck a few extra courses under your belt and worm your way into a better position at work makes sense for the average Joe, but let's be realistic, Vaughn, you can't sit still. I'm personally offended you didn't just spend your free time with me if you needed something to do. There is always a game on that needs watching and a case of beer that needs to be drank. And besides, you're being dramatic, I'm sure there are plenty of oldies like you about. You can't be the only one having a mid-life crisis."

Chuckling, I slid my prescription sunglasses up, fitting them on my head as I examined and counted my eye-wrinkles in the rear-view mirror. My chestnut brown hair was disheveled from a day at work. Finger combing didn't alleviate the issue; it exacerbated it.

"Can I have a midlife crisis at thirty-five? Isn't that reserved for forties or fifties?"

"Hate to break it to you, you are officially midlife, my friend. Average lifespan for us bros is only about seventy, so that makes you smack dab in the middle of a crisis. You know what that means, right?"

Giving up on my hair, I found my regular lenses in my bag and traded them out with my shades before leaning back and continuing to survey the bustling campus. "I need a new car?"

Evan laughed. "No, you need to find a hot young college boy to fuck."

"Not why I'm here." It always had to be about sex with Evan.

"Riiight. Suuure. Aren't you going to be late?"

I dashed a look to my phone. Six-fifty. "I have ten minutes. Gonna let you go. I should probably make my way in and find my class."

"Take me with, I want a play by play. I haven't been to college in over ten years."

I zipped my bag and cut the engine. Taking my phone off speaker, I exited the car and slung my bag over my shoulder. "You never went to college, what are you talking about?"

"Sure I did. I love me a college girl and dated plenty."

"Going to frat parties doesn't constitute going to college."

"Said who?"

"Said me." With one last look around, I headed to the stairs leading up toward the main entrance. "I'll bring you as far as the classroom, then I'm hanging up."

I dodged around a group of five people hovered together listening to some new-age pop and jogged up the stone stairs two at a time.

"Tell me what you see? Are there any girls in cute plaid skirts and white knee socks? Oh, God, say yes."

"It's not a Britney Spears video, idiot. You've never actually stepped foot on campus before, have you?"

Evan chuckled. "Not sober. A man can dream, can't he?"

In the front foyer, I glanced about, directionless. A winding staircase curved around on my left, leading up to the second and third floors, while two separate hallways were laid out in front of me. Everyone seemed to know where they were going except me. Signs on the walls indicated wings but were no help when I didn't remember what lecture hall I was looking for.

"Ev, I gotta let you go. I need two hands. I don't know where I'm going, and my course papers are in my backpack."

"Yeah, yeah. Okay. Call me when you're done or come over."

We said goodbye and I dropped my bag onto a bench to the left of the door. I wedged my phone into my pocket and rooted around for my paperwork. It'd been ages since I'd been in school. Every aspect, from the smell, to the sounds, and routine, brought me back over a decade.

Maybe I am too old for this shit.

Stuffed into the inside pocket of my binder, I found my course information papers and pulled them out. I noted the lecture hall where I needed to be, 206 B, and wedged them back in my bag. Glancing about, I vaguely remembered that rooms starting with a two were located on the second floor, so I took my chances and headed in that direction.

The congestion thinned the closer time ticked to the top of the hour, and I knew if I didn't ask for help soon, I'd be alone, lost, and late for my first night of class.

The next intersection had wall-mounted plaques with number ranges and arrows, and I was grateful to see it was the hall I was looking for.

Halfway down the corridor, double doors stood propped open to room 206 B, and I followed the herd of students as they shuffled inside. With less than five minutes until class began, I scanned the room and found a handful of seats in the upper left corner that were vacant. I climbed the gradient floor alongside the wall and dropped into the second seat from the back next to the aisle.

On a quick observation, I realized I was indeed probably the oldest person present. Not only that, everyone seemed to be somewhat acquainted. Clusters of people milled about, chatting, laughing, and hanging off seats and arm rests. When I caught hints of conversations, they seemed to mainly revolve around parties, alcohol, sex, or "my fucking parents this" or "my fucking parents that". It only added to my steadily growing weariness over my decision.

I pulled my textbook and binder from within my backpack before shoving it under my seat. Lowering the small arm with a writing table, I piled them on top and waited. I was surprised to find only about twenty or thirty students in attendance. When I'd been in college before, lecture halls were filled to capacity, easily accommodating a hundred people or more.

But, it *was* a night class, and it *was* marketing.

Shortly after seven, a man in a dress shirt and slacks, wandered in with a roller briefcase in tow. It would figure the instructor and I shared a generation.

"Good evening, welcome to Marketing 101. I'm Richard Spore. You can call me Richard. I'll be teaching you lot. If everyone can pull out their course outline, we'll go over what this class entails and the expectation on you."

Two guys a few seats over caught my attention as I pulled my outline from my binder.

"Richard's cool, he taught me economics last yea—Oh shit, look who's here."

When the man became twitchy and developed a devious eye for mischief, I followed his line of sight as the pair shared a chuckle. Entering the lecture hall was a man who appeared to be in his mid to late twenties. He glanced about with weariness, barely making eye contact with anyone before nodding to Richard who welcomed him by name.

"Good evening, Oryn."

"That's the crazy fucker from English class I was telling you about."

"Fuck no! You mean Man-E-Faces himself? Schizo-Boy? Space Ranger Bob?"

Flipping my gaze, I peered back to the two men making commentary. They'd sunk lower in their seats and were watching the newcomer with humored countenance, both staring from behind a raised paper. Deducing they were easily early twenties, their juvenile behavior didn't surprise me. But I couldn't ignore them when they started into a Twilight Zone whistling competition.

"Wow, grow the fuck up!" I growled.

They snapped their attention to me, unaware they had an audience, and stifled their follow-up laughter with poorly executed coughs. I glared until they decided to shuffle around in their seats and at least had the decency to look halfway ashamed.

Once I was satisfied they'd quit being a pair of asses, I refocused my attention to the man who'd entered. He was doing his best to find a seat without drawing attention. His eyes remained trained on the ground and he hugged his marketing textbook to his chest in an almost protective manner. The poor man looked like he wanted to disappear.

Our instructor, Richard, didn't waste time pulling the student's attention back to the course outline as he read aloud with a firm, clear voice.

The shy man—who he'd addressed as Oryn—sunk into a seat close to the doors in the front row. He drew the hood of his hoodie up, covering his light brown, almost blond hair.

"—hiding now, but seriously, man, wait for it. It's fucking hilarious."

I snapped my head back to the not-so-quiet pair beside me. They'd decidedly returned their attention to the obviously shy man who'd done everything to go unnoticed, and they were right back to mocking him. As my hackles rose, I slammed my hand down on my textbook to grab their attention. They both jumped, the one smacked the other on the shoulder and they exchanged a look before shuffling around and pretending to pay attention to the teacher.

In under five minutes, I hadn't just fallen back in time to my old college days, I'd tumbled more directly into those dreaded memories of high school, and I was anything but impressed.

"Definitely too old for this shit," I mumbled under my breath.

What had I been thinking?

As Richard gave a brief overview of the course, I took note of the surrounding people. Attentions seemed more focused on each other or cellphones than on what was being said up front. Only a random set of eyes even bothered to follow along.

Richard went on to explain the multitudes of assignments we'd be responsible for, including a full-term project worth forty-percent of our grade.

"I suggest using your time effectively. You will work in pairs for this activity, and it would be wise to find someone whose work ethic is on par with your own. I'm going to hand out a package detailing this particular assignment. Don't think you can do this overnight or leave it until the last minute; it won't work, and you will get a failing grade."

As he continued to explain, he handed stacks of papers to the people in the front row to be distributed.

"In essence, it will be your responsibility to develop a marketing plan using what you'll learn here in class to effectively increase revenue of a business of your choosing. It will require many factors. Determining your audience, your base starting statistics, and proving what you've developed actually works. There will be an oral presentation involved." He slapped a hand to his copy of the booklet which was still circulating. "Read this thoroughly. I'm always available to answer questions. My email is in your course outline. Use it."

A group project—even with one other person—wasn't what I had in mind. I tried not to worry over it as Richard continued with our first lesson. I'd missed the dynamic of school and quickly fell back into the routine of lectures and notetaking as though no time had passed. Before I knew it, Richard shut down his last power point and clapped his hands.

"It's twenty to nine. Ordinarily, I like to run class right to the end, but I want to give you some mingling time today so you can get to know one another and perhaps find a partner for your term project. Please note, you will be given minimal class time to work on this, so consider this a gift."

The eruption of bustle when Richard finished talking was abrupt. A number of well-acquainted people quickly gravitated into pairings, chatting, laughing, and sitting on desks as they visited and packed up. On a brief observation, hardly anyone seemed to be focused on our project and were mostly concerned over other things. It was beginning to look like an impossible task to find someone who was worth collaborating my time.

I shoved my books into my backpack as I scanned the room. There had never been a time in my life when I'd struggled making friends or being social, but for whatever reason, the whole 'find a partner' thing seemed like the biggest challenge of the entire project, especially among a room full of much younger students who made me feel old just by the way they spoke to one another.

From the corner of my eye, I caught Oryn as he slipped quietly from the room. I dashed a glance to the two men who'd felt the need to mock and bully him earlier for whatever reason, but they were preoccupied with a growing group of noisy friends.

Hustling, I zipped my bag and swung it over my shoulder before heading down the sloped aisle and out the doors in the front of the lecture hall. There wasn't a single person who'd caught my eye as a potential partner for our project—except the quiet man who the teacher knew by name for some reason. The same person who was instantly identified by the idiots beside me as being crazy.

I was beyond fed up with bully mentality and had hoped college students had moved past such teenage acts. I'd been wrong. Beyond appearing painfully shy and introverted, I couldn't see any reason why that Oryn man and I couldn't work together for the project.

Except he seemed to be in a hurry to get out of there.

When I made it into the hallway, he was already rounding the corner toward the front stairs. I picked up my pace and followed. It was less busy than earlier, and I only passed two other students before I descended the stairs after Oryn.

He'd made it outside by the time I reached the bottom but had abandoned his escape to rest against the concrete wall just outside the building. One hand dug fingers into his closed eyes while the other hugged the same textbook he'd been holding earlier. His lips moved like he was talking to himself, but as I stood with the door propped open, he didn't speak out loud. Something about his demeanor warned me not to startle him, so when I let go of the door and stepped outside, I waited for it to slam and grab his attention before approaching.

With the loud noise, his head jerked up and eyes widened.

"Hi," I said, standing my ground a few feet from the entrance. "I'm Vaughn. From your marketing class." I indicated over my shoulder from where I'd come.

He peered behind me and back at my face, creases deepening in his forehead. "Hi." He noticeably swallowed and tightened his grip on the book in his arms. "I'm O-Oryn. I p-probably won't be in that marketing class anymore."

He smiled sadly before his gaze darted our surroundings, eventually settling on his sneakers.

"Oh. How come?"

He shuffled before firming his lips and raising his head to answer. "Group p-project. It's... It's not really m-my thing."

I flinched, hating the defeated way he'd delivered that statement. His stutter only confirmed my suspicions over him being shy, but I certainly hoped that wasn't why he felt so defeated.

"And why is that? Because I followed you out here to see if you needed a partner."

Surprise flashed through his blue-grey eyes, and he wet his lips before speaking. "Oh." A sad laugh sang from his chest before he dropped his gaze shyly to the ground again. "That's really k-kind of you, but I m-may not be the best p-partner."

The conversation was almost painful. Oryn's discomfort seeped into me and I shuffled, adjusting my backpack on my shoulder. When compared to my options upstairs, Oryn was looking like a more promising choice. He lacked the cocky side most of the other students possessed, and on a guess, seemed more intent on learning than socializing. Why else would he be there?

"Well, unless you're dropping this class, maybe you'll reconsider. You see, I'm thirty-five years old surrounded by a bunch of guys and girls in their mid-twenties up there. It's almost uncomfortable for me and—"

"I'm only t-twenty-eight," he sputtered.

I cringed and chuckled. "Way to make me feel old."

He smiled and looked everywhere but at me. "S-sorry."

"No worries. I'm messing with you. What I meant to say is, I consider myself to be a pretty good judge of character and there wasn't a single person I thought I clicked with in that crowd. I can tell you're uncomfortable around people. Shy. I respect that—"

"I'm n-not like other p-people."

"Well, good. So long as you aren't like the two asswipes who were sitting beside me, I think we'll be fine."

He sighed and peered toward the street, a frown pulling at his mouth and eyes. "They're in my creative writing class on M-mondays. Did they s-say something?"

"Nothing worth repeating."

There was an awkward pause as Oryn watched the cars leave the parking lot. Classes inside had ended, and students flittered out into the evening. The sun had nearly set, and dusk gave the world a yellowy-orange tinge.

"So," I said after a minute. "What do you say? Or should I scramble to find someone else?"

Oryn pinched the bridge of his nose and closed his eyes. Pressing into one eye with a knuckle, he shook his head as if to rid himself of a thought or perhaps aligning them.

When he opened his eyes again, he glanced to me with uncertainty, worry marring all his features. "What? I'm sorry, I m-missed that."

The confusion he displayed transferred to me. "Umm... Partners? Did you want to give it a shot?"

"Oh, umm... okay. We... w-we should probably talk beforehand... Y-you need to know some things first... about me."

His unease was palpable, and he acted as though he'd given in to a suggestion he wasn't entirely comfortable with.

"Do you want to grab a coffee? I have nothing going on tonight. Maybe we can chat and read over the requirements for this project. You know, toss thoughts around."

"Umm... s-sure."

The pressure he applied to his textbook increased as he crushed it to his chest. He dashed a glance to the front doors of the college just as a group of rowdy men exited behind me. Oryn wilted on the spot. I turned, following his gaze. It was the same two men who'd sat near me upstairs. They'd been joined by another pair of guys and two women.

The instant they noticed us, jackass number one swatted his friend on the shoulder and whispered something I couldn't hear. When the comment filtered through their group, they laughed. It was rude and quite obviously directed at Oryn by the way they stared and snickered.

"Careful with that one, man." His friend smacked me on the shoulder as he passed us by. "He puts the loop in Fruit Loop."

I shoved him as he reached for Oryn, and I sneered.

"Have some respect. What's your fucking problem anyway? Grow up."

They laughed and continued toward the parking lot, unfazed by my comment. Had I really gone back to school to deal with pieces of shit like that?

Irritated, I turned back to Oryn to apologize. With a low-drawn brow, he scowled after the retreating group, eyes darkened with anger.

It was… an out of place and somewhat unexpected expression to see on his face.

The book he'd been intently hugging dangled from a coiled fist at his side, and he'd drawn himself to an impressive height I didn't know he had with squared shoulders and a raised chin. When I'd assumed he was relatively shorter than my six-foot frame, he was in fact equal to me in height when not slumped over.

The contrast in his demeanor was notable and significant.

After the group dispersed in the parking lot, he turned back to me and rubbed at his eyes once before blinking a few times. Then he stared at me with the same hard expression he'd shown the group. Subtly, he scanned the front doors to the college, almost with an edge of disorientation before meeting my eyes again.

"You got something to say, too? Wanna poke your fucking jabs at us? Go on, do it. I dare ya."

When all I could do was blink in confusion, he continued, "Are we done here?"

The soft-spoken side of Oryn, the near stutter and anxiety, were gone. His voice was deeper, raspier, and fringed with aggression.

My brain and mouth couldn't formulate a response in the presence of such a drastic turn of events, so Oryn brushed me off and walked away. His entire disposition and attitude had changed, and I couldn't quite catch up with whatever had happened.

"Oryn?" I grappled for my voice and called after him again, "Oryn?"

He continued walking as though I hadn't spoken. A confident walk, unlike before. I called a few more times, but he didn't respond.

"So much for coffee and a partner," I mumbled.

It was the most bizarre turn of events. Perhaps the group had upset him—understandably—they'd been rude and obnoxious. It was enough to raise my hackles and their jeers weren't even aimed in my direction. I guessed I needed to wait until the following class on Friday to determine if I was still in need of a project partner.

Or if I wanted one... *What just happened?*

I stood alone for a half-dozen minutes as groups of students left and drove off into the evening. Oryn continued on foot toward the main road, and I watched until he was no longer in sight. With nothing else to do, I fixed my glasses on my nose and headed to my car.

Once settled with the engine running, I linked my Bluetooth through the car's stereo system and called Evan. I was just pulling from the parking lot when he answered.

"Beer's cold. Are you coming over?"

"Just for one. I'm not staying all night, I have to work at eight, but I think I need a drink."

"Oh yeah? How was class?"

As I considered how to best answer him, I pulled into traffic. "The class itself seems decent. Probably easy when I consider what we'll be covering, but fuck if I haven't fallen back in time doing this. Since when are college students ignorant assholes?"

Evan chuckled. "Since always. You used to be one, you know?"

"No, I mean, was there always a bully mentality at *this* age? Wasn't that just high school?"

"I don't know, man, I never did college, remember? What happened? Do I need to kick someone's ass for picking on you? Did someone steal your lunch money?"

"You're a dick." I chuckled as I stopped at a red light. "We have to do this group project and there was this quiet guy I thought I'd try and partner up with. A few other guys were making jabs at him and it pissed me off. Anyhow, I approached him after class to see if he wanted to work together and..."

Unsure how to explain the radical change in behavior I'd witnessed, I paused. "Well he was painfully shy and seemed to struggle to accept my offer. Stuttered a little too, it was kind of cute actually. He kept insisting he's not like other people."

"Oooh, maybe he's gay. What did he look like? Did you ask him out? You told him you're gay too, right?"

"Would you shut up." I turned down a side street toward Evan's house. "Anyhow, I thought we were going to grab a coffee—to discuss our project," I emphasized. "When we were interrupted by these assholes who'd been teasing him during class. They said some things and instantly Oryn—that's his name—does a one-eighty on me. Like completely. He turns into that intimidating guy you didn't want to fuck with in school. The shy Oryn I was talking to was completely gone. Then, he totally blew me off. No mention of the coffee we'd planned or anything. Just a serious 'are we finished here' and gone. It was so bizarre."

"So, is he gay?"

I sighed and suppressed an eyeroll. "It's impossible talking to you."

"All right, all right, I'm messing with you. I don't know, man, it just sounds like he got pissed. Sometimes it doesn't take much to set a person off, and if those guys have been at him a lot, maybe he had enough."

"Maybe." It had seemed out of character. Not that I had grounds for comparison. I'd known Oryn for less than ten minutes.

"When is your next class?"

"Friday night."

"So, touch base with him then. Maybe he needed to cool off. Hey, where the fuck are you? I thought you were coming over."

"In your driveway," I said as I pulled in. "I'm hanging up."

Disconnecting the call, I decided I'd probably over analysed a rather simple situation. Evan was probably right. If Oryn was fed up, he could easily have needed to step away.

A niggling thought in the back of my mind didn't agree.

Chapter Two

Exhausted from a long day at work on Friday, I'd brought a coffee with me to class to try and keep me awake. Sipping from my paper to-go cup, I thumbed through our textbook, scanning the chapter headings. I'd arrived early and found a seat up front that evening, closer to where Oryn had sat before. He wasn't there yet, but class didn't start for another ten minutes, so I was hopeful.

With the ambiguity of his behavior and his declaration about dropping the class, I didn't know what to expect. When seven o'clock came and went, students had settled, and Richard had begun the lesson, I resigned to the fact that I would need to find another partner for my project. The thought alone was enough for me to consider dropping the class as well.

The focus that day was on determining your target audience. I followed along with each power point, took notes, read the passages when instructed, and kept a steady watch on the door. A half an hour into the lesson, the lecture room door pushed open a crack and Oryn slid inside.

He smiled apologetically to Richard and dashed his eyes to the front row where I sat. When he caught my eye, he paused his advance, uncertainty painting worry across his brow. It was momentary, and he quickly took a seat three down from mine, sinking low in the chair. After Richard returned to the lesson, Oryn dug through his bag and brought out a pad of paper and pen.

Without staring, I took note of Oryn's character and disposition. He was exactly that hesitant and apprehensive person I'd first met on Wednesday. None of the intimidating, assertive side was present at all, and for a fleeting moment, I wondered if I'd imagined it.

The class continued until eight when Richard issued a ten-minute break. Most students filtered from the room, but when Oryn didn't move, I remained put as well. He read from his textbook, using a highlighter to mark certain passages, completely uncaring—or unaware—that I watched him.

I cleared my throat to grab his attention, and when his blue-grey eyes found mine, I smiled. "So," I said, shuffling around to face him. "I'm not really sure where we sit with the partners thing. We never managed to grab that coffee and talk."

He gaped and scanned the room before settling back on my face. "Oh, I umm… I t-talked to Richard, h-he said I could do the w-work solo, due to personal reasons. I didn't th-think you were serious."

Well that was a kick in the nuts. Did he assume I was setting him up to be a jerk like those other guys? *Probably.*

"Oh. Well, I doubt I'll be given the same privilege." Taking note of the random students hanging around, I knew finding someone else to pair up with would be challenging at that point. "I was serious, for the record. And I'm not an asshole, if that's what you were worried about. I'd like to think I've grown up some since I was in school last."

The creases in his forehead deepened as I spoke, and he pressed a finger to his temple, squinting his eye on the same side. "It-it's not you. I… it's hard to explain. M-most people don't understand me."

He dropped his hand back to his book and stared at me directly, almost seeking understanding. I was lost. How was I supposed to *understand* something I was in the dark about?

"Well, I'm not all that judgy, so what do you say we try that coffee thing after class, you can explain the impossible, I'll listen, and we go from there?"

"You… You are really p-persistent."

"Have you looked around? I'd take the shy kid in the corner who apparently no one understands over any of these other yahoos."

He chuckled and smiled, his cheeks reddening as his gaze fell to his book. Between the nervous stutter and the way he easily embarrassed by a simple compliment, I was beginning to think he was incredibly cute.

"Okay. C-coffee after class," he said as he played with his highlighter.

"Deal."

"But... d-don't get your hopes up."

The second half of class zipped by and ended not a minute before nine. As students scurried from the lecture hall, I shoved my books in my bag.

"Where did you want to go?" I asked as Oryn organized his own belongings.

He looped the strap of his bag over his head and adjusted it on his shoulder before scratching his forehead and screwing up his brow. "Ah, maybe we can j-just go to the campus café d-downstairs. I walk here so everything else is kinda f-far away for me."

With his discomfort edging extreme, I didn't want to offer driving us anywhere, so I nodded and motioned for the door. "Sounds good. After you."

I followed Oryn down an unfamiliar back corridor, keeping a generous few feet between us. It didn't stop him from subtly eyeing me as we headed downstairs. He dug fingernails into the strap of his bag and gnawed his lip the entire way. It was hard not to feel sympathetically uncomfortable in his presence, and I caught myself more than once cracking my knuckles—my own nervous habit leaking through.

The campus food court consisted of a number of various food stalls including a small, intimate café set off in a nook in the corner of the huge room. There were couches and comfortable chairs along with many tables where students could sit quietly and study with their purchases. Oryn headed in that direction.

Since it was late evening, the food court was relatively empty, and the café was deserted. We both ordered a drink and settled at a small table near the far edge of the café which overlooked the rest of the food court. Oryn requested a vanilla latte and I asked for a black, dark roast. It was my second coffee since dinner, and I was asking for a sleepless night at that rate.

Oryn set his bag on the ground by his feet and wrapped his hands around his mug, peeking up at me as I got comfortable as well.

"So, what drew you to take night classes?" I asked, aiming to ease us into conversation. "You said you are taking creative writing as well?"

"Yeah, I am." The soft smile I'd seen only a few times appeared as he stared into his drink. "I am writing a b-book and I thought it might help, you know? The m-marketing was so I could figure out how to sell the book once it's f-finished."

"That's really cool." I shuffled upright and straightened my glasses. "What's it about? Or is it top-secret?"

His smile faltered, but he caught himself and rubbed at his temple briefly as he pinched his eyes closed. "It-It's about me. M-my life. I guess it's a biography."

His statement gave me pause. Average people like me lived uneventful lives. Nothing happened on a day to day basis that was near interesting enough to consider writing in a book. Oryn had me curious, but also tentative about asking questions. His constant nervous state gave me the impression I needed to let him talk and explain things at his own pace. So, I sipped my coffee and relaxed back in my seat.

"You must have a pretty exciting life. If I wrote a biography, it would put people to sleep. They'd need to make an audio version and sell it in the sleep-aid aisle at the drugstore or I'd make no profit." I chuckled and watched closely for a reaction.

My ridiculous comment earned me yet another shy smile. Oryn sipped his drink and then pushed it aside. He studied his hands a moment before meeting my eyes and swallowing with noticeable difficulty.

"I have dissociative identity disorder. S-so, if we are going to be p-partners for this project, you should know that. Just because it's m-me, Oryn, who decided to come take classes, it doesn't mean that while we are working together that it will always be the c-case. Which could inevitably p-put an end to study sessions quite ab-bruptly. Especially considering R-reed isn't too fond of this whole idea."

He blew out a shaky breath and rubbed at his face under his eyes. He snapped up his drink and took a hearty gulp as he peered across the table in anticipation.

I was lost. From the very first sentence, I had no idea what he was talking about.

"I'm sorry. Dissociative what? I don't know what that is."

He wiped a hand over his forehead and shuffled uncomfortably, massaging his temple again. He did that a lot. Always touching his face.

"Oh, umm… d-dissociative identity disorder, it used to be called m-multiple personality disorder. Basically, I have many p-people, I call them alters, living inside me who can r-randomly come forward and kinda t-take over sometimes. I don't always have control."

We shared a mutual pause, both staring at each other in expectation. Oryn clearly waiting for a response, me baffled by what he'd declared. Multiple personality disorder? Did people actually have such things? I'd heard of it, sure, but never stopped to consider what it truly meant, or if I believed it to be a real… disorder.

I wasn't sure what kind of face I was making, but Oryn frowned and dropped his gaze to the table. "You don't believe me."

"No, no that's not it at all. I… I just haven't known anybody with that before, and I… I don't really know anything about it, except a few movies I've seen—"

"P-please don't base your knowledge on the movies. They are ins-sulting and incredibly inaccurate." The slight flair of anger made me swallow a nervous lump from my throat.

"Okay, I won't. Umm…" I didn't know what to say or how to proceed. "Listen, like I said before, I'm not judgy. So, maybe help me understand. Tell me what to expect. I can't see why this needs to be a barrier for us to work together."

"It… It's n-not that simple. I can't j-just explain it over coffee."

"Oh, well, can you at least give me a vague idea?"

He glanced about the food court and settled his gaze back on me, nodding and picking up his drink again.

"What do you know?" he asked.

"Let's go with nothing." Considering all my minimal movie knowledge had just been blown out the window as false information.

"Okay, s-so without getting into any great d-details, basically, due to…" he paused and seemed uncertain. "Trauma… my brain was required to p-protect itself and me. In doing so, it created s-separate identities to handle certain situations, so I didn't have to. For the longest time, I thought I was going c-crazy. I had all these voices inside my head and they were as r-real as this mug." He tapped his fingernails on the ceramic side making them clink.

"I frequently lost chunks of time, would end up p-places and not know how I got there or own things I didn't remember buying. All kinds of crazy sh-shit. After years of being misdiagnosed, I was finally referred to a psychotherapist just over a year ago who officially d-diagnosed me with DID or dissociative identity disorder."

Oryn wrapped his hands around his mug and sipped his latte as he studied the table, deep in thought.

"Some people with DID have dozens of identities and others have only a f-few. It's really personal and d-dependant on situations. I've discovered five so far who have real significance in my everyday life. There are a few more emotional identities that fflit around, but they never come fully forward and are more just presences in the background…here." He motioned to his temple where he often rubbed.

My coffee forgotten, I leaned in, intrigued by what he described. It sounded so contrived and fantastical, I struggled to understand how it could be a real thing. Yet, it was fascinating.

"What does it mean when they come forward?"

He wormed in his seat and gnawed his lip. "In certain circumstances, other identities come to the front and Oryn goes away. S-so, my body becomes them. I… I don't always have control. Well… actually, I have m-minimal control most of the time. Switches for me are often triggered. I get limited warning, if any."

"So, you just become somebody else?"

He smiled sympathetically at the perplexity of my question and nodded. Wrapping my head around what he explained would take time. I could tell he wasn't pulling my leg. At least he seemed to truly believe in what he explained, but imagining gentle, shy Oryn becoming an entirely different person was…

Wait!

I flinched as a thought struck. Wednesday, there had been a notable change in Oryn as we'd stood outside the college talking. It'd been abrupt and confused me.

"Is that what happened on Wednesday?"

Confusion crossed Oryn's face as he thought back. Sighing, he pursed his lips and nodded. "P-probably. I lose chunks of time a lot. We were going to go for coffee on Wednesday. W-we didn't, did we?"

"No. Something strange happened, and you blew me off."

I almost thought for a moment he was going to cry the way his face fell.

"I didn't. It wasn't me." His brow furrowed as he worked to compose himself. "It was probably R-reed. He doesn't like the idea of me taking classes. He's been hovering." Again, he touched his temple.

"Reed?"

Oryn nodded. "He's one of my more p-prominent alters who comes forward."

"Oh." Yeah, cuz that just cleared everything up. They had names?

We shared another awkward moment. I had a million questions, but fought to know how to ask them without shining a spotlight on Oryn; one he was clearly happier avoiding. Every one of them made me sound ignorant, and I didn't want to make him any more uncomfortable than he already was.

"So," I treaded lightly, "is there anything specific I should know since we'll be working together? I mean, we are working together, right?"

Did I even want to work with him anymore? The idea of being suddenly sprung upon by random people was a little unnerving.

He chuckled. "If you can handle me, I'd like that." He shifted and let out a deep breath. "So, I guess if anyone else comes out, just r-remember, it's not me. They are their own person, and I won't necessarily remember what takes place if you are working with an alter. I'm who w-wants to be in school, and they all have their own lives, so d-don't be shocked if study sessions end abruptly. I haven't identified all my triggers, so it can happen r-really randomly. Just… treat them as individuals, because they are. They have their own names and will probably correct you if you call them Oryn."

The question on the tip of my tongue felt incredibly stupid, and I worked at keeping a straight face as I asked, because I didn't want to insult him. The mocking words of those other men in class came back to me, and I was beginning to wonder if they weren't right. It was all too surreal and impossible to imagine. But I tried to keep an open mind.

"Who… Who might I meet?"

"Well, I think you've met Reed, briefly. He's younger than me—t-twenty-three—and very protective. In his world, he's a competitive weightlifter. You might meet Cohen, he's nineteen, he's okay with this school thing, except I think only because it's s-social and he's really outgoing and likes to meet new people. Then there is Theo and Cove." He shrugged. "I'm not sure you'll meet them. Theo's role is more s-structured, and he helps with organizing and keeping our balance and roles. So far as I know, he is rarely out from t-triggers. And then Cove…" Oryn's gaze fell to the table and his lips curled in a subtle way I almost missed. "Cove is Cove. I don't want to explain him." He scratched the back of his head and struggled to meet my eyes again. "There is also Rain. Don't be startled if you meet him. He's f-five. Very chatty and excitable."

"Five?" I didn't intend to sound so shocked, but was he saying I could suddenly find myself working on a college project with a kid? He became a kid? It was too much. The questions I'd been slowly accumulating as he spoke, washed away at that revelation.

He frowned and sunk lower in his seat at my response, and I instantly felt bad.

"Sorry, I'm just trying to wrap my head around this."

"It s-sounds contrived and outlandish, doesn't it? People often react that way or d-don't believe it. I'm just giving you a fair warning of what it might be like working on a p-project with me. We don't have to. You can go find a more *n-normal* partner if you prefer. I won't be offended."

I didn't like the way he said normal. As baffled and skeptical as it was, I'd told him I wouldn't judge, so I tried to shrug it off. "I'm willing to give it a go if you are."

He couldn't hide his surprise. "Oh. Th-that's great. W-when did you want to start? I read a good chunk of our textbook already, so I have an idea of m-most of the material we will be covering."

He'd read the textbook!? I'd barely done more than thumb through a few pages and skimmed the assigned passages. At least he wasn't a slacker.

"Well, I work through the week until four, but otherwise I'm wide open. How about you?"

"I have creative writing on M-monday nights. Weekends are good, but maybe not this weekend," he amended quickly. "Tuesdays aren't good, how about Wednesday before class starts?"

"I can do that. We can meet up after I work and get a couple hours in before we have to go."

Oryn nodded and his shy smile returned along with a faint blush. "P-perfect."

The logical next question was where to study, and knowing Oryn's discomfort level, I wasn't sure the best course of action.

"Any suggestions where we can meet? I live alone, and you're free to come over, but I'm easy if that isn't good for you. We can go to the library or yours, whichever is best."

Oryn turned his gaze inward as he considered. Before answering, he dug a knuckle in his eye and shook his head. "Sorry, umm… maybe you could come to my place. It-It's probably better. I live on Birch St. The t-townhouses, you know them?"

"Yeah, I do. They're at the end of the loop, right?"

He nodded and pulled a sheet of paper and pen from inside his bag. On it, he wrote his address and phone number before sliding it across the table. "Here, w-what time do you think you'll be there?"

I accepted the paper and scanned it, waving for him to let me borrow his pen. Tearing a small piece off the corner, I then added my phone number. "I'll make a quick pitstop at home and grab a quick shower and a bite to eat. I can be there by about five, maybe sooner. Does that work?"

"Yeah."

The tension he'd carried loosened and his smile grew. I wondered how many people Oryn dealt with regularly who didn't try to understand him. Did the poor guy have many friends? Watching contentment bloom throughout his entire body made me feel good about my decision. I wasn't any less confused, but I planned to go home and do some self-teaching so I could be a little more informed.

Chapter Three

"**O**h, for fuck's sake, you ass." Evan yelled at the TV through a mouthful of potato chips. "They never should have drafted him. Biggest. Mistake. Ever." He turned his gaze to me and frowned. "Hey, you're missing the game. What the hell are you doing?"

It was Sunday, and since football season had officially started, I was a dedicated lump on Evan's couch every weekend until February. Except, that afternoon, I was more involved in my search results than the interception that had just pissed Evan off.

"Looking shit up..." I glanced to the TV to catch the replay before it flipped to a commercial. "I can't believe what I'm reading here. This is unreal."

"Are you doing school work on a Sunday? You don't have class until Wednesday, there has to be another time you can do this."

I grabbed my beer off the coffee table and adjusted the laptop on my knee. "No, I'm looking up the disorder Oryn has."

"Multiple personality, right?"

"They don't call it that anymore."

"Whatever, careful with him, man, he'll turn into an axe-wielding maniac and kill you in your sleep. I've seen the movies. He's probably got a serial killer inside him just waiting to strike."

"You're a fucking idiot. It's not like that. These people are victims."

The game came back on, and I lost half of Evan's attention to the TV. Ordinarily, I loved our Sunday game days, but the article I'd found had sucked me in.

"Just listen to this. It says most people afflicted with DID suffered extreme long-term abuse as children. Like physical, or sexual, or you name it, all of the above. Apparently, the brain goes into survival mode, and as a natural defensive mechanism, it creates identities who can better handle the abuse so the child suffering can go on living as normally as possible. Those identities will often not allow the host person to know about the abuse and will protect them by keeping those memories hidden."

"Mmhm." Evan was zoned into his game, no longer listening. Checking the score, and noting nothing had changed, I continued reading.

Oryn had mentioned some trauma. Reading the article, I concluded that was a vast understatement. However, perhaps Oryn didn't know the extent of his own past, only that it had happened. Based on the article, people with DID underwent extreme therapy which sometimes focused on drawing out those memories from alters.

It made me shiver to imagine having something so horrific happen to you but having no memory of it.

I followed one link after another as I tried to understand some of what Oryn had explained. By half-time, I was so engrossed in my research, I didn't notice Evan watching me until he cleared his throat, drawing my attention.

"What's the score?" he asked, brushing his dark brown hair back off his face.

The instant my head flipped to the TV, he turned it off.

"I'm sorry, I just got caught up in this. What is it?"

"You'll never know." Evan got up and grabbed our empties from the table. "You want me to order pizza?"

"Yeah, sure. Are you seriously not going to tell me?" I called after him as he headed into the kitchen.

Evan lived on the second floor of a shared house in the west end of our small town in southern Ontario. It was the equivalent to my single bedroom apartment, except more spacious. A majority of the kitchen was visible from a large window-like opening.

Evan grinned over the door of the fridge as he pulled out two more beers. "You tell me why learning about this project guy is more important than our football date and I'll tell you the score."

Laughing, I closed the laptop, placed it on the coffee table, and kicked my feet up. "If this is a date, I expect sex at the end of the night. Just sayin'."

Evan snorted laughter and flexed his disgustingly perfect muscles in show before popping the caps on our beers. "You wish. Seriously, what's the deal?"

"I don't know. I'm curious. Aren't you? Have someone tell you they have five distinct people living inside them who might randomly appear while your working on a project and tell me you wouldn't have questions."

Evan returned with our beers and handed me one. "It sounds like he wants attention. Are you sure he's for real?"

I threw back my head and took a swig. "Do you remember me telling you how he suddenly changed that first day we met? I've seen it, Evan. And with everything I'm reading, I believe him. Fuck, man, can you even imagine?"

Evan laughed. "No." He drank from his own bottle and pulled out his phone. "Usual?"

"Yeah."

Evan called in our order while I considered all I'd learned. According to my research, the identities who Oryn had referred to as alters, were as individual as the various people you'd meet in your daily life. They could have different voices, mannerisms, temperament, vocabulary, and even skills. Child identities, like the one he'd called Rain, were quite common. Some people had multiple child identities. Oryn only spoke of one. That in itself was one of the more unusual parts to comprehend.

"You should have taken psychology. Look at you all deep in thought."

I snapped my attention back to Evan who'd ended his call. "It's fascinating."

"Clearly. Twenty-eight to seventeen, if you care."

"Who's winning?"

Evan's gaze darkened with his frown as he narrowed his sharp brown eyes. "We are no longer friends if you don't even know that much."

I grinned and considered a moment. "Well, based on all your cursing over the last hour, I'm guessing Detroit is losing."

"They'll pull through."

He clicked on the TV again and leaned back on the couch, nursing his beer. He was devastatingly handsome, and he knew it.

The announcers were giving a detailed breakdown of the first half of the game and I listened intently, trying to catch up.

"Is he cute?" Evan asked after a minute.

"Who? Troy Aikman? Seriously? No." I shot him a dirty look.

Evan burst out laughing, choked and sputtered on his beer as he tried not to drown. "Yeah, that's who I meant, idiot. No, not Troy Aikman, Mr. Multi-Personality. The guy who has stolen my best friend on football Sunday and turned him into a psychology nut."

"Oryn?"

"You know more than one head-case?"

"Can you stop calling him that?"

Evan just stared expectantly with a raised brow.

"I don't know. Why? I never looked at him that way."

"Lies." Evan shooed a hand in my direction. "I'm single, and I look at every woman I meet *that way*, don't tell me you don't do the same."

"I'm not you. I don't, now shut up and let me catch up."

Once half-time ended and the game resumed, our pizza had arrived. We ate our fill and became absorbed in the second half. Detroit wasn't picking up their feet, and Evan ranted and cursed every play. Miami was killing them, which made me secretly happy. By midway through the fourth quarter, with no hope of a win in sight, my thoughts returned to Oryn and what I'd learned.

"What the hell do I do if he reverts to a five-year-old kid? I don't know anything about kids."

Evan blanched and passed me a blank look, not following my train of thought.

"Oryn," I clarified.

"Oh, good grief, watch the game."

"Detroit lost, get over it."

Evan's jaw fell, and he scowled from behind his beer. "You keep up with that negative talk and you'll need to leave. They have three minutes."

"And they are down by twenty-five points. In what universe are they coming back?"

Because Evan was Evan, he shushed me and continued watching with the most disgusted look, as though he could somehow force a win by simply showing revulsion toward their play choices. His easygoing, lighthearted sense of humor was one of the many things I liked about Evan. Most people took his edge too seriously, but we'd been friends since high school and I knew better. Evan rarely had a serious bone in his body. Except if I was in dire need of an ear or support, in which case, he'd be there for me in a heartbeat.

✳✳✳

After work on Wednesday, I zipped home and showered before heading to Oryn's house. As I fixed myself a quick sandwich to fill the void, I shot him a quick text to ensure we were still on since I hadn't talked to him since Friday.

Hey, it's Vaughn, we still good to go? I'm just grabbing some food and planning to head over.

I slid my phone aside as I added mustard and mayo to my turkey sandwich. After re-placing the items in the fridge, I leaned on the counter and ate. His response came as I shoved my last bite in my mouth. I washed my hands and snapped up my phone.

Yup, still on.

Short and no more than I expected from Oryn. Despite learning all I had about him, I'd been looking forward to working on our project together. There were things that made me nervous, but I wasn't the kind of person who shut someone out because they were different.

Since I was already dragging-my-feet tired and had many more hours left of my day, I planned to stop for a coffee on my way to Oryn's.

Grabbing a coffee. You want one?

That time his response was more immediate.

Sure. Decaf please. Milk and two sugars.

Before flying out the door, I checked myself in the mirror one last time, finger combing my damp hair in order and assessing the sleepy state of my pale brown eyes.

After a quick stop at the drive-thru coffee shop, I made my way to Oryn's. I knew of his neighborhood but needed to reference the paper he'd given me to ensure I went to the correct block of townhouses since there were two separate blocks of housing at the end of his road.

With a coffee tray balanced in one hand and workbooks in the other, I struggled to knock on his door. As I waited, I glanced around the street. It was a quiet enough dead-end area with large maple and birch trees on many lawns. It gave a peacefulness and serenity to the afternoon. Surprisingly, there weren't any people about, despite the balmy September evening. The little paradise at the end of his road sure beat the hell out of the busy corner where I lived.

After a few minutes, the door opened and Oryn peered out from the dimly lit interior. He wore a white, long-sleeved shirt and faded jeans. He threaded fingers through his almost blond hair and smiled shyly before dropping his gaze.

"Hi. C-come on in."

He stepped back but immediately noticed my loaded arms and jumped forward again without warning just as I entered. We nearly collided and I laughed, ducking back a step and swinging the coffees to the side so they didn't become crushed between us.

"Woah. That was close."

"I'm s-sorry... I should have offered to take something. I didn't—"

"No worries, here, if you don't mind." I passed him the tray and gave him a reassuring smile.

"This way." He went down the hallway then turned and passed through an arch which led into a small den. There was a big bay window which let in the sun, casting a glow across the floor and lighting up the room.

He placed the drinks on a side table and motioned to the room. "This okay?"

"Yeah." I scanned the space and settled on a cushioned chair which sat at an angle to a matching beige couch. Everything was clean and in order. Multiple bookshelves lined the walls. A desk sat in the corner with shelving above it, holding more texts and stationary. The colors were warm and earthy, a combination of browns, beiges, and deep burgundies. Almost every open space was filled with reading material of one type or another.

"Do you like to read?"

Oryn rounded the couch with his own workbooks and sat down, following my gaze. "I do."

With a warm smile, I got up and went to a nearby shelf to see what he had. "Anything in particular?"

"A-a little of everything really. I love h-history mostly and gravitate to historical fiction. But I also like to read about psychology. Especially since being p-properly diagnosed. The mind is pretty incredible."

"It is." I dashed a look over my shoulder. Oryn had stood and was hugging himself, watching as I went through his books. I wanted to tell him I'd been looking stuff up to better understand his condition, but I didn't know if that was weird or invasive, so I kept my mouth shut. "Do you mind if I look?" I nodded to the shelf.

He shook his head, and when he couldn't hold my gaze, he went for his coffee, removing it from the tray.

He owned a lot of books. Ken Follett, Diana Gabaldon, Philippa Gregory, and more. I wandered to a new bookshelf and picked through a few select psychology textbooks. One specific to Oryn's disorder caught my eye and I wanted to pull it out and leaf through it, but I refrained. Perhaps another day when we were more comfortable.

Just as I was about to return to the couch, an assortment of color on a lower shelf caught my eye, and I stepped back to see what I was looking at. It was a full shelf of Lego-made airplanes and cars, all on display with little men standing around each vehicle or positioned inside. Struck dumb, all I could do was stare in puzzlement at something that seemed so out of place in a grown man's home.

"T-They're Rain's. He's a Lego f-fanatic."

Breaking my gaze from the toys, I shifted around to meet Oryn's troubled face and scrambled for something appropriate to say.

"That... that's really cool. I loved Lego at his age too."

It felt incredibly weird talking like that, like I was referring to some imaginary friend who didn't exist. Except, there was Lego on his shelf and documented cases in highly renowned psychology textbooks that told me it did.

The corner of Oryn's mouth turned into a smile and he touched his temple, closing the eye on the one side. "He umm..." Oryn laughed lightly and shook his head as his face lit up more and more. "Sorry. He's chatting excitedly right now. It's... It's distracting."

Oryn radiated a joy I hadn't seen as he stared at the Legos. He continued to touch his face, moving his fingers over his eye on the same side then back to his temple.

He heard Rain inside his head? I'd read that could happen. As I watched Oryn in awe, I wanted desperately to ask questions.

Rain's presence had noticeably relaxed him. Was this like a switch? Or was Rain just *close by?*

When Oryn turned back, his smile remained but his cheeks heated and glowed pink. "We should probably do some work."

"Sure." I jumped on the distraction and shot my gaze to the little nook in the living room where the couch and chair flanked a square coffee table.

We settled in with our project package laid out in front of us and a blank pad of paper to take notes. Oryn flipped to the first page of the booklet and I saw he'd already highlighted what he found important.

"So, we n-need to pick a business first and foremost. We can't really do anything until we know our focal point. Any thoughts?"

With his focus directed entirely on work, Oryn relaxed significantly. His nervous stutter lessened and the stiffness he carried in his shoulders eased.

"Nothing in particular. You?"

Oryn shook his head and tapped his pen on the notepad. "What is it you do for a living? Could we use your work?"

"I work for Oliver Star Hotels as their accountant and bookkeeper."

"Well that's p-perfect, isn't it? We would have needed to make up a business plan to show places and seek their approval first to get numbers so we could show growth or loss, but now we don't. That makes it s-simpler since you'd be the go to guy, wouldn't you?"

Ideally, using Oliver Star was what I'd had in mind when I'd first heard about our project. It required getting permission from the owner, my boss, but I didn't see that as being a problem. Plus, it pushed me in the right direction. I was hoping to eventually move positions internally to something a little livelier.

"What about you? Where do you work? Shouldn't we consider all options?"

Oryn's gaze fell to the notepad where he doodled a star in the corner. "I don't work. I live off a government disability program. M-maintaining a job is difficult because of my DID."

I hadn't thought of that. "Oh, okay then. Are you good with using my employment? I'll need to clear it with the main man, but I can't see it being a problem. Free labor to potentially increase revenue. He won't say no. It's not like our profit margin isn't already known to me."

Oryn nodded and began to write Oliver Star at the top of the page. "I think it's a smart move, and who knows, maybe it will benefit you."

I remained quiet as he made subheadings based on our outline. He had an extremely tidy penmanship and was meticulous about keeping it organized on the notepad.

"Is that why you are considering writing a book? To make a career of sorts? From home?"

He underlined another heading before putting the pen down and shuffling from his spot on the couch to kneel on the ground in front of the table.

"Kind of. I've always wanted to write. My therapist says exploring a biography could help if…" He trailed off and brushed his hair off his forehead as he considered. "Well, I guess if I can collaborate with everyone, my alters, it could help us harmonize more and might facilitate some of the things he's working toward during our sessions."

Oryn ducked his head but didn't elaborate, and because of the nature of those sessions and what I'd learned had probably happened to him as a kid, I didn't ask. We moved back into work mode, and together drew up a business plan for me to bring into work the following day to present to my boss.

Time sailed by, and before we knew it, it was half past six and time for us to pack up so we could head to class.

"How do you get to school?" I asked. There had been no car in his driveway, and the other day, I'd seen him leave campus on foot.

"I walk."

"Did you want to catch a ride with me? I can drop you off after class too if you'd like. It's quite the trek from here, and I don't mind."

"Umm..." Oryn shoved his textbook and papers into his bag as he thought. It wasn't a hard question, but he seemed to struggle with an answer. "S-sure." And instantly, his stutter was back. The entire time we'd worked, it'd been barely present, and he'd been significantly more comfortable.

I smiled reassuringly as we stood to go. He slung his shoulder bag over his arm and I followed him out of the house.

My home I kept tidy, along with my desk at work, but my car was a different matter. Before Oryn could get in, I needed to clear a mess of papers, takeout containers, sweaters, and random other things that had ended up piled into the front seat over time.

"I swear I'm not a slob, it's just my car. It's the one place I allow myself the freedom to make a mess."

Oryn rocked on his feet and smiled. "It's okay."

Once everything was tossed into the backseat, we both got in. The drive was silent. Oryn stared out the window with his bag between his legs on the floor and hands folded in his lap. I eyed him numerous times, watching the concentrated look on his face. I'd never known anyone so painfully shy.

"Do I make you uncomfortable?" The moment the question left my lips, I regretted being so blunt.

He shifted from staring out the window and shook his head. "No. Not at all. Do... do I make *you* uncomfortable?"

"No." I flinched and screwed up my brow. "Why would you say that?"

He shrugged and watched out the window again. "M-most people don't want anything to do with me. I've always been different, but didn't have an explanation for it until not that long ago. S-so it makes people... well, they aren't always very nice."

"I'm not like that."

He turned back and studied my face as I drove. I pretended not to notice. "I can tell." Eventually, he shifted back to the scenery, and silence returned.

At the college, I found a parking space and we both made our way toward the building. A group of students, gathered around a bench under a tree, drew Oryn's attention and he watched them as we walked past. They chatted and laughed.

"Did… Did you have many friends in school?" he asked as we climbed the stairs to the front door.

"I did. Not a lot of close friends, but I blended into almost every setting and got along with everyone. I think I bent over backward to fit in though."

Oryn pulled his phone out and checked the time. "We're early. Do you want to sit out here a bit?" He motioned to a bench near the door.

"Sure."

We sat together and Oryn leaned back, biting at his lip. "What do you mean you went out of your way to fit in?"

I chuckled and turned to face him, folding a leg under my ass. "Well. I'm gay, and I feared telling anyone would instantly make me a target, so I didn't. Apart from my family and my best friend, Evan, no one knew until I went to college. I didn't want to be labeled different or be teased, which is what I assumed would happen. So, I went out of my way to be friends with everyone."

Oryn's eyes widened at my statement, and he stared at me a moment before ducking his head to his lap. The tips of his ears reddened slightly which made me smile. It was too easy to bring on that blush. Perhaps bluntly announcing my sexuality was too shocking for him. I didn't hide anymore and didn't think twice when telling people either.

"It sucks when people don't understand you. I've… I've never really had any friends."

The notion was heartbreaking. I couldn't imagine going through life without having someone to lean on or share secrets with. Oryn seemed like a decent person, although I didn't know the half of what it meant to live with such a peculiar disorder, it saddened me to think he'd gone his entire life friendless.

"Well, do you have plans for Friday night after class? I say we do something. Whatever you want?"

His head snapped up, confusion written all over his features. "W-what do you mean?"

"I mean, you and I hang out. Not because of a project, but because I have zero issue with you and think you are a decent guy, and I'd love to get to know you better. Are you free Friday?"

He nodded, his jaw slightly unhinged with disbelief. His utter bafflement was cute and made me smile. His blue-grey irises shone in the fading daylight, and for the first time, their innocence and sincerity caught my eye in a different way. There was a fragility to Oryn. A mistrust he carried everywhere. But as he returned my smile, I also saw hope and warmth radiate from his core. He *was* attractive—damn Evan—but I hadn't allowed myself to notice until then.

"W-what did you want to do?" he asked, sitting straighter and fidgeting with his hands in his lap.

"We can go out, or stay in. I'm easy."

"M-maybe a movie… at home… or something."

I wasn't surprised by his suggestion. If he'd suggested anything social, I'd have been shocked. "Perfect. Your place again?"

He nodded, as I assumed he would.

Following an awkward pause, we decided to head to class.

Chapter Four

Friday was a clusterfuck. We'd had an emergency at work that had taken me out of the office for over two hours, and by the time I'd caught up and was able to leave, it was after six. Class started at seven and I needed to eat, shower, and get out of the house in less than a half an hour.

Drying off from my shower, I shuffled through the clothing hanging in my closet as I decided what to wear. I was never so picky, but for whatever reason, going to Oryn's after class had me indecisive. Refusing to ponder why that was, I pushed it aside and grabbed a nicer pair of jeans and a grey t-shirt from within. Once I was dressed, I returned to the washroom to fix my shaggy brown hair into something acceptable and forwent shaving. Evan had begrudgingly made a comment years ago that scruff looked good on me. I'd teased him endlessly, but never forgot.

Without time for second guessing, I raced through my apartment and shoved my school books into my backpack and left. As I headed out to my car, I shot a quick text to Oryn to see if he wanted me to pick him up.

Before I reached the parking lot, I got a response.

No, thank you. I'm already walking.

A twinge of disappointment slowed my pace, and I shoved my phone back in my pocket. I should have insisted on Wednesday. He probably hadn't assumed my offer was meant for more than one day. I really didn't mind offering him a ride.

By the time I parked and raced up the stairs to class, I was almost late. The lecture room was a chatter of voices as I entered, but thankfully, Richard hadn't yet arrived. Oryn sat up front by the door, and without thinking, I slid onto the seat beside him.

"You beat me here." I chuckled, out of breath, as I pulled out my workbooks.

"Hi." Oryn shuffled over in his seat to put distance between us, but smiled despite the reaction. I hadn't considered the proximity until he reacted.

"Sorry, should I move over?"

He was quick to shake his head and break eye contact. "Did you t-talk to your boss about our project?"

"Yup." I withdrew the folder with the data sheets I'd printed off the day before. "Got all we'll need here."

He took the folder and leafed through the pages, nodding and reading. While he went over them, I couldn't help but take him in. He looked good. His hair was shaved close on the sides, but the length on top was gelled in a windblown style, spiked off his face. His long-sleeved button up was light blue and brought out the color in his eyes, washing away the hints of grey. His light facial hair was trimmed short, slightly longer than my days worth of stubble, and perfectly groomed. His eyebrows were nicely manicured, too.

And he smelled amazing. Almost a woodsy, citrus scent.

My attention was so completely on Oryn that I didn't notice him close the folder until he looked up and caught my eye. His pale cheeks immediately took on more color. Oryn became instantly awkward under my scrutiny, and I scrambled for something to say. I hadn't meant to overtly stare. He was attractive, and my body seemed to be just realizing it. Unlike Evan, physical appearance was not the first thing I noted about someone. Typically, it was personality that stood out first and foremost.

"Umm… we still on for tonight?" I asked.

He busied himself finding his notebook and wrote a few things down. "S-sure."

Thankfully, Richard entered and drew the class's attention before I could make Oryn feel any more out of place. Getting lost in the lesson helped him relax again, and I got to see up close and personal just what type of student he really was.

Where I considered myself to be relatively smart compared to the average person, Oryn's intelligence far exceeded my own. He was insightful and noted everything of importance, including marking pages in the textbook for future reference. The longer class went on, the more diverted my attention became. Watching him pen notes in his perfect script, and use various colored highlighters to categorize, was impressive. He was organized and meticulous.

Once we were dismissed, I knew I'd have a lot of catching up to do. If Evan had been present, I'd have never heard the end of it, especially with the way I'd been completely enthralled during the entire lesson.

"Ready to go," I asked once Oryn zipped his bag.

"Yup."

He was a man of few words, so we walked out to the parking lot in silence. The evening was warm and muggy, and I wondered how he was comfortable wearing long-sleeves all the time. I already regretted my decision to wear jeans. Summer clung, and Oryn didn't so much as even flinch at the heat or roll his shirt sleeves to his elbows.

Just as I pulled into his driveway, my phone rang. I killed the engine and squirmed to retrieve my phone from my pocket. It was Evan. Sighing, I dashed an apologetic smile to Oryn.

"Give me half a sec. It's my buddy, Evan. Probably calling to harass me."

Oryn lifted his bag from the ground between his feet and hugged it to his chest as he waited.

"Hey, you know I'm busy. What's up?" I asked as I answered.

"How's your date?"

I peeked to Oryn, who thankfully hadn't heard. "It's not and you know it. What do you want?"

"Thought you two might want to head over to Infernos in a couple hours. They have an amazing band playing tonight. We could shoot some pool or whatever. What do you say?"

"I told you, we are watching movies. Not really doing the bar thing."

"Come on. The guy needs to get out. You can show him a good time."

"Evan, we talked about this. Not his thing. I'm hanging up. We aren't going out. Goodbye."

I chuckled as I returned my phone to my pocket. "Sorry about that. Evan is a social butterfly. He wanted us to go out with him."

"Oh. Y-you can go if you want. It's not a big deal."

"Absolutely not. I spend enough time with him. He can get over it. I've been looking forward to movie night."

I gave him a warm smile, hoping he'd see my sincerity. It was true, I spent most of my spare time with Evan. A Friday night apart wouldn't kill him.

Oryn tried to return my smile, but it came across looking pained. He furrowed his brow and pinched the bridge of his nose before shaking his head.

"O-okay."

We got out of the car and he unlocked the front door for us to head inside. Somewhat familiar with his den, I followed him and made myself comfortable on the couch. Oryn deposited his bag on a chair by a desk in the corner and came partway to the couch, reconsidered, pivoted, and retreated to a secluded arched doorway that opened to another hallway.

He ran a hand over the back of his head and motioned to the TV. "I have an android b-box, so we can watch pretty much anything. I…" He blinked heavily a few times, rubbed his eyes, then stared into a distant nothing, not finishing his sentence.

"Are you okay?"

He didn't react to my question. A slow-moving hand came up and he pressed fingers into his temple before washing a hand down his face. He seemed disconnected, and I frowned as I watched him.

"Oryn?"

He rattled his head and roughly palmed his eyes, rubbing them intently as he licked his lips. Then, as though having cleared whatever confusion had taken hold, he raised his head again and met my worried gaze.

"Are you al—"

Something was different.

The moment he spied me, he smirked, and his eyes shone with a curiosity and energy unknown to Oryn. His stance changed. Everything changed.

Oryn ordinarily carried a nervous, almost awkwardness in the way he stood and walked. That was gone. His hip jutted out and a hand came to rest there as he fixed his hair and scanned me with an alluring smile I'd never seen.

The moment it happened, my heart jumped because I knew what I was witnessing but didn't know what to do. *This can't be real.* Instantly awkward, everything I'd recently read and learned disappeared from my mind.

"Hey, you." He strutted forward and sat on the edge of the couch, swinging one leg over the other, crossing them and balancing elbows on top where he held up his head on steepled hands. He quirked a brow, his smile shinning out his eyes.

"Hi," I croaked. What did I do? Did I introduce myself? Did he know me? Panic gripped my insides and all I wanted to do was race out the door. "I'm... Vaughn."

"I know. Damn, you're cute."

I flinched. His voice was different. Higher, and with a slight speech impediment he didn't have before. His r's weren't pronounced and came out almost like w's. He sounded... younger.

"What's your name?"

It felt like the most ridiculous question, but the man in front of me wasn't Oryn. With all I'd researched lost, I remembered Oryn telling me to treat his alters as the separate people they were. And I knew they didn't share a name.

He sat straighter and offered me a hand to shake. He didn't present it sideways like a man might shake, but palm down and with a slight downward turn to his wrist. "I'm Cohen."

Cohen. I searched my mind, trying to recall if Oryn had said much about Cohen. Why hadn't I paid more attention?

I took his hand and shook. His grip was light and dainty. With the contact, his smile grew, and he wet his lips playfully.

"It's nice to meet you." If I had to guess, Cohen was definitely gay.

I didn't know where to go from there. Oryn and I had planned a movie night and I wasn't sure if I was supposed to continue with that plan—or if Cohen even knew of those plans. Hell, I wasn't sure *I* wanted to continue with our plans. I was on the verge of bolting. Subconsciously cracking my knuckles, I glanced over my shoulder toward where I knew was the front door, out of sight down the hall. Considering my options, it felt like a dick move to abandon ship when I'd distinctly told him only days before that I wasn't an asshole. Our movie night was my idea.

So, what did I do? Did I wait for a cue from Cohen? It was like sitting in a room with a stranger. The contrast of Cohen and Oryn was so extreme my brain wasn't catching up. They were polar opposites.

"So," Cohen slapped his knee and jumped up, "Are we going out? I really want to dance. Let me shower and change and we can get out of here."

He skipped down the hall and disappeared from sight before I could respond. I stared at the place he once occupied, fumbling to catch up. Going out? Oryn didn't want to go out. He was a homebody, too shy to consider being so exposed in public situations.

But that wasn't Oryn. That man was nothing like Oryn. I guess I had my answer. No more movie night.

Grateful for the added time to adjust to such a drastic change of events, I worked to center myself so I could recall some of what I'd been so adamant to learn earlier in the week. Knowing something and witnessing it first hand were entirely different, and for whatever reason, I was nervous. Extremely nervous. The last thing I wanted was to do something wrong. Multitudes of unanswered questions returned and stirred my thoughts until I jumped up and paced the small room.

There was no reason I couldn't get to know his alters—since they were apparently as real as dirt. When Oryn had told me about his condition, and I'd learned for myself what it meant, I knew, unlike most people, I could look past his differences and be a friend. But I guess my mind hadn't been entirely convinced of its reality.

And I'm not a dick. I can do this.

So, it looked as though I was going out that night. With Cohen.

Like I'd told Oryn, I was decently good at making friends, so there was no reason I couldn't make friends with all his alters.

The shower stopped, and I sat back on the couch and waited. My eyes were drawn to the array of Legos on the bottom shelf of a bookcase, and I wondered how awkward it would be making friends with a five-year-old. And not just any five-year-old, but one who was stuck in an adult's body. I had little experience with children, so that outcome left a sliver of dread to run under my skin.

I'd deal with it if it happened. Maybe Rain wasn't an alter I'd meet.

When Cohen emerged from the hallway, I scrambled from the couch. He'd shaved and was finger-fixing his damp hair in a slightly different style than I'd seen on Oryn.

"Can we go to Majestics? They play good music."

His tongue poked out the side of his mouth as he checked himself in a mirror on the wall, pursing his lips to the side. I reminded myself to go with the flow. He'd changed into crimson skinny jeans and a black t-shirt that clung to his frame, something else I knew I'd never see on Oryn.

When he turned from the mirror, he rested his hands on his hips. With a slight tilt to his head and a smirk on his face, he waited. Only then did I realize, I hadn't answered his question.

Majestics was a bar just off campus where all the young college students gathered. It would be filled to capacity with nineteen and twenty-year-old kids, especially on a Friday night. Not exactly somewhere a thirty-five-year-old man was welcomed.

As I opened my mouth to reply, the inside of his bare arms caught my attention and I stalled. They were littered with extensive scars. Not one or two, but dozens on both arms. Most were thick and raised, while a few were just thin silver lines. There was barely a spot free from markings, and my mouth fell open.

When Cohen caught on to why I'd paused, he shrugged and rolled his eyes before turning back to the mirror. "Don't fret over it, babe, it keeps the bad stuff away."

Bad stuff? It was on the tip of my tongue to ask.

Sifting through broken memories of the articles I'd read, I remembered that often times, alters held the mysteries about the host's past trauma behind tightly vaulted doors. Inaccessible to anyone, including highly skilled therapists who could work for years to try and surface them, and weren't always successful.

"So, Majestics. What do you think?"

Cohen tore me from my whirlwind of thoughts and rooted me to the present. Perhaps bringing up his arms wasn't a safe direction and I should take the change of topic as it was offered.

"Umm... My friend, Evan, said there is a decent band playing at Infernos tonight. I'm not sure Majestics is up my alley."

Cohen chuckled and turned from the mirror. He crossed the room with a confident stride and patted my chest as he slinked by and exited to the hallway which led to the front door.

"Come on, you're not that old."

I hadn't felt that old until Oryn had left and Cohen had arrived. Going with the flow, I followed after him and found my shoes. I got the sense Cohen was a lot younger than Oryn, only I didn't remember how much younger.

The drive to Majestics was... strange. It was taking time for my brain to catch up with the fact that the man beside me—despite looking exactly like Oryn—wasn't Oryn.

He was self-assured and confident, two things Oryn wasn't. My tension must have been visible, because after a silent few minutes, Cohen's hand came to rest on my thigh. Higher than was within the realm of a friendly touch, and regardless of the unexpected circumstances, warmth bloomed over my skin at the connection.

"You okay, babe? If you aren't a dancer, we can just mingle and have a few drinks."

Earlier that day, I'd concluded that I was physically attracted to Oryn, but I'd also dismissed it for multiple reasons. First being, I wasn't sure Oryn was even gay. Second, he was so painfully shy, asking him or advancing in any way would have probably made him wretchedly uncomfortable. Cohen's touch did a number of things, none of which helped me be any less confused.

"I don't dance much, or well for that matter. But you can enjoy yourself." I smiled in his direction and returned my gaze to the road. He removed his hand after a minute and sat back, watching ahead.

When we arrived at Majestics, it was nearing ten-thirty. The bar crowd was just beginning to arrive, and many groupings of young college students hung around the parking lot, talking, laughing, and smoking. Cohen watched them with a spark of interest as we got out of the car.

Music sounded from within as we approached the front doors, and Cohen's smile grew. Oddly enough, he was in his element. Inside, he went ahead of me toward the bar, but checked over his shoulder a few times to ensure I followed. His hips swung with the music as he walked, and he smiled at a few people when they made eye contact.

He clasped my upper arm when I caught up and squeezed gently as he leaned in to whisper against my ear, "What are you drinking?" The crisp, fresh scent of his cologne and his breath against my lobe jarred my focus out of line. "My treat, just speak your desires." Then he chuckled, his lips brushing softly against me before he pulled back.

He was definitely flirting, but I was so torn on how to feel about it. If I flirted back, where did that put mine and Oryn's friendship? Besides, there were a number of things that felt out of place.

"Beer's good. Whatever's on tap. Thank you."

Cohen smiled as he ran his hand down my arm, squeezing my bicep once on his journey. "Relax."

There was a faint twinkle in his eyes under the low lighting of the bar, and I searched for any signs of Oryn. But he wasn't there. Not an ounce of him remained. It was surreal.

Cohen shifted to lean against the bar as he waited for someone to serve him. His ass jutted out and moved to the beat. While his back was turned, I scanned the room. It was busy and loud. I recognized a few guys from class at one table but otherwise the rest of the patrons were strangers. As I'd suspected, almost all of the people present were fairly young.

Cohen turned and handed me my pint of beer while he clung to some fruity concoction he'd ordered. "There's a table over there." He indicated with his chin. "Wanna sit?"

"Sure." I smiled through my unease and went ahead of him.

Once we'd sat, I drank deeply as I considered what to say. Cohen's attention was everywhere, and he glowed with excitement. Struggling not to stare at his shredded arms, the skin almost deformed from the mess of scars, I adjusted my glasses and subtly followed his gaze. He seemed unconcerned having them exposed, so I worked on not gawking.

When he started to sing to the music, I was drawn back. Two of his hands were cupped around his tall glass, and he swayed his body, singing a few lyrics as he watched me. There was no concern or self-consciousness, even though he was horribly off-key and fumbling most of the words.

When our eyes met, he laughed and shrugged. "Whatever, it's a good song."

I wasn't about to admit my unfamiliarity with it. It was some new-age stuff I never listened to. Cohen was clearly having a good time, and I didn't want to do anything to discourage that. I had no idea if getting out and having fun was something that happened frequently or not. At that point, I was walking blind and felt as though I knew absolutely nothing.

"So why are you back in school taking night classes?" he asked with a quirked brow before sipping from the twirly straw in his drink. His slight speech impediment only worked to enhance my appeal. It gave him an extra edge of adorableness I couldn't ignore.

I smiled at the question. It had been one of much debate between Evan and I. "Truthfully, and don't tell Evan I said this, but I needed change. My life has become monotonous and predictable. I go to work, I come home, I eat, I sleep, I do it again. On weekends, I hang out with Evan, or stay home alone and watch TV or read. Not much of a life. Crunching numbers all day is beginning to bore me."

He balanced his chin on an upturned palm. "And are you enjoying it so far?"

"I suppose. Not sure I've been at it long enough to judge. Some days I feel out of place. I'm not the same person I was ten years ago when I was in college."

Cohen's foot came to rest against my leg under the table. It was purposeful, and although I wasn't sure how I felt about his overt flirtations, I didn't move away. My body seemed convinced it was okay and tingled with the contact.

"And how have you changed?"

"More life experiences. Ten years wiser." I laughed. "I don't know. My focus isn't the same as it was ten years ago. Back then, I was more interested in being social and partying, whereas now I'm focused more on my career and future. I'm practically an old man, you know."

He snorted and covered his mouth before waving a hand, dismissing the notion. "Please, you are anything but. You can't forget to have fun sometimes. It can't all be serious."

It was an odd question, but I had to ask, "Cohen, how old are you?"

It earned me an age appropriate eye roll. "Nineteen. Why?"

Sixteen years younger than me. No wonder I felt out of place and uncomfortable around him.

"No reason. Just curious."

Likely sensing my discomfort, Cohen never forced me up to dance, and we spent the evening having a few drinks and chatting about random things. A number of times, as Cohen left to refresh our drinks, he detoured and chatted with random people. I didn't think he knew them, but was simply being friendly. His attention was solely fixed on me.

When I declined a fourth drink, because I was driving, he continued. The flirtations escaladed with a random touch here and facetious look there.

By the time it was last call, Cohen was significantly buzzed, and I suggested we leave. Halfway to the car, he latched onto my arm and shimmied closer to walk directly beside me. With enough alcohol to dampen my own apprehension, I enjoyed the connection and warmth of him against my side. The uncertainty of the situation had moved to the background—although it hadn't completely left altogether.

Part of me kept wondering where Oryn was and when he'd return. Above all, what would he think of our behavior that night and Cohen's extremely forward personality?

The drive was quiet. Cohen rested his hand on my thigh again, rubbing gentle circles with his thumb. The heat of his gaze was intense, but I worked on keeping my eyes on the road.

"You think too much," he stated as I pulled into his driveway.

I chuckled and put the car into park, not turning off the engine. "I know. It's a fault of mine. Blame my old age."

"Age is a number. Whatever. Sometimes, you have to just go with it. Life's too short to think so hard."

I turned to him and studied his carefree smile. His eyes glimmered with his intoxication, smoldering and eating me alive.

The lighthearted innocence of Cohen shone through. In that moment, he truly looked his age and nothing like the twenty-eight-year-old man whose body he occupied. His hand moved from my thigh to my hand and he held it.

"Do you want to come in?" he asked in a low whisper.

I focused on our connection as a thousand thoughts raced through my head. There was an attraction. Apparently on both ends, but when I really looked at the situation, I didn't think it was Cohen who'd drawn those feelings from me. It'd been Oryn... I thought.

"I... I don't think so."

When he remained quiet, I lifted my gaze again. We shared an awkward moment before Cohen removed his hand from mine and brought it to cup my face. "Okay." There was a hint of disappointment in the one word, but before I could respond, he leaned in and placed a delicate kiss on the corner of my lips. A huge part of me nearly turned to take more, but I held my ground. "I had fun tonight. Thanks, babe."

Without missing a beat, he hopped out of the car and waved before strutting to the door, working his skin-tight red pants for all they were worth. He let himself in without looking back. I sat baffled for a good five minutes, unable to order my thoughts enough to leave.

The night was... completely unexpected.

Chapter Five

At nine-thirty the following morning, I banged repeatedly on Evan's door as I balanced a tray of coffees and a box of donuts in my other hand. I'd barely slept. He was lucky I'd waited until then to wake him up, because desperation almost had me driving to his house at six in the morning.

Shuffling the coffees to my other hand, I kicked the door, wishing I had a key so I could wake the fucker up directly.

Without warning, the door swung open, and Evan peered back from his darkened apartment with a look of scorn. His dark hair was disheveled, he was unshaven and wearing only boxers.

"You do know it's nine in the fucking morning and I was out all night, right?"

I peered past his shoulder and scanned his apartment. "Are you alone?"

It wouldn't be the first time Evan had brought a girl home after a night at the bar. As much as he prattled on about wanting to find the right woman and settling down, I never saw a day when he would give up the single life.

He squinted and messed his hair, yawning. "I'm alone. What are you doing here?"

"I really need to talk."

As I went to let myself in, his hand came down on the center of my chest and he pushed me out the door again. "No fucking way. I'm hungover and going back to bed."

"That's why I brought this." I shoved the box of donuts in his hands and held up the coffees to show him. "Seriously, I haven't slept, and I need to talk."

His brow furrowed as he turned that information around and scanned me. I looked a wreck and I knew it. Deciding my pleas were honest, he stepped aside. "Fine, give me a minute to put something on. For the record, I feel like shit, so if I'm a miserable fuck with you, don't bitch."

He padded to the kitchen and left the box of donuts on the counter. As he went to find something to wear, I helped myself to one and sat at the table, sipped my coffee and waited.

When he returned, he'd put on a pair of tear-away sport pants and a tank top. I received a glare as he retrieved his own donut and coffee and joined me at the table. "Talk," he said around a mouthful.

I sighed and removed my glasses to clean them on the bottom of my t-shirt. "You were right. And you know I hate saying that shit." I fit my glasses back on and caught him smirking from behind his coffee.

"Go on."

"Oryn."

"You like him."

"This is complicated. Let me explain and you sit there and be as non-judgemental as possible. Can you do that?"

He licked icing from his fingers and sat back, crossing his arms over his broad chest. "Did you fuck him?"

"It's always sex with you. Shut up and let me talk."

He raised his eyebrows and made a point of pressing his lips together tight.

"I'm attracted to him. Definitely. I didn't sleep with him. I haven't even told him. I don't even know if he's gay. But last night—"

"How was movie night?"

"It didn't happen."

Evan tilted his head to the side and grabbed his coffee. "Go on."

"After class, we went back to his place, I talked to you on the phone, we went inside, and then he switched. I actually saw it happen. He flipped into someone else right in front of me."

Evan's face went from teasing humor to skepticism. "You actually believe this guy has multiple personalities?"

"He does, Evan. If ever I thought it was bullshit, I'm telling you, it's not. I saw it with my own eyes. And I spent all night with his alter, Cohen, who was completely different from Oryn. Apart from them sharing a body, there wasn't a single thing the same. Believe me. It was unsettling at first, and I didn't know what to think. We ended up at Majestics and—"

"You went to Majestics? Seriously?" Evan sat up and pushed his coffee aside. "We don't hang out there. How old are you?"

"It's where Cohen wanted to go. Shut up and listen, there's more."

Evan's sleepy hangover faded, and he got up to grab himself a second donut.

"So, Cohen it seems is Oryn's complete opposite. He's outgoing, nowhere near shy, and extremely self-assured. And he's gay," I added. "He spent all night flirting with me."

Evan pulled off a piece of donut and popped it in his mouth with a wide grin. "So you did get laid."

"No! Would you stop. I didn't let it go anywhere. It was too strange, and besides, Cohen is only nineteen so it felt incredibly weird and wrong."

Confusion dipped Evan's brow and he flinched. "Nineteen?"

"Yes. Alters can be whatever age, remember? So, I admit, I'm attracted to Oryn. I think he's a decent guy and he's smart and shy, and I'd kinda like to know him better, but I don't even know if he's gay. Cohen on the other hand, would have probably jumped at more last night, and part of me almost wanted to explore it, except… fuck, I don't know… it wasn't Oryn and it didn't sit right with me."

Evan ate his donut in silence, staring at me and saying nothing. When he finished, and I expected him to respond, he reached for his coffee instead and drank a few mouthfuls.

"Would you say something already!"

Evan shook his head and shrugged. "This is the weirdest fucking shit I've ever heard in my life. I've got nothing, man. I don't have a clue what to tell you. This is some Twilight Zone shit you have going on. Should have taken the bait and got your wanker yanked in my opinion."

I sunk back in my chair. "You're a big help. Thanks."

Evan scrubbed a hand down his face and scratched his stubble. "Okay, well, for starters, if this thing Oryn has is for real, then do you really want to be involved with that? I mean, are you interested in dating a guy who can flip around so unexpectedly?"

"You're missing the point. I don't even know if Oryn's gay."

"What if he is? You are attracted to him. You just said so. Is it enough you want to pursue something?"

"I don't know," I admitted honestly. "I was half-tempted with Cohen last night. The opportunity was there, but all I could think was, if I do this, it should be Oryn, not Cohen, shouldn't it?"

Evan pinched his eyes shut and shook his head, the magnitude of the conversation almost too much for Evan's hungover brain. "Okay, so if you and Oryn do have something, how does that work when he's not himself?"

I dropped my head to the table. "I don't know."

Nothing about the situation was that simple, and I realized talking to Evan wasn't going to give me those answers. We drank our coffee in silence. After we finished, Evan got up and tossed our empty paper cups in the trash. He leaned on the counter and appeared deep in thought.

"Can I make a suggestion?" he finally asked.

"Please."

He met my eyes and the seriousness of his expression wasn't one I saw often on my best friend.

"Don't get tangled up with this guy. There are plenty more fish in the sea. If he's confusing you already, that should be a sign. Be his friend, but keep it simple. Seriously, man."

I'd known Evan for twenty years and there wasn't ever a time I didn't take his honest advice to heart. We butted heads on a lot of things.

"Maybe you're right."

Only something didn't feel *right*.

***

Wednesday took forever to arrive. More than once, I verged on texting Oryn or driving to his house. I hadn't heard a thing since Friday night and had no idea what to make of the silence.

Arriving for class ten minutes early, I scanned the room. Oryn was seated in the front row, face buried in a book. Before approaching, I watched him carefully. He was as much Oryn as I remembered; hunched over his book with one arm wrapped around his middle. He wore a plain white, long-sleeved t-shirt—reminding me immediately of the mess I'd seen on his arms. When I'd spoken to Evan, I'd left that part out. It seemed an extremely personal side of him I was sure Oryn wouldn't appreciate having exposed.

"Is this seat taken?"

Oryn's head flipped up, but instead of the smile I'd hoped for, he frowned and dashed a look to the vacant seat beside him.

"N-no." He shuffled upright and closed his book. "You can sit there."

I slid into the open spot and placed my backpack between my legs. "How are you?" I asked, offering a warm, non-threatening smile.

"I'm okay." His grip on the novel he'd been reading tightened before he decided to return it to his bag in exchange for his notepad and textbook. "H-how are you?"

"Doing all right. Long day at work."

His discomfort was contagious, and instead of diving into conversation about Friday night—which we truthfully didn't have time to discuss—we sat in silence until Richard wandered in and class began.

Like before, once the lesson started, Oryn visibly relaxed into his work and his tension evaporated. For the second time, I found myself distracted and paying more attention to Oryn than the lecture. When class ended, we packed our bags and he rose to leave without so much as uttering a word.

"Can I give you a ride?" I asked before he could dart away.

He adjusted the strap of his bag where it rested on his shoulder and scrunched his brow as though surprised by my offer. "Umm… sure. Thank you."

Letting out a breath of relief, I snapped up my own bag and led the way. Oryn was always awkward around me, but as I started the car, his nerves seemed more escalated than all previous times combined.

"Are you all right?"

He nodded and continued to look out his side window, avoiding me. When we arrived at his place, I pulled in the driveway and cut the engine which drew his attention.

"Can we talk?"

He lifted his bag from the floor and placed his hand on the door handle as though ready to escape.

"Is this about F-friday?"

"Somewhat."

He licked at his lips and stared to his lap. "Sure. D-do you want to come in?"

"Or we could sit outside. It's a nice night." I thought perhaps it would be better if he didn't feel invaded.

He nodded and we both got out. There was a stoop before his front door and I sat there and glanced to the sky. The stars were making their slow appearance. It was a nice night. The air was warm still for September and I took in a lungful, letting it out slowly as Oryn sat beside me. He remained quiet, so I figured if I didn't start, we'd be in silence all night. I'd had a lot of days to consider what I wanted to talk about, but I still wasn't any more sure where to begin.

"I met Cohen."

The edge of his lip turned up in a hesitant smile and he wrung his hands. "Did you?"

"He's a lot of fun. He wasn't interested in a movie night, but we went out and had a good evening."

Oryn flinched and looked at me directly, mouth gaping in disbelief. "You... You went out? You s-stuck around?"

"You didn't know?"

He shook his head. "I d-don't retain any memories when an alter comes forward. I just lose time. It can be f-frustrating because I have no sense of where I am, what time it is, or what I've been doing. You and Cohen went out?"

I smiled at his shock. "Yup. He dragged my old ass to Majestics. Talk about being out of place."

Oryn chuckled and scratched the back of his neck. "Th-that's kinda funny."

"Oh yeah, funny as hell. That crowd would have made you feel old and I have over half a dozen years on you."

The humor behind Oryn's eyes was nice to see. "Yeah, but Cohen is—"

"Nineteen."

"And likes people."

Oryn glanced across the road and then up to the darkened sky.

"You didn't tell me Cohen was gay."

Oryn's teeth found his lip and there was a significant pause before he responded, "We both are."

Both?

His declaration made my heart jump involuntarily, and I lost all interest in our surroundings and watched Oryn's face. He refused to look at me, but even in the darkness, I thought I saw a hint of color bloom in his cheeks.

"Did... d-did he... w-was he...."

"He was quite flirty."

Oryn nodded, unsurprised. "He is."

Sensing his elevated discomfort, I jumped in with different questions. Ones I'd been wanting to ask, especially since Friday.

"Do you think you can tell me a little more about your alters? You know, in case I meet them at random like on Friday. So I know what to expect."

Slowly, he turned his head to examine me as though he didn't quite understand the question. "Why d-didn't you just go home on Friday? Why did you go out and do all those things even though they m-made you uncomfortable?"

"Umm…" I thought for a minute, considering if I should tell him the truth of how I'd nearly flown out the door. When Oryn had retreated to wherever it was he went and Cohen had appeared, it had taken time to adjust, but I was glad I'd stuck around. "Because we planned a night to hang out, and I know about your disorder and accept it as being a part of you. So, when Cohen showed up, I just went with it."

"M-most people wouldn't do that."

"I'm not most people."

With only the street lights and moon highlighting the gentle curves of Oryn's face, I couldn't look away. It was a rare moment when he held my gaze, and I became captivated by the vulnerability behind his eyes. There was something in his looks, a softness or tenderness, that warmed my insides. The notion that anyone would treat him unfairly, disturbed and angered me. He didn't ask for such a complicated life. From everything I'd learned, he was the victim, and one of unthinkable crimes I couldn't even wrap my head around.

Breaking the moment, Oryn looked back to the star-filled sky. As he spoke, I noted his stutter had petered off into non-existence, and I took it as a sign of his comfort level. "Since you've met Cohen first-hand, I assume he doesn't need much more explanation."

I chuckled, remembering the bubbly man I'd gone out with Friday. "Not really."

"Reed can be difficult. He's hard-headed and intimidating. M-my therapist describes him as my protector, which maybe I never realized before. He's straight. He doesn't trust anyone."

"I think I've had a small taste of Reed. Before you ever told me about all this."

Oryn's head whipped around. "You have?"

"The first time we were supposed to go for coffee after our first class."

"Oh, right. I forgot about that." He paused and rubbed at his forehead. "Umm... Rain is..." He drifted into thought.

"He's five, right?" That alter stuck in my memory because of the shock of his age.

Oryn nodded. "Yeah. Dr. Delmar explained, most people with DID have many child identities and they often are due to the robbed childhood we never properly experienced."

"I read that."

Oryn's eyes widened. "You read about us?"

"A little bit. I was hoping to get a better understanding. Is that okay?"

His head bobbed, the surprise not leaving his face.

"Umm... Whatever the case, I only have Rain. He loves animals, art, Lego, playing outside, basically anything a normal five-year-old likes. He's busy and chatty. Obsessed with Batman." Oryn smiled and brought fingers to his temple. "I hear him talking almost nonstop some days."

He'd mentioned hearing Rain in his head before and I wondered if he heard all his alters like that or just him.

"Does he come out often?" The thought of Rain's presence made me the most uncomfortable, because although I could visualize identities like Cohen or Reed coming from Oryn, I couldn't wrap my head around a child being in his body or how that might look.

"Yeah, a fair bit."

I did my best not to show my anxiety over his answer and graced him with a warm smile.

Cohen, Reed, and Rain. There were still two more if I remembered correctly, except Oryn went silent.

"Didn't you say there were five alters?"

Oryn shrugged and wrapped his arms around his body, hugging himself. "Theo doesn't trigger the same. He's been with me the longest and kinda has a place in my structured day. He's easy going. Not much to tell. Meticulous. Straight-forward. Organized. You probably won't meet him." He shrugged.

Again, silence.

"And the last one," I urged gently.

Oryn unconsciously rubbed his arms and squirmed. The action drew my attention and instantly reminded me of his scars hidden under his shirt. My stomach turned as I realized I may have inadvertently just asked about the man responsible for those scars.

Don't fret over it. It keeps the bad stuff away. Cohen had told me.

"I-I don't really w-want to talk about Cove." Oryn stammered.

Not wanting to frighten him, I cautiously and slowly reached out and took his hand. His eyes widened, and he flipped his gaze to mine once again.

He didn't wrench his arm free, but held himself perfectly still as though frozen in terror. The reaction tore a hole in my heart. Mistrust and fear swam behind his eyes, yet he couldn't even find the courage to pull away from me.

I didn't lift his sleeve like I'd intended. I didn't have to. Turning his wrist up, I touched his inner arm through his shirt, feeling the raised marks I'd seen the other day. The entire time, never breaking my eyes from his, I instilled as much reassurance as I could.

"Did he do this?"

Oryn's jaw clenched so tight, he vibrated with the pressure. Then he nodded as his eyes swam.

"H-h-he s-s-says—"

"It keeps the bad stuff away?"

I didn't think Oryn's eyes could widen more, but they did. "How d-did you know?" he whispered.

"Cohen told me."

Oryn nodded. "H-he hurts me too sometimes, but not like Cove. M-my therapist says I need to accept Cove as part of our s-system. H-he says if I keep trying to block him out, he will continue to cause trouble."

"What bad stuff, Oryn?"

He pulled his arm free and scrubbed at his face with two hands, pressing fingers into his eyes. When he looked back, his eyes darkened and his brow furrowed. The gentle lines of his face I'd seen a moment before became hard angles. There was no more worry in his forehead, no more tears in his eyes, and he instantly sat straighter. His once troubled expression turned harsh.

I shuffled away a few inches, my heart skipping as I realized Oryn was gone again.

Fuck that happens fast!

"I think it's time you go." The voice was one I'd heard before; outside the college on the first day of class.

Oryn—not Oryn, Reed—rose from the stoop, swung his bag over his shoulder and peered down to where I sat stunned and unmoving. He folded his arms across his chest and stood much taller than Oryn.

Jumping up as well, I stumbled to find words, telling myself to go with the flow and introduce myself nicely. "You must be Reed." Intimidating was exactly how I'd have described him as well. Amazingly, even though he inhabited the same body as Oryn, he somehow appeared so vastly different in every way, just as Cohen had. Bigger almost. Broader in the shoulder, even though it wasn't physically possible, the impression was the same. "It's nice to meet you."

I offered my hand to shake, but he didn't accept. His firm gaze never left my face. When he stepped forward, invading my personal space, I stumbled back and straightened myself, matching his height.

"For some reason you must be under the impression you're welcome here, but you're wrong. You want to work on your little school shit project, fine. But keep it at that. Let's get one thing straight. I don't like you and I don't want you around. We are not friends. Understand?"

I opened my mouth to speak, but closed it again immediately, not having a clue what to say. Trying again, I had no results and just gaped like a fish.

He raised his chin and peered down from under intensely dark eyes.

"I'm just trying to be a friend," I sputtered, finding my voice.

"I know what you're trying to do, so cut the shit." He stepped aside and motioned with his chin to my car. "Go."

I straightened my glasses, but didn't move. "I'm sorry if I've upset you or Ory—" I stopped myself, unsure if mentioning Oryn was wise. "I'm not a bad person."

"I'll be the judge of that."

When he continued to skewer me with his gaze, I submitted and went to my car. Even as I started the engine, Reed didn't move from the stoop. He watched me as I backed out of the driveway and was still there as I drove down the street.

Only once I was home did I allow the swarm of confusion and thoughts to hit me completely. Where had Oryn gone? Had *I* caused him to retreat? I had an unsettling feeling that Reed really didn't like me, although I had no idea why or what I'd done to cause him to feel that way.

I sat in my car for an hour playing the scenario around in my mind and considering everything; what Evan and I had discussed, what I'd read online, and ultimately, how I felt emotionally toward Oryn.

His entire condition puzzled me, and yet the more I witnessed, the more my heart pulled toward him. How many hundreds of people wouldn't give him the time of day, or teased, or bullied him because of something he couldn't control? I'd seen it on the first day of class, and the memory made me sick. The unfairness of what he experienced everyday cut me to my core, and I didn't want to be just another one of those people.

Even if friending Oryn wasn't cut and dry, and came with a plethora of bumps in the road, I wanted to learn to maneuver them any way I could. The poor guy deserved a friend.

Chapter Six

Taking a chance, I texted Oryn on Thursday afternoon to see if he wanted to work on our project before class on Friday. I didn't know what to expect. I'd spent the entire day at work, sneaking in articles and watching YouTube videos about DID. The more I could absorb, the better. With the disorder being entirely individual to the person involved, it made it difficult for me to understand what applied to Oryn and what didn't, but I tried.

Focusing my self-education on switches and alters, I learned—in a broad way—that the host may or may not be aware of the time when the alters were forward. Oryn, in his own words, was unaware and ended up with large chunks of missing time. Switches could be consensual, forced, or triggered. Based on the immediate way I'd been presented with Reed, I assumed Oryn may have been triggered into switching. Knowing what we'd been discussing, and understanding how Oryn's therapist had explained Reed as being a protective alter, I assumed I'd cause the switch unintentionally and felt horrible.

Alters were created to protect the host against whatever trauma they'd experienced. My diving in and asking directly about *the bad stuff* was far past the line of comfortable for Oryn, and I should have known better. If what I'd read was accurate, Reed was simply doing his job and protecting Oryn from a past he knew nothing about.

Uncertain how long Reed would stay present, or if he'd retreated immediately after I'd left Wednesday, I couldn't be certain I'd get a reply to my message. At half past nine, my phone buzzed on the coffee table as I was zoned out watching the comedy network. I sat up to retrieve it.

That would be great. Could we plan for after class instead?

A sense of relief filled me as I confirmed our study date. With Reed's insistence I stay away, I wasn't sure where I stood. At least Cohen had warmed up to me without trouble—maybe a little too much.

As I sat in the college parking lot before school on Friday, my phone rang. It was Evan.

"You have about ten seconds. I'm just heading inside for class."

"It's all I need. I bought beer. Come over after and we can hang out. Thought we could go shoot some pool tonight, yeah?"

I shut off the engine and made my way toward the front doors. "No can do. I have a study date with Oryn."

There was a groan on the other end, and I chuckled.

"Have I ever mentioned, I hate your decision to return to school? I've been cast aside for cute college boys. I knew this would happen. I hate it."

"You poor thing. Suck it up. I'll be there Sunday. We can go play a few games if you're still in the mood."

"Yeah, yeah. So how's it going with Oryn?"

"Umm, well I don't know. I met another alter yesterday and he didn't seem to like me very much, so we'll see tonight."

"Everybody loves you. What's his problem?"

Diving into my suspicions on how I'd possibly inadvertently triggered him wasn't fair to Oryn.

"Evan, I gotta go. I'll come by Sunday."

We exchanged goodbyes and hung up.

I was a few minutes late arriving, and Richard had already begun the lesson. I sunk into the seat beside Oryn and we exchanged a smile before I followed along with what was being taught. That day's focus was on the effectiveness of color in advertisement. How to use them and what combinations best called to the buyer. I took notes and read passages in the text as they were assigned.

By eight, Richard allowed us a ten-minute break, and many students slipped from the room. Oryn turned in his seat and smiled shyly as he fiddled with his pen, doodling on the corner of his notepad.

"I-I'm sorry about Wednesday."

I waved it off and tried to hide my nerves behind adjusting myself in my seat. "Not your fault."

All mine I think. Did he know what had happened? Was he aware Reed had come forward?

"We've been trying this new thing my doctor suggested where we write in a journal to communicate better with one another. It's been hard to get everyone on board, but Reed told me he sent you away. He sounds uncomfortable with you around me, although I'm not sure I know why. So," Oryn squirmed, put his pen down, and gnawed his lip a moment before continuing. "Just know it wasn't me sending you away and I'm sorry. They all do things their own way."

"It's okay. Really." I pushed my glasses up on my nose and shrugged. "I won't lie, Reed kind of surprised me, and I wasn't sure what I'd done to make him upset, but no harm."

I found the warmest, most genuine smile I could to show him I meant it. It worked, and he let out a sigh of relief.

"And we can still work together tonight?"

"I hope so."

He studied me for a moment, the unique color of his irises catching the light and shimmering with a joy I hadn't seen before. Much to my contentment, a hint of nerves released from his entire body and the shy smile I'd seen only a few times returned.

"You're a really nice guy. Thank you."

Everything about him sung through me in such an unexpected way. None of the challenges we'd experienced mattered in the least in that moment. Perhaps I could give Oryn something few others had; friendship.

Richard returned and called the class' attention up front, breaking the brief calm that had graced Oryn's world. As he shifted back in his seat, tension returned to his shoulders—even though he was in his element learning. I wondered if his whole life carried stress and if he ever saw respite from those feelings.

When class ended, we slipped out of the room first, beating the crowd, and raced down the stairs to the main level and the front doors. Oryn laughed as he tried to keep up with me, and the musical tone of his voice was so out of place in the man I'd come to know, I flipped around suddenly unsure if it was Oryn following me or someone else.

When he jumped from the last step and met my eyes, a smile covered his face and his cheeks were pink from either embarrassment or exertion, I knew it was still him.

"Why are we running?" he asked as he followed me out the door.

"I don't know. Just avoiding the crowd."

I slowed my pace and fixed my glasses. Oryn walked beside me, closer than I expected and our arms brushed together once before he increased the distance.

When we arrived at his house, Oryn found us a few cans of Coke to drink while I searched up our notes from our previous session.

"When we are finished, do you want to stick around for a movie? Umm... since we kind of m-missed it last time," he added quickly, darting his gaze to his hands.

The invitation was sweet, and based on Oryn's demeanor, difficult to make.

"I'd like that."

Oryn was easy to work with. We blended our ideas without argument and his insightfulness was unique and well thought out. Not for the first time, I was amazed with his intelligence.

"Did you go to school around here?" I asked an hour into our work.

Oryn eyed me from the paper where he was scrawling our notes. He shook his head and dropped his eyes again. "I was homeschooled."

He didn't elaborate and moved the conversation quickly back to our project. I didn't press.

"So," I suggested some time later, "how about we draw up a mock billboard, or at least sketch out a few possibilities." I chuckled. "Maybe we can see how much of that color lecture stuck with me."

Oryn smiled and immediately found his notes from earlier that day. "We have a reference," he said, placing them in the middle of the table. "Umm... I have m-markers. Let me find them." Oryn jumped up and disappeared down the hallway. "There are a few sketch pads on the bookshelf by the window. Near the bottom. Can you grab them?" he called.

Locating the correct shelf, I got up and found the specified sketch pads. They were on a lower shelf by themselves, a dozen or more of them. Squatting, I grabbed one from the top of the pile and opened it to see if it had available space inside for us to work. It was filled with childlike drawings on every page. I gaped, flipping through it in admiration before grabbing a second pad from the shelf and checking inside of it as well. It too was filled.

Most pictures were colorful and used every square inch of available space, while others were scribbled out with a black marker and left half-done, obviously rejected as not being good enough.

It was on one of the scribbled-out pages where I paused. The image had been drawn all in black marker and had the makings of a car. There were added flips and wings I couldn't quite decipher, but the emblem on the front was clear.

"Dat's a Batmobile. 'Cept I can't do it, it's too hard."

The moment I heard the higher tone and distinctive enunciation difficulties coming from the person standing behind me, I paused. Turning to face who I knew was Rain, a wave of nerves made the hairs on my arms prickle and stand.

There was no time to process, the moment he met my eyes, a toothy smile grew on his face. Fisted in one hand was a pencil case, and he bounced on his toes.

"I can show you da Batman. He's my favorite. Do you like Batman?"

He dropped to his knees beside me and removed the sketch pad from my lap as I remained frozen in shock. Rifling through the pages, he blew his cheeks to balloons and let the air out in little bursts making farting noises.

"Not dis one." He stuck the pad back on the shelf and dug through the pile until he found another. "Batman is my favorite."

"B-Batman is pretty cool." I stammered, watching in awe as he searched the next book.

When he found what he was looking for, he put it back in my lap and grinned. "Dare he is."

Eyeing the changed man beside me, I noted all the incredible differences that had taken place in the blink of an eye. Innocence sparked across his face. Pride at what he wanted to show me coupled with a sense of freedom and joy every adult left behind when they grew up. The permanent worry of Oryn, the firm tension of Reed, and the cocksureness of Cohen, weren't present at all. Rain was a person all to himself. A child in every sense of the word except form.

"You're Rain," I squeaked, barely finding my voice.

He giggled and scrunched his nose. "Dat's my name. You're Vaughn-d." Said with a distinct added 'd' on the end.

"You know me?"

He nodded, his head bobbing excessively with the gesture and making his hair flop.

"Do you know how to draw Batman? I can show you."

To call the situation odd was an understatement, but I'd prepared for the idea of meeting Rain and tried to look past the grown man's body in front of me to the child he clearly was.

"I admit, I'm not very good at drawing."

"It's super easy. Come on." He grabbed the sketch pad and tucked it under his arm, then took my hand and pulled me toward the hall.

"Where are we going?" I asked. Oryn had never invited me beyond the living room, and a faint sense of trespassing into his private space niggled my gut.

"We can only draw in da Batcave. Dat's the rules."

The Batcave?

He steered us into a dark room before flipping a switch on the wall. It was a child's bedroom, completely dedicated to what must have been his favorite superhero. Batman bedding, stuffed animals, shelves with figurines and other toys, Lego, and pictures he'd drawn were all over the walls.

"Is this your bedroom?"

"And da Batcave." He jumped ahead of me and flopped onto the floor, opening the sketch pad in front of him and finding himself a marker. His legs were folded out behind him in a w—like a child might sit—with his butt planted on the carpeted ground. Just seeing the awkward position made my hips and thighs hurt, and I wondered if Oryn ever had residual cramps or pain from Rain's behaviors.

There was no way Rain shared a room with Oryn—or the other alters for that matter. It was far too—young for an adult to find any comfort living there. But I wasn't about to conclude anything with the limited knowledge I'd collected on Oryn's condition.

"Does… Do you share your room or is it all yours?"

He snorted. "You're a noodle brain. Dis is all for me. Come on, I'll show you."

And now I'm a noodle brain.

Chuckling, I found a spot beside him and crossed my legs, folding my hands in my lap. "Okay, show me what you've got."

With a tongue poking out, Rain hunched himself over the sketch pad and began to draw. It wasn't a tutorial as I'd expected, just a young boy drawing a picture, but it was fascinating. A few minutes into his work, it dawned on me, he was using his left hand to color. Oryn was right-handed. How was that even possible?

"Can you use both hands when you color?" I asked, intrigued by the notion.

He shook his head and gave me a funny look. "Da other one doesn't work da same. See."

He flipped the marker and it was instantly clear he was telling the truth when he couldn't even find a comfortable grip to hold it.

Maneuvering the marker back, he continued to color. I sat quietly and watched. His skills were on par with a child of five, and even when he added his name partway through, the letters were blocky and proportionately wrong. As the picture was near completion, Rain paused, staring down at his work. When he didn't move for almost a minute, I grew concerned.

"Is everything okay, buddy?"

He rubbed his eyes before lifting his gaze to mine. Squinting and squeezing his eyes once more, he then scanned the room, worry marking grooves in his forehead. When his gaze travelled back to mine, I noted the carefree look had been replaced with anxiety. I knew right away, Rain had gone.

"Hey."

Confusion marred Oryn's face and he pressed a palm into his temple, sucking in air as though in pain.

"I-I..." He patted his pockets on his jeans, but didn't find whatever it was he searched for. "What time is it?"

My phone was in the living room, so I shrugged. "Probably around eleven."

"I..." He peered down to the open sketch pad and back up as the pieces clicked into place. "I lost time."

"Rain was showing me how to draw Batman. He was only out for about fifteen minutes or so."

Pink tinted Oryn's cheeks as he moved the marker to his right hand and adjusted the way he sat, matching my crossed legs.

"He loves Batman."

"I can tell." I indicated to the well-decorated bedroom, and Oryn chuckled.

"Did... I'm sorry, what were we doing? Everything is hazy." He pressed a palm into his temple again and his face pained.

"We were going to draw up a mock billboard. Are you okay?"

"Yeah, just a headache. It happens a lot with switches."

"We don't have to keep working today. It's getting late and we've been at it a while already. Especially if you aren't feeling great."

He nodded, closed the sketch pad, and stood, examining the room before moving to the door. I followed, and after we left, he shut off the lights and closed the door.

"That room is specifically Rain's. I don't use it."

"He explained."

Oryn ran his fingers through his hair and smiled shyly. "Of course he did. He's possessive with his space."

In the living room again, I packed up my workbooks as Oryn hovered nearby.

"Did... did you still wanna watch a movie?" he asked. "Or... it's okay if you have to go."

"For sure, if you're up for it." I shifted my bag aside and leaned back on the couch. "It's Friday night, I have no plans."

Oryn visibly relaxed and sunk onto the other end of the couch as he aimed the remote at the TV and turned it on. While he was distracted searching up movies, I stole a moment to watch him. I continually found myself in admiration of who he was. Anyone looking in might only see a socially introverted man, but spend time with him and you'd be introduced to the unique way he lived his life. Knowing society, I hated to think how it must feel to be so different. The simple act of watching a movie together had lit up his face. What did that mean for his life as a whole?

Deciding on *Deadpool,* a movie we'd both seen a hundred times but jointly loved, we relaxed together and let the unexpected twist to our evening become nothing more than a memory. The more time I spent with Oryn, the more I was able to read him. It was rare for him to be without tension or worry holding his body prisoner, so when moments of true requiescence shone through, I noted them.

It was late when the movie ended, and I could barely drag my ass off the couch. Groaning as I slung my bag over my shoulder, Oryn laughed.

"What?" I laughed with him. "Getting old sucks. You just wait."

He walked with me to the car and I chucked my bag in the backseat with the rest of the junk I hadn't bothered to take care of.

"Thanks for the company." He wrung his hands once before deciding to jam them in his pockets. He tentatively met my eyes and I was rewarded with the shy smile I'd come to adore.

"I had a good time."

Our gazes locked for a beat until Oryn looked away, scanning the night with an edge of discomfort. A warmth coated my skin as I studied his profile; milky pale skin contrasted against the dark night behind him. The delicate curve of his jaw and slight protrusion of his pouty lower lip worked in perfect harmony with the softer, gentler side of Oryn.

I reached out and rested a hand on his upper arm, drawing his attention. It was a move based purely on instinct and a rooted desire for contact with someone I was growing feelings for on a sublevel basis. Not once did I expect it to have a negative reaction. His entire body went stiff and his eyes widened with undiluted fear as he whipped his head around to look at me again.

Retracting nearly as fast, I held up my hands to calm him and show I meant no harm. "I'm sorry. I shouldn't have—"

"It's okay." He fought to catch his breath which had immediately found an erratic rhythm with the onslaught of fear. "You're going to think I'm completely crazy at this rate. I just…" He shook his head and dropped his gaze to stare at the ground. "I'm not sure I want to explain."

"You don't have to. And I don't think you're crazy. I can't imagine walking in your shoes. If I do things that frighten you, or say the wrong thing, just know I don't mean to. I would never want to cause you to be upset. I only want to be a friend."

It took time, but slowly his gaze found mine again, and he pressed his lips together as he fought an internal battle I might never understand. It played out behind his eyes, and my heart went out to him. In my core, all I wanted was to erase all that hurt and uncertainty.

"Thank you," he eventually whispered.

I shuffled and fixed my glasses. "You can call or text me whenever. It'd be nice to hang out. If you want."

My offer brought on a look of surprise, and he nodded.

"Take care."

Chapter Seven

After our night together on Friday, I made the decision to dedicate time each week to developing my friendship with Oryn. If I never moved forward on my budding attraction, it was okay. Part of me wasn't entirely sure Oryn was interested—or capable—of having a relationship anyhow.

"I feel like I'm being dumped," Evan said as he lined up his next shot. "I thought you said forever, Vaughn." He sniffled dramatically, but couldn't hold the façade of being hurt and laughed.

"I don't even feel bad for you. Every damn time you find a girlfriend, I'm the one who suffers."

"Not my fault. Women are *way* more demanding. They take up *all* my time." He sighed as his ball ricocheted off the side of the pool table, missing the pocket by a sliver. "You're right. I should have gone for dicks. You aren't half as annoying as all the girls I've dated combined."

"Too late. You had your chance. Should have taken me up on my offer in tenth grade." Examining the layout of the balls, I bent down to get an eye-level view of potential shots. "Ten, corner pocket." I rose and stretched across the table, finding the angle I needed.

"So, are you dating him now? Is that why you're dumping me to spend more time together?"

"No, I just think he could do with a friend who's willing to understand him."

"And this has nothing to do with that little ol' heart pitter pattering in your chest whenever you're with him?"

With the perfect amount of force, I hit the white ball at the exact angle required to knock my ten ball into the pocket.

"Are you finished?"

"Admit it, Vaughn, you're attracted to multiple-man. You have been since the day you met him."

"Don't call him that." Pointing out my next shot, I rounded the table. "I am, but he has some seriously huge barriers, and I'm not sure if it's a workable situation. I won't push myself on him, I'm fine with friendship."

Evan grabbed the chalk cube from the table's edge and worked it over the tip of his cue. "Here's a thought; tell him. See what he thinks. Worse comes to worse, he tells you he can't or doesn't want to be involved."

"Maybe."

I wasn't sure it was that simple.

***

The following Wednesday, Oryn was his usual quiet self, listening to the lecture and only engaging in conversation if I initiated. When class ended, I managed to pull him aside as everyone flooded out the lecture room doors.

"Do you have plans for Saturday?" I asked as he watched the few remaining students leave.

"No. Do you want to w-work on our project?"

"Nah, I just thought maybe you'd wanna do something. Hang out, you know?"

His gaze travelled to my face, confusion and surprise painted over his features. The combination was a recognisable reaction with Oryn, and I smiled. Hopefully, someday he'd feel more comfortable around me.

"Like f-friends?"

I chuckled at the perplexity of his question. "Yeah, like friends. Not sure what you like to do, but we can figure it out."

His gaze dropped to his feet and he shuffled. "I don't r-really go out much."

"I assumed, but if you aren't against it, I was looking up some things that were going on locally this weekend and there is an art festival in Grandview Park I thought we could check out. There are supposed to be all kinds of local artists, and the variety of displays is supposed to be amazing. What do you think?"

Even as I spoke, his eyes lit up. His fidgeting forgotten, he tilted his head in inquiry. "I've heard about that. It's an annual thing, isn't it?"

"I believe so. My friend, Evan, his mother goes every year and collects pottery from a lady who makes all kinds of neat things. I guess it just sounded interesting."

He nodded, agreeing. Biting into his bottom lip, his gaze drifted inward for a moment. "I-I like that. I'd love to go."

A wave of relief filled me. Evan and I never needed a reason to hang out. With twenty years of mindless friendship behind us, we knew each other inside and out. We could lay around the house and do nothing, zoning out on TV or watching a game. I'd worried Oryn might need more of a reason, so I'd spent a few days trying to find something he might enjoy. The art festival had been Evan's idea.

"Great. It's an all-day thing, so we can head over anytime we want. What time are you up in the morning?"

Oryn shrugged. "Early. I don't sleep well."

"How about I come by around ten. I'll bring coffees and we can head over."

With plans arranged, we said goodbye.

***

On Saturday morning, I woke at the crack of dawn. As I showered and got ready for a day out with Oryn, my thoughts got away from me.

What if while we were out, Reed suddenly came forward? The man seemed threatened by me. At the very least, he certainly didn't seem to like me. Or Rain? It *was* an art festival, and the child inside Oryn seemed interested in such things. I'd read more about triggers and how certain events could cause an alter to come forward. Triggers could be negative *or* positive. What if an art festival encouraged Rain out? What then? Did I spend a day with a child? How would people in public perceive that situation? As much as I'd read about Oryn's condition, I still found myself in the dark most of the time. Being around him was unpredictable.

Fall had snuck in, but the temperature was comfortably warm enough I didn't need a jacket. I fixed my shaggy brown hair with a squirt of mousse and a finger comb before deciding on wearing contacts instead of glasses. After putting them in, I stared at my reflection, scratching at the stubble on my chin and deciding if I felt the need to shave.

Pass.

I grabbed my wallet and sunglasses, perched them on my head, and headed out into the day. Because I hadn't eaten, I grabbed a few muffins to go with our coffees and headed to Oryn's.

It was almost exactly ten when I arrived, and he swung the door open after my first knock as though he was expecting it.

He looked amazing.

Refreshed.

Happy.

It wasn't the faded pair of jeans or the white shirt he wore under a long-sleeved, plaid button up, it was the freedom and joy that radiated from his eyes that caught my attention. He smiled and dashed his eyes to the ground as his cheeks grew pink.

"Good morning," he said, jamming his hands in his pockets. With effort, he found my face again, smile still intact. "How are you?" No stutter.

"Excellent." I held up the small baggie with our goodies. "Do you like carrot muffins? I haven't eaten yet and I needed food, thought you'd like one too."

"I do." Noticing my loaded arms, he relieved me of the tray of coffees, stepped aside, then hesitated, seeming unsure where to put himself. "Do… Do you want to have this first and then go, o-or are we taking it with us?"

"Let's bring them. Unless you need more time?"

"Nope, I'm ready."

He locked up and we piled in the car.

Grandview Park was an enormous expanse of land located near the harbor. There were countless gardens that the city maintained during the summer months, and paths that wound through forested areas for people to walk and explore. One specific area was more open than the rest and sat beside the waterfront. It was the location of many events put on by the city throughout the year.

Parking was plentiful, and I found us a spot in a lot a block away from where we needed to be, nestled close to the water's edge. Before getting out, I helped myself to a muffin and Oryn did the same. We ate and drank our coffees watching the boats pass through the harbor before heading out into the day.

He seemed relaxed—something I knew was uncommon for Oryn.

From our place in the parking lot, I could make out all kinds of tents set up in the field where vendors had their masterpieces on display. Oryn followed my gaze as he sipped his coffee.

"What kind of stuff do you think there will be?" he asked.

"I'm not sure. Evan says art of all kinds. Bead art, paintings, pottery, woodcraft, sculptures." I shrugged. "Let's go see."

We'd finished our food and there was no reason we couldn't bring our drinks with us.

It was still early enough in the day that the crowd wasn't too thick. Regardless, Oryn's tension returned once we were among people. Much to my surprise, he glued himself to my side, walking close enough one part of us was always touching. A surge of triumph washed over me at the contact, and I smiled.

It didn't take long before we became engrossed in all the various booths surrounding us. Not only was there an uncountable variety of displays, but many areas had live demonstrations with artists working at their craft or teaching interested people how they created specific effects in their art.

As we walked past a man selling blown glass, Oryn pulled away and wormed through the crowd to where certain twisted and bubbled pieces hung above the tent like crystal chandeliers or icicles. He touched them gently and smiled. Seeing his enjoyment elevated my own.

"They're so beautiful. The way the colors splash into one another is amazing," he said, turning another in his hand.

Beside the blown glass section was a man whittling wooden animals. His table was covered with finished pieces, all stained and arranged on raised display shelves. Oryn moved beside me again while I picked up a small dog with floppy ears. The detail was incredible; the artist had captured the perfect dog-pout with sad eyes.

Oryn chuckled under his breath and removed the dog from my hands, stroking a thumb over the grooved wood. In a flash, his hand moved to his head and he fingered his temple and shook himself subtly. Before I could ask him if he was all right, he grinned in my direction and motioned to his head.

"Rain… He loves animals and he's right here, chatting my ear off."

His eyes shone with delight when he spoke of Rain. As though his presence gave him a comfort he didn't ordinarily feel. It was contagious, and I smiled with him, watching his expression as he turned his thoughts to that small child's voice I'd met the week before. A voice only he could hear.

"I wondered if this event might bring Rain forward. I know he likes art."

Oryn replaced the dog on the shelf and shrugged. "I've told him not to, but that doesn't always mean anything. He's close today and really chatty."

He rubbed the middle of his forehead, contentment still present.

"Some days can be busy and distracting when they are all talking to me at once," he explained. He glanced around as weariness snuck in and stole the joy from his smile. When he found my face, confliction was the primary emotion present. "Y-you really don't think I'm crazy?"

"Not at all," I answered without missing a beat. "Although I can't for a second know what it's like to be you, I don't think you're crazy. I only wish I understood better. I get nervous I'll do or say the wrong thing."

My honesty washed away some of his concern, and when I thought he was going to say something more, he pressed his lips together and nodded to the next booth.

We wandered from one area to the next, stopping when something interesting caught our eyes. At the pottery art vendor, Oryn became enthralled watching the demonstration on the spinning wheel. When the man in a thick canvas apron created a simple bowl in no time flat, he asked if anyone else would like to try their skills.

"You should try," I urged. His interest was piqued, and I figured with a little coaxing he might enjoy making his own.

"I-I can't do that."

"Sure you can. And if you have no skill, I'll take the blame."

He flinched and his face quirked into an intrigued smile. "How will you do that?"

"I'll play out the whole *Ghost* scene."

"The what?"

"You know, the movie *Ghost* with Whoopi Goldberg, Patrick Swayze, and Demi Moore?"

He shrugged and shook his head, clearly lost.

"Wow, I feel *really* old right now. Basically, I'll slink in behind you, move your hands and make you mess it all up. So your poor skills will be hidden behind my disruption."

Oryn chuckled and turned back to watch a young girl who'd decided to try her hand at bowl making. "That happens in a movie?"

"Yeah. I can't believe you've never heard of it."

"Maybe we can watch it sometime. Is it black and white, or one of those silent films from the olden days with the writing you have to read?"

I stared at Oryn, dumbfounded. He'd never been relaxed enough to crack jokes before, and it was so refreshing I could hardly believe my own ears.

"Making digs at the old man? Look at you. I don't even know you anymore."

He kept his eyes forward, but the tips of his ears and the crinkled smile in his eyes told me he was enjoying himself.

"Come on, let's check out some more."

We passed a few booths that didn't interest us; a seamstress who designed some eccentric clothing with unusual patterns, a soap carver, whose stand was so heavily perfumed we both ended up in coughing fits, and jewelry art.

Scanning the grounds, I pointed out a man who crafted intriguing works of art using pounded steel and suggested we head in his direction. Oryn agreed, but part way there he came to a halt without warning.

When I peered back to see why he wasn't following, I immediately noticed Oryn had paled and gone still as a statue, staring unseeing at something in the distance.

"Are you all right?"

"Windchimes," he whispered.

"What?"

He backed up a few steps nearly colliding with a group of teenagers before he caught himself. Then in an instant, the worried creases in his face vanished and he stood straighter. An intense firmness took over his features and his eyes narrowed—not with worry, but defensiveness.

Reed.

There had been no warning signs that time. No eye rubbing. No head shaking. Nothing.

He didn't look at me, but continued to focus on the crowd and booths where we'd been headed.

He shook his head fervently before scowling in my direction. "I knew this was a bad idea."

Without missing a beat, he turned and worked his way through the crowd back toward where we'd come. It was a race to catch up, and I wasn't entirely sure chasing down Reed was a good idea, but I did anyhow. Something had clearly upset Oryn, only I didn't have a clue what.

Reed went straight for the car and didn't stop until he was beside it. When I caught up, I gave him space, ensuring he knew I was there, but unsure how to approach. He leaned on the hood, glancing across the harbor. The rapid rise and fall of his chest eventually calmed, and when he peered in my direction again, he frowned with confusion, worry creasing his forehead.

Oryn?

Fuck, how the hell did someone keep up with all that?

Squinting and blinking heavily, he scanned the parking lot before checking his watch.

"I'm sorry," he whispered. "I... I don't know..."

"It's okay." Cautiously, I moved in and leaned beside him. "Do you know what happened?"

"Not really." He hugged himself and clutched his chest near his heart. "My heart is racing."

"I think something frightened you. We were heading to a new booth and you just stopped walking. You... you said..." I feared repeating it would bring back Reed, but maybe it would help jog Oryn's memory and explain why he'd fled. "You said 'windchimes', then Reed was there without warning."

"W-windchimes," he whispered. "I d-don't like windchimes." He shook his head and pinched the bridge of his nose, sucking in air through his teeth like he was in pain. "I can't really explain it, but I hate them. I don't even know why. When I hear them, it's almost p-paralysing. A chill runs up my spine and I get this jumpy feeling inside like I have to run away, but I can't m-move." He sighed. "I know that sounds incredibly stupid, but welcome to my life where nothing makes sense."

"We all have our things. It's not a big deal."

"It is a big deal. Do you know what it's like to live in a perpetual state of fear, but not have any clue why you are so afraid or what is causing it? That's my everyday life. The t-terror never goes away. Ever. Then something like that happens, and I have no idea why."

Debilitated by fear? Enough, Reed had come forward to handle it. When struck by such an emotion, I generally always knew the cause, I couldn't fathom it being unexplainable.

"Is that why Reed took over?"

Oryn shrugged and massaged his temple. "My therapist would tell you yes."

"You don't agree?"

He dropped his hand and pushed off the car, heading toward the railing overlooking the water. "I don't know anything. There are more things I don't know than I do. It feels a little bit like I'm going insane some days. I'd really hoped to know more by this point, but I don't feel any further ahead."

We stopped at the water and Oryn leaned on the rail, absently rubbing his temple periodically.

"I'm not sure I understand," I admitted.

He chuckled. "Welcome to my life. Neither do I."

"Do you have a headache?" I asked when pain took over his face again.

"I always have headaches. My doctor said people with DID frequently complain of headaches. He called them switching headaches. They're lovely because no amount of pain killers will take them away."

Just another inconvenient element to Oryn's already complicated life. The more I learned, the more my heart went out to him. Ten minutes passed in silence as we stared at a flock of seagulls floating nearby, and a motorboat sped past in the distance.

I'd spent only sporadic time with Oryn, but every one of those times had built-in challenges and obstacles to overcome. I could see why people might give up on him easily. Whenever I tried to envision life in his shoes, I couldn't. It was hard to get to know him when our time was continually interrupted.

"What's it like?" I asked as a large cargo ship slowly passed us by.

Oryn looked to me and then back at the water. "What part?"

"I don't know. Everything. Your life. I can't pretend to understand or imagine."

"It's... busy. Complicated. Maybe confusing is the better word."

I turned to him and leaned sideways, no longer interested in the ship. "How so?"

He thought for a moment, then copied my lean. "Think about your understanding of time. For you, it's straightforward. You have twenty-four hours in a day, maybe you sleep for eight of those hours, work for another eight, have routines, deadlines, a schedule. It all happens in an order that makes sense. I don't have any of that. Time is probably the most difficult concept for me. No matter how hard I try, I can't find that same order you can. My life is full of gaping holes. Blank spots with no memory. One minute I'm walking to the grocery store, then the next I know, I'm at the train station with a ticket in my hand bound for British Columbia. I don't know how I got there. I don't remember buying the ticket. Hell, I don't even know what day it is. When I find out, I may have missed hours, days, weeks..." He paused, and his eyes glassed over before he looked away across the harbor again. "Maybe years. Now imagine living your entire life like that. Not one day. Not one week, but every single day for as long as you can remember. Oh, and the kicker, the 'as long as you can remember part' only goes back a short way, because your entire childhood is gone. All you have are bits and pieces of memories that don't go together and barely paint a picture."

He stopped speaking. Despite the bustle and busyness of the day around us, there was a heavy stillness in the air. Never could I have imagined a life where time was an element of confusion. For me, time was concrete, something that was universally understood and something I relied on unconsciously in my everyday life. Imagining what Oryn described was almost impossible. The things we took for granted in life.

"Is it because of your alters?"

"In essence, except when I tell you I only learned who they were and identified them properly just over a year ago. Before then, they were all a jumble of voices in my head. Imaginary friends I thought. I could talk to them. They could talk to me. They were always so real, so when I say imagined, I just didn't have a better word to use. What I didn't know was why they were there. I was an adult and they never went away.

"Only when I was about twelve did I know it wasn't normal. I never could explain the missing pieces of time. So, my imaginary friends turned out to be alters. They are like my own homemade army according to my therapist. They were created to protect me. When any one of them come forward, I retreat, and consequently, time disappears."

It was almost haunting to hear him explain it.

"What's it like when they come forward and you have to retreat? Can you tell it's happening?"

Oryn glanced to the blue sky above and turned all the way around to lean his back on the rail. "Depending how immediate a switch is. Sometimes there is no warning, but other times I get foggy and whoever wants to come forward will be hovering in front and talking. So I can feel them there. It's like going to sleep in a way, except not completely. You know that feeling right before sleep takes you? Where you are maybe aware that things are going on but couldn't ever describe what? It's foggy and nothing makes sense really?"

"Kinda, yeah."

"It's sort of like that. When someone else is forward, they are in control and I'm in the dark." He chuckled. "It's like someone taking you for a ride in the car, but you are travelling in the trunk. You know you're moving, you know things are happening, but when you get out, you don't have a clue how you got there, all the places you were in between, or how much time has passed. Do you understand?"

"That's terrifying."

"And frustrating."

Silence slipped in once again as we watched the goings on at the festival from a safe distance. Based on what I'd read, I could only assume, the holes in his memory were likely times when Oryn had been tucked away from whatever harm was taking place. An entire childhood gone? The implication made me sick.

The thought itself was horrifying to imagine. Because of its nature, I didn't tread in those waters. But there were still things I was curious to know and carefully formed another question.

"Will it always happen, or is this something that can be resolved with therapy? I'm sorry if that sounds dumb, I just don't know how this works."

"Not dumb. It's a process and I've only just begun. Right now, my therapist is working on us all getting along. I struggle with that because certain alters upset me."

"Cove?"

Oryn nodded. "He hates me. I've tried to block him out, or control him, and it makes everything worse. My doctor wants us to communicate and come to an understanding in our internal structure. All of us. The main goal is for something he calls co-consciousness or co-sharing. All of us working together in an agreed upon way. Which would mean awareness while others were fronting and agreed switches. There is also integration, which would basically mold all identities back into one person. But I'm not even close to making that decision yet. We... we have a lot of work ahead of us."

It sounded complex. Did he have support from anyone? He didn't speak of family, and I didn't ask, fearing the segue wasn't safe.

"Well, if you ever need an ear, I hope you can consider me a friend. Maybe I don't understand everything there is to know, but I'm trying to learn and I'm just a phone call away if you ever need to chat."

Oryn turned his attention from the busy festival in the park and stared at me in wonder. The grey in his eyes was more prominent outside in the sunny day and there was a glimmer reflecting off their surface. His near blond hair blew in the gentle breeze as I examined and memorized the curve of his cheekbones and nervous smile that made him chew his lip. He was a gorgeous man, and the calm surrounding us only elevated that awareness.

Taking a chance, I reached out and cautiously took his hand in my own. His fingers were warm. The moment we touched, his gaze fell to our connection before returning to my face.

"You're a beautiful person, Oryn. Inside and out. Anyone who has discarded a chance to know you better is an idiot. Nothing about you is crazy or frightens me off. I just want you to know that."

His fingers moved in my own, not gripping so much as testing the hold we shared. Slowly, so I didn't surprise him, I brought my other hand to his face. He watched the movement, saw it coming, and his eyes widened a fraction, but he didn't flinch away. With a feathery touch, one that hardly connected us, I held his cheek in my palm. With the ghosting touch, his fingers formed a grip around my own, and only then did I fully rest my hand on his face.

"Do you believe me?" I asked.

The nod would have been missed had I not been looking for an answer. His lips moved, but no words surfaced, and he eventually dug his teeth into them instead.

Getting the sense he was quickly overloading, I dropped my hand, letting my fingers dance down his cheek until they fell. Then I stepped back, retracting my hand as well.

"I saw a food vendor selling caramel apples. Wanna go grab a few? Maybe we can take a walk?"

"I'd like that," he whispered. His eyes hadn't left my own, and I desperately wanted to know what he was thinking. After a beat, he dropped his gaze to the ground and shuffled ahead of me, making his way back toward the festival. There was a soft blush in his cheeks I hadn't missed, and it warmed my heart.

Chapter Eight

After the small hiccup with the windchimes and Reed, our day together on Saturday had been amazing. We hadn't spoken since, but I looked forward to seeing Oryn again in class on Wednesday night.

Arriving early, I found a seat in the same area we always sat and arranged my text and workbooks so I was ready for the lesson. On the hour, Richard showed up and began the evening with some short videos. Oryn hadn't arrived, and I paid as much attention to the classroom doors as I did up front. By ten after seven, I began to wonder where he might be and pulled my phone out to check for a message.

We didn't communicate much between classes, so I didn't assume I'd received one, but I hoped if there was a reason he was late, or planned to be absent, that he'd touch base.

Nothing.

I re-pocketed my phone and tried to pay attention. The least I could do was take proper notes so Oryn could copy them later. Maybe he wasn't feeling well. Maybe something had come up.

The longer class ran, the more concerned I became. At the top of the hour, when Richard gave us a ten-minute break, I sent Oryn a quick text.

Hope everything is okay. I'm taking notes for you. Let me know if you need anything.

I hesitated before sending it, wondering if it was intrusive. Saturday, I'd taken gentle strides toward letting Oryn know how I felt. Ignoring my internal debate, I hit send. When class resumed, I still hadn't received a response.

At the end of class; my phone remained silent. My classmates packed up around me while I contemplated sending another text. If I knew he was all right, I could rest easier. Deciding against it, I filled my bag and dragged my feet to my car. The sun had gone down a while ago and it was dark. The night was cloud-filled, blocking the moon and stars. A cool breeze blew and reminded me it was early October and summer was long gone.

Rotten leaves crunched under my feet as I crossed the parking lot. Once I'd settled in my car, I checked my phone again. The endless quiet from his end bothered me and gave me an unsettled sinking feeling in my gut.

Needing reassurance, I dialed his number. After a half-dozen rings, an automated voice informed me the person I was trying to reach didn't have a voicemail box set up. I hung up and tried again.

No answer.

For ten minutes, I sat in my car and contemplated what to do. Unable to shake or explain my worry, I drove to Oryn's.

It was after nine-thirty when I arrived. Sitting in my car, I examined his townhouse. The curtains had been drawn over all his windows, but there were no lights on beyond. All was quiet.

I decided to knock regardless. Maybe he was home and had gone to bed, or was watching a movie in the dark. After I knocked, I listened for approaching footsteps. None came. I knocked again and stood for another few minutes before giving up.

His street was quiet, and no one else was about. I wondered if his neighbors knew him well or if Oryn had remained in the shadows with them as well.

With nothing else to do, I headed home.

All evening I waited with anticipation for my phone to buzz with a message from Oryn. By midnight with no word, I sent another text and crawled into bed.

The following day at work was riddled with much the same distraction as I'd had in class. I still hadn't heard from Oryn, and another attempted phone call that morning had gone unanswered.

Remembering his explanation regarding time, and the holes in his memory he carried everywhere he went only escalated my concern.

Next I know, I'm at a train station with a ticket in my hand, bound for British Columbia.

Had that happened before? Where the hell was he and why wasn't he answering his phone?

A small niggling thought wondered if I'd upset him somehow on Saturday, but apart from the conversation we'd had near the water, everything had gone smooth.

I was baffled.

Evan invited me out for a drink after work which I wanted to decline but decided would work well to distract me. We met up at our favorite bar and grill, The Monkey Barrel, so we could have some dinner as well.

Evan worked in real estate and liked to brag about making his own hours. When I arrived at The Barrel, he was already watching some soccer game on the big screen while nursing a beer.

"Hey," he said as I sunk into the seat across from him. He tore his gaze from the TV and shoved a beer in my direction. "Ordered us burgers and fries. Should be here soon. How was your day?"

"Long." I drank deep and relaxed back, glad to be away from the office, but still tense from all the worry I couldn't let go of. "How about you?"

"Not bad. I have a showing at six, so I can't hang out long."

I quirked a brow. "And you're drinking?"

Evan shrugged it off like it was no big deal.

I pulled my phone out and placed it beside me on the off chance I'd hear from Oryn.

Evan scowled, sensing something was up, but turned back to the game instead of voicing it. The waiter showed up with our food shortly there after, and we dove into our meal.

"So, since you dumped me, I have a date Saturday night. Asked out that girl at the café."

"The one with the red hair you've been ogling for months?"

"Yup, her name's Krystina. We are going to Rock and Bowl."

"You hate bowling. Why are you doing that?"

Evan shrugged. "Her idea, not mine. You and lover boy should come too. Unless you have other plans." He wiggled his eyebrows for emphasis.

"Enjoy your Rock and Bowl. Oryn and I aren't dating, and I don't think he's ready to put up with you quite yet. You'll scare him off."

"You haven't wooed him? Good grief what is taking so long. Didn't you go out together Saturday? I've never known you not to express yourself. What's the deal?"

I checked my phone and grabbed a fry, shoving it in my mouth to give me a moment before answering. "I think he needs a friend more. Maybe down the road. His life isn't exactly straightforward. But… I may have given him a clue how I feel. I won't push myself on him. I get the sense that would be a bad idea."

"So come bowling. I'll behave. No raunchy comments. I promise."

"Why do you want me to intrude on your date so badly?"

"Because I hate bowling."

I rolled my eyes and shoved another fry in my mouth without responding while checking my phone for the hundredth time since I'd sat down.

"What's wrong with you?"

"What?" I dashed my gaze to Evan's. "What do you mean?"

"You've been staring at your phone all night."

I sighed and grabbed my napkin to wipe my mouth. "Oryn wasn't in class last night and I've messaged him a few times and called, and he hasn't got back to me."

"So?"

"So… I don't know. I get this feeling something isn't right."

Evan shrugged off my concern as though it was a non-issue. "Go see him."

"I did after class yesterday. He wasn't home."

"So go after dinner. Why the hell are you so worried?"

I sighed and shoved my phone back in my pocket so I didn't look as desperate. "I don't know. Never mind. Let's drop it."

Evan dissected me a moment more before deciding not to push the matter and turned back to the TV and his game. After we'd finished eating it was edging six o'clock and Evan had to split for his house showing. Since I had nowhere else to be, I drove across town to Oryn's once again in hopes that I would find him home and alleviate the unsettled gnawing in my gut.

It was dark at six when I pulled into his driveway, thanks to the arrival of fall. A light in Oryn's living room glowed from behind the drawn curtains. The minute I put the car into park, I yanked my phone out, expecting a response to the umpteen messages I'd sent. Still nothing.

Disappointed at being ignored, I slid my phone on the dash and killed the engine. Maybe I was pushing myself on him too hard—even as a friend. Oryn lived a secluded life, and perhaps he preferred it that way. My attempt to make friends had only been out of kindness, but maybe he didn't appreciate or want that in his life. It wasn't the impression I read from him, but maybe I was seeing something that wasn't there.

As I approached his front door, I scanned the dead-end road. It was vacant and quiet as always. No people milling about, just a few brightly lit houses among a sea of darker ones. That far off the main road, there wasn't even any traffic.

I knocked once and shoved my hands in my pockets. Unlike the previous time I'd been there, I knew someone was home and I expected an answer. When one didn't come, I furrowed my brow and brought my hand up to knock again. Just as I was about to connect, the door swung inward and Oryn stood tall on the other side, sneering and glaring back.

"What?" he snapped, his eyes not leaving my own.

I opened my mouth to respond and then shut it again just as quickly when I realized it wasn't Oryn who'd opened the door. I scanned him, noting all the indicators that told me I faced Reed.

His squared shoulders, raised chin, deeper voice, intense eyes, and stance which didn't cower from my unexpected arrival.

He wore a t-shirt and jeans. The moment my gaze parted from his face to observe him more closely, I saw the thick bandage wrapped around his left arm. It covered the majority of his forearm and was secured in place by multiple pieces of white medical tape.

Instantly concerned for his wellbeing, forgetting I was facing off with Reed, my mouth hung open, and I reached out to grab his arm.

"Holy shit! What the hell happened?"

My fingers barely grazed his hand when he snapped his arm away and stepped back to get away from me. I lifted my gaze to his as his irises darkened with further distrust and anger.

"I told you not to come here. What are you doing?"

I fumbled briefly with my nerves, thrown off finding Reed in place of Oryn, but I straightened myself and forced a steadiness into my voice.

"I was worried about Oryn and came to make sure he was okay."

Maybe bringing up Oryn wasn't a good idea. I honestly had no clue, but Reed didn't flinch. He propped his foot to hold the door and crossed his arms over his chest. It was almost uncanny how different they were. Even though I knew it wasn't the case, he looked bigger.

"Oryn isn't your concern. We've done just fine without you until now, so go on home."

"No." That time he did flinch. I even startled myself. "Oryn is my friend and no matter what you want to believe of me, I do care about him and want to make sure he's okay." I dashed a glance to the bandaged arm. "What happened?" I asked again.

Reed continued to study me with an air of uncertainty. When enough time passed, and I realized I wasn't going to get an answer, I heaved a sigh and backed up a step.

"All right. Never mind."

I didn't want to leave. Everything in me wanted to fight my case and prove to Reed I was genuine in my concern, but I didn't know how to do that.

When I turned to my car, I heard the door close behind me.

"You need to understand, I will do everything in my power to keep him safe."

The sudden gruff voice behind me made me spin in surprise. I'd assumed Reed had gone back inside. He approached and stood closer than I felt comfortable, but I didn't retreat. His intimidating stance made me feel small, but I drew on all the courage I could find and matched his hardened glare.

"If that's true, if you're supposed to be keeping him safe, then why did you allow that to happen."

I nodded to his arm, knowing what the bandage probably hid. My stomach turned relentlessly.

Reed's jaw hardened. When he spoke, it was barely above a whisper. "Don't cast judgement on things you don't understand."

"You act as though I'm a threat, but you haven't spent a minute even trying to get to know me. I've gone to great lengths to understand Oryn, and I tread very carefully around things I know nothing about. But I would never hurt him. Not like you."

He stepped in closer bringing my heart rate up another few notches. "That right there proves how little you know about us. We are protecting him, not harming him. I'll tell you one more time. You don't belong here. In my eyes, you *are* a threat. Go home."

With another step forward, I stumbled back, losing my nerve along with my footing. When my back hit the car, Reed stopped and held his ground, waiting for me to flee. I didn't know what else to say or do so I reached blindly for the handle at my back and yanked the car door open.

"When will Oryn be back?" Perhaps it wasn't a safe question and I steeled myself for Reed to react in anger. He didn't. Like a statue, he stayed strong and firm.

"When he's ready," was all he said before turning back to the house.

When he shut himself inside, I climbed back in my car and squeezed two hands over the steering wheel. My palms were slick on the leather, and only then did I register the inner tremble that had taken root.

Doing my best to ignore the growing turmoil inside, I drove home and collapsed on my couch. When I'd explained to Evan that my friendship with Oryn was complicated, it was moments like that which encompassed those feelings and made them even more true and real. I felt like a yo-yo, being jerked in one direction then another without warning, and my poor heart didn't know what to do.

I knew what lay under that bandage. I'd seen the scars from many before. Based on what Oryn had shared, I had a pretty good idea who'd put them there too. What I didn't understand was how a system that was created to protect him, did him harm.

Sleep didn't come that night. Long into the early morning, I lay staring at the ceiling, wondering about the man who'd come into my life unexpectedly. It made complete sense why so many others turned their back on Oryn. No matter how carefully I approached, being around him was a constant rollercoaster of unexpectedness. I never knew who I'd be talking to one minute to the next, and although I hadn't met all his alters, more than half of them made me uncomfortable or nervous.

I could hear Evan mocking me and asking what the hell I saw in Oryn that kept me so interested. But, I couldn't explain it. Understanding enough about his life, realizing the kind of isolation he saw everyday, just made me want to reach out more. Plus, the more I got to know Oryn as a person, the warmer and more undeniable my feelings for him became. Had he been any other person, that day beside the harbor would have certainly gone further.

***

I stopped texting after I visited Oryn's house Thursday night. Not surprisingly, he didn't show up to class on Friday either. Come the weekend, I was consumed with worry but did everything to ignore it. Evan had his date Saturday, so I didn't hear from him until Sunday at noon when he texted to confirm our football plans.

I wasn't in the mood but begrudgingly forced myself into a shower before heading to the beer store and then over to his house.

Evan unloaded the case of beer from my arms after he yanked the door open and ushered me inside. It was evident his date night had ended at his apartment—and likely only a few hours before our text conversation. There were empty wine glasses on the coffee table and the distinctive smell of women's perfume hung in the air.

"Date went well?" I asked, nodding to the pair of glasses.

Evan chuckled and took the beer to the kitchen where he started unloading it into the fridge.

"Extremely."

I grabbed the dirty dishes and brought them to the sink to wash. Evan was the furthest thing from a neat freak and had succumb to the fact that I tended to tidy up after him whenever I came over.

The TV was already on and set to the Detroit pre-game show.

"How'd it go with Oryn on Thursday? Was he around?"

I balanced a cleaned wine glass in the dish drain and pursed my lips deciding how to best answer without causing Mr. opinionated Evan to jump all over the situation.

"Not technically. I talked with Reed." *Talk* was a loose term. More like got put in my place and shipped out with the garbage.

Evan scratched his stubble and squinted. "Which one is he again?"

"The one who doesn't like me."

Evan's face turned pained as he popped the cap on both our beers and handed me one. "How'd that go?"

"Not well." I shrugged, not really wanting to dive into complexities. "Let's watch the game, I'm not sure I want to talk about it."

Evan slapped my shoulder and steered me into the living room again. We didn't need words to communicate. His subtle gesture, squeezing my shoulder before releasing me, said enough for me to understand if I wanted to talk, he'd listen.

The game wasn't any easier to follow that week than it had been the previous few. My preoccupation with Oryn was extreme, only that week, I hid it better.

When my phone buzzed during the fourth quarter, I jumped and ripped it from my pocket.

It was a text from Oryn.

Can you talk?

Dashing a glance to Evan who was entranced in the game, I ducked my head and typed out a reply while I headed down the hall to his bedroom.

"Gotta take a call, be right back."

He mumbled a reply but didn't tear his eyes from the TV.

Yes, I can.

Within a minute my phone rang, and I accepted the call as I closed over Evan's bedroom door. His bed was a pile of rumpled, un-made bedding, and it reeked of sex, so I shuffled a few things over on his end table and sat on its edge wanting to avoid the bed at all costs.

"Oryn?"

"Hi." The timid voice was unmistakable. When I heard it, my entire body let go of the mountain of stress it had been carrying around all week. "I'm s-s-sorry."

His stutter was heavier than usual. The simple apology he had no business making tore at my heart.

"You have nothing to be sorry for. Are you okay? I've been worried about you." There was no sense in lying, the concern was evident in my voice and I couldn't hide it.

"Umm... Y-yes." He paused, and my mind raced with a hundred questions.

"Oryn, I was at your house. Reed, he... he told me to butt out and leave you alone. Your arm. What happened?"

He moved the phone in his hand, muffling the sound for a brief moment before sighing. "I d-don't want to t-talk about it on the ph-ph-phone. Would you like to m-meet me after my writing class Monday?"

I nodded frantically at the chance to see him. "Yes! Yes, please. When are you done with class?"

"Eight-thirty. Will you c-come by my house?"

"How about I pick you up? Can I pick you up at the college?"

"Okay." His voice went soft and quiet, and silence grew between us.

I didn't want to hang up, but if he didn't want to talk on the phone, I hated pushing the matter. "Oryn, please tell me if you aren't okay. I can be there in five minutes. Even if you just need company."

"I'm really okay," he assured, his voice still airy and hard to hear. "I'm s-sorry I didn't respond to your calls and m-messages. It was j-just... I just—"

"I understand. It's okay. I'll see you Monday?"

"Thank you."

When the call disconnected, the urgency to go to him was almost more than I could bear. More than anything, I needed to see him with my own eyes and judge how he truly was for myself. Deep inside, a growing part of me yearned to pull him into my arms and hold him until his distress and inner turmoil calmed. Knowing that it may never, and that it was probably a permanent part of who he was, only intensified the ache in my chest.

Chapter Nine

Monday evening took forever to arrive. Work tested my patience at every turn, and as a result, I ended up behind and needed to stay late. By the time I arrived at the college, my hair was still damp from my shower, so I worked some semblance of order into it with my fingers while I waited for Oryn's class to let out.

He'd sent me a text, assuring me he was in class, and as I waited, I sent him one back letting him know where I'd parked.

Just after eight-thirty, a crowd of students spilled from the front doors and scattered through the parking lot. Sitting up straighter in my seat, I scanned for Oryn. Only when the crowd had thinned did he emerge, cradling his textbook to his chest, eyes trained on the ground, and bag slung over a shoulder. He wore long sleeves, as usual, so the bandage I'd seen before was hidden away.

When he reached the stairs which led to street level, he looked up for the first time and scanned the lot. Spotting me, he ducked his head again and continued on his way. I started the engine and watched him with a heaviness in my chest as he approached. The hunched shoulders and white-knuckled grip on his books told of his anxious state. It was exactly like he'd described. The poor man lived in a perpetual state of fear.

When he slid in the passenger seat and turned to me with a warm smile, relief flooded through my every pore. The all-consuming worry I'd carried for him over the past week eased slightly seeing Oryn as opposed to an alter.

"Hi," I greeted. "How was class?"

He shrugged and gnawed his lip, unable to hold my gaze. "It was okay. I don't like that class as much."

Pulling from the parking lot, assuming we were heading to his house, I asked, "Why is that? I would have thought creative writing would be the better class."

He shuffled, and the tips of his ears pinked with his shy smile. "Because…" He passed me a quick glance and clenched his jeans as he fidgeted nervously. "You… you aren't in it, so it's lonely. N-no one talks to me. They talk a lot *about* me… behind my back, but I'm not s-stupid."

The confession did a combination of things. It irritated me that people could be so cruel and shun someone who was a little different without even knowing them—especially at an age that was past dramatic teenage-hood. Also, the statement warmed me in a way I didn't expect. Knowing Oryn found comfort in my presence was a win I'd been hoping for.

"Their loss," I said, keeping my features soft in hopes of helping him relax. "Sorry the class isn't as much fun."

He shrugged and watched out the window as he continued his assault on his pant legs. When I parked in his driveway and shut off the engine, I turned in my seat and indicated with a nod to the house.

"I assumed we were okay to come here. Yes?"

He dashed a look my way then dropped his gaze to his hands which were folded together in his lap. "It's m-more comfortable for me. Is that okay?"

"Absolutely."

We got out and Oryn collected his bag without passing more words. At the front door, he unlocked it as I hovered behind him a few feet. The fresh hint of woodsy citrus hung in the air when I was near him, and it took all my self control not to step in and inhale.

He peered over his shoulder as he pushed the door inward, and a shy smile came and went before he looked away again. I followed him into the den and got comfortable in the same place I always sat when I was over. Oryn dumped his bag on the floor by the desk and shuffled between feet as he indicated to the kitchen.

"C-can I get you a drink or something?"

"Sure. Whatever you have is fine."

His gaze fell to the ground as he escaped to the kitchen. When he returned a short time later, he carried two mugs full of a steaming hot drink. Little brown sticks poked out of the top of the mugs and it took me a minute to realize they were cinnamon sticks.

"Hot apple c-cider. Is that okay? Theo p-picked it up at the market this afternoon. They have all kinds of f-fall things now with the season, I guess."

Theo? I didn't ask.

I accepted the mug and inhaled the sweet yet spicy scent. "It's perfect. I don't even remember the last time I had cider."

He smiled with a hint of pride and sunk to the ground in front of the coffee table, settling on his knees. I'd noted before, he seemed more comfortable there and often gravitated to the ground instead of the couch itself.

He wrapped his hands around his mug and focused on the steam rising, brows drawn together as though forming words before voicing them.

"I… T-Tuesdays and Thursdays are therapy days with Dr. Delmar. S-sometimes it doesn't go well. Progress can be… umm…" He thought a minute, clearly struggling with what he wanted to express. With a heavy sigh, he met my eyes. "There is a lot of resistance." His gaze dropped along with his volume. "Cove and I don't get along and," he whispered. "Sometimes it makes things worse between us."

Leaving my place on the couch, I joined him on the floor to be at his level. With hesitance, I crawled a hand across the table toward his own. He released his mug as I closed the distance and watched with caution swimming in his eyes. The left arm, which I knew was bandaged under his long sleeve, laid closer, and I took that hand in my own with a loose hold, enough he could pull away if he didn't want the touch. He didn't move. Turning the arm so the affected area under his shirt would face up, I pressed the balls of my thumbs into his palm, massaging it delicately, hoping to keep him relaxed. His tension visibly mounted; his shoulders stiffened, and his Adam's apple bobbed with a difficult swallow.

"May I?" I asked, nodding to the arm, requesting permission to see what had happened.

His lips twisted in uncertainty, the blue-grey eyes which hadn't left mine became glassy, but he nodded. It was barely enough movement for confirmation, so I didn't move until he worked a simple squeaking 'yes' from his throat.

With continued care, I drew up his shirt sleeve to his elbow, exposing a new white bandage taped over the length of his arm. I trailed my fingers down over its surface, feeling raised lumps underneath. I wanted to see more but was unable to explain why. Rooted deep inside was a swelling, burning desire to care for the man in front of me, which also meant understanding everything there was to know about the self-abuse he fell victim to.

With my fingers rested against the affected area, Oryn began to explain. His voice was barely audible, and I needed to strain to ensure I didn't miss anything.

"He knows about my past. He hates me. Maybe he blames me, I don't know. To achieve co-consciousness like I explained before, Dr. Delmar says I need to accept Cove. Except... he's angry and violent. I try to hold him back and not let him out, but he gets free and then he does this. Dr. Delmar doesn't understand. I sometimes think Cove is trying to kill us. He cuts. He burns. Anything he can do to make us hurt. I'm trying to stop him, Vaughn... I really am."

When his voice broke, he fell silent. I couldn't stop myself and took hold of the end of one of the pieces of tape. When I pulled it from his skin, his face scrunched and he bit his lip. Otherwise, he didn't stop me. One by one, I removed the tape holding the bandage in place. After the last piece was removed, I lifted the cotton covering, carefully, in case it was stuck to his wound. What I found underneath stirred bile in my stomach, and it rose up my gorge forcing me to swallow a few times.

His arm had been opened in two places. Long distinctive cuts with clean edges, probably made with a sharp blade. Both were equal in length; roughly two and a half or three inches long. Both had been stitched cleanly and were showing evidence that the skin had begun knitting itself back together.

A million questions pummeled my brain, but I sat mute, staring at the wounds on his arm, hurting more on the inside with each passing minute.

"How... How do you know this is Cove?" I hadn't met that alter—and wasn't sure I wanted to—but I had met Reed, and for whatever reason, I didn't put that sort of aggressiveness past him.

"He told me. The journals we share. Sometimes he says he's sorry, and that he has no choice, but I don't believe him. He's promised in the past that he won't hurt me anymore, but it always happens again." Oryn shook his head. "Maybe if he didn't know about them, he wouldn't hate me so much. It's not my fault."

Them? The memories?

"You don't remember him doing this at all?"

Oryn shook his head and watched as I traced a thumb alongside the closer cut. "I lost almost a week."

Not releasing his arm, I glanced up and studied the contortion on his face. His eyes were downcast toward his arm, only he wasn't looking at it. He was lost in his mind. "I came by. I was worried about you."

"I'm sorry."

Without a second thought, I brought a hand to his face and encouraged his chin up so he'd look me in the eyes. He flinched at the initial contact, but relaxed faster than every time before. So, I left my hand on his cheek.

"You have nothing to be sorry about."

With our eyes locked, Oryn's breathing noticeably increased. Although his entire body had gone still when I'd cradled his face in my hand, an unmistakable inner tremble resonated throughout him.

Seeing the stormy, blue-grey worry in his eyes was enough for me to lose myself. His features were so delicate and soft. Every gentle curve pronouncing his beauty in the most subtle of ways.

I couldn't pull away. His gaze flicked about my own face and twice fell to my lips before shooting back up with an edge of panic.

I moved toward him before I had enough sense to stop myself. Simultaneously, I drew him closer, sliding the cupped hand to his nape. As fearful as I knew he was, he didn't resist. Within inches of his face, I stilled. Our foreheads brushed close and his breath ghosted my lips, but I didn't move further.

His sharp intakes of air were audible, and I locked my gaze on his lips as he licked them repeatedly. The invitation might have been obvious had it been anyone else, but with Oryn I knew enough not to jump the gun.

"I want to kiss you," I whispered.

His nose brushed mine and he spoke on a wobbled breath, "I know."

I smiled at his response. It wasn't permission, so I pressed closer, until our lips were a hairsbreadth apart. "Is that okay?"

He nodded at the same moment his fingers hooked around my arm and secured themselves with an uncertain hold. Almost like fear required him to ground himself in some tangible way.

Heedful of any signs I should stop, I closed the final sliver of distance and pressed our mouths together. The only part of him that wasn't stiff with apprehension were his lips. They softened at my touch and an unexpected sigh whimpered from him as we met.

Grazing a feather light touch against his mouth, I kissed him tentatively, only tasting along his lips when his hold on my arm loosened. It remained chaste and light; small pecks as I tested his resolve. When I made attempts to encourage him to part his lips and go further, Oryn pulled away.

I relaxed my hold behind his neck and sat back on my heels, widening our gap so his shuttered breathing might calm. Wild eyes examined mine, and he unconsciously lifted a hand to his mouth where he touched his lips. His uncertainty left him searching for a response, and more than once he lost his nerve and looked away.

"I like you, Oryn. I hope that… kissing you didn't scare you off. I would never purposefully want to make you uncomfortable."

The hand that hadn't left my arm tightened again reflexively, and his lips worked to form words. It was painful to watch him struggle, but I waited patiently for a response.

"W-why?"

Why? Why did I like him?

I chuckled and laid my hand over his. "Why not? You're incredible and I've loved getting to know you. Your strength and determination... you fascinate me, Oryn."

"I'm n-not those things." His gaze fell to the table. "I'm a barely functioning adult with more issues than I can count."

"I don't see that."

When he found the courage to lift his gaze, he examined me skeptically. "I like you too," he whispered. "But..."

A crushing sensation surrounded my heart with that single *but,* and I firmed my jaw as I waited for him to explain, certain I was about to hear rejection.

"I-I don't know if I... It's j-just..." He visibly trembled more as he stuttered in his effort to explain. "P-physical r-rela..." He blew out a huff of air in frustration and tried again, "Physical relationships m-make me uncomfortable. I don't t-think I can do that." With the admission, he pulled his hand free and scrubbed it over his face. "I'm s-sorry."

He scrambled to collect the bandage and pieces of tape, then jumped up and flew down the hallway out of sight. A door slamming was the last thing I heard before the house fell silent. My mind raced with what we'd shared, and I instantly felt like an ass. If he had been severely abused as a child—sexually abused of all things—of course physical intimacy would be a struggle. *Fuck!* I wouldn't be surprised if it was downright impossible.

Waiting long enough to conclude he wasn't coming out, I rose and left our cooling drinks on the table and followed after him. Perhaps I should have left, but I couldn't shake the need to ensure he was all right and to let him know I would never in a million years push myself on him. The kiss had been a mistake, and I needed him to know it wouldn't happen again.

The door to Rain's room was closed over and a second door further down stood open to another bedroom, but it was dark inside. Across the hall was a third door which was closed. A light shone from underneath, telling me where I'd find Oryn.

I knocked lightly and waited. No response. With a second knock, I added, "Please talk to me, Oryn. I shouldn't have done that. I'm the one who should be sorry."

A full minute later, when I was set to give up and leave him alone, the door creaked open. Inch by inch, the bathroom was exposed along with Oryn, a medical kit cradled in his arms.

"Can you help me re-cover this please. It's t-tricky."

He backed up a step, welcoming me into his space, and I advanced with caution.

"Of course."

He handed me the first aid kit and sat on the closed toilet lid. The bathroom was small, and the edge of the tub was close enough I sat there to work. He wouldn't look at me and kept his gaze fixed on what I was doing. As I cut a piece of gauze bandage to fit over the wound, his soft voice came to my ears.

"No one has ever been as kind to me as you have. I've n-never even really had a friend before. I'm too different for most people. Too unpredictable. I'm not always me, and I certainly don't have control right now over who is forward and who isn't." He blew out a frustrated breath. "Vaughn, I... I like you, too. But I can't give you what you want."

I worked a piece of medical tape from the roll and eyed him before fitting it along the side of the cloth. "You don't know what I want."

He made a noise that was almost a strained chuckle. "You are a good looking guy and are probably itching to have that perfect relationship with someone. One that includes... you know..." He squirmed and hung his head even lower so I couldn't see his face. "The stuff normal people do in relationships," he mumbled.

What he clumped into that *normal relationship* box, I could easily guess.

"Can I explain something to you about me?"

I affixed another piece of tape and waited for him to respond. He nodded but wouldn't lift his head. So, I secured the last two pieces of tape in place, ensuring the bandage was secure, and pulled his sleeve down before taking his chin and turning his face up.

Once his eyes were on mine, I released my hold, sensing the anxiety it caused.

"You tell me all the time how you aren't like other people, and I see that and understand it in the only way I can. I'm really trying to learn. But, *I'm* not like other people either. I've had all kinds of offers to date men and I've taken a few of them up on it, but they're all the same. There is always something we don't click on."

Sex. But I didn't want to be so bold as to say it out loud. Unlike Evan, I'd always had a much lower need for that sort of thing. Intimacy was important to me, but I was probably one of the only guys on the planet—or I *was* the only guy on the planet according to Evan—who just didn't feel the draw to have a hugely active sex life. Boyfriends in the past couldn't get past that and eventually gave up. It wasn't that I didn't enjoy sex, I did, but the intimacy that surrounded it was far more important to me when building a relationship. Sex was always a bonus, but I didn't go seeking it like Evan, nor did I require it with the same urgency as I did oxygen, or food. I wasn't like other men.

"Evan teases me and tells me I'm looking for Mr. Perfect, but he's wrong. I'm just looking for someone who understands me as well and sees things the way I do. Someone who appreciates the smaller things, not someone who is narrowminded or entitled. Someone kind-hearted. There are fewer and fewer people out there like that. But you are, and I like that about you.

"I'd never ask you to take on anything you didn't feel comfortable with. If announcing how I feel about you like that was a mistake, I'm sorry. I guess you know how I feel now, but I'd be more than happy to be by your side as a friend if that was all you wanted."

His teeth found his bottom lip as I spoke, and he gnawed it mercilessly. The uncertainty behind his eyes hurt, but I couldn't begin to imagine being in his shoes.

"I wish it could be more," he finally said.

"Is it impossible?"

"I... I don't know." His gaze fell to his lap before he continued, "But if we tried, and it all went badly... I-I don't want to lose you as a friend. I don't want to see you be frustrated because..."

Again, he stalled on something he couldn't voice. I was convinced if I stated flat out I was okay waiting on sex, he'd call me a liar and never learn to trust me, so I remained quiet.

I wanted to reach out and touch him. Comfort him in a way I doubted anyone in his life ever had. However, his boundaries were clearly marked, and any uninvited contact was quite clearly a potential trigger for him.

"You take control here, Oryn. If friendship is all you are able to give me, I understand. If any part of you wants to test the waters of a relationship, I think you'll find I'm more than patient. Okay?"

There was a long expanse of silence. Without a word, Oryn's hand slipped closer and grazed my fingers with a hesitant touch. I didn't move and allowed him to explore the connection on his own. Opening my hand, the balls of his fingers danced over my palm before coming to rest fully against my own. He curled them around my hand and held on. Only then did he raise his eyes to mine.

My internal desire to kiss him was strong, and I had to fight off my body's urge to advance more than once.

"You understand that we kinda come as a package, right? I'm not just me. All of us are kinda housed together and you can't really just take one and not the rest." His lip curled into an attempt at a smile and his shyness returned full-force.

Was he trying to say he was willing to attempt a relationship?

A package. That was something I'd considered but it still confused me more than anything. Oryn was who'd caught my eye.

The other alters—the ones I'd met—were simply other people who, despite their uniqueness at being a distinctive part of Oryn, they weren't Oryn. Rain was a child. Reed an indignant jerk. Cohen, although outwardly flirty and attractive in his own way, was *very* nineteen. I wasn't sure how I felt about that.

None of them were Oryn. The object of my true attraction, and the person who'd caught my eye and made my heart beat with more vigor and my insides flutter.

"That may prove challenging," I admitted honestly. "The last time I saw Reed, I was certain he might kick my ass just for expressing concern over you."

The chuckle that followed my statement was more free than before. "See, we aren't cut and dry. Probably not a good mix for a normal relationship."

So, is that a no?

I squeezed his hand and stood, helping him up as well. Dropping my hold on him, I closed the first aid kit before returning it to his hands. "Can you do me a favor?" I waited for him to nod before continuing, "Stop with the *normal*. No two people are the same. I like you for you."

He conceded and returned the medical box to its spot under the counter. To break the tension, I suggested a movie, and Oryn was quick to agree. He reheated our beverages and settled beside me on the couch. No more was said about our shared kiss, the cuts on his arms, the direction of our friendship, or what—if anything—might transpire after that day. We simply enjoyed the evening.

Midway through the movie, Oryn reached across the small expanse separating us. He slinked his hand into mine. Our fingers weaved together, and he held me tight. I didn't draw attention to it, but spent the rest of the movie caressing over his warm skin with my thumb. It was a simple and uncomplicated connection.

Safe.

It warmed my heart knowing, despite his uncertainty, he sought more.

Chapter Ten

Christmas vacation approached faster than I anticipated. My free time until then had been consumed with Oryn. We spent many evenings together working on our term project and others simply hanging out either watching movies or walking the nature trails by the harbor—an activity I'd learned Oryn enjoyed.

Nothing more had happened between us apart from a scarce number of fleeting touches that never lasted more than a second. Oryn's comfort level around me had grown and his stutter was always my indicating factor on where that level hovered. It was encouraging to hear it slip away and to see him smile more.

With two weeks off from class and a much needed few days holiday break away from work, I looked forward to having a little more time with Oryn. I knew he was without family—or at least he'd never mentioned any in our time together—so I'd invited him over for a small dinner at my apartment. He'd been reluctant to change our routine and hang out at my place, but in the end, he'd agreed.

Over the past two months, I'd had a number of encounters with Reed. None had ended well. Each time I found myself in his presence, I was shuffled out the door and told never to return. I took each episode with a grain of salt—outwardly. Inside, I had to admit, it hurt. Reed wouldn't talk to me, or listen to reason when all I wanted to do was explain that I wasn't a threat and that I liked Oryn. The dejection always hit hard, especially since his appearance was always abrupt.

Rain had surfaced one other time and Cohen twice. My awkwardness with Rain remained, but because his appearance was as short lived the second time as the first, I had no time to really acclimate to the idea of a child inside Oryn's body.

Cohen… was determined to win me over. When I'd shared that with Oryn, he'd only giggled and assured me he knew all about it.

Journals… ones I wasn't privy to.

There were days I felt like the outsider in a close-knit family.

Cove and Theo remained a mystery. I had yet to meet either of them, and some days, selfishly, I hoped I never did. Oryn and three other identities were complex enough. Balancing two more alters, who may or may not like me, was unnerving.

I opened the oven door and checked on the whole roasted chicken and potatoes. A wave of heat hit my face and instantly steamed my glasses. I drew my face to the side and waited for my vision to clear before poking a look inside. The savory smell of lemon and herbs hit my nose, and my stomach growled in response. The skin on the chicken was a golden brown; as were the potato cubes I'd tossed in olive oil and sprinkled with garlic and rosemary. Everything looked cooked, including the carrots steaming in a pot on the element.

I checked the time as I drew the items from within the oven and placed them on top to cool. It was a quarter to six.

I clicked off the heat and typed a quick text to Oryn letting him know I was on my way. He'd insisted on walking over, but I'd adamantly refused. The temperature was below freezing, and it had snowed significantly two days before, leaving the sidewalks only moderately passable.

As I pulled on my coat, I scanned the living room and dining area. Everything was tidy. The table was set for dinner, including my fancier dishes I'd inherited from my grandmother, folded napkins, and a Christmas candle arrangement in the middle. It looked intimate and date-like.

"It's not a date," I reminded myself as I pulled on my boots.

I'd repeated that statement to myself all afternoon, but hadn't been able to resist making the entire atmosphere exude that exact sentiment. From the air fresheners I'd purchased to the soft music which already played in the background, it was exactly how it appeared.

Deep inside, I still couldn't shake those feelings I'd developed for Oryn. In fact, the longer I knew him, the more pronounced they'd become. And he hadn't really been clear on whether or not we were proceeding on *relationship* status... nor had I asked, because it seemed uncomfortable conversation for him.

The drive to his house was slow. The roads were semi-plowed but slushy. The side streets were even worse. Night had fallen early with the season and the Christmas bustle at that time in the evening was intense. Everyone was out shopping for the upcoming holiday season and traffic was heavy.

When I pulled in his driveway, it was after six. He waited outside the front door bundled in a black knitted tuque, matching scarf, black winter coat, and boots. He hugged himself against the cold and scurried over the moment the car came to a stop. When he got in, he removed his hat and brushed fingers through his light-colored hair as he smiled.

"Hi," he said in the meek tone I was accustomed to. He'd come out of his shell significantly over the past two months, but his timidness was something he couldn't escape. It was simply a part of who he was.

I returned his smile and backed out of the driveway. "I hope you're hungry. I made a ridiculous amount of food."

"Starving." He shivered and held his bare hands over the vents, seeking warmth.

With his action, I cranked the heater to max, blasting the hot air over us both.

At my apartment, I didn't miss Oryn's curious observation of the dining room table and music selection. He didn't comment, and I worried momentarily I'd gone too far, until I caught him smiling to himself when he thought I wasn't looking.

"I'm just going to make a couple of plates and bring them out. Can I get you something to drink? I bought wine, but I didn't know if that was your thing."

In all the time we'd spent together, I'd never seen him drink alcohol. Cohen had, but not Oryn. When his forehead creased at my offer, I regretted not grabbing a variety of alternate options.

"I'm not *really* supposed to drink. They have me on an anti-depressant, but I love wine and, it's the holiday season, right?"

It was an actual question and the look he gave sought a real answer as though he wasn't sure he could make that choice on his own. I had no idea he took meds that conflicted with alcohol. Cohen had never mentioned it. Nor had he seemed concerned.

"I can run to the store and grab a bottle of Coke or something instead, I should have asked ahead of time."

Oryn shook his head at the suggestion and pressed a knuckle into his eye. "N-no… It's okay. I hate that rule to be honest. Everyone else breaks it. Why not me too. Wine is perfect."

Reluctantly, I excused myself and went to make our plates in the kitchen. When I returned and placed them at our respective spots at the table, I hesitated. Part of me had planned to light the candles in the centerpiece display—which had rung as a good idea when I'd thought of it earlier—but in the moment, I shied away, knowing it hedged into date territory and I wasn't sure if that was acceptable.

The ambience rang of intimacy regardless, and Oryn's posture and constant fiddling, coupled with the random shy smiles when our eyes met told me he'd noticed. With my already obvious failure, I snatched a book of matches and lit them anyway.

Fuck it, it's a date.

Oryn watched the flickering flame and again scanned the apartment before settling on my face and issuing me yet another warm smile. It brought a tickle of nerves to dance over my skin. He had the most beautiful eyes and mouth, and I adored seeing them shining with contentment.

Without exchanging words, we settled in to eat.

"This is really good," he said, pointing his fork to the roasted chicken.

"Thank you. My mother used to insist I help out in the kitchen growing up, so I may have picked up a thing or two."

"I can't sort out how to combine herbs and such to make stuff taste good. Theo is the cook. He goes all out and fills the freezer with all kinds of…" He trailed off and lifted his gaze to mine as he pressed his lips into a tight line. "S-sorry."

His chin fell to his chest as he shoved a small bite of chicken in his mouth. Speaking of his alters often caused him to become awkward. I knew he labeled himself as odd or abnormal—two terms that bothered me more than he knew.

"There you go, making me jealous again. We can't all have an army of people inside us whose combined skills turn us into the ultimate super human who is good at everything, you know."

He tried to hide his chuckle as the tips of his ears pinked. "That is so far from the truth it's scary."

"Maybe, but it made you laugh. So, Theo cooks?"

I did my best to make him feel comfortable about who he was. Especially since the entire world seemed out to do the opposite. By that point, I hoped he understood, I'd never judge or tease him about his condition and only supported him wholeheartedly.

"He does. Loves trying new things. I never know what I'm going to find in the fridge or freezer. And the amount of recipe books he's accumulated are insane. I'm going broke with what he spends on groceries."

I took joy in the fact that his nervous stutter was almost nonexistent. It spoke volumes of his comfort level and I used it as a guide to know how he was feeling in certain situations.

"My mother would love Theo. They'd talk recipes and food for hours."

He shifted in his seat, dashing his eyes from his plate once, but didn't respond.

Using the segue, I laid my fork beside my plate and wiped my mouth with a napkin. "Speaking of my mom, she's putting on a family Christmas dinner next week on the twenty-second. Did you want to come?"

Oryn gaze shot to my face. Color drained from his cheeks making him pale. He looked away again, focusing intently on his food. With his fork, he speared a potato a little too hard, and I didn't miss the small tremble in his hand.

"Umm… I d-don't want to intrude on f-family functions. But thank you." The potato never ended up in his mouth and instead was dragged over his plate numerous times before he removed it from his fork and poked a carrot instead.

"I'm always encouraged to bring a friend. In fact, my mother would be over the moon if I brought someone."

"L-like a date?" he whispered. "Sh-she probably means a d-date. Not me."

That was exactly what my mother wished for. Because even if I dragged Evan along, she prattled for half the night how I needed to settle down and find a man. But why not Oryn?

"My mother would love you to bits." It wasn't an answer—and seeing as I'd have loved to have called him my date, I hoped he saw through my clever avoidance.

Leaving his fork on the edge of his plate—with the uneaten carrot still attached—he reached for his wine and took a bigger gulp than the menial sips he'd been doing before.

"I d-don't think I want to." His cheeks flushed, and he tipped his glass to his mouth again, emptying more of the wine down his throat.

I placed my hand over his and encouraged him to put down the glass. He still couldn't look at me, but he didn't pull away and allowed the connection.

"How come?"

"Umm… I j-just…" He withdrew his hand and dug a knuckle into his eye. I recognized the action as one he did often when alters were close. "P-people don't understand me. S-stress can trigger switches… I…" He swallowed and shifted in his seat before shaking his head in determination. "I c-can't go."

"It's okay. I shouldn't have asked." Because I couldn't leave it there or have him group me into that self-made category, I added, "Not *all* people. You know I understand, right?"

"I know you t-try."

Feeling ten kinds of stupid, I remained quiet for the rest of our meal. Oryn didn't eat anymore but worked hard to look as though he was by pushing food around his plate. At that point, I regretted everything. Pushing a romantic atmosphere down his throat wasn't the way to go with Oryn, no matter how I felt. Relationship lines weren't clear between us, and I had no business forcing them.

I cleared the table after we'd finished and ran water in the sink to wash the dishes. Lost in my head, I didn't hear Oryn come up behind me until a hand rested on the center of my back. It was the lightest of touches and completely unexpected considering he'd rarely—if ever—initiated any form of contact.

I shut the water off and glanced over my shoulder to where he stood less than a foot away. When our eyes met, he retracted his hand and stepped back, hugging himself.

"I-I'll try," he breathed. "To go to your parents for dinner."

Shifting around, I leaned on the counter wanting to take the hands he held so securely around his body for stability.

"You don't have to. I shouldn't have asked."

He shook his head, stopping my words. "It's not f-fair. You've tried so hard with me. Been an amazing friend. I… I need to try, too. I'm just afraid…"

Unable to resist, I unclasped a hand from his body and wrapped it in my own. "Don't be. I have the most amazing parents. If anything happens, they will understand. Believe me."

His focus was entirely on our joined hands and I wasn't sure if he'd heard me until he nodded. His fingers moved in my own, testing the connection in the frightened way Oryn always had with everything in life. I brushed gentle touches in return, grazing the pad of my thumb over his skin and encouraging him to calm.

His lips parted a fraction and he dashed a quick glance to my face before refocusing on the contact we shared. With slow movements, watching his face for any signs of distress, I brought his hand to my chest and pressed his palm over my heart, linking my fingers over top. Without realizing it, he stepped forward again, still zeroed in on the action.

My heart pounded, and I could only imagine his was working to break through the cavity of his chest as well.

"I'll always have your back, Oryn. When you are with me, you don't need to be afraid. I hope you know that."

Slowly, his chin lifted until our eyes connected. The blue-grey irises, ones that held more pain than I would probably ever understand, shone with uncertainty and disbelief but also with a sliver of hope. It was that hope I needed to reach for and draw to the surface. More than anything, I wanted him to believe me. A cruel world was all he'd ever known, and I wanted to show him a better life.

For many minutes neither of us spoke. Touching, watching; our connection grew and rivaled the intimate atmosphere I'd inadvertently created. I pulled against the instinct that drew me toward him, urging me to capture his mouth and kiss his troubled soul. Knowing it wasn't the right move, I tightened our hold on each other. With my free hand, I brushed fingers along his cheek and temple until I held the back of his head. Even that small action made his eyes widen and pupils dilate.

Because I couldn't resist, I leaned in, closing our minimal gap, and ghosted a barely-there kiss against his forehead. His fingers by my heart tightened their hold, anchoring to my shirt and keeping me from stepping back.

One kiss turned to a second, that time by his temple, and a third next to his ear. That was when his arms wrapped around my waist and he leaned into me, burying his face in my neck. So, I held him, securing my own arms around his body and wishing I could calm the turmoil I could physically feel trembling through his every limb.

How did I ever think Oryn was in a position to have a relationship? The simple act of being held and hugged was almost more than he could handle. Yet, he didn't pull away. He'd initiated, and there wasn't a chance in hell I would deny him what he needed.

His scent, his warmth, and the delicate way his fingers clung to my shirt at my back was amazing, and I filed all those sensations away for safe keeping.

Little did I know, my next action would tip our entire evening from sweet and sensual into chaos.

Enjoying the hold we shared, and the feeling of Oryn against me, I squeezed him tighter, pinning and caging his slightly smaller frame to mine and inhaling deeply as I buried my nose against the side of his head.

That marked the precise moment his entire body stiffened. Initially, I registered the action as typical Oryn fear and was about to loosen my hold, but I was wrong. Only a fraction of a second passed from his whole-body tightening to him violently shoving from my arms. If the counter hadn't been against my back, I'd have stumbled with the force.

Oryn, on the other hand, did stumble and clattered against the wall opposite me. My confusion and shock instantly evaporated with the look of venom in his eyes. He pulled himself straight and fixed his shirt, craning his neck to the side and making an awful popping noise as he cracked his neck. The square set of his shoulders when he stood to his full height, coupled with the firm set of his mouth, stopped the words I was about to say—which were to encourage him to take a deep breath and relax.

Reed.

I swallowed my near spout of concern and held his death stare, not backing down. He'd never displayed violence, and Oryn had laughed when I'd asked if it was in his nature. Reed didn't need muscles and fists, the fire in his eyes would have a man twice his size backing down without question.

He pointed at me as his lip curled at the side of his mouth. "Never touch us like that again," he growled through gritted teeth.

"I wasn't—"

He stalked forward, finger still raised, furrow in his brow deepening. When he invaded my personal space, I shrunk back against the counter. "I know your type. I know your intentions."

The deep raspiness of his voice had thrown me off every time I'd met Reed. That day was no different. As quickly as Oryn was capable of switching, my brain never caught up as fast. It became tangled in a torrent of thought as I immediately tried to discern what had been the cause.

"Let me make a few things clear, lover boy."

He licked his lips, and only then did he lower the finger that nearly poked my chest. Reed never had much to say. He'd ordinarily expressed his animosity toward me through clipped words and nasty, seething glares before either tossing me out the door, or leaving me alone in the middle of the street.

His irises darkened as he hovered in front of me. "This little experiment you have going on ends right here and now. We aren't interested."

"I'm not sure what you're talking about."

"You're plenty aware. Don't play games with me." He spun on his heels and crossed into the living room where soft music continued to play in the background and candles burned low in their holders mid-table.

He scanned the room and his gaze landed on the two wine glasses I hadn't cleared.

I spoke before I could stop myself.

"It's not how it looks."

Why the fuck was I defending my actions? It was exactly how it looked. Exactly as I'd intended. It was a date without my having ever called it a date. I knew it and Oryn knew it.

But Reed...

"You don't seem to understand." His voice dropped to a whisper as he picked up a wine glass and shifted it to swirl the contents. "This isn't okay. None of it. Being here. Doing this. You."

"What's wrong with me? I've done everything I can to be a friend to… you." *Oryn.*

What the hell was I defending? Who?

His gaze shot to mine and he crossed toward me in two strides. I held my ground, not allowing him to see how his actions affected me.

"This," he held the glass up, "and this," he waved a hand through the air, indicating the music, "aren't the actions of a friend. It's gone beyond harmless studying, and I know where your mind is going. You're all alike. It will *never* happen. Do you hear me? Never!"

I opened my mouth to respond. To explain that Oryn seemed to feel differently, but I snapped it closed again, knowing I wouldn't get anywhere with Reed.

"I'm sorry," I said instead. "I swear to you on my life, I would never hurt him…or you. Any of you."

The stare down that followed was intense. Minutes ticked by and Reed refused to move. His penetrating glare ate into my core, and I tried to see through him and find Oryn.

But he was gone.

"I like him, Reed." It was all I had left. The confused feelings that had been tumbling inside for months surfaced. A huge draw to a complicated man. One who'd managed to catch my eye and my heart. Why did it have to be impossible?

Without a word, he returned the glass to the table and collected his coat and hat from where I'd laid it over the back of the couch. After he'd zipped it, he raised his chin and pursed his lips.

"It will never happen, so stop trying."

Then he turned to leave.

No, not good enough!

I jumped into action and raced after him, catching the door as he opened it and slamming it closed again, much to his surprise. I left my hand on the hard surface, preventing him from trying again.

He shifted to face me and narrowed his eyes. "What are you doing?"

"Tell me why. Why can't it happen? I understand him—the best I can at least. I like him, a lot, more than I've ever admitted to anyone. I would never hurt him. So why? Why can't I try?"

Reed's lip curled as he dashed a look to the hand preventing his escape and back to my face. "Because we don't trust you. End of story. Move your fucking hand."

The finality of his statement hit me in the chest and I stood stock still, windless and gaping from the metaphorical punch. I slid my hand from the door and Reed immediately yanked it open and disappeared down the hallway.

I closed it again and leaned my head on its surface. Oryn's scent lingered in the air around me and I closed my eyes, returning to the moment in the kitchen when he'd been in my arms. Where had it gone wrong? What had I done?

Did I frighten him away? Or was Reed always close by, lingering and waiting, determined we couldn't proceed in the direction I strived.

He hadn't broken through that one evening two months back when we'd shared a kiss. Oryn had been just as nervous then.

Perplexed and unable to sort through my own muddled thoughts, I kicked the door in frustration and returned to the kitchen to clean up.

Chapter Eleven

As was custom, Oryn texted me the following day, apologizing for something he had no memory of. All he knew was that our night hadn't ended together, and because Reed hadn't bothered sharing in journals, Oryn was in the dark.

I hated telling him how Reed had behaved, because I knew it bothered him and he assumed responsibility and felt guilt when he shouldn't, so I glazed over the details, and changed the subject.

Although he'd seemed uncertain at dinner about attending my family Christmas, he assured me through text he was definitely going. I couldn't help but wonder if his guilt drove him to agreeing when he'd have much rather backed out.

I'd given him the date and time, and since that day, we hadn't talked.

On the morning of the twenty-second, I sent Oryn a text to confirm our plans. He was quick to respond, and I reminded him I'd be there by two that afternoon to pick him up.

My mother liked to hold Christmas dinner early so we could spend many hours afterward doing Christmas puzzles around a roaring fire while digesting our food. That way, we'd have plenty of room for late night desserts. It was tradition in my house and had been for as long as I could remember.

That year, the expected turn out was supposed to be seven people. Mom, Dad, me, Oryn, my older brother, Lucas, his wife, Ally, and their son JJ. I'd given my mother a heads-up I was bringing someone and dodged about a hundred and one questions when she found out that someone wasn't Evan.

Evan was pissed—on the outside. He liked my mom's cooking and had long ago become a part of our family. That year, although he played the disgruntled card well, I knew he wasn't as sore as he let on. He and Krystina were still dating, and giving up time with his woman was unheard of. So, I assumed he was secretly relieved Oryn had agreed.

At half past one, I checked myself in the hallway mirror one last time. I much preferred myself without my glasses and decided I needed to wear my contacts more often. I'd gelled my hair and blow dried it into a sweep off my forehead. I'd recently had it cut, and the sides were close cropped, giving it a much cleaner look than the shag I'd been sporting. With my dark grey button up and slacks, I looked put together enough to please my mother. Except, I hadn't shaved in two days, and the stubble across my jaw would likely cause a frown and verbal reprimanding.

Deciding I was decent, I snagged my coat from the closet along with a scarf and a pair of gloves. Not wanting to ruin my hair, I decided against a tuque and settled for cold ears. The temperature was well below freezing and had been for weeks. Snow covered the ground and trees and the wind howled, especially by the harbor which was where my parents lived.

While my car warmed a minute, I sent Oryn a text, letting him know I was on my way. He didn't respond, so I assumed he was probably finishing getting ready.

It was ten to two when I pulled in Oryn's driveway. I left the car running while I scurried to his front door and knocked. Hunched against the cold, I did my best to cover my ears with my shoulders—unsuccessfully. They were going numb as the door in front of me flew open.

Oryn was bundled in a short, black and red winter coat with a fur-lined hood hanging in back. It was one I'd never seen on him. He didn't have a tuque either but wore a matching scarf around his neck and red mittens with black snowflakes on them. He was completely coordinated. His black skinny jeans were tucked into black, fur-lined boots that came up to his calves.

"Hell, I can't believe how cold it is today. This is crazy," he said, bouncing on his feet as he locked the door.

His voice was muffled from his scarf, but the slight impediment was prominent and gave me pause. The flashier ensemble should have been the giveaway, and I blamed my half-frozen brain for missing the obvious.

He spun from the door and buried his face in my chest, arms automatically wrapping around and squeezing my torso.

"Brr, warm me up, babe, I'm a popsicle."

Cohen.

With his abrupt action, my arms automatically encompassed him, and I found myself hugging him back as my brain caught up.

Why Cohen's appearance shocked me, I had no idea. I shouldn't have been surprised. Oryn's apprehension over dinner and social affairs was well-known and likely had caused him to seek out a way of coping.

The whirlwind I constantly seemed to be in around Oryn had me fumbling and fighting my own internal emotions. Had he abandoned me on purpose?

Trying not to let disappointment sink in, and forcing myself to go with the flow, I rubbed Cohen's back and gave him a squeeze. It wasn't like I could tell him he wasn't invited. As hard as it was, I'd tried to be level-headed and accept the ambiguity of what it meant to be friends with Oryn.

It looked like Cohen was my dinner date.

"The heats blasting, get in."

As I drove, he fixed his hair in the vanity mirror. His cheeks were pink from the cold but radiated with a smile that twinkled in his eyes.

"I haven't eaten all day. I love turkey dinners with all the fixin's." He pushed the mirror back in place and leaned back eyeing me. "You look nice."

I stole my eyes from the road a moment to smile in his direction. "Thank you. So do you."

The traffic was heavy with the upcoming holiday rush. Last minute shoppers were on the prowl for the perfect gifts and courtesy and manners went out the window. People drove with more rage and aggression the last few days before Christmas then they did all year.

I turned down Harbor Rd.—the ritzier end of our small town—and was grateful for less traffic.

"Your parents live down here?"

"Yup. Their property backs onto the lake. I grew up here. Love it."

Cohen continued to watch out the window with a gleam in his eyes, sitting forward without an ounce of the nerves Oryn would have shown.

I regretted not explaining more to my mother when I'd told her I was bringing someone. All I'd told her was I'd met a man who I *wasn't* dating but who I'd grown close to. All she knew was his name was Oryn and he was a bit shy. Why it hadn't occurred to me there was a possibility I wouldn't be bringing Oryn to dinner, I had no idea.

I pulled into the driveway a few minutes later and parked behind my brother's truck. The house was a significant way off the road and surrounded by trees on either side, giving privacy from their neighbors. The two-story brick home was much larger than my parents needed any longer—since my brother and I had moved out—but they had no intention of moving. The backyard sloped toward the lake, and we had our own small private beach space which was always nice in the summer months. As a child, I'd spent a lot of time down there, playing in the sand, fishing, and swimming.

I shut off the engine and hesitated, turning to Cohen. "Ready?"

He tilted his head with a wide smile before answering. "Of course I am. Are you? You look more worried than me. Are your parents monsters or something? Should I be concerned?"

I chuckled and let out a breath. "Not at all."

My dinner date had changed suddenly, and I needed to adjust to the idea of introducing Cohen to my family instead of Oryn. He was a little more flashy and vibrant than anyone I'd ever brought home in the past, so I anticipated unusual looks—from my brother at least.

I rounded the car and waited while Cohen caught up. He'd fit his mittens back on and skipped over to my side, instantly linking our hands. The action stalled me in place, and I worked through how the introduction would go in my head. If I showed up holding his hand, my family would automatically assume we were dating. There would be no convincing them otherwise.

If it had been Oryn's hand and Oryn beside me, I would have been okay with their assumptions, but Cohen's bold ways and eagerness for more always induced conflicting feelings that made me standoffish. As natural as his advances always were, they left me with an odd yet equal mix of yearning and concern I couldn't quite sort out.

Oryn had never expressed anything but sly humor when I'd told him about how Cohen acted. Because he was an alter, I didn't always ward off his clinging behavior. There were times it sent tingling heat and longing to course through me, but then it would be swiftly followed by profound guilt and I'd stew over it for days.

Cohen was the biggest source of puzzlement.

As I worked through the conglomeration in my brain, I kept our hands together and guided him to the door. When we gathered on the front stoop, I detached from him to knock before letting myself in. Instead of rejoining us, I worked at removing my jacket as I called down the hall toward the kitchen. The house was warm compared with the cold outside and the savory smell of turkey and stuffing filled the air.

"Hello!"

My mom scurried from around the corner, dressed in a holiday sweater and slacks, with her silver and brown hair done to perfection, curled and styled in the short bob she always wore.

"Vaughn!"

It wasn't like I didn't visit her frequently, but every time I saw my mother, she acted as though we'd been apart for a decade. I barely had my coat undone before she wrapped me in her arms, pinning me to her chest. Her floral perfume was strong and tickled my nose, but it was a scent I was familiar with—one she'd worn for as long as I could remember.

"Hey, Ma."

When she pulled back, she clapped her hands and turned a sweet smile toward Cohen who was looking anything but shy. His grin put hers to shame and he automatically opened his arms for a hug as well.

Because of who my mother was, she didn't hesitate and hugged him in return as though I'd been bringing him to dinner for years. "You must be Oryn," she said over his shoulder as they rocked side to side in a tight embrace—one the true Oryn would have wanted no part of. "It's so nice to meet you."

I pressed my lips tight and waited for Cohen to correct her. Why hadn't I thought to explain more to my mother? I knew what could happen. I'd been friends with Oryn long enough I should have anticipated that a social dinner with strangers would probably be too much for him to handle. No wonder he'd been adamant about not going.

"Umm, Ma," I started as she pulled from Cohen's arms, "This is Cohen, actually."

Her brow furrowed, and she flipped her gaze between us in confusion. "I'm sorry, sweetheart," she said to Cohen. "My mind is all a muddle with the holidays. Forgive me."

As expected, Cohen didn't flinch at the required correction, and I assumed it was a common occurrence in his, their, lives. "It's nice to meet you."

"Let me take your coats. The boys are all in the living room. Dinner will be a half an hour yet."

We removed our winter gear and placed it in my mother's outstretched arms. Before she disappeared down the hall, she gave me a quizzical glance. My mother was sharp as a whip and nothing passed her by. Her mind wasn't muddled, and she was simply being polite until she could ask me what the heck was going on. I'd said Oryn, and she'd heard Oryn.

The next problem was, did I attempt to explain something as complicated as dissociative identity disorder on a night that was supposed to be for us to celebrate the holidays, or did I wait and deal with it at a later date?

Why didn't I just tell her before?

Cohen wormed up against my side, and because I'd forgotten to be mindful of keeping our distance, he weaved his warm fingers with mine again.

"Did you tell her we're dating?" he asked openly and without a hint of reserve.

I guided him down the long hallway and to the back end of the house where the living room was and where people were gathered.

"We aren't dating, Cohen." I stopped just outside the door. Whatever game was playing on the big screen TV in the other room drifted into the hallway, along with the chatter of voices. Again, I unlatched my hand and turned to face him.

"I don't want to give my family the wrong idea. I told them I was bringing a friend."

He smoothed a hand down my shirt, working free the wrinkles and fiddled with a button. He was rarely without a smile. "Is it such a bad idea? I know you are attracted to me, and I know you've wanted more for a while." He batted his eyes and couldn't have looked more nineteen in that moment—even with a twenty-eight-year-old body.

My heart betrayed me and picked up its pace at the contact, despite my words. I caught his wrist gently and smoothed a thumb over his hand. I hated how my body seemed to adamantly refuse to respond to my requests to ignore Cohen's flirtations.

I didn't know if it was the right thing to say or not—or if I'd hurt his feelings—but I needed Cohen to be on the same page as me—at least that evening. Whatever it was I couldn't sort out needed to be examined another night.

"Cohen, I'm attracted to Oryn."

He eyed me with the hint of a smirk still evident in the soft turn of his mouth. There was something he wasn't saying, and it glowed in his eyes. He rubbed my arm and nodded to the door.

"Shall we?"

My dad, brother, and nephew were engrossed in a football game when we entered. Lucas was splayed across the couch with JJ on his lap. Lucas had the same dark hair as me, but his was cut much shorter. His son was his spitting image, but his brown locks had been grown long and curled on the ends around his ears. Both grinned in my direction as we entered.

My dad was reclined in his black, leather Lazyboy. My mother had obviously insisted he wear his ugly Christmas sweater again that year it seemed, and he wore it proudly over his potbelly.

We made introductions, and Lucas shifted up on the couch to allow Cohen and I room. JJ slipped to the floor.

With our close proximity, Cohen's hand rested on my leg and he snuggled into my side, an action my brother didn't miss, and he grinned that knowing grin in our direction a few times. There would be no allaying their suspicions that evening, I could tell already.

By the time my mother and Ally called us all for dinner, the game had gone to half-time and we moved to the formal dining room without complaint. The long, heavy wooden table was set up for the festivities. A red runner spanned its length. Christmas platters filled with food spanned its surface.

Cohen asked to use the washroom before we sat, so I steered him down the hall in the right direction. The moment he wasn't by my side, Lucas and my mother pounced.

"Boyfriend?" Lucas asked, a grin wide on his face.

"No," I said, conflicted on how to explain. Had Oryn been present, that answer wouldn't likely have been any different, especially considering his tentativeness. "Just a good friend."

"Yeah right. Does he know that? Because he's glued to your hip."

Wasn't that the truth. But that was Cohen and completely his nature.

"I thought you said you were bringing a man named Oryn," my mother piped in.

I washed a hand down my face and pinched the bridge of my nose. The handful of minutes Cohen would be in the bathroom wouldn't be near enough time for me to explain. It was barely a conversation that could be discussed over coffee. I'd spent the past few months learning and was still in the dark most days.

"Oryn couldn't make it tonight, Ma. Umm... Cohen is..." I stalled, fumbling for words.

Before I could come up with an explanation, my mother got pulled away when my dad announced he'd finished carving the turkey. The moment she was out of sight, Lucas leaned in as a smirk filled his face.

"Come off it, Vaughn, you two are totally into each other. I can see it. You're dating, aren't you? You don't hide shit well."

A string of guilt pulled in my chest at his words. Was that how it looked? Of course it was. I sighed and shuffled back a step, peering down the hall to where Cohen had disappeared. "It's complicated, and I can't explain right now."

Lucas tilted his head and gave me a shit-eating grin I knew would be followed by a statement I wouldn't like. "Who's Oryn? Fuck, how many guys are you messing around with? Are you playing the field?"

More guilt.

"Stop," I said with more firmness to my tone. "I said it's complicated."

At that moment, Cohen bounced up beside me and rested a hand on my lower back. That hand rubbed circles before looping around my waist and drawing Lucas' attention. When my brother met my eyes again, I stopped his comment with a hard look. Thankfully, he had more respect than when we were teenagers and shut his mouth, but I knew his silence would only last so long.

Dislodging from Cohen was impossible. As steadfast as I'd been in explaining to him earlier that we were friends and nothing more, I gave up the fight far too easily and just let him cling. Deep down inside, no matter my denial, I liked it.

All through dinner, he leaned against my side, brushed our hands together under the table, and kept his leg permanently glued to mine. Unlike Oryn, he chatted the meal away. There wasn't an ounce of shyness to him. He asked mom about her gravy and how she'd made it so full of flavor, while commending her cooking with each moaning mouthful. With my dad, he engaged in conversation about football, openly admitting he knew nothing about the game, and allowed Lucas and my dad to tease him about it good-naturedly all through our meal. He was over the top, funny, and engaging.

Without a care in the world, he also paid exclusive attention to me. Not a single member of my family could possibly have missed the flirtatious way he acted. Everyone was relaxed by the end of dinner as Cohen weaved himself into the family like he'd been there forever.

As was tradition, once the meal was cleaned up and dishes washed, we retired to the lounge where my dad lit a fire. A large folding table had already been set up and a thousand-piece, holiday puzzle was awaiting our attention.

Over the following hour, we all found our spots and worked to turn pieces face-up while sorting through and collecting all the edges. Due to the crunch of bodies, Cohen ended up shifting onto my lap, and as much as I wanted to argue—for face sake—part of me didn't mind. The stir of guilt in my stomach had been growing since dinner, and I couldn't sort it out.

My focus was shot, and I wasn't much help with the puzzle. Cohen worked on the edging while I slid pieces his way when I found them. A mindless task that helped me appear occupied while I continued to mull over my inner clutter.

"I'm missing this piece. It has a smidge of evergreen on it," Cohen said.

I dashed a look to where he indicated on his line of edging that was nearly complete. Scanning the table more thoroughly, I quickly found the exact piece he was missing and glided it over.

He squealed and jammed it in place before leaning back against me and bringing his face close to my ear.

"Thanks, babe."

I brushed my nose against his cheek before he sat forward again, and it earned me a heart-stopping smile.

I couldn't help but inhale the familiar scent of his cologne. It warmed my heart and made my skin tingle. The longer we sat engaged in puzzling, the more my thoughts drifted and the deeper the guilt rooted. The position where I'd wound up that evening was messing with my head, and I couldn't sort it out to save my life.

Over the past couple of months, Oryn had definitely become the object of my affection. I knew and understood the complexity of that notion, but as I sat with Cohen on my lap, I was more than confused by the feelings and sensations he stirred in me as well. In essence, the physical form of Oryn was planted in my lap. *His* body, *his* smell, *his* warmth.

But it wasn't him.

And it was Cohen's personality that was worming around all those things, amplifying the chaos in my brain. A personality that was innocent, pure, and indeed growing on me.

I didn't know at what point I'd wrapped an arm around his waist and dragged him closer, but when his fingers linked with mine against his abdomen, the realization hit. I didn't remove it, although I focused on that connection more readily, unsure how to feel or what exactly I was encouraging.

Cohen was everything Oryn wasn't. But yet they were the same person, weren't they?

Not according to everything I'd read.

Alters should be treated as separate individuals.

Yet they seemed to have moments where they functioned as a unit. As separate and individual as they were, they housed and ran one system. One being.

My mother stood, breaking me from my thoughts.

"I'm going to throw the pies in the oven. Can I refresh drinks?"

I accepted a second glass of wine and Cohen declined. I'd seen him struggling with his first glass at dinner and assumed wine wasn't his drink of choice. I wondered if Cohen understood the same repercussions drinking might have while taking antidepressants. Oryn had seemed mildly concerned, but not overly. Then, I wondered if alters understood to take medications if they were out and Oryn wasn't. The complexity of his life boggled my mind. I wasn't sure there would ever be an end to my questions. I needed to read more.

Another half-hour into the puzzle, Cohen leaned back against me and nuzzled his face to mine. I didn't pull away, but snuck a glance about the table to see if his actions were being noted. Of course they were.

Not a single member of my family had an issue with my sexual orientation, and having boyfriends over in the past had never been an issue. But I'd made it clear Cohen wasn't a date. That line had been blurred into non-existence. Lucas' look alone made that clear. Casual friends didn't touch, flirt, and sit on each other's laps.

"I need to stretch my legs," Cohen whispered against my cheek. "Wanna take a small walk before dessert?"

My lips brushed his cheek in return as I found his ear. "Sure. How about I show you the lake?" I removed my hand from his waist and he stood. I missed the heat of him against me immediately.

A walk would be a good idea. I needed a minute to think; to process. The fresh air would work wonders to clear my brain.

We promised to return shortly for pie and slipped from the room to find our coats. Once bundled, we stepped outside, and I guided Cohen around the house and through a tall gate into the backyard.

A few years back, my father had installed motion sensor flood lights near the house. There had been problems with kids sneaking onto properties by way of the beach area and causing trouble. The moment we rounded the house, they kicked on, washing a large section of the backyard in bright white light.

There was no path and over a foot of snow covering the yard. I knew the land like the back of my hand, but concern for Cohen and the unsure footing leading down to the water—especially hidden under the snow—I felt obligated to take his hand so he wouldn't fall. *Excuses.*

We walked in silence down the sloping property a few hundred yards until we were far enough away from the house, the motion light couldn't see us and switched off. The rushing water further out brought a steady lull to the atmosphere—one I'd grown to love as a kid, and one that would always calm me during the stressful periods of my teenage-hood.

Closer to the water, there was a significant three-foot drop-off to the beach area. I knew it was coming, but slowed my pace since the darkness had a tendency to mask it. Somewhere there were stairs, but we'd never find them in the snow. Once we'd maneuvered down the edge, I slowed my pace and eventually came to a stop a few feet from the frozen shore.

Even in the dark, the ice glistened. I'd been taught from a young age never to trust the ice. With the current coming in off the harbor, it was never safe to test your luck. Its thickness could never be trusted, and I'd heard of a few tragedies over my lifetime of people who'd gone through while goofing around in the winter.

Cohen's hand fell from mine and wrapped around his body as his gaze passed over the moonlit water.

"I can't believe you grew up here. It's amazing."

"Even better in the summer. Used to spend days down here as a kid. Soaking up the sun, laying in the sand, swimming in the water. It was great."

Even without light, his smile glowed, uninhibited and free across his face. I stared, unable to look away and full of more confusion and confliction than I'd felt in a long time.

He caught my eye and turned to face me, tilting his head to the side. "What's on your mind? You seem troubled."

Troubled barely encompassed my inner turmoil.

All those growing, budding feelings I'd been having for Oryn sang through me every time we were together. I was attracted to him in every way, yet he was always just out of arms reach. The small amount of intimacy we'd shared the other night at dinner had been shattered when Reed had stepped in.

In my heart, having something with Oryn didn't seem impossible. Difficult, yes. However, every attempt I'd made to advance on those feelings had proven me wrong. Was Oryn unreachable? Was I yearning for something I could never have?

And there I was, facing Cohen because Oryn was again out of reach. I couldn't explain.

Cohen stepped forward and rested his mitten-covered hands on my chest. I couldn't take my eyes off him. Eyes that were Oryn's. A body that was Oryn's. Yet the man in front of me was as different as night from day. And those differences were pulling me with just as much force.

When he nuzzled into my neck and slipped his arms around my waist, I was torn in two different directions. There was a distinctive pull to the young man in my arms. I'd felt it all night. But I didn't know where that pull was rooted. Only when his lips grazed my chin and went to claim my mouth did I finally react.

I gripped his forearms and held him back. My heart thudded restlessly as I searched his all too familiar face for some sign of the man who had wormed his way into my heart.

He truly wasn't there.

Everything in me wanted to pull him back to the surface. I wanted it to be Oryn against me. Oryn holding me. Oryn seeking my lips.

But he was gone. Sunk somewhere inside. Too afraid to even manage a simple dinner because it posed a threat to his being.

"I can't," I croaked. Shaking my head, I worked to find an explanation, tried to find appropriate words to explain my confliction.

Before I could speak, Cohen jumped in, "Babe, listen to me." He removed his mitts and cupped my cheeks in his warm hands, before stroking a thumb through my stubble. "I can see your confusion. I can feel the pull in your heart." He moved a hand to rest on my chest. "Understand me when I tell you this; I can give you things Oryn can't. I know the intimacy you want with him, and I can give you that intimacy. You don't need to fight it, or feel guilty."

How did he know my thoughts?

Searching his face, I pondered his words. I'd been struggling to understand Oryn since I'd met him. Spent sleepless nights Googling and researching. I heard what Cohen explained. Maybe a part of me understood as well, but I didn't know how to separate people, feelings, and emotions. I didn't even know if it was okay.

He drew me closer again and brushed his lips to mine. It fluttered in my heart and seeped heat through my veins. I closed my eyes and sighed against his mouth. He didn't take it further and I didn't go seeking. The feather light connection was brief, and he lingered, the warmth of his breath ghosting against me.

Shielded in darkness behind closed eyes, my body came to life with desire and need. The aching pull to grow that bond between us, to nourish it, and to help it come to life. I'd burned the memory of our one shared kiss in my mind and it was that thought and the vision of Oryn's worried face which helped me close the gap with Cohen.

That time when our lips pressed together, it was my initiation. Cohen's softened and parted almost right away, seeking more. The dance of his tongue across my mouth tingled over my skin, but when he drew my bottom lip into his mouth with a bit of suction and nibbled, taking control, and pressing us further, something changed. It felt so right and yet incredibly wrong. The kiss wasn't the same at all, and my body flooded with guilt.

I pulled off his mouth and opened my eyes. His lips remained half-puckered and the moonlight shone in his eyes.

The spinning confusion and drowning sense of wrongness made me step back.

What was I doing?

Shaking my head, I wiped at my mouth. "I can't do this."

In all my adult years I'd never cheated on a boyfriend, yet that was exactly the disgusting sensation that was crawling over my skin in that moment. Regret and profound guilt.

And Oryn and I weren't even dating. Were we?

I hated that my body was equally drawn to Cohen, and I pushed those sensations away as well. It was enough to make me want to pull my hair out.

Desire and guilt combined weren't comfortable feelings. They didn't feel natural together and didn't belong side by side.

"It's okay, babe. It's a lot to take in. I get it. Come on, I'm cold."

He fit his mittens over his hands and waited for me to lead the way back to the house.

Cohen was less affected by what had happened than me. I spent the evening mulling, reprimanding, and shaming myself for what had taken place.

My family was more focused on puzzles and dessert to notice, and by the time we said our goodbyes, everyone was winding down and Cohen's attention on me had become expected and normal. I knew I'd need to explain things at a later date.

How do I explain something I don't even understand?

It was nearing ten by the time I pulled in Oryn's driveway. Cohen's driveway. He didn't jump out and turned in his seat when I put the car in park.

"Do you want to come in?" he asked.

I couldn't look at him and stared out the windshield. "No thanks. It's getting late. I should probably get home."

He remained silent, but didn't move to leave. Eventually, I turned to him and caught him studying me.

"Just remember what I told you, okay? You're making it complicated in your head and it doesn't have to be. I like you, Vaughn, and I think, even though you are fighting it, you don't mind me so much either." He caught my chin and leaned in, pecking a soft kiss in the corner of my mouth. "Have a good night."

Then he was gone. He scurried to the door, found his keys, and let himself inside. I sat in the driveway for another five minutes, lost in thought.

Evan's words from months ago came to mind, and I wondered if I truly was in over my head. I should have stopped at friends. It had been my intent. But my connection to Oryn had grown beyond my control and without my knowledge. So, there I was, guilt-ridden, confused, full of shame, and yearning for a guy—possibly two guys—I had no idea how to have a relationship with. What was worse; I was falling for him and I knew it.

Like an impossible picture, the longer I stared at it, the more the answers eluded me. Maybe there weren't answers. Maybe that was all it could ever be.

Chapter Twelve

Since Lucas had a family of his own, and my parents travelled to visit distant relatives on Christmas day—ones I wasn't close with—the twenty-fifth was typically a day I spent alone at home. I'd never minded in the past, but that year was different. Since dinner at my parent's house a few days back, my mind had been in knots.

Evan was busy with his own family celebrations, and that year, he had his girlfriend's family added into the mix. We'd both been busy for almost a week, so my comforting ear had been unavailable, and I'd needed to deal with my thoughts on my own.

Trying to find comfort in my Christmas routine, I made myself a big breakfast of scrambled eggs and toast and brought it to the couch to enjoy the marathon of holiday movies playing on the TV. I didn't own a tree, and never bothered decorating, so it was the only reminder I had that it was Christmas day.

Unlike past years, I found no enjoyment in my solitude, and the harder I worked to stay focused on the present, the further my mind drifted.

The evening with Cohen played on repeat whenever I closed my eyes, and the mixed, conglomeration of feelings I'd been unable to shake returned full-force. I thought of Oryn and re-lived every day we'd spent together, going over the details of our friendship in my mind. My efforts at remaining purely focused on that friendship failed, and the heart-aching yearning returned.

It was impossible.

The more I knew about Oryn—despite it becoming more and more unsettling some days—the more I was drawn to him. While reflecting, I noted how he'd become more comfortable around me and how he'd begun to open up about himself more each day.

I knew in my heart, growing anything beyond friendship was likely impossible, but I couldn't help wishing we could try. When I plunged into those waters, I envisioned what obstacles stood in the way.

Everything.

Oryn had proven that physical intimacy was trigger inducing. Never mind sex or being naked, I could barely kiss the man without issues arising.

Yet I'd kissed him once.

He'd been shy, and trembling, but I hadn't lost him. Why was that moment different?

It budded hope, and I knew better than to allow such a seed to be planted. Regardless, there it was, worming its way alive in my gut, begging to be given a chance.

My breakfast had grown cold, and when I remembered it, I placed my untouched plate on the coffee table and sighed. As I debated tossing it in the microwave, my phone buzzed in my pocket.

I pulled it out and was surprised to find it was a message from Oryn—or possibly Oryn. Although the other alters had never texted me in the past.

Merry Christmas.

Those two words made my skin come alive, and I sat up straighter, staring at them and formulating a response. It *was* Christmas. What was he doing? Was he home alone as well?

Merry Christmas!

I hit send then added.

Was Santa good to you?

My phone remained silent for many minutes, and I slumped down, wishing I had more to say. Wanting to ask if he'd like to come over, or needed company. I'd have given anything to talk to him. I hadn't had a proper conversation with Oryn since he'd been at my place for dinner—and Reed had ended our night.

When my phone buzzed in my hand, I jumped.

It's not snowing anymore, so I'll go with yes. How about you?

I smiled and typed out a quick response.

Nah, I must have been on the naughty list, I got nothing.

The following text came through much quicker as I removed my plate to the kitchen. I left it on the counter and debated brewing a pot of coffee. I stared at my phone and back to the empty pot and then to the clock on the microwave. Ten-forty.

Did Santa at least bring you coffee? I typed.

When I hit send, I bit my lip and waited.

Not yet. Apparently, I need to make my own. Must have been naughty too.

Not missing a beat, I typed a quick reply.

I'm not Santa, but can I bring you coffee?

The extended pause following my question brought my hesitation back to the surface.

Nothing is open. How did you plan to do that?

Shit, I hadn't thought of that. Tossing my phone on the counter, I rummaged through a few cupboards and found a couple of travel mugs shoved way in the back.

"Bingo."

I snatched up my phone and snapped a picture, then sent it along with a few short words.

Got it covered. So yes?

I got an *LOL*, but he added the word *sure* which grew a huge grin across my face.

I'll be over shortly.

I set the coffee pot to brew and jetted down the hall to find something to wear. I'd been lounging in pajamas for two days and hadn't even showered. Finding clothes, I jumped in a quick shower and washed before dressing. I cleaned my glasses and fit them on my face before giving myself a once over in the mirror.

Forget that, I switched to contacts.

I examined myself; navy polo shirt and faded jeans. It wasn't as though I was attending a fancy dinner, but I questioned my appearance nonetheless, wanting to look nice for Oryn.

Before filling the travel mugs, I gave them a wash—since I didn't have a clue how long they'd been sitting in the cupboard—and then I was set to go.

In the front hall, I checked myself again in the mirror, the nerves of seeing Oryn prickled my skin and brought self-consciousness to the surface.

With a heavy sigh, I searched for my warm gear.

I had it bad.

The roads were empty, unlike the previous few times I'd been out that week. The desolation surrounding my neighborhood could have made it a passable set for *The Walking Dead*. Not a single solitary person was out, and no cars passed me the entire time I drove to Oryn's.

Dark clouds in the distant sky threatened another storm, and I chuckled to myself as I remembered Oryn's joy at finally having a reprieve from the snow.

Once I'd parked, I headed to his front door with the two mugs in my hands. Their warmth bled through their stainless-steel frames and heated my cold fingers. After knocking with my foot, the door flew open a few minutes later and the man I'd come to know waited tentatively on the other side. Deep in my core was a sliver of gratitude that Cohen, or Reed, or any of the other alters weren't there to greet me.

He smiled with his typical shyness as he accepted his coffee.

"Hi." When he couldn't meet my eyes any longer, his gaze drifted to the floor.

"Merry Christmas."

"Come on in." He stepped back, and I banged my boots before entering. As Oryn held both of our drinks, I shed my coat and the rest of my winter gear before finding a vacant hanger in his closet.

There was a moment of uncertainty when he handed my drink back, and neither of us moved down the hall to the den.

He was dressed in a beige, knitted, turtle neck sweater and dark jeans. His chin held the perfect amount of stubble which he'd groomed in such a way it accentuated his jawline. The gentleness of his eyes melted the chill I'd brought in from the outdoors. More than anything, I wanted to reach out and touch him.

I didn't.

"Were you alone on Christmas, too?" he asked, before breaking our standstill and shifting down the hall.

"Every year. Lucas celebrates with his family, and Mom and Dad go visiting distant relatives I don't know as well."

"Lucas?" he asked over his shoulder.

I stumbled with my response, momentarily confused how he'd forgotten my brother, before remembering it was Cohen who'd met my family, not Oryn.

"My brother. He has a young son, JJ, and his wife, Ally."

He nodded and kept his eyes forward. I didn't miss his frown or the way he drew his lip between his teeth to gnaw.

Instead of the den, Oryn steered toward the kitchen, so I followed. It was small but cozy. A two-seater dinette sat off to the side and a glass-doored curio was angled in the corner. It held an assortment of dishes and glasses. Oryn had two trays on the counter and looked to have been working to fill them with an assortment of snacks.

"I thought maybe you'd want something to eat. I didn't have a lot on hand, but you brought coffee so…" He trailed off and grimaced before shrugging and taking up a knife that I assumed had been abandoned when I'd arrived.

"I let my breakfast go cold, so this is great. Is there anything I can do to help?"

He squinted and rubbed at his forehead as he took stock of the items he had arranged.

"You could check the freezer and see if there are any frozen, mini quiches. I know Theo likes to make them and keeps us stocked."

I smiled at the mention of Theo. Oryn's back was turned, so he didn't witness it. It was indication of his comfort level with me. At a time, he would have never casually mentioned an alter without flinching.

When I opened the freezer above the fridge, I had to stifle a gasp. He'd mentioned Theo enjoyed cooking and often stocked the house with his favorite meals, but what I found was nothing like what I'd envisioned.

Neatly stacked rows of Tupperware lined the freezer. Each individual sized container was clearly labeled with its contents. Lasagna—separated by slice—cabbage rolls, soups, stews, chili, shepherds pie, and so many more. It was incredible.

"I told you he likes to cook. At least I eat well. I'm not much of a chef, and I'm lousy with a knife so I really appreciate all he does."

I spun at his words, still absorbed in my discovery. "That's really amazing."

It was the truth. There were a million things that could be said about dissociative identity disorder, but having alters with abilities like Theo's was definitely one of the positives.

Oryn slinked up beside me and lifted a few containers. His sweater brushed my arm, but he didn't step away or even note how closely connected we were. He was too absorbed in his search for quiche. I tried not to notice the distinct hint of citrus that clung to him... or to lean closer.

"Here they are."

He withdrew two containers with mini quiches inside. Six in total.

"Do you mind popping these in the toaster oven? It will give us a hot addition to the cold food."

Nodding, I accepted the containers and set to work as Oryn returned to slicing strawberries and setting them on a tray.

By the time we'd finished, there was a beautiful assortment of foods laid out. Cheese, crackers, fruits, veggies, quiche, and even

Christmas cookies in the shape of candy canes. We made a fresh pot of coffee and settled in the den.

Like my apartment, there were no signs of Christmas about. It could have been any other day of the year.

As I sipped my drink and nibbled a quiche, my thoughts drifted to Rain. Eyeing Oryn, I wondered if the child inside him got to celebrate the holidays. Too uncomfortable to bring it up, or question such a bizarre realization, I dismissed the thought, somewhat sad at the notion that any child should miss Christmas.

Following that line of thinking, I considered Oryn's growing up and wondered just how many Christmases he'd missed or what the holidays had been like for him. Never once did he bring up his parents or even if he had any siblings, and knowing the subject was heavy, I remained quiet.

Oryn sat on the opposite end of the couch as me and picked at the few items he'd piled on his plate. It was quiet between us with the television off and the streets deserted. A few times, he lifted his gaze and we exchanged a smile. Heat would rise in his cheeks, and before long, he focused on his plate again.

The past few days had left me with a number of lingering questions and avenues for conversations, but I worried when the best time might be to bring them up. I always felt I verged on ruining our day if I ventured into territory that might stress him out and cause other alters to come forward. It was stressful and weaved a lot of anxiety around our time together.

"I'm sorry about dinner with your parents," he mumbled as he nibbled a cracker.

Forgetting my food, I lifted my head, stunned he'd managed to read my thoughts and target exactly what I'd been mulling over in my mind.

"It's my fault." I shifted upright and placed my half-empty plate on the coffee table. "I know social situations aren't really your thing and I—"

"Don't make excuses for me. Please. I really wanted to go. I wanted to try and do something that challenged me some. Like school does. I guess I didn't know how affected I was by the idea."

He replaced his cracker on his plate and brushed the crumbs off his shirt before putting his plate beside mine. He sighed and tugged his sweater sleeves over his hands as he rocked a bit and forced himself to meet my gaze.

"I don't mean to be like this. It's why so many people just can't—"

"Stop." I reached out and placed my hand beside his knee where it was folded on the couch. I wouldn't touch him unexpectedly for any reason, but needed to catch his attention. "I've told you, I'm not like that. When I showed up at your house, and Cohen greeted me at the door, I think deep down, I wasn't surprised."

He stared where my hand rested and hugged his arms around his torso. "Okay." The submission in his voice wasn't what I'd wanted to hear, and it stabbed at my core.

Sighing, I wished I could help him find comfort in my presence.

"Do you like music?" I asked when the silence became too much.

His head lifted, and a light shone in his eyes. "I do."

"Much Music is playing non-stop Christmas tunes all day today. Mind if I put it on?"

He nodded as I jumped up to find the remote for the TV. After I located it and found the right channel, setting the volume to a distant background lull, I returned to the couch. A gentle smile washed away the shadows he'd been carrying a moment before, and his body visibly relaxed with the music.

For a long time, we both rested back on the couch and enjoyed the serenity around us. Neither of us spoke—words weren't needed.

After a short time, I took our empty coffee mugs to his kitchen for a refill, and when I returned, I sat a smidgen closer to him on the couch. He either didn't notice, or didn't care.

"Can I share something with you?" I asked after we'd drank through another round of coffees.

"Sure." He shuffled around to face me, the action bringing his knee to rest against mine. "Is something wrong?"

I hated that he always assumed the worse.

"No. But I have been feeling really uncomfortable about something that happened the other day, and I want to get it off my chest."

Worry creased his brow, but he nodded for me to continue.

I cleared my throat and brought my arm to lay across the back of the couch as I turned to him more as well.

"I told you Cohen came with me to dinner at my parents house the other day?"

He nodded, and a hint of a smile turned his mouth. Seeing it, I sneered playfully and smacked his shoulder.

"You gonna laugh at me now? You know I told my mom I was bringing *you* and never went into any details about your DID. So, when I showed up with Cohen on my arm—yes glued to my side—what do you think she assumed?"

The faint smile turned into an all-out chuckle, and his hand shot to his mouth in an effort to hide it. Swelling pride bloomed in my chest as I watched him laugh. Such manifestations of joy were infrequent, seeing it was enough to make my Christmas complete.

"Well," I continued, drawing on the moment, "I'm sure I'm probably some man whore in her eyes now."

Oryn bit his bottom lip to contain his humor and his cheeks reddened. "Did you tell your mom I was supposed to be your date?"

"No, but you know how mothers are."

I regretted my words the moment they left my mouth and panicked on the inside. Luckily, Oryn didn't react adversely to the comment and continued to smile.

"Did you explain after that?"

"No," I admitted. "It wasn't really the time for that. So, I just let her think whatever she wanted and figured I'd correct it next time we talked."

He chuckled and fidgeted, pulling his sleeves over his hands again and running them over his jeans.

"So my entire family is probably convinced I'm dating Cohen now," I continued. "He certainly didn't help matters." *Nor did I.*

Oryn remained focused on his jeans, the smile still tugging at his lips. When he didn't respond, I took a deep breath and pressed on.

"Oryn, I know we've said that this between us is complicated, and we haven't really called it dating exactly, so I'm never sure in my mind where we sit. Something happened at my parents, and it's eating me up."

His eyes found mine and the smile was replaced with a frown. "W-what happened?"

With the return of his stutter, I knew his stress was mounting so I trudged carefully.

"I've shared how... interested Cohen is in me. Dinner was no exception. There wasn't time to talk or sort out how to manage the evening, so I just went with it. Allowed him to be flirty and hang on my arm. Among other things." I dropped my gaze with the onslaught of nerves that had returned. "We went for a walk later that evening down by the water. Cohen, he... he really pushed the issue. Told me he could be what I wanted and..." My heart raced and clenched simultaneously. "He kissed me—which I stopped—at first... Then I didn't, because half of me wanted it to happen. I was inexplicably drawn to him, so I allowed it. But a rush of guilt swept over me and I stopped it again. I've been so fucking confused since that day, and I'm not sure how to tell you this, because I don't know where we sit or how I feel. Cohen, he draws on something inside me, and..."

My words ground to a halt when I caught a gleam of humor in Oryn's eyes. I frowned, gaped, and stumbled over how to respond.

"What...Why are you smiling?"

Surprising me, Oryn leaned in and rested his hand on my knee so he could bring his mouth close to my ear. Then, he whispered, "I already knew."

His breath ghosted my ear, and the words he spoke had two completely opposite effects on me. Warmth coated my skin and tingled in my belly, but I jumped back to stare at him in shock.

"You knew?"

He pressed his lips together, fighting a smile that seemed so out of place on the shy man I'd come to know, then he nodded.

Before I could open my mouth and question him, he held up a finger and hopped off the couch. He disappeared down the hall, but returned a minute later carrying a thick, leather-bound book. When he'd got comfortable again in his spot on the couch, he flipped through and found a page before placing it in my lap.

I recognized it immediately as his journal and glanced to him before looking at the handwriting on the page. I'd seen Oryn's penmanship enough times while we worked in school to know it wasn't he who'd written the passage. Oryn always wrote with a neat and even cursive script. The writing staring back at me was a mixture of printing and the odd loopy letter that mimicked cursive poorly. The sizing was all over the place and it was far more bubbled than Oryn's tall thin scrawl.

Taking it as permission, I started at the top and read.

Had Christmas dinner with the sex god who is Vaughn. His fam was sweet, and the food was fab. Vaughn seemed uptight at first, but I managed to help him relax. Maybe took advantage of the fact he was too much of a gentleman to say no to me in front of his 'rents. Finally got him alone and tasted that delicious jawline I've been eyeing. Even managed to encourage a kiss from him. It was short lived, and he panicked, but fucking hell, I could use me more of that. Would you set him straight already! I can tell he feels it too.

Cohen-

I read it three times with my jaw slack. For days, I'd been consumed with guilt and self-loathing over that moment of weakness with Cohen and the feelings surrounding it. I'd puzzled how to bring the subject up with Oryn, and he'd known the entire time.

"You knew." I repeated, dragging a finger over the writing on the page. "Oryn, I don't know what to say."

When I eventually met his eyes, there was no anger, and his smile was radiant.

"You seem upset," he said.

"I'm a wreck," I admitted. "I really like you. I've wanted this to be dating since I first kissed you. I understand there will be challenges, but I felt in my heart that you and I could at least test those waters and see where we ended up. Cohen, he…" I shook my head as my confusion returned. "I don't even know how to explain this without sounding like a complete asshole."

Oryn removed the notebook and placed it on the table. Then he did something I didn't expect; he took both my hands in his own and shuffled toward me until our legs touched.

"Just tell me what you're thinking."

It was insane, but the entire situation with Oryn was unique, so I forced myself to bite back the ugly feelings inside and just speak.

"I am so attracted to you, and I've been worried over how to take those next steps and how you'd react. When Cohen is out, he is everything you aren't. Having him clinging to me, touching me, and openly flirty it…it's messing with my head. I get those same intense feelings inside. When he tried to kiss me, I wanted it to be you… I stopped him. He told me you couldn't be what I wanted but that he could. When I closed my eyes to process and think I could smell you and when he touched me, they were your hands and your body and I thought… I don't know what I thought… but I kissed him." Shaking my head, I worked to swallow around a lump that was growing in my throat. "But that kiss wasn't you, it was him.

And what's worse is, I didn't hate it. I liked it. A lot. But then a wall of guilt hit me, and I was almost sick with what I'd done."

His hands tightened in mine bringing my attention back from the vision of that night I was seeing inside my head. There was no disgust or upset on his face, only concern and worry.

"You feel guilty," he whispered.

I wet my lips and nodded, hating the rotting pit growing in my belly. "I don't even know for sure if we are dating. But I do know it's what I want for us. Yet, kissing Cohen, liking it, it felt an awful lot like I'd stepped out and it's not who I am, Oryn. Only I'm so confused with all this."

Consumed with shame, I stopped speaking and swam in the blue-grey of his eyes. The hold on my hands released, and my stomach fell, thinking he was pulling away. Within a second, those two hands took my face and pulled me forward. I didn't have time to process his actions and moved automatically.

Our lips met, and I needed to supress a whimper at the sheer magnitude of what was happening. His mouth moved against me, and I melted into him, taking all he gave. It was chaste and sweet, never advancing into anything more. When his tongue teased along my lower lip, I tentatively took a simple taste of him. I didn't reach out to hold him like I wanted, fearing any movement might break the moment.

When he parted from my mouth, he continued to cup my face and remained close. "Will you be my boyfriend? Will you make it official? I can't promise you anything. There are a lot of things you don't know about me. And there are probably things I can't give you. Maybe ever. But if you know that and it's what you want—"

"Yes." I rested a hand against his waist and leaned my forehead to his. "I know there are barriers, but I want to try, Oryn."

He lingered, and I closed my eyes, breathing him in. My heart didn't know what it was doing anymore. One moment it jolted with fear at my confession, the next it skipped from overwhelming lust.

When Oryn pulled back, I released my hold. He stayed near and kept one hand on my cheek, ensuring I remained focused on his face.

"There should be no guilt," he said. "I explained how, although we are all individual, separate people, we are as much a part of a whole. If you accept me as your partner, you need to accept all my alters as well. They were all created for a reason and each of us has a purpose. Cohen excels at being social and is the furthest thing from shy. I think you will learn that he's right; he can give you things I can't—"

I opened my mouth to protest but he pressed a finger to my lips.

"And that's okay, Vaughn. There should be no guilt. Cohen is a part of me. Where I cower, he thrives. I would hope you two can form a bond as well. And if it's an intimate one, that's really okay. It's not weird to me in the least and it doesn't make me jealous. How can it?"

I waited until he freed my lips before I spoke. "It's so confusing. I'm not sure I can do that and make it okay in my mind."

Oryn sighed and examined my face pensively. "Just don't dismiss it."

Sensing it was important for him to hear, I agreed. Silence returned and Oryn remained close. I wanted to feel his lips again with mine, and touch him. The yearning for his soft kiss was one I'd been feeling for weeks.

I nuzzled into his hand and lost myself in his stormy eyes.

"Will you kiss me?" I asked.

He wet his lips before swallowing what could have been nerves. His other hand, the one that had fallen from my face a few moments ago, moved to my knee as he shifted closer. He touched our mouths together briefly and pulled back again, seeking something in my eyes.

"Please," I urged.

He closed his eyes, and eliminated our remaining gap, pressing his damp lips to mine with more force. With less reservation, he moved against me, gliding our mouths together with more confidence than before. When I requested invitation against the seam of his lips, he obliged. His taste sang through my body as our tongues met and we tested that connection a little more freely.

It didn't escalate past a few tantalizing kisses, and as much as I wanted to pull him up against me, I refrained. The only free-roaming I allowed myself, was threading fingers through his hair and brushing a thumb along his stubbled jaw. It was enough, and an action I'd dreamed of doing for weeks.

The remainder of the day was spent watching Christmas movies. Oryn remained close on the couch and kept his hand linked with mine the entire time. It was simple and uncomplicated, which I knew he needed.

As night descended, Oryn yawned.

"I should probably head out and let you get some sleep."

I shuffled off the couch and he followed me down the hall. Once I'd collected my winter gear and put it on, I paused, eyeing Oryn. His hands were jammed in his pockets and he looked about, not meeting my gaze.

I touched his arm to draw his attention and stepped closer, testing the comfort level we'd been growing all day. He didn't retreat or react with any indication of fear.

"I had a great day. Much better than spending Christmas alone."

He smiled as his cheeks pinked, and he dipped his gaze to the ground. "Me too."

His shyness and level of comfort reminded me so much of how I'd been when exploring my first ever relationship at fourteen. Perhaps it wasn't any different for him.

I caught his chin and drew it up as I stepped in and placed a soft kiss on his mouth. He sighed, and a minor amount of tension released from his body. I kept it safe and removed my mouth a moment later.

"Goodnight," I whispered against his lips.

"Goodnight."

Chapter Thirteen

Classes resumed a few days past New Years. I'd seen Oryn a handful of times since Christmas, but we chatted more frequently in texts. His reservations remained, and I often found each visit with him always began at square one with nerves and distance. Hours in each other's company lessened that constraint, and eventually we moved back into the safe territory of hand-holding and the odd cautious kiss. It was a relationship with severe limitations, and I found myself overtly conscious of my every move.

It was Monday evening and I planned to pick Oryn up after his class so we could go for a late night walk with hot chocolate by the water. For the first time in two weeks, the temperature hovered just above the freezing mark, and the night was perfect for a winter stroll.

I parked in the nearest spot I could find to the front entrance of the college and left the engine running so I could bask in the heat a short while longer. I sent Oryn a text to let him know I was there and cranked the tunes while I waited.

Shortly after eight-thirty, Oryn exited the college. There were a number of other students surrounding him on either side, but he walked alone, shoulders hunched, and head down as though trying to disappear or become smaller. The action sprung a leak in my protective barrier, and I scanned the other people looking for any indication they'd been targeting Oryn recently. None of them seemed to pay him mind.

He separated from the group and eventually lifted his head to scan the parking lot. The moment his eyes found my car, his face lit up and his pace quickened. The action brought a twinge of warmth to wash over me.

"Hi," he said as he pulled the door open and climbed inside. He plunked his bag between his legs on the floor and smiled shyly.

"Hey, it's good to see you." When I wanted to lean in and kiss him, I settled for rubbing his leg and returning his smile. "How was your first day back?"

"It was okay. I got my expository essay back, ninety-six percent." His pride lit up his face.

"Holy shit!" My eyebrows shot up as I put the car in reverse and backed out of the parking spot. "I knew you were insanely smart, but that's incredible."

He ducked his head, but the smile growing on his face was impossible to miss. "Thank you. I'm not that smart. The things he marked me on are things I should never have messed up."

And modest too. Oryn studied hard and I knew it. His dedication to school was something I admired, yet I was also beginning to see a lot of self-criticism outshining the well-deserved satisfaction he should have been feeling. He was really hard on himself.

I pulled into traffic and aimed us in the direction of the harbor and Grandview Park. The trails were some of Oryn's favorites and I knew of a coffee shop with a drive-thru nearby where we could grab a hot drink.

Oryn went quiet beside me and fiddled with the zipper on his coat. The nervous habit wasn't unusual, but I sensed an added uneasiness to it that day. As we waited in line at the drive-thru, I noted his frown and repeated lip biting.

"Is everything okay?" I asked.

The restless squirming instantly stopped, and he folded his hands in his lap and peered out the front window. "Sorry."

I waited on him to elaborate, but he fell silent. The car in front of me drove off and I needed to pay for our drinks before I could press him for more.

With our hot chocolates balanced in the middle console cup holders, I continued toward the water, deciding it might be best not to press the issue and let him talk when he was ready.

With the fall of night and the cooler temperatures, the park was deserted. I found a spot right beside the harbor-front path and killed the engine. Before getting out of the heated car, we both found hats, gloves, and scarves to wear, knowing the breeze off the water would only make it feel even colder.

With our hands wrapped around our hot chocolates, we wandered to the railing and leaned, looking out over the half-frozen lake. An ice breaker had gone through a day or two before and thick slabs of ice were piled along the coast in all directions. The night was peaceful and calm.

When with Oryn, we could easily pass great expanses of time without saying a word to one another. It was never uncomfortable. That was one of those moments.

We sipped our hot drinks and rested against the railing for a long while. The crisp air made the stars above shine brighter, and the water seemed to glisten in the dark.

"Do you want to walk some?" I asked when we'd both finished our drinks and found a garbage to deposit them.

"Sure."

Oryn still carried a lingering uncertainty about something he wasn't sharing. He fidgeted more than normal, but I hoped with fresh air and some company, whatever bothered him would either pass or be brought up.

We followed the cement path along the edge of the water. It was intended as a bike path in the summer time, but more people used it for strolling than anything. In the midst of winter, it saw little traffic and was mostly snow covered with a few random footprints from people who'd walked it earlier.

Before we'd gone far, I shifted closer and grabbed Oryn's hand to hold. It was an action that had become normal and comfortable, and he didn't flinch away anymore. He squeezed me tight and passed me a sideways smile, letting me know everything was all right.

After venturing half a mile, the path veered in toward a forested area. We chose to turn around and retrace our steps toward the car, staying where there was some element of light.

A large tanker ship had been slowly moving into the harbor as we walked, and when we changed directions, he was close enough we chose to stop and watch him trudge his way through the slushy waters. As we leaned on the rail again, I rested an arm across Oryn's shoulder and encouraged him to shuffle closer.

One step at a time.

When the closer proximity became more comfortable, he rested against me and I kissed the top of his head. Although there were a million things I wanted to explore with Oryn, I took great pride at the daily successes between us.

"I have a new assignment for my writing class," he whispered into the night. "And I don't know what to do about it." It had been silent for so long, I was surprised when he spoke.

Turning from the water, I released my arm and leaned sideways on the rail to face him. "What do you mean?"

He blew out a breath and I watched it fog into the air as he hugged his arms around his body. "Well, we've been told to write a f-five-thousand-word m-memoir of our childhood. I don't think I can do that. I-I mean I can, but…" He pinched the bridge of his nose and squeezed his eyes closed a moment before continuing. "What do I do, Vaughn? I b-barely remember my childhood. What I do know is ch-choppy and broken. It's all disconnected and n-not really a real life. It's all holes. I-I feel ill even thinking about it and…" He sighed and forced a knuckle into his eye before shaking his head. "N-never mind. I sh-shouldn't have brought it up."

My stomach sank as he struggled to explain, and when he fell silent again, I scrambled to know what to do. What to say. His past was forbidden territory—or at least I'd accepted it as such and never pressed, knowing what truths it probably held. That was the first time he'd referenced it directly.

His stress mounted with each passing moment, and the obsessive eye rubbing turned to massaging his temple, and wiping hands over his cheeks. They were signs I recognized. Pulling his hands from his face, I turned him so his back was to the rail and I was in front. I cupped his face and held it firm, encouraging him to look me in the eye.

"Stay with me, Oryn. Focus on me a minute and just breathe."

I was going to lose him, and I knew it. His breathing was out of sync and I wasn't sure he heard me. The touching of his face and temples, the squeezing shut of his eyes, and the random way he shook his head as if to rid himself of an unwanted thought were escalating, not decreasing. Was it even something I could prevent?

"You don't have to do anything that makes you uncomfortable. No one is forcing you to write on a topic you can't handle. Oryn, look at me. Listen. Are you listening?"

He opened his eyes and searched my face with a creased brow, worry pressed into his every feature.

But he nodded. With the connection, his breathing evened out, and although his gaze shifted frantically about my face, he appeared to be visibly calming.

"Mr. Jackson understands your condition. You've told all your professors. I'm certain he will allow a slight variation in the assignment. You don't have to give reasons, he should respect your privacy and understand."

Oryn nodded and his manic fidgeting lessened.

"W-we don't like going there. To the p-past. Therapy is already incredibly hard most days, b-but the idea of writing—"

Whether it was the fact that my heart ached so hard for him, or that I wanted to make it better and forcibly draw him from those terrible thoughts, I didn't know. Not letting him finish, I slammed our mouths together and kissed him, backing him right up tight against the rail and wrapping him in my arms, determined to never let anything hurt him ever again. Determined to stop the forward motion of thought and stress before it went too far.

It backfired.

Any ordinary man would have been taken aback and stunned silent by my action—which was the goal. However, logic had decided to fail me with that decision, and instead of showing Oryn how passionately I cared for him and wished to protect him, I tossed him right over the edge I'd only saved him from falling over moments before.

The split second it took for me to realize my actions were wrong was one too many, and when Oryn's back hit the rail and I engulfed him in a smothering kiss, he exploded.

…or rather, Reed did.

The shove to my chest was enough to make me stumble and almost lose my footing on the slippery ground. Wind-milling my arms, I managed to remain upright and flipped my confused gaze to Oryn—no, Reed.

He wiped at his mouth with the back of his hand and turned to spit over the rail before glaring back in my direction.

He raised a finger and opened his mouth to speak, but pressed his lips together and squeezed his hand to a fist instead before turning back to the water and running his mouth against his scarf.

"What the fuck were you thinking?" he asked, fisting the rail and leaning heavily as he worked through a few deep breaths.

"I was kissing my boyfriend is what I was thinking."

"Attacking or smothering is more like it. I told you to back down. Accept that and walk away."

He rolled his shoulders, and when I didn't respond, he peered back. "Did you hear me?"

"I heard you. But that's not going to happen, Reed. Oryn and I are trying this and—"

He flipped around and scowled before stalking toward me. Even though we were relatively on par when it came to height and weight, I backed up a step and held my hands out, warding off what I assumed would be an attack.

He swatted my hands away with a dry laugh. "Put your fucking hands down. I'm not going to hit you. Jesus. You don't get it."

"Then maybe explain it, because every time we meet, you blow up in my face and threaten me. I like Oryn. I know there are limitations and I know it won't be smooth sailing, but—"

"But don't even pretend you understand, Vaughn... You can't." The final statement was choked off and he cleared his throat trying to cover it. His anger remained, but there were hints of something else that passed through his eyes. Pain. A pain unlike I'd ever seen from Oryn. It softened his hard edge against his will. "You never will."

We remained in a silent standoff for more than a minute before he spoke again. His voice had hushed and was almost lost in the night. "I know what you want from him, and we don't really work that way. We've learned to get by, and we've learned to move forward. This..." He indicated to me as a whole with a finger. "You... It's not safe."

"You don't trust me."

"No."

"What will it take? I'm not a bad person. I will never cross lines Oryn doesn't want to cross." When his brows shot up, I sighed and added, "Knowingly. I didn't mean to... Reed, the world isn't all bad. There are good people in it. Oryn doesn't see me as evil, why are you so sure I am?"

"It's my job in the system."

We were at an impasse. Reed refused to find trust in me, and I refused to let Oryn go. Alters were each individual people, yet all part of one as Oryn had explained it. If I wanted to date him, it included Reed... somehow.

But Reed was determined to keep us apart. Being with Oryn meant finding a means to balance a relationship with all his alters. Including the brute in front of me. Somehow, I needed to prove I was trustworthy and not a threat... to his *system* as he called it.

Reed pulled the hat from his head in irritation and shoved it in a pocket before running a hand through his hair. He puffed out a warm breath of air into the chilly night. After passing a glance to the tanker, which had moved off down the channel, he shoved his hands in his pockets.

"Listen, I don't wanna be an ass, but this isn't going to work. Accept it and move on. I wish you'd listen. Take care."

Without waiting for a response or retort, he spun and marched across the field toward the road. Where the fuck was he going? The harbor was on the opposite end of town from Oryn's house.

"Wait, where are you going?"

"Home."

"You're walking?"

He turned to face me but kept pace through the snow going backward. "It won't kill me. Have a good night, Vaughn."

Idiot!

Cohen and his flirtatious ways were nothing compared to the stubborn mule who was Reed.

"Fuck's sake." I jogged to catch up and caught his arm. "Would you stop." He instantly yanked it free and spun on me.

"What are you doing?"

"Let me drive you home."

"No. I'm fine."

"Would you drop the dick attitude for five minutes. It's fucking freezing, and your house is over an hour away on foot. I can drive you home." He opened his mouth to respond and I jumped in faster, "Shut it. I'm not asking. Get in the fucking car."

I didn't think he expected me to grow a backbone and stand my ground. His intense gaze—one that always made his eyes seem darker—held on my face for many beats before he huffed a dry chuckle.

"Fine." He spun and crossed toward the parking lot instead, leaving me behind.

Small victory. Reed was not going to be easy.

When he reached the car ahead of me, I hit the door unlock button on my fob and he got in. He scratched his chin and watched the harbor as I approached. Seeing the man who was in so many ways the same, but in more ways different than Oryn, I mourned my lost evening. Again.

I knew the reality of having a relationship with Oryn meant accepting unexpected switches and drastic changes to plans, but it didn't make it hurt any less. We were only just getting to know each other. Reed, of all people, was bound and bent to see that didn't happen.

I got in the car and started the engine. Once it had run for a few minutes, I cranked the heat and removed my gloves. Reed didn't acknowledge me and remained focused on the outdoors. The silence was nothing like the one Oryn and I frequently shared. Those ones were comfortable and mutual. That one made me squirm and fish for something to break the tension.

As I pulled from the parking lot and onto the road, I filtered through the information I knew about Reed, trying to find something we could talk about.

"So, you like weightlifting?" The first time Oryn had discussed his inner world, I recalled him saying something along those lines about one of his alters. It'd stayed with me, because at the time, an *inner world* was beyond my understanding, and I'd found it weird. Knowing more about who his alters were, I guessed that Reed was probably the weightlifter—based strictly on his personality. It fit.

"We don't have to talk."

I blew out a breath and continued in silence. At a red light, I drummed my fingers on the steering wheel, hating the oppressing weight of the silence surrounding us. Two more stop lights and I couldn't take it and tried again.

"Do you like football?"

When I didn't get told to shut up immediately, I glanced over. Reed examined me with his telltale furrowed brow and frown. So, I pressed.

"Do you?"

"Love it," he mumbled, turning back to watch out the window.

I sat up straighter, a surge of energy passing over me at his simple answer. It wasn't much, but it was something.

"Favorite team? And please don't say Detroit." Evan and his obsession with the Lions was about all I could take.

He snorted and chuckled. "As if. Detroit sucks. Broncos fan. You?"

"I try to remain neutral."

"Bullshit. You have to have a favorite. That's a pussy answer."

I laughed as I stopped at the next intersection. "Fine, but if Evan ever asks, I'll deny ever saying this. I'm kinda a Miami fan."

"Dolphins, really?"

"I grew up watching Marino play. My older brother was a huge Dolphins fan, so I guess that's where it started."

As the light turned green, an idea struck. I glanced at the time on the dash. Nine-thirty. It was a longshot, but I felt like I'd broken the ice somewhat between us and needed to try.

"I have an idea." I passed a glance to Reed as I pulled into the next driveway to turn around.

"Idea? What are you doing?"

As I waited for a clearing to pull out again, I grinned. "It's nine-thirty on a Monday night, and we've only missed the first quarter. What do you say we head to Infernos, have a few beers, and watch the game? It's playoffs. I don't know who's playing, but the Broncos made it this year, didn't they?"

He nodded and the easy expression he'd adopted as we'd talked football faded as his harsher examination returned. When he didn't answer immediately, I waited before pulling back into traffic.

"Well? What do you say?"

"If this is some kind of date invitation, then no. I'm straight."

"That's nice, and I'm gay. But I'm not asking you out on a date, dipshit. I'm asking you to go have a few beers at the bar with me and watch the game. If that's dating then someone should inform Evan, because we've been at it for twenty years and he has yet to put out."

When Reed unintentionally laughed at my response, he coughed to try and cover it then shifted around to peer out the window again.

"Not sure if the Broncos are playing tonight. What's the date?" he asked.

"The tenth. Does it matter? Football is football."

He nodded and glanced back briefly before shrugging. "Yeah, sure. I could use a beer."

With his agreeance, I pulled back into traffic and headed toward Infernos with one goal in mind.

Build trust with Reed.

Chapter Fourteen

Monday night football at Infernos always saw significant traffic. We found a couple of open stools at the bar—surprisingly in front of the big screen—and settled in with a couple of drafts. It was a Wild Card game and the Packers were already crushing the Redskins as half-time approached. We'd managed to wander in just after the second quarter started.

"He's gonna get sacked. Wait for it... wait for it... and boom!" Reed jumped up and laughed. "Sucker. Kirk didn't even see it coming. Nicely played."

He shifted back in his seat and swigged his beer. Since our explosion by the harbor, Reed's mood had shifted significantly. Broncos may not have been playing, but he clearly had a preference for Green Bay and had been rooting for them since we'd arrived. To make life interesting, I'd decided to root for the opposing team, even though Washington had been down by fourteen since first quarter. Reed and I had placed bets—loser paid for drinks at the end of the night.

Washington went into half-time down by twenty-one, so unless they pulled their shit together, it looked like I was buying that night.

When the panel began breaking down the first half of the game, Reed dropped his gaze to his mug of beer and spun it on the bar top, leaving a trail of condensation smears behind. Without the game to distract us, it became awkward again.

I drank deep, drained my glass, and pushed it forward, waving for the bartender to bring us a couple more before turning to face Reed.

"Is it so wrong for us to get to know one another?"

He didn't respond and traced a finger through the puddle his wet glass had left behind.

Not enjoying the extended silence, I shrugged and just started talking. If he didn't like it, too bad.

"Okay, so me... I like being busy. If life is too stagnant, I get bored. Work doesn't challenge me enough, so that's why I went back to school. I need to do something different. I'm a math whiz, but an English failure. However, I love to read. Mysteries mostly, but when I'm feeling sappy, I tackle a good old fashion romance, like Gone with the Wind."

Reed snorted at my confession and shook his head. "Why am I not surprised."

"Go ahead. Laugh. In fact, sometimes I like to curl up in a blanket and watch romantic comedies on the TV."

"No wonder you and Oryn get along so well. He has this skewed perception of romance because of that sort of shit. He doesn't seem to understand, we don't need that in our lives, and it only poses unnecessary problems."

I pursed my lips and tried a new angle. "Cohen seems interested in romance. Maybe it's just you."

"Cohen will hump legs with anyone who pays him attention. Ask Cove. They've been on again off again for years."

That was interesting information.

"I don't understand. How does that work?"

Reed sighed and pulled his new beer closer. "It means, in our inner world, Cove and Cohen date. They make it very clear it's an open relationship. But they fight a lot, hence the on again, off again part."

The inner world. Right.

"So, Cove is gay too?"

"Cove is bi. You didn't know that?"

I shook my head. "I haven't met him yet."

"That's because Oryn won't allow it."

That statement made me wonder if Oryn had asked Reed not to interfere as well, and Reed had simply chosen to do his own thing.

Deciding against asking, I mulled over what he'd explained.

"What about Theo?"

"What about him?"

"Is he gay?"

Reed shook his head as he swigged his beer. "Asexual."

"Huh." Somehow that didn't surprise me with what little I knew about him. "I'm still trying to sort out and understand the whole inner world thing. Sorry if I sound stupid. Can you tell me what it's like?"

Reed chuckled and scratched his chin, tilting his head to the side and popping his neck. "It's our world. It's where we live when we aren't fronting. Just like this is your world. You're an accountant, you swoon over romance reads, you go to college. Same thing. We all have our own lives there."

Sensing I might be getting somewhere, I chanced asking the same question he'd ignored earlier. "And you're a weightlifter?"

"Yeah. I compete all over the country. I also teach Taekwondo when I'm not training. Theo and I are brothers. Did you know that?"

"Really?" I had no idea. Oryn and I hadn't gone into great depths when discussing the inner world of his alters, and I suddenly felt as though I was missing a whole lot about him.

"Yeah. Rain is Theo's adopted son. I help him out with the brat on occasion. He's a good kid actually."

It felt odd asking, but everything about Oryn and DID was so unusual, it seemed it was more a matter of getting used to the functionality of it all.

"What does Theo do for a living?"

"He's an in-home support worker with the elderly and disabled. It's right up his alley. Basically, he cooks, he cleans, and he takes care of people who can't take care of themselves. Which is also kinda his role in the system. He manages and nurtures and cares for everyone. Kinda mister bossy pants sometimes."

Hearing more about Theo made me less apprehensive about meeting him. The way Reed spoke, he gave the impression of a man I'd get along with well. I wondered why I hadn't had the pleasure yet. Had Oryn given him the same warning as he'd apparently given Cove?

"What's your role in the system?" I already knew from what Oryn had explained, but it would be interesting to hear it from the horse's mouth.

"I protect it. Keep it safe from threats."

"Threats like me?"

"You're catching on."

I bit back arguing that he wasn't giving me a chance, because it wouldn't get me anywhere. Actions spoke louder than words. Instead, I pondered the inner workings of Oryn's world and what little I knew about some of his alters. As aggressive as Reed portrayed himself, it was Cove who concerned me the most. We hadn't met—apparently for a reason—and I knew he was responsible for Oryn's severely disfigured arms.

"What's Cove's role in the system?" I asked somewhat hesitantly, unsure if I was crossing into areas I shouldn't.

Reed's attention had been drawn across the room and he remained fixed on something over my shoulder for a moment before meeting my gaze again.

"He protects it as well. Only in a different way than I do."

The hardened glare I received with his explanation warned me not to elaborate. When he saw I understood, he shifted his focus back over my shoulder. Curious, I turned and followed where he was looking.

A woman leaned on the far end of the bar; blonde, petite, huge breasts—which were on display and spilling from her too-tight tank top. She was a knockout. I flipped my gaze back to Reed to confirm the direction of his stares, and there was no denying it; that woman had consumed his full attention.

A mixture of annoyance and jealousy stirred in my gut. I'd analyzed and accepted a lot of things when deciding to date Oryn, but it'd never occurred to me that his alters might have different plans.

Reed was straight. Did that mean he dated women while—*what did he call it*—fronting? Cohen was nineteen with raging hormones. Did he pick up guys at the bar? Did dating Oryn mean that I'd inadvertently agreed to allowing his alters—the ones who claimed his body so randomly—to have alternate lives?

I wasn't okay with that.

"Stop freaking out."

"What?" I snapped out of my thoughts and focused on Reed. He was watching me. For how long?

"We all have a contractual agreement with Oryn. I may break rules on occasion when I feel it's best for him, but that's one rule I won't cross. So relax. She has nice tits and a man can look, can't he?"

"What does that mean? What agreement?"

"No dating outside the inner world." He hesitated and broke eye contact, turning back to the television before mumbling, "Only Oryn can date."

It took everything in me to hide the smugness from my face. Reed may not agree with Oryn and I dating, but at some point in time, he *had* agreed to the eventuality that it could happen.

The second half began and we both became reabsorbed in the game. Packers were a sure win, and Reed celebrated early with another round of drinks.

By the time we left Infernos, the heavy tension that had been present between us by the water was gone. I wasn't naïve enough to believe we were okay and I'd have no more issues, but I hoped we'd made positive headway at least.

Once I'd parked in the driveway, Reed wasted no time unbuckling and jumping out of the car. It was only then when I once again mourned the loss of my date with Oryn. The sweet moments we shared when we went our separate ways were among my favorites. The lingering soft kisses and the way he clung to my hand a little longer, only letting go when our physical gap was too great to stay connected. His smile that was so different than anyone else's. The way his eyes shone with the two-toned color. His shyness and the way he bit his...

"Later."

I snapped from my thoughts as Reed bent and peered in the car.

"Yeah. Take care."

Thanks for trying. Thanks for not decking me when I kissed you and not Oryn. Thanks for letting me in—if only a little.

I bit back each statement as they popped into my mind, begging to be voiced. The car door slammed, and Reed moved toward the house. Clutching the steering wheel, I closed my eyes and tried to wash away my disappointment, reminding myself that *was* what I'd signed up for. Oryn had warned me. Evan's laughter and admonishment rang in my ears. If he knew the half of it, I'd never hear the end of it. Vaughn Sinclair, dating not one, but six men... well, four. Rain was an accepted part of the system, but only a child. And Reed, no matter if he became accepting or not, was definitively straight and wanted nothing to do with *dating*.

A pounding on my car window made me jump, and I popped my eyes open and swung my head toward the noise, startled. Reed glared in and made motion for me to roll down the window. I complied and stared back confused.

"Why?" he asked.

"Why what?"

"Why dating? Why not simply friendship? You have no idea the shitstorm you're causing in the system doing this."

I flinched, but answered him the only way I could. Honestly.

"Because he means more to me than that. I can't deny the connection we have and the way he makes me feel when we're together. He warms my heart in a way I haven't felt in a long time... maybe ever. I'd never hurt him, Reed. I wish you could believe me."

He pressed his lips together into a thin line and stared for longer than was comfortable without uttering a single word. Then he straightened to his full height and went into the house without looking back.

***

"What do you want to do for your birthday?"

Oryn's fingers paused over the keyboard and he glanced up with a blank expression. I chuckled. When he buckled down and focused on work, Oryn tuned out the world—including me.

"Pardon?"

"Your birthday. It's next month. Is there something you'd like to do?" Stepping carefully into territory we hadn't explored, I added, "Maybe we could go away for a weekend."

Laptop forgotten, Oryn blinked a few times at the suggestion before dashing his gaze to his empty glass beside him. He clamored to his feet in a rush and snapped it up before disappearing into the kitchen.

"I don't know," he called as he left.

It was mid-March and Oryn and I had been dating for two and a half months. In that time, I'd learned a great deal more about who Oryn was and how his system operated. Reed continued to front at the most inopportune times, wrecking any and all progress Oryn and I made intimately. Kissing and a moderate wandering of hands was about as far as anything had progressed.

And we'd never spent a night together. Hence my delicate attempt to offer a weekend away.

Oryn's head poked out from the kitchen. "Did you want more ginger ale?"

"No, I'm okay, thanks."

When he returned, he fit himself back on the ground in front of the laptop and shuffled through our notes, avoiding my gaze.

In two and a half months, I'd paid attention and learned his cues; when he was stressing out, when he was uncomfortable, when I could press forward, and when I needed to step back. I'd also learned to let Oryn take the lead when it came to intimacy. If it was his idea and his initiation there was less chance of me losing him to Reed... or Cohen.

Despite Oryn's insistence that Cohen and I should develop an intimate bond—due to his own personal limitations and reservations—it had been challenging. We'd become closer—Cohen and I—and even ventured on a handful of dates, but I struggled. His immaturity shone through at times, and where Oryn couldn't seem to move *our* physical relationship past timid make-out sessions, *I* couldn't move mine and Cohen's past the same invisible wall.

Oryn squinted at the screen and continued typing.

"Oryn? We can get separate beds. I just thought it would be nice to get away and do something fun. We could go to Toronto, maybe, visit the museum, or go see a play. I've never been up the CN Tower. There is a beautiful, rotating restaurant that would make a perfect location for your birthday dinner. What do you say?"

His teeth found his lip. Removing his hands from the keys, he folded them in his lap, but wouldn't look at me.

"Do you trust me?" I asked.

Immediately his head shot up and he nodded too quickly. "Yes."

I'd asked him that question a lot, and knew he had yet to be completely honest when answering. In his heart, he wanted so badly to trust me, but the damage from his past was significant, and I saw in the depths of his eyes the skepticism he wasn't willing to voice.

"Okay, we can go," he submitted, dropping his focus again.

My heart sank, knowing he'd only agreed because he feared upsetting me. It was instances like that when I understood Reed's point of view and why he fought to keep us apart.

I couldn't force trust any more than he could will himself to believe. No matter how many times I told him—or Reed—that I would never bring harm, his experiences told him differently. Someone close to him—someone he should have been able to trust with his life when he was just a young child—had done irreparable damage. Oryn may never learn to trust again and that was something I was slowly coming to realize.

I dropped the subject, knowing I had another month to build his confidence over the idea. We dove back into our project, smoothing out the finishing touches and ensuring our tallies of data matched. In two weeks, we presented to the class and the week after that would be our final exam.

It was Saturday night and we'd been at it half the day. Oryn resumed typing, but the worry I'd caused was pressed into his forehead. A surge of guilt bled through my veins, and I shifted from the couch to join him on the floor.

He pretended not to notice me watching him until I reached out and took his hand.

"Let's be done for the night. It's almost eight and we haven't eaten since noon. What do you say to some dinner?

He blew out a breath and finally met my gaze. "Yeah, I'm kinda hungry."

He saved our progress and closed the laptop. We tidied up the rest of our mess and retreated into the kitchen. Oryn went straight for the freezer and began shifting through the frozen meals Theo had made. I'd still not had the pleasure of meeting him, and when I'd mentioned that to Oryn, he'd shrugged and explained Theo's place in the system was specific, and I just wasn't around when he needed to front.

I moved in behind Oryn and placed a hand on the freezer door to let him know I was near. Sneaking up on him, or startling him, was a sure-fire way to bring Reed forward. Once I saw him acknowledge my presence, I rested a chin on his shoulder and wrapped an arm around his waist to look at our choices with him. He leaned back against me and turned his face, smiling and joining us in a soft kiss. It sang through my body and tingled over my skin—always shorter lived than I wished. When we came apart, Oryn resumed looking. I planted a few more kisses along his cheek and nuzzled into his neck, inhaling the fragrance that was all him. It was a scent I loved more than any other.

"What about…" He lifted a few more containers, reading the labels before shifting them aside. "Take out?"

"Theo will be pissed you just chose junk over his hard work."

Oryn chuckled and it rang through my body. I loved hearing him happy. "He won't. He's not like that. Besides, I'm craving crap food."

"What level of crap are we talking? Greasy, deep-fried or the stuff that has the appearance of being healthy but we all know it's not?"

Oryn closed the freezer and turned in my arms. He kept a small distance, but rested his hands on my waist and clung with a light grip. "The first one. The clog your arteries and hug the toilet all night because we shouldn't have eaten that, type."

"Excellent."

We both laughed, and he leaned in taking the kiss I'd been craving. His initial contact was always tentative at first, grazing and pecking lightly, as though testing our connection. Then, when he felt comfortable, he pressed his supple lips more firmly to mine before finally teasing with his tongue. Each shared kiss began in the same agonizingly slow manner, aching through my body and testing my wills. I'd learned not to advance before he was ready, and basked in the slow burn until I tasted him against my tongue.

Never in my adult life had I gone so long in a relationship without sex. I was thankful I didn't have the inflated sex drive Evan had. He could screw every night of the week and act like a starved man by noon. However, I'd never actively needed to refrain when I'd wanted to move forward with someone. Most boyfriends were quick to jump into bed when we decided it was time, but with Oryn that bridge was extremely fragile. Attempting to cross before he was ready could have a detrimental effect on him. I'd known that going in—accepted it may be a place we could never go—but there were times my body craved more, and fighting those cravings left me aching.

As our kiss moved to new heights and his tongue explored more freely, his hands gripped my sides and pulled me closer. With our chests touching, I wrapped my arms around him in turn, cautious not to crush him against me or make him feel trapped.

When we came apart, he remained close, smiling. It was free and full of an emotion I was seeing more readily on him with each passing day; optimism, contentment, and bliss.

"This isn't getting food," I said.

"I know."

He chuckled and in the same instance his right eye squinted briefly, and he drew a hand up to wipe at it as he shook his head and refocused on my face.

"Is it Reed?" I asked, learning the signs of when an alter was hovering close by.

"Yeah."

He didn't allow for anymore discussion over it and withdrew from my arms, tugging fingers through his hair as he moved into the hallway.

"So, food?" he called over his shoulder.

Probably for the best.

Crap food turned into an attempt at semi-healthy as Oryn decided he was in the mood for Chinese. Balancing veggie stir-fry and rice with an assortment of deep fried chicken balls and wontons seemed to satisfy both ends of his craving.

We got our food to go and ate in Oryn's den, since his dining room table had been taken over by school books and papers. Following Oryn's lead, I sat opposite him on the floor, and we pigged out as he shared about the English assignment he'd gotten back the previous day. Back in January, his professor had assigned a paper about memoirs based on childhood. Oryn had received permission to alter his somewhat and instead wrote as Rain, deconstructing his inner world to show how the five-year-old lived.

Surprisingly, Oryn had allowed me to read the paper before he'd submitted it, and I'd enjoyed the opportunity to peek into Rain's world. He'd surfaced a handful of times while I was around, and each consecutive appearance made me more comfortable.

Oryn had earned eighty-nine percent on the paper and gloated quite proudly.

"Who knew I could get a grade like that talking about Batman and puppy dogs. I almost feel like I cheated. Rain was easy to write, he's fun and open-minded. Free-spirited and so full of life and energy. He was thrilled when I told him I wanted to work with him and write his story."

Rain was exactly what all children *should be*. He experienced life in a way that was so normal, Oryn didn't recognize it and assumed it to be something of awe.

I smiled as I finished chewing. "You should consider adding it to the biography you want to write. I don't know how you are including everyone, but it would be really neat to add it in."

"I should."

He glowed as he mulled over the idea, and we finished eating.

When the takeout containers were disposed of, we relaxed on the couch and Oryn flipped on the TV. Once we settled on a station showing repeat episodes of The Simpsons, Oryn shuffled closer and leaned against my side. I automatically wrapped an arm around him and threaded fingers through his hair, playing with the soft strands as we laughed at Bart's repeated antics.

When the second episode began, Oryn rested a hand on my leg and moved his fingers against my inner thigh. He'd been testing our connection lately. Touches had moved past holding hands and stroking cheeks, to exploring my abdomen, biceps, and thighs. Always over top of clothing. Always with timid restraint.

The smooth, light tickle of his fingers as they drew circles on my leg tingled across my skin, and I caught myself focusing on them more than the show, willing my body not to react. The heat germinating in my core spread through me and my breath came short despite my determination.

Oryn turned his head where it was rested on my shoulder, probably sensing or noticing the sudden change in my behavior. He smiled with a hint of mischief in his grey-blue eyes.

Shifting, he brought his other hand behind my head and pulled me against his mouth.

For the first time, there was no shaky start, and he sucked on my lower lip before dipping his tongue inside. The warmth that had begun a moment before turned to fire and I fought to avoid pulling him on top of me and taking more.

His taste permeated and sang across my tongue, and I returned his affection with as much limitation as I could handle. The urge to palm his skin, remove his shirt, and bring our flesh together in a crushing, tangled way, was almost painful.

Instead, like I'd dared before, I traced one hand down his spine, stopping slightly below his waist, while clinging to his nape with the other. He shuffled to face me, moving the hand from my leg to my chest and smoothing it down until it sat at my hip. Then, he did something I didn't expect. He moved onto my lap, straddling me and pressing us together in a closeness we'd never experienced.

My head buzzed with need and I couldn't stop myself and slid both hands to cup his ass. A long moan escaped him as he continued to kiss. His hands found the bottom of my shirt and crept inside, smoothing over my stomach and rising. It wasn't until he rocked against me, and I felt the effect of our actions pressed into my abdomen did all the pieces fall into place.

I tore from his mouth and grabbed his face in two hands when he attempted to re-join us. He stilled, panting and out of breath as he stared back into my eyes. The lust and desire pouring off him was wrong. Sitting in my lap, climbing hands under my shirt, his lack of reservation…

…his erection. Something wasn't…

"Cohen?"

The corner of his lip twitched as he fought off a grin, but the humor in his eyes shone through. I patted his ass and frowned.

"Off."

"Ah, come on."

Regardless, he slid to the side and allowed me to get up. My heart raced. I was semi-hard, brimming with a similar hunger that was radiating off him in waves. I paced, readjusting myself as I tried to align my thoughts and calm my suddenly overactive libido.

"That wasn't fair," I said, spinning on him. "You can't trick me like that."

"We've made out before, what does it matter. When you didn't know, you didn't worry so much and you let yourself enjoy it."

"It matters, Cohen. I'd like to know who the fuck I'm making out with."

God, I never thought I'd say those words in my life.

His face fell when he realized how upset I was. "I'm sorry."

I let out a long breath and flopped beside him on the couch again, leaving space. Leaning back, I rested an arm across my eyes. There wasn't necessarily guilt any longer associated with Cohen, but there was a deeply rooted confusion over how I felt about becoming romantically involved. The lines were definitely beginning to blur.

"But you were enjoying it, weren't you?" he asked, his hurt feelings glaringly obvious.

Yes!

Enough my body wasn't coming down as quickly as I'd have liked. My blood had all drained south and ached with the sudden halting of activity and turning of direction.

I couldn't tell him, though, because it would encourage something I didn't know for sure I wanted. So, I remained silent. If I claimed I *hadn't* enjoyed it, he'd know damn well I was lying, based on the evidence he'd surely felt.

We sat in silence for a while before he shifted closer and wedged himself against me. Cohen adored snuggling. He wrapped his arms around my body and rested his head against my chest. Sighing, I draped an arm around him and held him close. Kissing the top of his head, I inhaled the one piece that never changed. He carried his natural scent everywhere, no matter who he was, and it reminded me that as separate and different as his alters were, they were all part of a whole person.

He can give you things I can't. It's okay, Vaughn. Cohen is part of me.

Oryn's words played on a constant loop, especially when Cohen was fronting. Even more so when I was relaxed enough to allow that affection to bloom and grow.

The Simpsons continued to play, and Cohen remained in my arms for the next hour. When another episode ended, I shuffled and encouraged him to get up.

He moved to his knees and faced me, dejection still present behind his attempt at a smile. I fixed his hair and stroked his cheek. The tiny action wiped it away. Cohen fought so hard for affection and my inner turmoil got in the way every time. Some days, I felt he needed a reminder that he wasn't an object to be used. He'd truly grown on me in the past few months, but he was worth a lot more to me than what he desperately tried to pursue.

"We should go dancing next weekend," I said.

Cohen flinched, but the flash of excitement my suggestion brought wasn't masked.

"But you hate dancing."

"I never said I hated it, I said I wasn't good at it."

He shimmied closer and kissed my nose. "I can teach you. It's all in your hips."

I chuckled, knowing I'd be making a fool out of myself, but not caring. "These hips are a lot older than yours. Go easy on me."

Cohen laughed and flopped down across my lap, turning to look up at me. It amazed me how the look in his eyes was so much younger than the look I saw in Oryn's. Almost like his irises shone brighter somehow.

"Are you serious about dancing?" he asked peering at me with a contented smile.

I played fingers in his hair as he got comfortable. "For sure, on one condition."

He furrowed his brow. "What's that?"

"You'll have dinner out with me beforehand."

His smile was crooked and nothing like Oryn's. "Deal!"

We fell silent and I continued to roll strands of hair around my fingers as he watched. When he rolled to face my abdomen, smoothed a hand up my shirt, and planted kisses on my bare skin, I fought the pleasure it induced and stopped him.

"I should probably get going. It's getting late."

Cohen sighed and pulled himself upright without argument. His disappointment was evident. He followed me to the front hall where I collected my jacket from the closet. It was beginning to thaw outdoors, and we'd managed to shed the need for hats, scarves, and mittens. Cohen watched me don my coat and put on my shoes. As much as he smiled, I didn't miss the hint of rejection in his eyes.

When I'd tied my second shoe, I stood and pulled him into my arms. He automatically wrapped his own around my torso and we shared a silent pause.

"You can't trick me like that anymore. It's unfair."

His gaze fell a moment and he nodded. "I'm sorry. I know. It's just…"

"Shh." I lifted his chin and pressed my lips to his, kissing his argument away. When my body wanted more, and screamed for me to back him into the den and continue where we'd been before, I pulled away. "Don't rush it, Cohen. Give it time. It will happen."

Those few words were all the gift he needed. It proclaimed for the first time that I wasn't dismissing the possibility any longer and may in fact decide we could move forward.

Chapter Fifteen

I turned the key in the ignition for the third time. It clicked, but nothing happened. The engine didn't roar to life like it was supposed to.

"Dammit!"

I sunk back against the seat and pinched the bridge of my nose. Blowing out a frustrated breath, I checked the time on my phone. Ten after four. Taking a chance that he wasn't involved with a showing or meeting with a client, I called Evan.

"Hey, give me a sec."

The sound muffled, and I faintly heard voices as he talked to someone in the background. A moment later, he was back.

"What's up?"

"Are you busy?"

He sounded busy. The last thing I wanted to do was call a tow truck.

"I have a closing tomorrow, so a bunch of paperwork to do for it, but nah, not busy. What's up?"

I sighed and braced myself for the backlash I'd receive the moment I opened my mouth.

"I need gas."

"What do you mean." He was eating something, and his words were muddled.

"For my car. I ran out."

Evan snorted. "Crazy as it sounds, they actually have places all over town that deal directly with that issue. They are called gas stations." He emphasized the words slowly, enunciating them like I didn't understand English. "They're a rip off, but what are ya gonna do."

"That's brilliant, dipshit. Who knew."

"Yeah, well, I help when I can."

I loosened my tie and unbuttoned the top two buttons on my dress shirt. It was strangling me, and I needed to breathe.

"Okay, knock it down a peg. I'm serious. I'm in the lot at work and I'm out of gas. I don't want to pay a tow truck. Can you help me out?"

Evan laughed. "You *are* serious, aren't you?"

"Yes."

"Give me twenty minutes. I just need to close down here. I'll take my work home with me tonight. Then I'll grab gas for you on my way over."

I blew a strand of hair off my forehead. "Thanks. I'll pay you back."

"Fucking right you will. I ain't buying your gas. You owe me dinner, too."

"You'll need to take a rain check on that one. I'm meeting up with Oryn tonight."

With both of us dating, our time hanging out had diminished. Football season was over, so there was no longer an excuse to gravitate to Evan's on Sunday either.

"Yeah, whatever. I won't forget this."

As I waited for Evan to show up, I sent a text to Oryn, letting him know I was running behind. Tuesdays and Thursdays were his therapy days. Ordinarily, he was too worn out and asked we not visit on those days. But, he'd texted me that morning to check in since we'd not said a proper goodnight the previous evening after Cohen's appearance.

I didn't get a response, which wasn't unusual. I'd learned it meant either someone else was fronting—Theo, perhaps, as he managed the house, cooked, or cleaned—or Oryn was resting.

It was a mild March day and I cracked my window for some fresh air while I researched ideas for Oryn's birthday on my phone. Toronto had a variety of options, but it was a three-hour drive north. It only made sense to plan for the weekend instead of driving back and forth in one day. I knew the idea unsettled him, but if I could find something appealing enough, I was sure he'd agree.

The Royal Ontario Museum or the ROM was my first thought. With Oryn's love and knowledge of history, I knew we could spend an entire day there without question. Just as I clicked their website to see if they had any special exhibits running, a car pulled up beside me.

Evan.

I got out as he did and scowled when he didn't even attempt to hide his humor. He popped the trunk on his black KIA Rio5 and removed a red jug full of gasoline.

"You know," he said as he set it on the ground and slammed the trunk again. "If you pay attention to your instrument panel, there is this little flashy light that comes on when you are almost out of gas. Looks like a little pump. They put that there so things like this don't happen."

"Yeah, yeah, I know. It came on yesterday on my way to work. I planned to get gas after, but was running late and needed to pick Oryn up at school. Then I was going to get gas on my way home from his place last night and…" I paused, not sure how much to explain. "Things didn't end how I expected and I was caught up in my head and forgot."

"And this morning on your way to work?"

I shrugged and picked up the jug from the ground. "Didn't notice I guess. Kinda forgot all about it."

My confession earned me a well-deserved eyeroll and chuckle. For the next few minutes, Evan helped me transfer the gas into my tank. To be sure that was indeed the problem, I tried starting it and it roared to life.

Evan returned the empty jug into his trunk and searched his own keys from his pocket.

"What do I owe you?" I asked, pulling out my wallet.

"Dinner and beers. Keep your money."

Knowing it was useless to argue, I returned my wallet to my pants.

"So how are all the boyfriends?" Evan asked, leaning against his car and crossing his arms over his chest.

He didn't look in a hurry to leave, so I joined him and leaned on my car across from him. He liked to tease that I'd turned slut and was dating half a football team. I ignored the comment, knowing better than to correct him.

"Last night was interesting."

Evan raised a brow in query, so I continued.

"It was the first time, that I'm aware of, that an alter tried to pull a fast one on me and pretended to be Oryn."

Evan's face split into a wider than was necessary grin. "Nice!"

"Not nice. I kinda like to know who I'm locking lips with and who's trying to get into my pants."

Evan snorted a laugh. "Oh to have your problems. You poor thing. Why does it matter who you're fucking? Be it Oryn or the other ten guys. It's all the same body."

When I deadpanned, he held his hands up and apologized. It held no heart.

"There aren't ten. There are six in his system and I'm not dating all of them... exactly. Rain is a kid, Reed is straight, and I haven't even met two of them."

Math wasn't Evan's strong suit, so I almost chuckled when his face screwed up as he thought.

"So... you're fucking two of them." He mouthed counting as he held up fingers before meeting my eyes, more confident about his statement.

"I'm fucking none of them."

Evan flinched. "Say what now?"

Why was I delving into a conversation with Evan about my sex life? That was the last thing I needed to be doing.

I sighed and waved a hand, dismissing the whole thing. When I went to get in my car, Evan spun me by the shoulder.

"Whoa, you don't get to run away yet. Are you telling me you've been dating Oryn since Christmas and you haven't had sex?"

The notion was utterly baffling to a man like Evan, and his face moved through many stages of disbelief.

"It's complicated. I don't expect you'd understand."

"What does that mean?"

"It means, sex is important to you. If you found a woman who wanted to wait until she got married to have it, you'd run in the opposite direction… and there is nothing wrong with that. It's who you are—"

"Are you saying he's abstaining because he wants to get married first?"

"No. I swear you never listen when I talk." I shuffled and knew Evan wouldn't let me get out of the conversation without at least a feasible answer. "Many people with DID suffered long term sexual abuse as children. I'm certain that is probably Oryn's history. I don't know for sure, and I don't ask. As a result, the likelihood of him being comfortable having a sexual relationship is slim. It might never happen. I knew this going in and," I held up a finger when Evan opened his mouth to interject, "and, I'm okay with it."

Evan's mouth hung slightly askew as though he couldn't quite fathom a relationship where sex wasn't the key element.

"Anyhow, Cohen does have an interest in a sexual relationship with me and I haven't gone there yet. It…" I searched for the right way to describe my hang-ups. "It just hasn't felt right."

Evan remained speechless and continued to stare dumbfounded. I wasn't sure I was looking for advice, but his gaping silence made me drop my hands in frustration.

"See, I told you, you wouldn't understand."

He shook his head. "I can't believe you aren't having sex and you've been with the guy almost three months."

Biting back a retort, I fished my keys from my pocket. "I'm leaving now. Thanks for the gas, Evan. I'll call you."

"You're mad. Why are you mad?"

"When you figure it out, let me know." I pulled my door open and got in.

"Oh my God, you are as bad as a woman."

He caught my door before I could slam it in his face. I glared, unimpressed and no longer in the mood to deal with him. We'd been friends forever, and sometimes, Evan was a piece of work. What I needed was the Evan I could talk to without judgement, but apparently, he was nowhere to be found.

"Would you stop," he said.

I stared him down and his face softened.

"What's the hang-up with Cohen? What about it doesn't feel right?"

I shifted my gaze out the windshield and sighed. "He's not Oryn. I like Cohen. A lot. In a completely different way than Oryn. Enough it confuses the hell out of me because I didn't think it possible. We've become close, and I don't feel the guilt like before and I... I've been fighting those urges with him for weeks now. I want more with him, Evan, but what does that say about me?" I turned back to Evan, not expecting an answer, but pleading silently regardless. "I want everything with Oryn, too. I want him comfortable and happy, and I want to bring him pleasure and make love to him, but I know I can't. Instead I—"

"Vaughn," Evan interrupted. I swallowed my next words and waited for him to continue. "I think Oryn is telling you that you can have all those things. Just not in the same fashion regular people do. This isn't a typical relationship, so the answer isn't as straightforward. You told me before they are individual, but together are part of a whole. So, all that passion you're feeling... the stuff you can't express to Oryn because it could be damaging... give it to Cohen. I can tell just by how you're talking about him that you want to. In a backward, non-typical, weird-ass way, it's the same thing. You just need to learn where to direct your feelings. They all balance his system—or whatever the fuck you called it—so you need to balance the way you express yourself."

It was my turn to gape.

"Yeah, shithead, I do listen when you talk to me, so shut your mouth, you're attracting flies."

I hated how much sense he made, even rambling.

"And by the way," Evan continued, standing so he wasn't hunched in the way of the door. "You have totally fallen in love with this guy and probably don't even realize it."

With that, he slammed my door and walked around his car to the driver's side. He got in and waved before driving away.

Love?

I contemplated the possibility and knew instantly, Evan was right. Oryn meant more to me than I could describe. No one had ever captured me so completely. The last thing I wanted to do was disappoint him in any way. Which was probably why I couldn't shut my brain off and didn't know the answer when it came to Cohen.

Overanalyzing my predicament with Cohen had everything to do with my standard notion of how relationships worked. Ours was no standard relationship. It didn't follow the same rules and never would. I needed to stop trying to fit it into a category where it didn't belong.

Maybe Evan was right.

It was after six-thirty when I arrived at Oryn's. I'd run home—after topping off my tank—showered, changed, and grabbed us a couple of hot chocolates on my way to his place. He hadn't texted me back, but I thought nothing of it as I killed the engine and strolled to his front door.

Balancing the tray of drinks in one hand, I knocked. Many minutes passed without a response, so I tried again, only harder and louder.

When there was still no answer, a seed of concern sprang to life in my gut. The last time Oryn had disappeared without warning had resulted in a hospital visit, evaluation, and stitches down his arm.

I snapped my head to the window and noticed the curtain to the den was drawn open. Disregarding the unkempt garden, mucky from melted snow, I moved in front to look inside. The den was vacant and dark. I pressed my face closer and held a hand to block the light so I could see inside with more clarity. It was still. No one seemed to be about, yet there was a light coming from down the hall and another shining from the kitchen.

Leaving the cocoas on the front stoop, I walked around the long stretch of building, counting how many units from the end Oryn's was—something I'd never needed to note before—and went around back. His kitchen had a door leading out to a ridiculously small excuse for a backyard. He'd explained he never used it, even in the summer.

Double checking I'd passed the right number of units, I let myself through the back gate. The curtain over the kitchen window was always drawn shut, but there was definitely a light on. I went to the pane and tried to find a hole where the two pieces of fabric met so I could peek inside. As I searched, a distinctive shadow moved beyond. I froze. Someone was inside.

In a moment of panic, I stumbled back a few steps. My inquiry and concern hadn't felt creepy in the least until that second.

But… He was home.

Why hadn't he answered?

Not thinking, I approached the back door and knocked. Hard. There would be no mistaking my presence.

In less than a heartbeat, the door flew inward. But the man who'd jerked it open and who stared back at me with bloodshot eyes wasn't Oryn. His left cheek twitched, and his gaze flickered nervously about, scanning the world behind me before returning to my face. His hair was dishevelled and oily like he hadn't bothered washing it—or brushing it for that matter. I'd never seen it less than perfect. Dark shadows circled his eyes like he hadn't slept. They made his irises appear darker and menacing. His brows met in the middle and he radiated anger.

A flicking noise drew my attention, and I searched for its source. A lighter. He ran his thumb along the flint wheel, bringing it to flame with each pass. Over and over, releasing it after a beat and letting the flame die before repeating.

I took him all in and knew immediately who I faced.

"You're Cove."

Flick... Flick... Flick.

"You're intuitive."

Having had no time to compose myself, I fumbled for a response, a direction, or a next step. Oryn had shared next to nothing about the man in front of me, and what knowledge I had managed to piece together, was worrisome.

"It's nice to finally meet you. I'm Vaughn." I offered my hand to shake, but he only stared and didn't reach out.

He likely knew who I was, but the pleasantry of an introduction seemed as good a place as any to start.

"I brought hot chocolates. They are around front. I tried knocking, but you didn't—"

"This isn't a good day. You probably should go."

I stalled, mind racing. It was a therapy day, and if Cove was fronting, it was a pretty good indication of how things had gone.

Flick... Flick... Flick.

The steady action with the lighter continued at even intervals as a matching fire burned hotter in Cove's eyes.

My ears perked in the absence of noise. The flicking stopped abruptly, and Cove's face pinched. His lips were white under the pressure he applied, and his nose curled. I travelled my gaze down to his hand.

The flame burned high and he'd maneuvered a finger overtop of it. There it sat as the flames licked around it, encircling the digit. He didn't remove it and held it steady. Confused by what I was seeing, I didn't react immediately and continued to stare. Then, the smell of charred hair and flesh hit my nose. Only then did it sink in what he was doing, and I jumped forward, knocking the lighter from his hand.

It flew through the air before hitting the ground, slid across the linoleum floor, and only stopped when it hit the baseboard on the far side of the kitchen.

"What the fuck are you doing?" I asked, panic making my voice almost an entire octave higher.

My abrupt action had caused his arm to swing backward and he stumbled into the open door. He brought his finger up and examined it, sneering, but with no indication of pain on his face. The finger was well and truly burnt; the skin had blistered and broken, peeled back to reveal the vulnerable pink layer underneath. There was evidence of charring around the edges.

I shoved past him and ran to the fridge. Yanking open the freezer, I dug around in search of an ice pack, but when I couldn't find one, I settled for a bag of peas.

When I returned to him, I snagged his wrist and brought the afflicted digit up to examine it myself before surrounding it with the bag of frozen peas.

"What were you thinking?"

Our eyes met, but there was no longer any emotion on his face.

"It's not a big deal. I can take it. It doesn't even hurt."

He tried to pull free, but I clung tighter and glared. Guiding him to the kitchen table, I encouraged him to sit, not releasing my hold. He complied without argument, but his face was a blank slate and his gaze was lost in nothingness. He became unresponsive as I doctored the finger, and my concern grew.

"Why did you do that?"

He didn't respond.

I shuffled a chair in front of him and sat down. A moment later, he snapped out of whatever daze had trapped him and he studied my face.

"What?" he asked.

"I said, why did you do that?"

He pulled his finger free from its frozen coffin and held it up, squinting and turning it to see the damage.

"Physical pain is nothing. It's easier. And I told you, it didn't hurt."

I took his finger back and wrapped it again. Bullshit it didn't hurt. I'd had enough unintentional burns in my life to know the searing sensation took a long time to pass. Cove allowed for it, at first, but when he'd had enough, he dislodged from my grasp and tossed the peas on the table.

"It's fine."

It's not fine!

He got up and moved immediately to get the lighter he'd lost. My heart jumped into my throat, but he shoved it in his pocket and went for a glass on the counter instead. It was full of an amber liquid. Scanning the counters, my gaze fell to a bottle of Rye.

He upended the glass, his throat moving with multiple swallows as he downed over half. When he placed it back on the counter, he winced and blew out a breath, shaking his head and squinting his eyes. He was drinking it straight up based on his reaction.

He passed a glance in my direction before pulling open a drawer. The cutlery drawer. I was on my feet in a heartbeat, but stalled when he snagged a packet of cigarettes from within. Then he slammed the drawer and crossed to the back door.

"Where are you going?"

He held up the packet and shrugged. "Not allowed to smoke in the house."

Befuddled by his actions, I barely knew how to respond.

"Oh, umm…" Feeling the urgency to stay with him, I rose and motioned to the door. "Mind if I join you?"

He removed a cigarette from the package and stuck it between his lips. "Whatever."

Outside, he lit the cigarette, drew deeply, held it in his lungs, then let it out, watching as it wisped away into the air.

I didn't know what to say, so I stayed silent. It was as awkward as keeping company with a stranger. I didn't know Cove, and the twenty minutes I'd spent in his presence had unnerved me.

He smoked silently, and I watched him, analyzing his movements and trying to pick his brain from a distance without asking what was on his mind.

The cool March wind blew, and he shivered. Holding the cigarette in his mouth, he rubbed warmth back into his bare arms as he paced.

"Kinda cold for a t-shirt." I didn't know how else to kick off conversation.

He shrugged and blew more smoke into the air as he turned his face to the grey, cloudy sky. I couldn't help staring at his arms. There were no new cuts—thank God—but the thick scars knotted my belly. That man was responsible for them, and I'd just witnessed a small taste of the ease at which he managed such a task.

"Dr. Delmar tells us that facing it is part of the healing process sometimes. Bringing them to the surface."

His voice came on the breeze, barely loud enough to be heard even from my place less than five feet from where he stood by the fence.

The void of silence that followed those few words was uncomfortable. The pulsing of my own heartbeat waved in my ears. I was aware of every uneven breath I took into my lungs. What did I say?

Cove turned and watched me with a cold, dead glare. "I told him I'd rather die than reveal those things. Now wouldn't that be fucking blissful." His eyes glazed over as he spoke, "No more." His face twisted in vile disgust. "I deserve it. To die."

I couldn't swallow the ugly lump from my throat. It lodged there so thick and painfully, I thought I might choke. Was he waiting for a response? What had I read about self-destructive alters?

They carried the memories of the abuse, and they would protect those memories at all cost—even if it meant destroying the host body. They were built for that reason.

So, I said what I hoped he wanted to hear. I needed to gain his trust. It was up to the professionals to poke at him and encourage him to speak, not me.

"Thank you for protecting him," I whispered, barely able to spit out the words.

The flinch that followed my statement was subtle, and had I not been watching him carefully, I would have missed it. Cove continued to stare in the most unsettling way, as though he was tearing me open and searching for any evidence of dishonesty. Mistrust radiated off him in waves.

I was standing in front of the man who'd seen it all. The alter who'd been tortured and tormented for years. Witnessed things no child should ever know. My knees wanted to give out.

No wonder he was angry, violent, and untrusting. He'd only ever understood pain and suffering. And to a degree no one could possibly comprehend.

Robotically, his gaze shifted to the cigarette burning low in his hand. He turned it, examined it with a distant wonder.

When he moved it to his arm, and I saw his intent, I sputtered, "Please." His head lifted, and his hand stilled as he found my pleading eyes. "Don't... don't do that."

He shook his head with a pain so raw and unhidden all over his face. "I don't want to hurt anymore."

My feet moved before I could think, and I took the butt and tossed it away. Then, I folded Cove in my arms and squeezed him to my chest. He didn't return the embrace, but went limp in my arms. I stroked his hair from his face and kissed his forehead, the ache in my own body overwhelming me.

And I trembled. Not from cold, but from fear.

"You're safe," I whispered.

Maybe not from his haunted mind, but I'd be damned if I ever let harm come to him again. Not to Cove, not to Oryn, not to Cohen, Rain, or Reed. Not even to Theo who I had yet to meet.

His skin was cold to touch, and I traced a hand up and down a bare arm as I hugged him, soothing and doing what I could to give him warmth and comfort. Minutes ticked by, but he made no effort to move, and I couldn't find it in me to break the moment. So long as he accepted my support, I remained put.

The first movement he made was when he turned his head toward me and buried his face in my neck a moment before his arms came up to my waist and he pushed me back gently.

There was a world of vulnerability behind his eyes. His forehead creased, and he glanced about the backyard in confusion. From his pocket, he withdrew his phone and checked the time before shoving it back in again. Then he pressed a palm to one eye and winced.

I watched it unravel. Noted the disorientation and evident change in temperament.

When he lowered his hand and blinked a few times, I cupped his cheek and redirected his attention to my face.

"Oryn?"

He nodded and furrowed his brow. "I'm s-sorry." Then he winced again and brought his finger up; the one Cove had burnt. He didn't ask how it had happened. I suspected he already knew.

"Come on, let's put ice on that. I bet it's still pretty painful."

Another nod and he allowed me to take his other hand and guide him back inside. The peas didn't hold enough cold to be worth using, so I fished inside the freezer for something else.

"Grab a container of food. I'll just use it for dinner."

I did as he requested and returned to the table.

"Thank you," Oryn said, as I held the frozen container to his burn. He made a face I mistook for pain before he shifted to stand. "Give me a sec." He moved his tongue along his lips and grimaced. "He was smoking, wasn't he?"

I nodded, "And drinking."

"That accounts for the way everything is waving about. I just want to brush my teeth, then we can ice this." He held his finger up and sighed before disappearing down the hall.

For the following hour, we iced the burn and eventually treated it with burn cream Oryn had in a medical kit. It wasn't the first time Cove had injured him in such a way. I peeled back the paper from a band-aid and secured it around his finger.

Oryn was sullen for the rest of the evening. We ate lasagna without sharing words, and moved to the couch where he shuffled close and rested his head against my chest. We watched a random show we'd never seen on HBO, but it failed to hold my attention. My short visit with Cove ate at me. I wanted to talk about it, but respected that Oryn didn't seem in the mood.

The ambiguity of our relationship meant letting that brief visit pass. I acknowledged it for what it was and remained determined to learn more as I went about the complex nature of Oryn and his disorder.

He yawned, and peered up from my chest with tired eyes and a weak smile.

"I should go," I said, brushing hair off his forehead. "You look whipped."

At the front door, I zipped my spring jacket and put on my sneakers. Oryn reached out when I'd finished and took my hand. He stepped forward, closing our distance and brushed his lips to mine with hesitation. That was the Oryn I knew.

Tiny pecks along the seam of my mouth grew braver, and within a minute, he wrapped his arms around me and we shared a proper kiss. His tongue sought mine and they joined, interlacing in a way that made me feel alive. I could kiss him all evening and not get tired. Dreamed of his mouth most nights and longed for more.

With a little more suction, I drew his bottom lip into my teeth and nibbled. His hands tightened around me, but when I didn't allow that higher level of intensity to peter off, he pulled back, breaking our kiss and looking away.

We were still pressed together, and his racing heart pounded through my own chest.

"I'm sorry," he whispered.

I took his chin and turned it so I could see his blue-grey eyes. "Don't be. Don't ever be sorry for your limitations."

"But you want more from me. I know you do."

"I will never take from you what you can't give, Oryn. Do you understand me? Never!"

He nodded, but there was that hint of uncertainty that always lingered, and my heart ached. Would he ever believe me? *Could* he?

"Cohen wrote and told me what happened yesterday."

It was my turn to look away. I'd dismissed it. It was between Cohen and I, and I didn't want Oryn to fret.

"Vaughn?"

I met his eyes again and saw the sadness he failed to hide. "He can give you what I can't. He is part of me. The part of me who is able."

"I know," I admitted. "I'm considering it."

If I wasn't mistaken, a hint of relief passed through his eyes at my confession. "Thank you."

Chapter Sixteen

"Are you sure you want to split this? You can always run the slides and I'll do the talking."

Oryn shoved me and laughed. "I'll be fine. I told you."

He fit the rest of the printed papers into the right section of the three-ring binder we'd bought to hold all our presentation items. Clear sleeve protectors covered each print-out, and the slides and presentation notes had been organized into proper sections.

I'd been asking for a week if he was sure he wanted to speak, and instead of being annoyed, he was in good spirits. I knew how social situations affected Oryn, and I was only trying to save him unnecessary stress. However, it seemed I was the one doing all the stressing.

"Fine, don't say I didn't offer. How do you want to split this up?"

Oryn snapped the rings closed and turned to the first section which contained all the preliminary data we'd collected about my work; the average revenue, the target audience, the length of stay, and any complaints that we'd looked up that were filed on those travel apps people could download when searching for hotels.

Based on our findings, we'd created a low-budget advertising campaign that focused on the hotel's assets, what people wanted and looked for when seeking accommodations, and geared it to be appealing to our target audience. We ran multiple ads on popular webpages during peak usage hours. Tracking the amount of hits our promotion received, we adjusted the times and locations accordingly.

After a solid month, we re-ran all the numbers and proved a surprising increase in bookings and ratings. We considered it a win—especially since winter months after the holidays were over were generally the slower months.

Everything was ready for our oral presentation the following day.

"How about you open with all the preliminary data, and show our base starting point. Then explain a little about Oliver Star Hotels, since you work there. Then, I'll take over with what our marketing plan entailed and show the results. Does that work for you?"

I still found it hard to believe he thought himself able to get up in front of a classroom full of people and present. His stutter alone was sure to be a problem and I knew how it embarrassed him. But I didn't mention it again and agreed.

"Sounds perfect."

Oryn studied one of the diagrams for a few minutes before closing the binder and shifting it aside. "Are you ready for the final? Only a week away," he asked.

"I think so. I'll cram a few more hours of studying in before next Wednesday. I'll be good to go." He smiled at my confidence. I didn't need to ask if he was ready, he'd been quizzing me constantly. He knew our material inside and out. "Are you ready for Toronto?"

I'd convinced him to spend two nights away from home. In ten days, on his birthday weekend, we planned to drive to Toronto. We'd travel Friday afternoon, spend the night together in a hotel, do sightseeing Saturday, including dinner at the rotating restaurant atop the CN tower, spend another night, then visit the museum the following day. It would be busy, but I was beyond excited to have that time together.

"I think so," he answered honestly. The immediate fidgeting when he broke eye contact told me he was still uncertain.

Although I'd insisted we could have separate beds, or even rooms if he needed it, he'd firmed his lips and told me I was being silly.

We're dating. We can share a bed. I trust you.

His eyes deceived him. As much as he wanted his statement to be true, the truth was, inside him lived a sliver of doubt he couldn't shake.

The following day, I picked Oryn up early for class. We'd volunteered to present first so we could slip out early and have more time together in the evening.

Richard was there early as well and gave us space up front to unload our arms. Oryn—the brains of our operation—set up the power-point system on his laptop and made sure it displayed correctly on the screen upfront. He clicked through our slides once to double check they were presenting in order.

As students filtered in and found their seats, I noted the first signs of anxiety creeping over Oryn. He hugged his arms around his body and flashed glances about as people chatted. His breathing changed, and he rubbed at his temple.

I stepped forward, prepared to make a final offer to take the role of speaker when he shook his head abruptly.

"I'm okay. D-d-don't."

He was not okay. That was clear, but I stayed my ground and let him decide for himself what was best.

At seven o'clock, Richard called the class's attention and explained the layout for the evening's presentation schedule. Then he passed the floor to us.

Oryn remained sitting in a seat upfront with the laptop, ready to flip through slides when I began. Public speaking never bothered me. People and their opinions never bothered me. The classroom was filled with students who were considerably younger and who'd proven themselves to be less than mature, but even that didn't bother me.

Once I had everyone's attention, I began.

We'd worked hard on our project and it flowed like silk as I explained what business we'd selected, why, and how we went about choosing the right advertising campaign that worked for us.

In twenty minutes, I had finished my section and passed a nervous glance to Oryn to see if he was ready to take over.

He was watching with an even smile and stood the minute our eyes met. He adjusted his sweater on his shoulders and fixed the sleeves before moving up front. There was confidence in his stride as he took his place and faced the class. I sunk into his vacated chair and took over running the power-point.

With his chin high, his voice came out strong and clear. There was no stutter, and I found myself forgetting to do my job flipping slides because of how impressive he was to watch. He reminded me of a prosecutor addressing a jury—one who knew he'd hammered out a flawless case. He made eye contact and held his audience captive, even when all he talked about was boring, dry number data and the way it had shifted over the course of a month.

I studied him. Squinted and puzzled the man in front of me. There was no way in hell that was Oryn. Oryn couldn't do that.

I shot my gaze to Richard to see if he'd noticed. He seemed as enraptured as the rest of the students. Was I wrong?

"Vaughn?"

I flung my head back to Oryn when he called my name. It flowed like silk off his tongue in a way I'd never heard.

"Can we have the next slide please?"

I nodded but couldn't take my eyes from the confident smile that was focused on me. Who was he?

I changed slides, and he continued.

When we finished our presentation, Richard thanked us, congratulating us on a job well done. He gave the class a ten-minute break while the next group set up. Oryn and I collected our notes and handed in the finished project. As Oryn packed up his laptop, I hung close by and waited. The confident posture and smooth motions hadn't left him. When he slung his laptop and shoulder bag over his arm, he turned and raised a brow.

"Ready?"

Even that single word was delivered in a tone that contrasted Oryn.

"Yeah." I raised an inquiring brow, but he only smirked and walked out of the room ahead of me.

His walk was definitely not the same.

I kept pace as he moved down the hall, not engaging in conversation or making eye contact at all. Once we'd made it outside, I stopped and crossed my arms over my chest as he continued toward the stairs that descended to street level.

"Theo?" I called after him.

His paced slowed, and when he shifted, a humored smirk shone across his face, but he didn't respond.

I closed our distance and held his gaze, smiling despite myself.

"Was this his idea or yours?"

"Oryn's. But don't fret, it was only meant to be for the presentation. Your evening plans haven't changed."

"Can... are you able to control the switching?"

"Absolutely. A lot of the time, it happens unexpectedly or for reasons, but we can agree to switches when necessary. Oryn hasn't gone far. He's ready to come back."

Theo's gaze fell, and the smile slipped from his face. Contortion marred his features briefly and he closed his eyes a second before opening them and running a hand over his forehead.

When Oryn had slipped to Theo in front of a classroom of people, I hadn't even noticed. But the indicators were subtle and becoming more recognizable if I knew to look for them. Perhaps, switches didn't always have physical indicators.

When he lifted his gaze again, his face scrunched in pain and he pressed a knuckle into his temple.

Switching headache; Oryn had explained about them.

He blinked a few times and looked around before landing his gaze on me.

"Hey," I said, smiling. "Welcome back."

"Hi." His own smile was shy and one hundred percent Oryn's.

"Theo blew it out of the water with our presentation. He kinda kicks ass with that stuff, doesn't he?"

Oryn's gaze turned inward and his smile grew. "He does. I watched him. He was good."

"You remember?" I couldn't hide the shock from my voice. Oryn had always explained that switches caused amnesiac periods which left him with blank chunks of time he couldn't account for.

"Mostly. It was an agreed switch, so I was able to be more consciously aware. Theo and I are much better at reaching that level of co-consciousness. I've never had it with anyone else."

"That's really amazing. Isn't that what your goals are eventually?"

Oryn nodded and wiped at one eye again, his headache definitely ailing him. "In a perfect world, that's exactly what I would hope for."

***

After my surprise introduction to Theo during our presentation, his presences became more frequent. On the night before we planned to leave for Toronto, I'd shown up at Oryn's only to find Theo scrupulously packing his bag and ensuring he had everything he would require for the trip.

Theo was a man of few words, extremely straightforward, kind, and meticulously organized. He held no animosity toward me, and although I couldn't describe him as warm, he never shut me out either. I understood immediately how he fit into the entire system and was surprised I hadn't met him earlier.

On Friday morning at ten, I pulled into Oryn's driveway with two steaming cups of coffee in the cup holder and a bag of breakfast sandwiches for our ride. Before I was out of the car, his front door swung open and he stepped out carrying an overpacked duffle bag with his belongings.

"Holy crap, that bag wasn't that full last night. What the hell happened?"

"Theo. He decided on a few more items." Oryn rolled his eyes and laughed. "You'd think I was going away for a week, not two days."

I chuckled as I ran up beside him to grab the second bag he had slung over his shoulder. "So, how's the birthday boy? Do you feel older yet? You're cresting on thirty."

Oryn dropped his duffle bag into the trunk when I popped the lid and he chuckled. "My birthday is next week. Early celebration does not mean I turn twenty-nine sooner."

"I disagree. Birthday cake with candles marks the crossing of time. If you refuse to age until next week, then no cake at dinner."

Oryn stuck out his tongue good-naturedly and got in the car. It warmed me to see the ease at which he could tease me back nowadays. In the beginning, any amount of torment, even in fun, resulted in uncontrolled stuttering.

"Do your alters celebrate birthdays the same as you?" I asked once we were on the highway.

"Not really. Reed, Cove, and Theo are the only ones who have birthdays and grow older. But they aren't the same day as me. Reed's birthday is in August, he'll be twenty-four, and Cove's was on February eighth. He just turned twenty-six. Theo and I have basically grown up together, even though he's older. I have broken memories of him going back to when I was four or five I think. Nothing solid. His birthday is in May. He'll be thirty-one. The others are frozen in time I guess you'd say. They don't age."

Having acquired a comfort level with Oryn's alters and learning where I belonged among them, I groaned and threw my head back against the headrest. "No, don't tell me Cohen will be nineteen forever."

Oryn snorted as he tried to cover a laugh. "Yes. Sorry."

"You mock my pain."

"You exaggerate your pain. I think you two are just fine."

I rubbed his leg and offered him a smile. "Yeah, yeah, don't tell him, but I think he's grown on me."

Oryn's smile turned smug and he dashed his eyes to his lap where he fiddled with his hands. I could only imagine what he was thinking. There were days I felt like an outsider when up against his entire system.

We arrived in Toronto in the early afternoon and went straight to the hotel to check in. Our room was decent, but small. I'd been hoping for a couch to go along with the queen-sized bed, in case Oryn changed his mind about sharing. No such luck.

We set our bags down and unpacked a few personal belongings into the bathroom. Even I had to admit my nervousness. Even though Oryn and I had been dating three and a half months, it was a first step for us. Spending the night with a new boyfriend always encouraged those pit-of-my-stomach butterflies to become erratic.

When I'd organized my shower supplies, I returned to the room and found Oryn sitting on the bed, a stiffness present in his posture. His nervousness was nowhere near the same as my own.

"Everything okay?"

He nodded a little too quickly, giving himself away. "Wh-what did you want t-t-to do now?"

My stomach sank with his stutter presenting. I sighed as I considered. Our plans for the following two days required Oryn to be quite social, so a restful, quiet evening sounded better.

"How about we drive around and find some amazing food we can't get back home, order takeout, and just watch a few movies. We have a busy few days planned, and I'm kinda whipped after all that driving."

His face lit up with my suggestion. "Sure. That will be n-nice."

By the time we'd driven around so many blocks we were dizzy, we settled on a small Vietnamese restaurant whose sign we couldn't read and whose staff barely spoke English. We both shrugged, deciding it would probably mean it was more authentic than any place we had back home.

With two bags full of random menu items I couldn't pronounce, but which Oryn assured me I'd enjoy, we headed back to the hotel. He set to work 'preparing' our soup thing while I sorted through our options for movies.

Once I'd selected *X-Men First Class* and settled in, propped up against the headboard, Oryn carried our bowls over one at a time.

"I can't believe we are eating soup in bed. This is going to be a disaster."

Oryn chuckled as he climbed in beside me and grabbed his from the side table where he'd sat it.

"Just eat carefully."

I moved the spoon he'd given me through the broth and shifted the items inside, examining each of them with a frown. There were a few different kinds of meats—or I assumed they were meats—bean sprouts, some green leafy thing I'd seen Oryn add a moment ago, noodles, and unidentifiable white things with tiny bumps that concerned me.

"What is this called again?"

"Pho," he said, bringing a chunk of what could have been beef to his mouth and eating it.

I screwed up my nose and looked in his bowl. It was the same as mine.

"Just try it. It's good."

I didn't consider myself to be picky, but I generally stuck to things I could pronounce...and identify.

I stirred the contents around and chose a safe looking mini meatball-ish looking item with broth and slurped it up. Oryn examined me as I ate.

"It's got good flavor," I said once I swallowed.

"I wouldn't steer you wrong."

Feeling braver, I filled my spoon with one of the white things and held it up to examine it. The edges were a little jagged and it definitely had an odd-looking texture.

"What's this?"

Oryn smirked. "Tripe."

I furrowed my brow and dashed a glance beside me. "What is tripe?"

"Just try it."

I stared at it hesitantly and Oryn reached over and put his hand over mine, steering the spoon into my mouth. "Open."

I laughed, but complied. He shoved it in and I prodded at the strange item with my tongue before chewing slowly. The texture was nothing like what I expected and instead of it being chewy like meat it almost broke apart in a way cartilage did. After an excessive amount of chewing, I eventually forced a swallow and looked at Oryn expectantly.

He turned back to his food with the biggest grin and kept eating.

"What is tripe?"

"Did you like it?"

"It has a bizarre texture."

"Just eat dinner and don't worry about it."

Oryn focused on the movie as he continued to eat his Pho. I stirred my broth around more, moving the contents and noticing just how many of those strange white things there were floating among the other items. I set my bowl on the side table and pulled out my phone.

"What are you doing?"

"Looking it up."

"You don't want to do that. Just eat and enjoy."

I glared at Oryn for a moment while he fought off a smile, then dropped my head to my phone and typed *what is tripe* into the Google search bar. When the results came up, I read...

The edible lining from the stomachs of various farm animals. Most tripe is from cattle.

My hand flew to my mouth at the same instant I heaved. I was off the bed and bolted to the bathroom just as bile climbed my throat, and I heaved again.

As I hugged the toilet and barfed the two mouthfuls of Pho I'd eaten, Oryn's laughter rang through the air. Because that was the first I'd eaten since breakfast, I had nothing else to come up and continued to dry-heave for the next few minutes.

Once my stomach settled, I wiped my mouth, brushed my teeth, and returned to the room. Oryn had set his own bowl down and had a pillow hugged to his chest, doing everything he could to calm his laughter.

"You are an evil, evil man."

He chuckled more and buried his face. It was hard to be even a little upset seeing the humor radiate off of him. When he calmed enough to speak, he pointed to the bags he'd left on the window ledge.

"There is Pad Thai, too. I promise all normal ingredients."

"You cannot be trusted."

I collected the new container of food while piercing him with an evil glare. It only induced more laughter.

Once we'd finished eating, we changed into pajamas. I'd brought a pair of plaid, cotton bottoms and a t-shirt. Ordinarily, I slept in boxer briefs, but I knew I needed to maintain a level of comfort with Oryn, and underwear alone wouldn't have been a wise decision.

Oryn pulled back the comforter and shuffled about, avoiding getting in. I sensed his discomfort and decided to act cool and calm and let him see it wasn't a big deal. I crawled in and sat against the headboard. Flicking through channels, I motioned to the TV.

"What movie now? I picked the last one. You get over here and decide."

It was enough to help him break the barrier of uncertainty and he shuffled into bed beside me. Confiscating the remote, he flipped through the options. As he busied himself, I drew the covers to our waist, paying no attention to his squirming.

Once a new movie was playing, he'd calmed.

The sun had set, and with it came the reality that Oryn and I were spending the night together for the first time. Not just one night, but an entire weekend. Even when I knew our limitations, the entire notion felt intimate.

Oryn caught me watching him and smiled shyly, dropping his gaze to his lap. Within a minute, he shuffled closer on the bed and rested his head on my shoulder. I took it for permission, and draped my arm around him.

We often snuggled close during movies. We'd just never been in a bed, with blankets covering us before. I kissed the top of his head, inhaling the fragranced scent of his citrus shampoo before I returned my focus to the TV.

A short time later, his hand found mine under the blankets. He didn't grab or hold on, but simply traced our fingers together, testing the hold. It was his way of asking for more, and I would never deny him. I wrapped my hand in his and stroked my thumb across his skin.

The movie became background noise as Oryn's gentle advances continued. One tiny step at a time was all he could ever manage, but for him, they were huge steps.

He turned his head on my chest, nuzzling closer to my neck and tilting his face to mine. Joining our foreheads, I let him absorb that closer connection a moment. When he moved his face closer, I took the initiative to close the remaining gap and pressed our mouths together. But, that was when I relinquished control again.

I allowed Oryn to command the kiss. His lips glided with mine, pecking and licking small tastes along the seam. Tiny moments of suction when he'd draw me into his mouth. I monitored his every move, as I'd learned to do. When he opened and allowed my tongue to find his, a warm tingle sprung up over my whole body. Butterflies came to life in my belly like I was sixteen again. Oryn did that to me, and the slow progression of our relationship had only intensified those feelings even more.

His uncertainty faded as he leaned in and kissed me deeper, nibbling and tasting with more bravery as the minutes ticked by. I brought a hand to rest on his nape and encouraged a little more, holding him against me and kissing with more vigor.

He turned on the bed, bringing himself to his knees beside me. He framed my face with his hands, peering deep into my eyes. His nerves shone through, but his determination was fiercer. Our mouths were apart for only a moment before they collided again. Surprising me, Oryn shuffled closer, trying to wrap his arms around me, but with his position at my side, it was awkward.

I broke our kiss, working to control my ragged breathing. I was becoming worked up and quickly.

"Straddle me," I suggested, nudging his side.

His gaze fell a moment and he licked his kiss-swollen lips before nodding. His trembling was evident, but he moved a leg to the other side of my lap and sat. We'd never been that close. I took a minute to run my hands up his spine and down again, before applying a small amount of pressure to his lower back.

He took my meaning and leaned closer. His knees squeezed around my torso, and his chest aligned flush with mine. I rejoined our mouths, my entire body buzzing with that new step forward. Oryn's bravery astounded me.

Our kisses heated with the passing minutes. No hesitation remained. They were hungry and daring, bringing my blood to near boiling. I may not have had Evan's inflated sex drive, but I was still a man. A man who'd gone an exceptionally long time without sex. One who had a gorgeous man straddling his waist, whose tongue was lodged down his throat and who had emitted more than one soft moan of pleasure at what we were sharing.

It was inevitable.

The moment I felt my dick begin to swell, I tore from Oryn's mouth and tried to hold him back. I was out of breath and lightheaded.

"Oryn," I started, trying to lift him from my lap.

"I'm o-okay," he stuttered.

Using his weight, he pressed me back against the headboard and joined our mouths as he repositioned himself on my lap.

Then, he froze.

There was no denying what he felt and why he was motionless. I reached up to take his face in my hands, ready to calm him down, but I didn't get that far. He flew away from my mouth just as his hand came up and clasped my chin in a tight grip. His eyes were ablaze, lips curled back off his teeth in anger and disgust.

I held my hands up in surrender. "Reed," I said through pinched lips, "I can explain."

Chapter Seventeen

He was off the bed like a shot, scrambling from me just as fast as I scrambled from him—only I had the headboard at my back, and my retreat was foiled.

"Just calm down," I said, silently urging my traitor dick to hibernate immediately.

Reed couldn't seem to formulate words and paced, ripping a hand through his hair as he forced even breaths. Finally, he stopped and turned to face me, lips pinched together as he sneered and breathed audibly through his nose.

"This has to stop."

"I couldn't agree more."

I swung off the bed and stood, subtly adjusting myself as Reed shook his head.

"Why do you push limits? Why can't you just be happy—"

"I didn't push anything," I snapped. "I've never pushed anything. All this," I swung a hand at the bed, "was Oryn's initiation. I'm sorry my body responded the way it did, but fuck man, I'm human."

"You… You don't understand."

"No, maybe you don't understand. The way I see it, Oryn is exploring something he wants when he feels comfortable, and every goddamn time that happens, you jump in and stop it. Why not let him try?"

Reed huffed a dry laugh and shook his head incredulously. "That's how you see it, huh? You think I want to be tossed into the middle of your fucking make-out session with a hard dick wedged against my ass?"

"Right, tossed, sure."

Reed's face darkened with anger. "Yes! Tossed." He stormed toward me and I retreated in alarm, backing against the wall. He was in my face, somehow seeming a million times larger and more intimidating than Oryn's frame allowed. "I didn't choose this moment to front, asshole. Oryn fled because whatever was happening between you was more than he could process. The terror level was too high, and he retreated. When that happens, I get shoved forward, because he's in danger and it's my fucking job. So, before you go thinking that he is okay with it and I'm just being some jerk, try again."

When I didn't respond, he backed down, allowing me to breathe. From the TV stand, he scooped up a room card and held it up to show me. "I'm taking a walk. I need air."

Before he could leave, I jumped forward. "Reed, wait!"

"What?" he said without turning.

"You have to know I *have never* and *will never* push myself on him. Oryn is the one who's been determined to try more recently. Do you know that? Have you talked to him?"

"Of course, I have. But until he truly trusts you, we *will* keep meeting like this."

"You mean until *you* truly trust me."

He turned and his face had lost the edge of anger he'd carried only a moment before. "No. Until *he* trusts you. My trusting you is fully dependant on Oryn. We take all our cues from him."

"Oh."

He put his hand on the door, ready to depart when I stopped him again, "Reed?"

"What?" he said through gritted teeth.

"You might want to put clothes on. You're in pajamas."

His chin dropped to his chest as he peered down, and he growled under his breath. In less than two minutes, he found jeans and a shirt and was out the door.

I waited for two hours for Reed to return, or Oryn, or anyone for that matter. Worry consumed me as I imagined Reed wandering blocks from our hotel and Oryn coming back with no clue where he was.

I never intentionally wanted to bring Oryn fear. But I had, and it made me sick. I never wanted to hurt him. Was I supposed to put a stop to everything, even when he was the one initiating and pressing us forward?

I didn't have the answers. I never seemed to have the answers.

Eventually, after waiting another hour in vain, I crawled into bed and tried to sleep.

Some time in the middle of the night, the bed dipped beside me, and I stirred from semi-sleep to alertness.

"S-sorry. I didn't mean to wake you."

A stutter. Definitely Oryn.

"It's okay." My voice was rough from disuse, and I shuffled to face him, leaving a generous gap. "Are you okay?"

He rested his head on the pillow and pulled the blankets to his chin. "Yeah. Just chilled. Need to warm up."

More than anything, I wanted to draw him into my arms and hold him. But after what had happened, I refrained. It was silent for a long time, and a veil of sleep surrounded me yet again, pulling me down and making my eyelids heavy. Just as consciousness slipped away, Oryn's soft voice drifted to my ears.

"Vaughn?"

I startled awake and rubbed my eyes, yawning.

"Yeah?"

"I'm sorry about earlier."

"Do you know what happened?"

"Reed told me. We talked. I… I'm really sorry."

The bile that had been churning my stomach returned. I found his hand under the covers and gave it a gentle squeeze. "Never be sorry for stuff like that. It's not your fault."

"But—"

"But nothing. We're okay."

"Okay."

It was quiet for a long time. Only Oryn's light breathing sounded through the room. I knew he wasn't asleep, so I kept holding his hand and brought it to my mouth to kiss his fingers.

"Goodnight, Oryn."

"Goodnight."

The sun woke me up the following morning when it shone through the window and across the queen-sized bed into my face. Instinctively, I buried my head and groaned. It took an added few minutes for me to remember I wasn't at home, and another two or three after that to realize the bed beside me was vacant.

I threw back the covers and glanced around, concerned Oryn had fled. He was still there. He'd perched himself on the windowsill and was staring down toward street level deep in thought. A frown creased his forehead and his bottom lip was jutted out a fraction in a pout.

I rustled around to draw his attention, and when he turned, he wiped whatever thoughts had disturbed him away.

"Good morning." His smile was strained, and his gaze fell to his lap when he knew he'd failed.

"Did you sleep at all?" I asked, stretching long on the bed and yawning.

"Yeah. Some."

More fidgeting.

"Are you ready for a fabulous birthday adventure today?"

I grinned with pride when my comment brought a real smile to his face.

"I can't wait."

Our entire morning was spent exploring over half a dozen outlet malls in the area. With spring on the horizon, we both used the opportunity to replenish some of our wardrobe.

Oryn was distant and quiet for the most part, and I knew something was bothering him. By lunch, we stopped at a café on the second floor of one of the malls and ordered sandwiches and coffees. We chose a seat near the balcony's edge which overlooked the lower section of the mall. No one was around us, so once we'd finished eating and Oryn zoned out again for the hundredth time that day, I reached for his hand and drew his attention.

"Hey, I feel like I've lost you today. We're supposed to be having fun and you look miserable."

Oryn let out a breath and drew his bottom lip between teeth.

"I'm sorry." It was his automatic response and I cringed hearing it.

"Stop being sorry and just talk to me. What's got your mind so tormented?"

"Umm..." He withdrew his hand from my hold and squirmed in his seat. "I... I'm not a very good b-boyfriend. I can only imagine how frus-fr-frustrated you must be."

"Why would you say that?"

He shrugged and refused to meet my eyes. I held my hand out, inviting him to take it again. He hesitated, but eventually slinked his closer and re-linked us.

He hadn't answered, so I pressed, figuring I knew the cause for his concern. "Is this because of last night?"

He nodded rapidly and peeked a quick glance to my face. "Boyfriends should be able to... to... it... doing that... w-we should be able to have that."

He'd never once said the word, and I was beginning to wonder if he was able.

"You mean have sex?"

His eyes widened, and he dashed a look around the food court. "Yes," he croaked, his cheeks immediately flaming.

"Look at me." He struggled, but found my face again. "Why are you trying so hard to go there? Is it because you think it's what I want? Or because you think it's what is supposed to happen? Do you think I'll leave you eventually if we don't?"

He didn't respond, but his worried expression deepened and told me one of those things were correct—if not all.

"Oryn, I knew going into this relationship that sex was probably off the table. You ask a million other men and they'd never be okay with that, but I'm different. We've never been blunt enough to have a discussion about sex, because I know it's a hard topic for you. But you should know, I don't have a raging sex-drive. It's been a relationship killer for me in the past. So, I really don't want you to worry about it. If needs arise, us men have been given other ways to handle them, believe me."

I chuckled and squeezed his hand, aiming for that statement to be lighthearted. Oryn's brow drew down with a frown.

"But that's just it. You d-do have urges. I know you do. Can… can I ask you something honestly?"

"Always."

"Do you wish you could have that with me?"

My heart ached as I looked into his pleading eyes. I couldn't lie to him.

"Honestly? Making love to you would be the most beautiful thing in the world. Do I wish I could have that with you? Yes. Am I okay without it and being intimate in other ways? Also, yes."

As he mulled that information around, I thought of the previous evening and how he'd tried so hard to take us further.

Before he could respond to my confession, I continued, "I'm going to ask you the same question. Do you wish you could have more with me?"

"Yes." There was no hesitation, and he rose his head and looked me square in the eyes with more confidence than I'd ever seen him have. "More than anything. I don't think never is good enough for me. I'm so tired of being afraid."

I didn't have to know details to understand how sex had become such a deeply ingrained terror that it triggered switches without warning. I wished more than anything, I could alleviate those fears. So much had been taken from him as a child, all I wished was for him to experience a better life as an adult.

I released his hand and cupped his cheek instead. He leaned into the touch and a real smile warmed his face.

"Don't push yourself," I said, stroking his cheek.

Surprising me, he leaned across the table and planted a soft kiss on my mouth. It lasted only a moment, but when he pulled away, a new light shone in his eyes.

"What's next today?" he asked.

With time to kill before our dinner, we wandered around a few more shopping centers before returning to our room in the late afternoon. The restaurant was somewhat fancier and we both changed into nice dress shirts and slacks so we were suitable for dinner. It was the first time I'd seen Oryn so dressed up. His ash-grey shirt brought out the stormy quality in his eyes. As he worked on adjusting his tie, all I could do was enjoy the sight. He was breathtaking.

"Can you help me with this?" he asked, looking up from yet another failed knot.

I moved to him and skillfully fixed his tie without looking. I couldn't break my gaze from his face. He smiled shyly.

"You're good at that."

"I wear a tie everyday to work. I have to be."

When I finished and straightened it, I took his face in my hands.

"Can I kiss you?"

"Always."

When I joined our mouths, Oryn leaned against me and his arms went around my waist like it was the most natural thing. They might have only been minor bouts of progress, but for him, they were huge. His hesitation was lessening everyday. Maybe we could never cross certain roads, but I believed we could build a loving bond together in many other ways.

The CN tower was only a few blocks from our hotel room, so we chose to walk. The massive building stood over five hundred meters high, and at one point in time, had been the tallest freestanding structure in the world.

The ride up the elevator was nothing short of amazing. One entire wall was a glass window, and as we shot up in the air, the emerging skyline was incredible. Oryn clung to my shirt, but swore he wasn't nervous.

The view from within the restaurant was breathtaking. I had been a little concerned over it being a *rotating* restaurant. I didn't do spinning and wasn't sure if it would make me nauseous, but it didn't. The room was dimly lit with candles on every table. It was intimate and romantic—more so than any other place I'd eaten before. Our table was nestled by a window, a private distance from others, and the view was incredible. The city spanned for miles, and since the sun had already set, lights sparkled below. I knew at one point we'd eventually face over the lake, and I couldn't wait to see it from our vantage point.

"This is unreal," Oryn said as he leaned against the window, peering down. "We're so high up."

"Do you approve? Good restaurant for a birthday feast?"

Oryn turned to me with a smile. It was pure and joyful. One that sang through every part of his body and leaked into mine. He'd shed his funk from earlier and had been enjoying the rest of the day in a much more carefree manner.

"Best birthday we've ever had." He glanced back out the window, grinning.

We. It still struck my ear funny sometimes hearing him refer to his system as a whole. I wondered if he had any good memories of past birthdays, or if those were all vaulted away with the rest of his childhood. Either way, I hoped to give him one he'd cherish.

"Are you excited about the museum tomorrow," I asked as our appetizer salads arrived.

"I am. I was looking it up this morning while you slept. Did you know they have a Viking exhibition going on right now? How incredible will that be?"

I chuckled as I speared my salad. "I did know. I looked it up when I got our tickets. I thought you'd like that."

"I've never been to this museum. Did you know it's one of the largest in North America?"

"How much time did you spend on their site this morning?"

He swallowed a mouth full of his own salad and shrugged with a grin. "A while. It's going to be great."

I'd known it would be a hit, considering Oryn's love for all things historical.

The meal was out-of-this-world amazing. Oryn and I indulged in a couple of glasses of wine, and because it was his birthday, I convinced him to have dessert as well.

By the time we wandered the busy streets back to our hotel, we were stuffed. Oryn was more relaxed than ever and held my hand the entire way while leaning against my shoulder. Not wanting to lose the precious closeness, I suggested a few extra blocks to walk off our food.

"Thank you for dinner." He smiled as he watched the night sky, the city lights catching a gleam in his eyes.

"Thank you for sharing your birthday with me."

"It's not until next week," he reminded me with a chuckle.

"Anything to hold onto your youth. God to be twenty-nine again. Wait until you're in your thirties."

"Don't rush me."

Around the following corner, Oryn leaned in and pecked my cheek. He didn't move his face away, so we shared a few light kisses as we walked. We laughed, kissed, and tried to maneuver the sidewalk without stumbling as we returned to our hotel. The atmosphere was almost surreal. I only hoped one day, Oryn's daily life could be as happy as that moment right there. Not watching where we were going, we tripped over more than one curb and had to catch ourselves before crashing to the ground. It couldn't have been more perfect.

In our room, I pulled my tie loose and unbuttoned a few buttons on my shirt as Oryn dug through his bag.

"Do you mind if I grab a shower?" he asked.

"Go for it. I'm gonna put on pajamas and find something to watch. Any requests?"

When he didn't respond, I glanced up from my buttons. He watched me with a smile that shone out his eyes.

"Nah," he said.

Our eyes stayed connected and the moment thickened with unspoken words. I wasn't sure what message he was trying to convey, but I couldn't look away. Leaving his search for clothes, he crossed the room and continued to unknot my tie, removing it and tossing it on the bed. Then he touched my cheek.

"Thank you for tonight. You're the kindest person I've ever known."

His fingers trailed along my jaw as his gaze followed. He touched my lips and lingered there a moment before leaning in and kissing me. His fingers fell to my chest and sat motionless at the opening of my shirt, their tips ghosting my skin and warming me from the inside out. Such a small action, but it affected me so profoundly.

Our tongues joined as he pressed our mouths more firmly together. I would never tire of those precious moments we shared. When the kiss ended, our gazes remained locked. There were no words to describe how I felt seeing his blue-gray irises shimmering with such hope.

Or maybe there were.

I brought my hand up and copied his move from before, gliding fingers along his jaw and ending at his lips. He kissed their tips and smiled.

"Oryn, you are the most amazing person I've ever known. There is no one in the world I'd rather be with. I've completely fallen in love with you."

I'd known for a while but was never sure how he'd react to such a declaration. My heart soared when his smile remained, and a shimmer came to his eyes. His lips parted, but before he could speak, I pressed a finger to them.

"You don't need to say it back. I only wanted you to know how I felt. You mean everything to me. I understand you have many obstacles in your way when it comes to forming relationships, and I'm glad you've allowed me the chance to be part of your life."

Oryn removed my finger and stared in awe. When he managed to find words, he simply said, "No one has ever loved me before."

"That's their loss. They don't know what an amazing man they're missing out on."

He blinked heavily, warding off the tears I'd caused with my confession. I kissed him softly and indicated to his bag.

"Go shower. I want to snuggle you so hard."

He nodded and backed up a step, our gazes lingering. Eventually, he found some clothes and disappeared into the washroom. While he showered, I changed into my plaid pajama bottoms and a t-shirt and drew the covers back on the bed before getting in.

The shower turned off as I flipped through the movie options. When I saw *Ghost*, I paused and chuckled to myself, remembering the pottery stand and our conversation months before at the art festival.

When I heard the bathroom door open, I called out, "Hey, *Ghost* is playing. Remember at the—"

My words caught in my throat when he came into view. He hadn't bothered with pajamas at all. The only thing he'd put on was a tight pair of black underwear. Time jarred to a halt as I drank him in. In four months, I'd never seen Oryn with even his shirt off, let alone one piece of clothing away from being nude.

The lines of muscles along his abdomen were a lot more pronounced than I'd expected. His chest was bare except for a small patch of light blond hair that traveled from his navel and disappeared below the band of his underwear.

He moved into the room and tossed his dirty clothes on top of his bag before facing me.

My mouth dried. I couldn't take my eyes off him. When I found his face, and noticed the half-smirk glowing down at me on the bed, I wasn't fooled. Oryn would never be so open and confident around me.

My breath came short, and I swallowed as I worked to force words. "Cohen?"

It came out like a question, but I knew him well enough I didn't need to ask.

"Hey, Vaughn."

I dashed a glance toward the bathroom and back, trying to sort out why Oryn had suddenly gone. There'd been no stressors that I was aware of.

Cohen crawled across the bed and knelt in front of me. He smiled like he knew my thoughts before I spoke them.

"Why are you here?" I asked.

He shrugged and rested a hand on my knee. "Oryn asked me to switch."

A small seed of worry came to life in my gut, knowing moments before his shower, I'd shared something pretty profound. "Did I upset him?"

"Not at all."

He reached for my hand and guided it to his chest. When he pressed my palm to his bare skin, my heart jumped, and I sucked in a shuddered breath. He was shower-warm and soft.

In my head, I knew what Oryn was doing. He'd been so determined, and so utterly frustrated with himself recently because he couldn't move forward like he wanted.

Cohen released my hand, and without thought, I glided it over every curve and muscle I'd admired from afar.

"Why?" I asked. "Why doesn't he believe me?"

Cohen moved onto my lap and I brought my second hand to explore his skin as well.

"He believes you," Cohen said against my ear. "But there are two sides at play here, Vaughn. Two people make a couple. Two sets of feelings should be considered. Oryn wants to have this with you, and, babe, right now, this is the only way he can do it."

He sucked my lobe into his hot mouth and I gasped, digging my fingers into his sides. It shot crimson fire through my entire body, and I closed my eyes, leaning my head back as he continued. When he unlatched, he sat up, took my face, and crushed our lips together in a breath-stealing kiss.

Our tongues found each other, and I couldn't deny the feelings it elicited. I buzzed and hungered for more. My mind was tearing itself apart. Could I happily go without sex and have a satisfying relationship with Oryn? Absolutely. Did I still yearn to share that bond with him, to make love and be closer to him than anyone else? Also, yes. Did his feelings matter? Without a doubt. Could Cohen, Oryn's alter who was more suited to such a role, help us bridge that gap?

But what of Cohen?

I broke us apart and stared into his eyes. They shone with the same youth and vibrancy I always saw when he fronted. In the beginning, his presence had been such a dilemma. As he sat on my lap and waited for my decision, I knew we'd moved far past those initial barriers.

"He wants this?" I asked, needing reassured again. "And don't lie to me, Cohen."

"He wants this."

"And you?"

"Babe, I've wanted this a long time."

I knew that. I touched his face, trailed fingers over his lips and stared into his gorgeous eyes. All those equally strong feelings I felt in Cohen's presence came alive and consumed my body. A separate person on his own. One I cared for very deeply, but also an extension of the man I couldn't be with on an intimate level.

"This switch was consensual?"

"Yes."

Remembering Oryn talking of consensual switches with Theo, I asked, "Is he aware of what's going on. Can he… is he…" I couldn't remember the word he'd used.

"Co-conscious? No. You'll understand he can't be for the same reason it can't be him here right now. Not for this. He'll know only what I tell him. Or what you tell him."

I nodded. Relieved.

I took in the man sitting on my lap, coursed my hands up his sides and around to his chest. Examined his every curve and feature. Each side of Oryn was different, but every piece fit together to form a whole. They were all a part of the man I loved. And I'd do anything for that man.

If I was doing it, if I was crossing that line, it was important Cohen understood that it was as much for him as it was for Oryn. Because his spot in the equation was just as significant, and his feelings counted too.

"Okay," I whispered. "But, Cohen, your feelings are just as crucial. In no way do I want you thinking that you don't count." I kissed his mouth and spoke in a hushed tone, "because you count."

"I know, babe. We've just been waiting for you to catch up."

Chapter Eighteen

The minute I agreed to proceed, my anxiety went through the roof, knowing I was about to cross that line, and in a round about way, bring our relationship that much closer. As many times as Cohen had attempted to jump the gun with sex, he remained reserved in that moment and allowed me to take the lead.

I wanted to explore every piece and part of him. Memorize his body and absorb every aspect of who he was. It was the first time I'd been allowed beneath clothing, and his near naked form had already encouraged my blood flow to increase.

I started with hands, smoothing them over every inch of exposed skin. The hard cords of his muscles, coupled with the softness of flesh, was the perfect balance. Cohen's lips parted, and his eyes closed as I inspected every inch of him. My thumb rolled over the nub of a nipple, and it hardened at my touch, making him draw in a faint gasp. I noted all of it; the way he breathed, the way he moved, and the sounds he made.

Travelling to his back, I inched my hands down his spine and pulled him closer. Nuzzling my nose to his chest, I inhaled. Under the fresh scent of woodsy citrus was the familiar essence shared among them all, one that belonged to Oryn's body, and one I couldn't ever get enough of.

I kissed his chest, moving slowly around, teasing a taste of his skin as I climbed toward my eventual goal—his mouth. When I paused by a nipple, Cohen anticipated my move and sucked in a breath. He reached out and clung to me as I feathered a sweeping tongue over the stiffened nub.

"Oh God," he moaned. His fingers dug into my arms, and he squirmed as I applied a minute amount of suction.

When I released him, he shuddered with desire and opened his eyes. Before we could join mouths, he tugged at the hem of my shirt and lifted it over my head. Once he'd tossed it aside, he examined me in much the same way I'd been doing to him.

It was difficult to find words. Nothing quite fit the grandeur of the moment.

I rested back against the headboard as he journeyed his hands over my body in turn. My muscles were less defined, and my chest wasn't completely bare, but he seemed to like what he saw based on the quirk of his lip. I'd never been an avid gym-goer, but my genes worked to my advantage.

He leaned in and joined our mouths, licking and nipping at my lips. It didn't take long for it to escalate into something far more heated and for my body to respond. I didn't panic like the previous night, and instead, I slid my hands over his ass and positioned him where he'd feel what he was doing.

Perhaps I didn't crave sex as much as the average man, but it didn't mean I didn't enjoy it. Cohen lapping at my lips, sucking at my tongue, and exploring every contour of my mouth had me set to burst.

In no time, there was a constant jab into my abdomen as he rocked his ass against my dick while simultaneously pegging me with his own erection. He was as hard as me, and I couldn't take it any more. I broke free from his mouth, and he panted as he struggled to catch his breath. I squirmed up, while securing him in my arms, and flipped him to his back. He chuckled and immediately took hold of my pajama bottoms and yanked them down along with my underwear. Aiding the process, I kicked them off and reclaimed his mouth.

The kisses were never the same. If I paid attention, both Oryn and Cohen had different styles. Equally tantalizing, and both with the ability to make me weak in the knees. The same in so many ways, yet completely different. Somehow, they both owned a section of my heart. As much as I yearned and wished to have more with Oryn, in that moment, it was all Cohen. Every blissful feeling growing inside, every pulsing need moving through my body. All him.

His hands were all over me. Starting with a smooth glide over my ass cheeks, they eventually ended around front where he cupped and massaged my balls. With deft hands, I worked his underwear free, and they joined mine somewhere at the bottom of the bed.

Mutually tearing from our kiss again, we both drank in each other's bodies, touching and seeing what we'd not seen before. He was beautiful. All of him.

I couldn't get enough and kissed down his chest, tracing over his skin as I went. As I kissed around his navel, he moaned and squirmed.

"You are so incredible. Look at you," I said between more nibbling tastes.

His sounds quieted, and I peeked up to see a momentary frown on his face. He wiped it away the second I looked, but I stopped my attacks and crawled up his body again.

"What was that?"

He took my face and brought us together for a deep kiss before responding, "Nothing." He joined us again and kissed longer.

"Cohen," I said when I came up for air. "How do you want this? I can go either way, but—"

"Will you top me?"

"But," I continued. "I'm not in the habit of carrying condoms around."

He turned thoughtful for a second before nodding toward our bags. "Let me up. If Theo packed, then we might have some."

I doubted it, but I rolled off him and let him search. Why would Theo assume Oryn and I would or could ever have sex? We were nowhere near that and he would know.

"Bingo." Cohen jumped up and waved a foil wrapped condom in the air.

I must have visibly flinched because Cohen smiled and climbed back over the bed toward me, dropping a condom and lube within reach.

"Theo and Oryn talk a lot. Oryn has expressed his frustrations many times. Theo listens. He also is super smart and knows a weekend away could amount to something... somehow." Then he winked.

His matter-of-fact explanation and the faint speech impediment he always had when he spoke made me smile. Cohen was expressive in a way none of the other alters were, and when he told stories, he was vibrant and showy, almost dramatic.

"Well thank you, Theo, I guess."

I took Cohen by the waist and pulled him down on top of me. Our bodies crushed together completely, and it took no time to return to that heightened place we'd left a moment before.

When we could no longer coordinate our kiss, we gave up and focused on grinding our rigid lengths together. Cohen was more vocal than I expected and threw his head back on a steady stream of moans as he moved against me. Things were becoming slick, and the tingle through my body was mounting.

His exposed neck called to me, and I latched on, licking and sucking with a hunger that consumed me. Then, his neck wasn't enough, and I wanted to taste more of him. All of him.

Fueling his whimpering moans, I made my way down his body, devouring all of him I could as I journeyed lower. When I reached his begging dick, glistening with the results of our activities, I salivated. Cohen met my eyes and nodded.

With his permission, I took his dick and stroked it a few times before bringing it to my lips. Tenderly tracing a tongue along his tip, I tasted him. The combination of his hearty flavor and the gasp from Cohen made my own dick drip even more. I wasn't sure how long I could drag it out. The overwhelming urge to take him was almost unrecognizable in myself.

When I swallowed him down in one pass, I thought he was going to come off the bed. His hands found my hair and gripped painfully as he cried out. I rose slowly, rolling my tongue as I came up and then sucked him down my throat again. Over and over until he was bucking into my mouth and dripping a steady stream.

His body was taut and became more and more rigid with each pass, and I knew if I didn't slow my pace, he was going to come.

He groaned as I pulled off and moved up the bed. I slammed our mouths together and drank away his complaints, working him with my hand a few times before finding the lube.

In the back of my mind, I worried Cohen bottoming might be an issue. First, his experience was zero, and second, how would Oryn deal with the remnants of an aching ass tomorrow? Would that be a cause for stress or alarm?

Before I could voice my concerns, Cohen removed the lube from my grasp and squirted a good amount into my hand.

"I'm ready."

"Cohen, this could hurt some. Especially if you've never—"

"I'll be okay."

"But afterward, it will probably be tender, or at the very least noticeable. I'm just thinking—"

"Of Oryn?"

I nodded. "How will that affect him?"

"It will be okay. We've talked, and he knows how I wanted this to happen."

Sometimes, it was hard not to feel a bit like the outsider in my own relationship. I wished Oryn had expressed some of it with me, except he knew I'd have halted any discussion.

"Okay. Open up for me. I wanna make sure you're good and ready."

I wouldn't take any chances on hurting him. It was already going to be a challenge to make him comfortable, but I remembered my first time and it had been perfectly enjoyable, so I knew it was possible.

I kissed him while I spent a great deal of time working to prepare him for my length. Once he'd become comfortable with a couple of fingers, I nudged his prostate and made him vibrate with need. It took time and patience, but when I was able to work three fingers inside and he begged for more, I knew he was ready.

I fit the condom over my length and coated it with a generous amount of lube. Then, I rolled to my back and encouraged him to straddle me.

"You have all the control. Only go as fast as you can handle," I instructed.

It was the first time I'd seen any signs of nervousness in Cohen's eyes.

"You can change your mind at any point," I added.

He nodded and rocked his ass against my slickened dick. I held it up and glided it over his crack as he tested and teased a little.

When he pressed against me and met resistance, he bit his bottom lip. Instead of pulling back, he pushed harder.

"Slowly. A little at a time," I encouraged.

He rose and tried again, slowly working himself past the tight muscle barrier. When he broke through, he gasped and held himself perfectly still. The extreme pressure surrounding my tip was mind blowing, and I had to breathe through the incredible sensation as he adjusted. Slowly, he rocked himself in and out, taking a bit more each time he went down. When he bottomed out, I held his hips steady.

"Get comfortable a minute."

I said it as much for his sake as my own. His heat engulfed me, and any movement was sure to make me come on the spot. I needed to calm my body.

Cohen looked down into my eyes, and for a moment, the creased brow and hesitance behind his grey-blue eyes reminded me of Oryn. It was gone just as fast, and he braced himself on my chest as he smiled.

From that point forward, it was a hopeless struggle for control. The moment he moved, everything tingled and came alive. Growing and building, the steady ache for release became excruciating, and I had to bite back all urges to go faster and drive into him deeper.

He rocked us together, lifting and lowering himself in a steady, mind-numbing rhythm. Cohen's eyes fell shut and his mouth hung open as his own bliss grew. In that moment, I closed my eyes and brought myself to where I knew Oryn wanted and intended for us to be; not just with Cohen, but with him as well. Our relationship was unconventional in so many ways. The bonding moment I shared with Cohen was just a small example of how differently we operated.

With the ever-growing warmth in my core, my balls pulled tight against my body and I knew I wasn't going to last. When I opened my eyes, I was gifted a vision of beauty. Beads of sweat coated Cohen's brow as he moved. The force of his drives increased by the minute, and a steady stream of cum dripped onto my chest from his painfully hard dick.

"Stroke yourself," I said on a panted breath. "Come, I'm so close."

He leaned an arm beside my head and worked himself in time with his movements. His face was close, and I rose my head to meet our foreheads. I watched his orgasm grow and burn through his eyes. When he lost rhythm, I helped him find it and rose to meet his thrusts. When he pinched his eyes closed and growled through clenched teeth, hot jets of his cum coated my chest. As his ass clamped around me, I toppled over the edge as well. The intensity made it impossible to keep our coordinated rhythm, and instead of trying, Cohen kissed me and let me take over as I rode out the wave of pleasure.

Out of breath and exhausted, we laid together for a long time, clinging to one another, too absorbed in the shared moment to say anything.

My heart raced as I hugged Cohen tighter against me. I searched for any signs of guilt or unease over what had taken place, but apart from a tiny thread of worry over having made his body sore, I couldn't find any. I knew in my heart it was how he wanted—and needed—things to progress for us.

My wandering thoughts brought me back to the man in my arms. As much as I loved Oryn, Cohen and I had become closely bonded in a way Oryn and I weren't. I couldn't deny the way he'd wormed his way into my heart as well. He carried a naivety around and an insecurity he'd never admit to, but he was truly a loving, caring man.

"Why did you respond the way you did when I complimented you earlier?"

I hadn't forgotten, and the look I'd seen cross his face bothered me.

"When," he breathed against my chest. "I don't remember."

"I told you how incredible you look, and you frowned."

Cohen's fingers danced at my sides, but the gap in the conversation grew.

"Cohen?" I asked raising my head to peer down at him.

"Because this body isn't me. Maybe it's what you physically see, but when I see myself, I don't look anything like this. It's just the body. Oryn's body, I guess. Not mine."

I considered that a moment as I rested my head back down and played with his hair. Each alter was unique and individual. I'd never considered that they might see themselves differently. But it made sense. Rain was five years old. His perception of himself certainly wouldn't be a twenty-nine-year-old body.

"I never thought of it that way. I guess I always see what's in front of me."

"I know. And that's to be expected. I guess when you told me I looked incredible and I saw you looking at this body, it made me sad because you aren't seeing me."

His comment crushed me. I'd never done that intentionally. Cohen's personality was such a reflection of who he was, I wished in my mind I could see what he saw.

"Tell me what you see when you look at yourself."

He lifted his head and looked me in the eyes. "Really?"

"Yeah. I'm sorry I made assumptions. I want to see you for you. So tell me. Please."

His crooked smile lifted my spirits, and he brought a hand to cover my eyes. "Then close your eyes and see it in your mind. Don't look at the body in front of you."

I chuckled and held my hand over his. "Okay. Go."

"My hair is the color of mahogany. It grows a little past my ears and curls on the ends, but I like to make it windblown and messy looking. You know, styled like that, not messy for the sake of messy. I'm not tall. Only five-foot nine and kinda skinny. No muscles really. At least none that are prominent. My eyes are green, and I never grow facial hair. I hate it."

He fell silent, and after a moment, he went to remove his hand. I held him in place, not letting him go. Keeping my eyes shielded, I reached out and blindly felt for him. Rubbing a hand over his arm, I envisioned all he'd described and smiled.

"You're beautiful, Cohen. I can see you perfectly, and what's more, the man you describe suits your personality so much better."

I let him remove his hand, and I opened my eyes. We stared at one another for a moment longer before he spoke.

"Do you really think so?"

Uncertainty and doubt shone where he normally held such assuredness.

"Absolutely. I'd never lie to you. From this day forth, I will see you for who you really are. But you should know, this physical form you wear means very little. It's your heart I love and your kindness."

He turned thoughtful and worried his lip. "Oryn said you love him," Cohen whispered, a hesitance in his eyes.

"That's right." I took his chin and leaned up to kiss him. Our lips brushed together once before I continued, "And I love him whole. Not one part, but all."

"So me too?"

"So you too."

His smile was bashful as he laid his head back on my chest. No more was said as we enjoyed a quiet moment, taking in all we'd shared. When sleep started to draw in, Cohen shuffled from my arms and looked around the end of the bed.

"What are you looking for?"

"We should clean up some. And at least put on bottoms. I promised not to steal you all night, but Oryn can't handle this." He motioned to our nakedness.

One-hundred percent agreeing, I got up and retreated to the bathroom to find a washcloth and clean up. Cohen followed me with pajama pants in hand.

He cleaned up as well and we returned to bed wearing bottoms. No t-shirts.

"Shouldn't we grab shirts?" I asked as Cohen got comfortable under the covers.

"Nah, Oryn will be okay. He needs that little nudge. I'll keep Reed distracted. It'll be fine."

I had to smile. At no time in my life did I ever think I'd have a conversation like the one I was having. An outsider would never make sense of it, but for me, it was becoming normal.

I snuggled in beside him and he curled against my side, an arm over my abdomen and head on my shoulder. I played with his hair for a while as my eyes became heavy once again.

I didn't remember drifting off, or for how long I'd been asleep, when Cohen stirred. He lifted his head and peered down at me through the darkness for a moment before resting back against me. Whether it was a hunch or merely that I was learning to read him more, I wasn't sure. I kissed his head and smiled.

"You're back."

"We're shirtless."

I chuckled. There were no hints of unease in his voice, only plain observation.

"Cohen said you'd get over it."

He buried his face in the crook of my shoulder and neck and I could feel the smile on his face. "I'm fine."

His fingers moved tentatively against my side and over my abdomen, exploring new territory. They got braver the longer they were there until it was his entire palm touching and gliding around.

"Thank you," he whispered into the dark. "It was important to me."

"You could have told me."

"You'd have said no."

He was right. I would have exhausted all energy explaining how taking our relationship to that level wasn't necessary for me, and I'd have never listened to him telling me how important it was for him.

"For the future, I understand now."

He pressed against me as close as he could get, and I wrapped my arms around him. That night, he slept against me.

Chapter Nineteen

The following morning neither of us woke until much later. The last thing I wanted was to get up. All night with Oryn in my arms was sheer bliss, and I didn't want to spoil it. We planned to drive home that evening, and I didn't know if spending nights together was something that would continue on occasion or be reserved for trips out of town. With all we'd shared, I could only hope to have many more mornings waking with Oryn in my arms.

"Can we stay here all day," Oryn said against my chest where he'd moved his head. "I like it."

Feeling his breath across my skin tickled and reminded me how there had been no adverse reaction to coming back to his body and finding us clung together—and shirtless. Perhaps those bridges were hard to cross, but once on the other side, it was okay.

"Me too," I agreed as I brushed fingers through his messy hair. "But what about the museum? I know you're looking forward to it. Besides, this right here," I kissed the top of his head, "can happen again any time you want it to. I happen to love cuddling… Just don't tell Evan. I'll never hear the end of it."

Oryn laughed and peered up. I lifted my head and kissed him cautiously, but he only smiled against my mouth and moved himself higher up to reach better.

"I really am looking forward to the museum."

"Then we should get moving. Coffee, breakfast, then Viking exhibits and more."

Within an hour, we were up, dressed, and caffeinated. We packed the car, since we intended on heading home after our day at the ROM, and were at the museum by the time they opened at ten.

It'd been years since I'd been to Toronto, and even longer since I'd visited the ROM. When the lobby area was moderately crowded, and Oryn found my hand and clung tight, I worried it was going to be too much for him.

That concern evaporated once we paid our entrance fee and made our way into the first gallery. There were plaques describing how the exhibits and floors were mapped out, and we stopped near one to plan out our day. There were three levels to the museum, so we decided to start on one and make our way up, hitting the sections that interested us most.

Because Oryn couldn't wait, we had to start with the Viking exhibit before anything else. It was a separately ticketed area, so the density of the crowd was much less.

Immediately, Oryn drifted toward a display of various artifacts and hovered as he read the plaques.

"That's an animal-head shaped brooch. Look at the details that went into that." I leaned over the display case as Oryn read out loud the information tag.

We moved on to old weapons, including an axe head, iron sword, and a helmet that was constructed of both iron and links of chainmail. The fascination on Oryn's face as he analysed each piece brought me more joy than the exhibit itself. He was lost in learning about each item, and his concern over his surroundings had vanished. He was in his element.

An hour later, we'd circled the room twice, and Oryn had read and examined every item on display in great detail. We were set to continue our journey and wandered our way into another section of the museum.

In the Chinese Architecture room, we focused mainly on the interesting displays of ancient weaponry and devices. From there we travelled into the Sigmund Samuel Gallery of Canada and explored the culture of our own country.

Oryn talked endlessly as he read and shared the artifacts and displays that interested him. His knowledge of history was astounding. Most of it went over my head, but the trip was for him and I'd hit the nail on the head. He'd never looked more happy.

After a thorough exploration of the first level, we wandered to the staircase and climbed to the second floor. Huge totem poles were displayed in the middle of the winding stairs and spanned from the first to the third floor. Beautifully carved and painted, it was art in itself, and we admired as we climbed.

"Did you want to grab a drink or take a break for a bit?" I asked. "We've been here over two hours already."

"Have we really?" Oryn didn't take his eyes from the large wooden pole as he climbed beside me. "I'm okay. Do you?"

"Maybe after the second floor we should grab lunch and take a break before hitting the third. Says here there is a café in the museum." I pointed to where I was reading the pamphlet we'd been given.

"Sure." Oryn finally peeled his eyes away from his examination and beamed a smile in my direction. "This is a lot of fun. It's so fascinating."

"I'm glad you're enjoying it."

"I am." He quit walking and leaned in, pecking my cheek with a soft kiss. "Thank you."

The second floor was vastly dedicated to the history of living things. Animals that had roamed the Earth since the beginning of time. The moment we stepped out onto the floor, it was evident that section of the museum was designed to entertain the entire family. The more technical and advanced galleries, dealing with cultural histories were kept on different floors because they may not appeal to families with children.

The landing where the stairs opened up was home to a four-and-a-half-meter long cast of the skeletal remains of a giant sea turtle. There were a few people gathered around it and Oryn and I stood back as we read the large plaque displayed in front.

"It's huge," Oryn exclaimed. "I can't imagine coming face to face with that."

"Me either," I laughed.

We rounded the bend and into the open section of level two. There was a vast open space that dropped to the first floor and was sectioned off with a clear plexiglass, waist high wall. Beyond, dangling in the open air, was the skeletal remains of a huge flying dinosaur. Its wingspan had to be over twelve-feet wide. It was daunting the way it was displayed, as though in flight and heading directly toward onlookers.

"Woah!"

Oryn's clasp on my hand was gone, and a moment later, so was he. Bolting to the clear barrier, he gawked in awe at the ancient beast soring through the sky.

"Vaughn-d, das a dinosaur!" he squealed.

Registering his exclamation, hearing those few simple words as they rang through my ears, the hairs on my nape stood on end. My heart responded immediately and jumped into my throat.

"No," I said under my breath as I dashed a look at all the people surrounding us. "Not now."

"Vaughn-d! Look!" The distinctive childlike voice called to me as the man whose body he'd claimed jumped up and down with excitement. "C'mere. Do you see it?"

A few nearby adults turned his way and odd looks were exchanged before they resumed their own tours with their families. What the fuck did I do? I'd had only a small handful of visits with Rain. Our interactions were still among my more awkward moments when dealing with Oryn's DID. It was one thing to gradually get accustomed to being around a child in a man's body while we were at home and alone. But in public, where his behavior was already attracting attention, I didn't know how to proceed and froze.

Rain didn't allow time for my deliberation and ran toward me yelling my name.

"Vaughn-d, come see da dinosaur!" He yanked my hand and dragged me toward where he'd been standing.

"Yeah, buddy, I see it. Super cool, huh?"

"It's scary. Das gonna fly down here and eat me up. Nom, nom, nom, nom." He continued making chomping noises until he burst out into giggles and smiled with a wide toothy grin.

With my heart thrashing, I chased my thoughts as I tried to think of what to do. An older couple standing next to us stared openly at Ory—Rain with matching curled noses before sharing whispered words and shaking their heads.

"Hey," I snapped, "Got something to say?"

Their humored guises immediately turned to matching looks of shame, and instead of responding, they turned and walked away.

Maybe it was unusual to see a grown man acting like a child, but I'd be damned if I was going to allow him to be mocked. He didn't ask for that. God knew, he'd been through hell already in his life, he didn't need added shit from strangers who judged him without knowing a damn thing about him.

"Why you mad, Vaughn-d?"

I turned back to Rain once the couple had departed and wiped the annoyance from my face.

"I'm not, buddy. Umm…" I looked up at the dinosaur he'd been admiring and tried to bring his attention off my momentary irritation. "You aren't really scared, are you? You know that big guy isn't alive anymore, right?"

Rain joined me, craning his neck and smiling wide again. "Das a skeleton and not real. I know. Waz his name?"

I looked around for the plaque and read with a fumbling ability as I tried to pronounce it correctly. "That's a Quet-zal-co-atlus? I think."

Rain's eyes went wide, and his jaw fell. "Woah, das a big name."

"Says here we can call him Q. That's easier, huh?"

Rain's head flopped up and down as he nodded dramatically. I dashed another look around and swallowed a tight lump that had been building in my throat. My heart thudded so hard against my chest, I needed to resist the urge to clutch it.

Rain held the edge of the barrier wall and jumped up and down as he watched the soaring creature. I stared and waited, wondering if the switch was momentary like all the times he'd appeared before. When the bouncing stopped, he pivoted and scanned the open floor in awe. There were at least a dozen other dinosaurs on display, and he was off like a shot before I could stop him.

With barely a second for my mind to catch up, I bolted after him. He'd stopped at the hanging barrier links that blocked off the Tyrannosaurus Rex.

"A T-Rex!" Rain's head flipped in my direction and he pointed—as though I'd somehow missed the looming carnivore. "I saw him in a movie. He was racing, racing after a car with da people. He was gonna eat them."

"Jurassic Park?" I asked, quirking a brow. "Aren't you kinda young to watch that movie?"

"It's not scary, noodle brain." He giggled and made his hands into mock claws as he snarled. "Rawr! I gonna eat you up, Vaughn-d. I'm a T-Rex."

In that moment, time became suspended as I watched Rain stomp around like a dinosaur. Was it awkward being with him? Nerve-wracking? Absolutely. But when put into perspective, and I viewed the entirety of the complex man who played dinosaurs in front of me, it brought tears to my eyes.

I'd fallen so completely in love, and the knowledge that something so terrible and traumatizing had happened to him as a child, causing his mind to split into separate people, utterly broke my heart. There was no need to think or wonder how I would handle being around Rain in public. I would just be. No matter what part of Oryn I faced, be it Rain, Cohen, Reed, Theo, and even self-destructive Cove, it didn't matter. It didn't change how I felt for him, it only confirmed what I already knew.

"Oh no," I gasped, playing along. "Don't eat me, Mr. Dinosaur!"

Rain burst into uncontrolled giggles, and he covered his face. "I'm teasing." He went over to the Tyrannosaurs plaque and squatted down. "Waz it say, Vaughn-d?"

I knelt beside him and skimmed the information. It was a lot of technical mumble jumble that I wasn't even sure I could pronounce, so I just told him what I thought he'd be more interested in knowing.

"It says the T-Rex was the king of the dinosaurs. He ruled the Earth billions of years ago and his favorite thing to eat was other dinosaurs. That means he was a meat-eater."

"A carvenor," Rain corrected

I chuckled and mussed his hair. "Close, it's a car-ne-vor."

"Oh." He peered up at the gaping mouthed beast and made biting motions as he touched his teeth. "How come they not alive anymore?"

"Don't know, buddy. They believe maybe a huge meteor crashed into the Earth and wiped them all out."

He thought about that a moment before losing interest in the T-Rex and skipping away to a large Wooley Mammoth.

"Is dat an elephant?"

"Nope, but it's the elephants really old cousin. He's called a Wooley Mammoth."

Searching out the plaque, Rain plopped himself beside a group of children who were admiring the pictures on its front.

"Read dis one, Vaughn-d, read dis one."

"Excuse me," a woman around my own age scurried over and glared down at Rain. "What the hell is your problem? Since when is it okay for you to shove children aside like that?"

"Hey," I jumped forward just as Rain's face crumpled at her harsh words. "It's okay, bud, read with the kids."

I took the woman's shoulder and spun her away. "Back down. He doesn't know any better." I wasn't sure how the hell to explain, but I'd be damned if I was gonna let people shove him around.

Rain laughed out loud with the kids behind me, and their child-like banter over the displays were loud enough to hear from where we stood.

"What the hell is wrong with him?" The woman looked as though she were about to march back over, but I got in her face.

"Don't judge things you don't understand, lady. You leave him alone. Do you hear me?"

She sneered, but didn't move. "Matthew, come on. Time to go."

One of the boys behind me groaned. "But, Mama, I wanna stay here."

"No! Now."

I waited until she moved off with her son before I turned back to Rain. There were still two other children beside him and they were all talking about the Mammoth.

"Are you a kid?" one of the young girls beside him asked.

"Yeah, I'm five." Rain held up his hand to show her.

"Why are you so big like a grown up?"

Rain shrugged. "I dunno, cuz I have to be."

"Okay."

And that was all there was to it. The conversation ended, and they resumed talking dinosaurs. It amazed me how open and accepting children were compared to other adults.

I stood back for a while and watched him interact with the children until they ran off to find their families. Rain stood and came up beside me and took my hand. His joy was gone, and he looked glum.

"What's wrong?"

"How come dat lady was yellin' at me?"

I sighed, hating that he'd needed to witness her negative attitude.

"She just didn't understand."

When his smile didn't return, I scrambled for what to do or say.

"Come on. There are a lot more dinosaurs to see. Wanna keep looking?"

Although reluctant at first, Rain continued to the next display. My experience with kids was minimal. I didn't spend a great deal of time with my brother and his boy, so I was out of my element and made it up as I went along. When Rain's spoiled mood eventually turned a corner, and his happy bubbly personality emerged again, I took it as a win.

After over an hour exploring dinosaurs, I wondered if Oryn was going to be returning any time soon. Being on the second level with all the family oriented exhibits probably wasn't helping, so when Rain was finished examining fossilized dinosaur eggs, I suggested we take a look at some other parts of the museum.

Together we climbed the stairs to the third level. It was slow going since everything was a distraction for a five-year-old. By the time we landed on the top floor, I took his hand.

"We need to stick together and look quietly now, okay?"

"K."

I guided him into a gallery which housed historical Egyptian artifacts and displays. Much like on the first level, many of the items were behind glass display cases and the plaques were smaller with no added pictures.

The area was absent of the bustle from the second level, and immediately I realized how much more Rain would stand out among museum goers. Everyone milling about were quietly observing, reading, and studying the displays.

We walked the perimeter of one room, then another. I watched for any indication of a switch, but Rain remained.

When we stopped in front of a group of mannequins wearing period costumes, Rain became restless.

"Vaughn-d, dis is boring."

But Oryn couldn't wait for this trip.

Mourning the loss of our birthday adventure, I ran a hand through my hair and thought. I couldn't force a switch, and as much as a small weight of disappointment sat in my belly, I wasn't being fair to Rain.

"You're right. This is boring."

I pulled out the pamphlet I'd been given and flipped through. Rain looked over my shoulder and when I flipped the page, he gasped.

"What?" I asked, peering from him back to the pamphlet.

"What's dat?" He jammed his finger on a picture of a bat. "Is dat Batman?"

I read the title out loud, "Discover the mysterious creatures of the night at the ROM's very own Bat Cave."

Rain's mouth dropped, and his eyes almost bugged out of his head. "A bat cave," he whispered. "Like Batman."

That was that. The rest of the day was spent in the darkness of the bat cave where Rain pretended he was Batman. Creatures flew over our heads and panels explained all about the bat habitat, what they ate, how they hunted, and where they could be found. Rain was in his element.

As much as I was saddened that Oryn was missing out on his day, it had given me more time than I'd ever had before to get to know Rain.

After well over an hour in the bat cave, I convinced him it was time to leave. It was nearing five in the evening and we hadn't eaten all day.

"How about fast food for the long drive home?"

"Can we have McDonald's?"

"We can have anything you want."

Before leaving, Rain dragged me to the gift shop and picked out a bat-hat souvenir. He put it on immediately and wore it proud.

All I could do was smile.

As promised we pigged out on McDonald's as I drove to the highway to take us home. Once his belly was fed, Rain couldn't stop yawning.

"Are you tired, bud?"

He rubbed his eyes and shook his head. "No."

As adamant as he was to stay awake, within twenty-minutes, he was fast asleep beside me.

I turned the radio on low and thought over the weekend as I drove us home. Being with Oryn for two solid days had given me a sense of just how often his switches took place. I'd shared time with Cohen, Oryn, Reed, and Rain on that trip alone, and I was wiser because of it. The more time spent with each alter was just more of Oryn to know.

About an hour from home, Rain stirred beside me and lifted his head. Wiping the sleep from his eyes, he then squinted out the window with a furrowed brow. I glanced over in time to see him grimace in pain and rub his temple. It was then I knew, Rain had retreated and Oryn had returned.

He pulled his phone out and checked the time, before looking out the window again.

"Where are we?" he asked.

"About an hour from home. Head hurting?"

"Yeah."

When he went to massage the sore spot again, he frowned and reached higher, removing the bat-hat from his head. He examined it and his cheeks flushed.

"Please don't tell me you spent the entire day with Rain."

I laughed and patted his knee. "I spent the entire day with Rain. But it was awesome, and we got to know each other a whole lot better."

He turned the hat in his hands and peered at me for a long moment. He placed the hat on the dash and took my hand in his.

"You're pretty incredible, you know?"

I smiled before returning my focus to the road. "Nah, it's you who's incredible."

Chapter Twenty

The beginning of July was too hot and muggy to be stuck in a dress shirt and slacks. The minute I hit the parking lot after work, I yanked my tie off and rolled my sleeves to my elbows. Beads of sweat gathered at my temples and along my nape. As I started the car and blasted the air conditioning, I pulled my phone from my pocket.

I hadn't heard from Oryn all day, but knew he was over his head in writing. Since classes had ended in April, he'd gone full-force with his biography. He treated it like a full-time job and wrote his ass off for at least eight hours a day, five days a week.

I unbuttoned my shirt a little more as I glanced around the parking lot then sent him a quick text.

You ready to go out? I just got off work. Gonna swing home and shower then pick you up.

When I didn't get a response right away, I headed home. I wasn't surprised. When he was writing, he was in the zone.

By the time I'd pulled into the parking lot and wandered to my apartment, I still hadn't received an answer, so I called him. If he'd switched, I knew I'd get no answer, but I had the feeling he was simply distracted.

He picked up on the second ring.

"Oh my God, tell me it isn't four already!"

"It's four-thirty, and I'm showering and coming over. Evan and Krystina are expecting us at six."

"So I have some time?"

I chuckled and used my free hand to remove my shirt and pants as I headed to the bathroom. "You have a half an hour. Then get your ass in a shower."

He sighed and didn't respond. The sound of keys clacking drew my attention and I shook my head.

"I'm hanging up, Oryn."

"Okay, see you soon."

I savored the cold water coating my body for a bit longer than I should have, but I knew Oryn wouldn't care if we ran behind. More time for him to work. He was dedicated to his book, and I loved seeing him so absorbed and pleased with himself. He hadn't shared any of it, and I waited patiently for him to announce that he was finished.

After dressing in a nice pair of cargo shorts and a navy polo t-shirt, I fixed my hair with a bit of gel. With my electric razor set to a close trim, I cleaned up my stubble and headed out the door.

Oryn and I had been officially dating for nearly seven months. I'd made solid connections with almost all his alters—save Cove—and Oryn and I had become closer every day. There was still that minor hesitation in his eyes at times, but his confidence around me soared, and for the most part, his stutter had become non-existent.

Since our trip to Toronto, we'd spent the night together a handful of times. Although intimacy remained a huge barrier, Oryn had made great strides. Without the pressure of sex looming in the air, he willingly explored new things at his own pace while continually encouraging mine and Cohen's relationship to wander where it would.

And it had... a few times.

When I reached his front door, I pocketed my keys and knocked before poking my head in and calling out.

"Hello?"

"Yeah, in here," Oryn called from the den.

I kicked off my shoes and wandered down the hall. "If you are at that keyboard still, I'm gonna physically remove you."

The sound of clacking sped up as I approached and rounded the corner.

"I knew it!"

"Two... more... seconds."

"No more seconds." I went up behind him and clasped his wrists, pulling them against his body as I nuzzled into his neck. "Time's up, and I took my sweet ass time in the shower too, so you can't say I didn't give you enough time."

He peered up with a wide grin, arms still bound to his chest. "Can I finish my sentence?"

I glanced at the screen and he squirmed in my hold. "No peeking!"

Instead of looking to his progress, I released an arm and took his chin, drawing his head around for a kiss. The squirming ceased, and he wormed free to hold me down and kiss me deeper.

The initial hesitancy that used to prelude each kiss was nothing more than a memory. He took with gumption. Even his startle reflex had diminished, and I was able to initiate things more or—like I'd just done—sneak up and wrap arms around him without making him jump. Small steps, but huge for Oryn.

His tongue licked at the seam of my lips, and I spun his chair and kissed him proper, sharing the offered exchange with greed. When he wrapped his arms around my waist and tugged me down to straddle him, I pulled away.

"No way. Get your sexy ass in a shower before I put you there myself."

He chuckled and allowed me to pull him to stand. "Fine." Reaching back, he closed his laptop and pointed a finger in my face. "But no looking."

I narrowed my eyes and he threw his hands up in defeat. "I'm going, I'm going."

It was ten after six when we arrived at the restaurant. Tony's Smokehouse was more of a bar and grill type of restaurant with a laid-back atmosphere. Evan wasn't one for fancy and was determined to squeeze in a few games of pool after we ate. The building was divided into two sections. One half was more restaurant-ish while the other was more of the bar style with TVs hung on the walls, dart boards, and three pool tables. Although you could eat and order off the menu in the bar half, we decided on a slightly more formal meal in the restaurant section first.

It wasn't Evan's first time meeting Oryn, but his initial introduction had been brief. He'd popped over for a quick beer in the evening about a month or so back and didn't know Oryn was visiting. So, we'd planned an official meet and greet with Evan and Krystina.

The waiter guided us to our waiting party at the back of the restaurant. They'd been given a booth by the window and I slid in first and allowed Oryn to sit on the outside.

"Hi," Oryn said as he sat. "Good to see you again, Evan."

"You too. This is Krystina. Kryssy baby, this is Vaughn's boyfriend, Oryn."

Oryn smiled shyly and dashed his gaze to the surface of the table. Evan was already well informed that Oryn was shy and knew enough not to pester him, and I assumed he'd probably mentioned it to his girl.

"We need to blast through this meal like pronto, super fast because the Yanks and Tigers are playing and I'm missing it."

"Dude, we are having dinner," I said. "Life won't end if you miss a half an hour of the game."

I chuckled, knowing already that in Evan's world, it already had. He was addicted to his sports and had been for as long as I'd known him.

"How do you stand it?" I asked Krystina.

She laughed and shoulder bumped Evan. "He makes it up to me."

Evan wiggled his eyebrows and grinned. "I balance my sports and my woman equally. It can be done."

"That's a first. You must be something special. I've been friends with him since we were fifteen and I've always been second to sports."

"I told you. Grow a vagina and we'll talk."

Evan chuckled and swigged his beer as Krystina rolled her eyes as his quip. When Oryn squirmed, I rested a hand on his leg under the table. Talk of sex, or organs involved in sex, always gave the same reaction. He shimmied closer on the bench and laced his fingers in mine.

As unfiltered as Evan was, we made it through dinner in one piece. He really did tone it down for Oryn's sake, even though outsiders may not have noticed. Krystina was exceptionally nice and ensured to involve Oryn in conversation all through dinner. She asked about his schooling and the plans he'd made for the following year.

"So are you planning more college courses in September?" she asked Oryn.

Oryn pushed his food around his plate and dashed a glance in her direction. "P-possibly. I've been l-looking into some English classes. T-to improve my writing, you know? But not night classes. I might try doing part-time studies during the day. N-not sure yet."

Oryn had been toying with the idea for a while, but attending school in the company of a larger body of students made him uncomfortable. But he was determined. I'd noticed he seemed to be slowly working himself up to it.

After we ate, we relocated into the bar area where Evan lost himself in his baseball game. Krystina showed a strong knowledge of sports and joined in on commentary. It was the missing piece I'd been baffled over. Evan had never had a relationship last more than a few months. But no woman to date was as knowledgeable, or interested, in sports as Evan. Krystina showed her true colors, and the longer I watched them, the more I understood why they worked so well together.

"Wanna shoot a game of pool?" I asked Oryn.

He peered across the bar to the tables and shrugged. "Sure. I don't really know how, but you can walk me through it."

After I explained the basic rules, I broke the balls, scattering them over the table and sending the five ball to drop into a side pocket.

"So I'm solid," I explained, pointing out where the ball had fallen.

"Is it my turn?"

"When I miss," I said, lining up a shot.

I sunk two more balls, purposefully missing my third to give Oryn a chance to play.

"Okay," Oryn said, leaning over the table and lining up an easy side-pocket shot. "Am I holding this right?"

"Don't hook your finger over the cue. Let it glide over top."

He moved his finger down and the cue slipped from where it was balanced.

Oryn laughed and tried to reposition it only to have it happen again.

He laughed. "Oh my God, this is harder than it looks."

When he finally got the cue balanced, he adjusted his aim, but before he took his shot, I went up behind him and took hold of his waist.

"Wait," I said. "You need to get down at eye level. You'll never make the shot like this."

He peered over his shoulder and grinned before bending over the table. I slinked my arms around his waist and bent with him, resting my head on his shoulder.

"I think I'll never make the shot with you laying over me."

I moved my hands over his and nipped at his ear. "I'm just helping show you how."

He turned his face and pecked my lips. "Sure you are."

I walked him hand over hand through his shot—which he missed because we couldn't coordinate our bodies together to make it happen.

The game was less than serious, and we laughed and goofed around, tossing rules out the window. By the time all the balls were pocketed, we had no idea who'd won and who'd lost. Evan and Krystina were still engrossed in their game, so we decided to call it a night and said our goodbyes.

The summer heat hit like a wave the instant we walked out of the air-conditioned building. Oryn snagged my hand as we wandered through the parking lot toward the car. He pulled me closer and kissed me twice as we walked, beaming the entire time. It was amazing to see him so happy.

"I had fun," he said as he pulled open the door on his side.

"Evan wasn't too much?"

"No, not at all."

That was a relief. I'd been overly worried about us spending any time with him. He was a great guy, but he was a little unfiltered and crude at times.

Back at Oryn's, I pulled into his parking spot and checked the time. It was nearing ten.

"So what are the weekend plans? Anything you'd like to do?" I asked, stretching our time together so it would last even longer.

"I don't know. It's been so hot, the thought of doing anything outdoors is almost unbearable."

I shrugged. "Not unless we hit the beach. There is a quieter section not far from where my parents live. I used to go there as a teenager. What do you say?"

Oryn's eyes gleamed as he thought a moment. "Yeah, that could be fun."

"Perfect."

We shared an awkward moment of silence where I knew it was time to say our goodbyes. It was always the hardest part. I never wanted to push for more from Oryn, but I longed to spend every night with him. Not just one here and there.

"So, how about I give you a call in the morning when I'm up and we can sort it out then."

Oryn nodded, but dashed his eyes to his lap. "Yeah."

With an ache in my heart, I took his cheek and turned his face back around toward me. "Sweet dreams tonight. I'll miss you."

I joined our mouths and kissed him with all the love I carried inside. It was never enough. Being apart from him was becoming harder and harder.

"Goodnight," he whispered against my lips.

As I was about to pull away, he caught my arm. "Vaughn?"

I paused, waiting for him to continue.

"Stay the night. I don't want you to go."

My heart swelled, and I nodded, taking him back into another longer, deeper kiss. There was nothing I wanted more. The few occasions I'd stayed over had been amazing. Not only was Oryn feeling safer around me, but he'd become more comfortable with our intimacy, and often we would spend a little time exploring each other before he'd curl in my arms and sleep.

I killed the engine and we made our way out of the heat and into his air-conditioned home. He immediately took my hand and guided me down the hall without exchanging words. His room was small but furnished in a fashion that made it cozy and welcoming.

In the bedroom, he flipped on the bedside lamp and messed a hand through his hair as he smiled shyly.

"I'll need to borrow some pajama bottoms," I said. "I wasn't planning to stay."

Oryn hopped over to his dresser and dug through a drawer. He pulled out two pairs of lounge pants and handed me one.

"Thanks. I'll just," I indicated to the door, "use the washroom and change."

I still didn't chance changing in front of him. Too many times, lines had been crossed unexpectedly and the result had been a switch. I didn't want to miss that night with Oryn, so I remained respectful.

"Theo bought extra toothbrushes the other day. They are under the counter."

I retreated to the washroom and took my time dressing and brushing my teeth, ensuring I gave Oryn enough time to change as well.

When I returned, he scooted down the hall to brush his teeth, too. Thanks to Cohen, being shirtless around each other had become safe. Oryn didn't think twice about it anymore—despite his countless scars along his arms—and when he bounced back into the room and jumped into bed beside me, I took a moment to subtly admire him. I knew every part of that body and had explored it thoroughly, memorizing and loving it. But it wasn't the same when the person occupying it wasn't Oryn. Somehow, it made it different. Mysteries remained, and there was a world I still didn't know when it came to Oryn.

He rolled to his side and propped himself on an elbow. "What are you thinking?" he asked, seeming genuinely curious and content.

I moved a hand to his bare side, and smoothed my palm over his warm skin. "I was just thinking how much I love learning you. Inside and out. Mind, body, and soul." I moved my hand to the small of his back and encouraged him closer. He came without question, and his face rested close to mine. "I love you, Oryn. All of you. I hope you know that," I whispered against his mouth.

"I do." He pressed our mouths together, taking my breath away. Fluttering, tingling warmth coursed over my entire body, and I sighed against him, never more happy in my life. He hadn't returned the sentiment, but I didn't expect it yet. With love came full trust, and we still hadn't broken that barrier completely. Every day was better, but with Oryn, time and patience were necessary.

Oryn pressed me flat on the bed and deepened our connection, tracing his tongue along mine and laying against my side. Over time, I'd seen his bravery grow, and our make-out sessions had escalated. Since our trip to Toronto, and the progress in mine and Cohen's relationship, Oryn hadn't carried the same self-induced pressure to go further, however, that night, determined Oryn had re-emerged.

His hands glided over my bare chest like they never had before as his tongue invaded my mouth. His steady movements escalated my growing desire, and I met his forceful kisses with my own, nudging us further down that path. Between his taste and the deft fingers that continually brushed my hard nipples, I couldn't supress the moan when it climbed up my throat.

Breaking free from my mouth, Oryn moved over top of me and buried his face against my shoulder. His exposed neck called to me. I didn't hesitate and licked and kissed to his ear. It made him gasp, and the hands clung to my sides tightened. I'd never seen him react that way. Hearing those noises so close to my ear drove me to continue. I flipped him to his back and straddled his waist, licking, sucking, and kissing his neck with a hunger I couldn't satiate.

His eyes fell closed and lips parted. He craned his neck, giving me permission and access. As I continued the assault, I braved tracing a hand over his chest as well.

I carefully kept my lower body off of him. Between his sounds and movements, my own body reacted, and I didn't want to startle him into stopping. He was in heaven, and I wanted to keep him there as long as I could.

When I'd nibbled my way down his neck again, I took a chance on maneuvering further. I'd journeyed and tasted my way over Oryn's body before, but only when Cohen fronted. It was a different story with Oryn beneath me. Hearing him in such bliss made me want to try.

Slowly, so he could register and anticipate what I planned, I kissed over his Adam's apple and down to his chest and scraped teeth over the coarse stubble of his neck. I shimmied lower and licked a trail to the middle of his chest, inhaling all that was him. I braced two arms on either side of his body and glanced up to ensure he was still okay.

There was no worry on his face, so I feathered my lips over flesh until I reached a nipple before drawing it into my mouth. I flicked a tongue around the hardening nub and then applied a small amount of suction. I wasn't there long when he clasped my shoulders and pulled me off on a breathless gasp.

"V-Vaughn. St-st-op, please."

I scampered back up the bed in a panic, took his face between my hands, and peered down into his widened eyes. His pupils were blown with desire, but his features told another story.

I'd gone too far.

"I'm sorry. God, Oryn, I'm so sorry."

He shook his head fervently and bit hard into his lower lip. Tears flooded his eyes and I felt like the worst person in the world. What had I done? How stupid was I to think that was okay?

"Oh, God. Shit, I'm sorry."

He kept shaking his head. Then he pulled my face down and brought his mouth to my ear. "It feels really good," he whispered. "It's just… I'm sorry. I panicked."

I raised my head to look at him. His cheeks had flushed a deep crimson like he was embarrassed. There was no way in hell he needed to apologize or feel shamed, and I was about to ensure he knew that, when he took my face in his hands and turned my gaze between our bodies.

His lounge pants were distinctly tented in the front. Then it dawned on me. He was getting hard from what I was doing. Sexually aroused. And it had surprised him enough he'd panicked.

Oryn struggled so hard with anything sexual. Our make-out sessions were a form of intimacy he'd slowly become accustomed to, but they didn't bridge into sexual for him. They were purely romantic and a form of emotionally bonding. The poor guy wasn't even capable of voicing the word sex or the anatomy that went with it, so his current state was shocking—for both of us.

I found his eyes again, and among the worry there remained that determination that had begun our evening. I had no idea how to proceed.

"Were you enjoying what I was doing?" The answer seemed obvious, but when closely coupled with fear, which emotion was stronger?

"Yes." His voice was barely audible.

I studied the glassiness behind his eyes and tried to calm my racing heart. "Do you want me to keep going?"

That time, he could only nod.

"If you need me to stop—"

"I'll tell you."

I kissed his mouth for a while, ensuring he was calm before travelling back down his body where I'd been. I traced fingers over his muscles and circled a nipple with a thumb before capturing it in my mouth once again.

He sucked air between teeth and his body grew taut at the connection. Mindful of his every reaction, I went slow and played tenderly with one nipple before moving to the other. A quick glance showed me that my actions were having an effect. I smoothed a hand down his abdomen and around to his outer thigh as I licked and kissed toward his navel. His breathing increased, and every so often, a whimper left his lips.

I longed to touch him, to build that pleasure he was feeling—possibly for the first time—to levels he'd never felt. Even though I'd said it a million times that I was content where we were, I yearned to make love to him—to Oryn—to take away his fear and to show him how special he was to me.

Keeping my hands safely on his sides, I kissed lower, licking a wet trail along the waistband of his lounge pants. That was when I noticed he'd gone still. He didn't squirm any longer and the tiny sounds he couldn't hold back were gone.

I darted my eyes up. He stared blankly at the ceiling, unmoving, as though he no longer registered what was happening and had zoned out. I watched him for a minute, but he didn't move—I wasn't sure he even blinked.

"Oryn?"

No response.

I shuffled up the bed and only then did his gaze shift to me. Emptiness stared back, a darkness unlike anything I'd ever seen.

I brushed his cheek and studied him. "Hey, are you okay?"

His brow furrowed. "I'm bad." He shook his head glaring from behind eyes that quickly turned venomous. "I'm bad. Bad, bad, bad." Each punch of the word came from behind gritted teeth.

What was happening?

There was no time to process. His hands flew to his head and he clasped two great hands full of hair and screamed through a clenched jaw.

"No! Bad. I'm Bad."

Thrashing, he threw me off and rolled to his stomach where he screamed into a pillow as he tugged his hair.

My brain stuttered. Knowing only that I needed to prevent the assault, I took his wrists and unwound his fingers from their grasp before pulling them back.

"I'm sorry," he cried, thrashing against me. "I know… I know I'm bad. Bad!" He slammed his head against the pillow. "Bad! Bad! Bad!" Each time he screamed the word, his head fell in an attempt to hurt himself. Thankfully, he wasn't in danger of cracking his head open on a mattress.

A rush of panic hit me in the chest and I didn't know what to do.

That wasn't Oryn restrained in my hold. Based on the little I knew, I'd have bet anything I was facing Cove—an extremely unstable Cove.

"Let go of me," he hollered as he arched his back and tried with all his strength to knock me away. "I'll be good now, I promise. Let me go. I'll be good."

The horror of his words hit me in the chest, and I let go, fumbling off the bed and retreating as Cove spun and backed himself against the headboard. He craned his neck and clawed fingers down his arms leaving flaming red marks with the pressure he applied.

"I hate it. I hate it. No… no… no…"

He continued to gouge his arms and shriek as though I wasn't even there. All I could do was watch it unfold. Helpless and desperately wishing I had some guidance on how to handle what I was witnessing, tears filled my eyes.

The raking of nails was incessant, and when a few thin trails of blood trickled from deeper wounds, I couldn't be still any longer. There was no way I could stand by and watch him hurting himself, pouring that much pain and not do something.

"Cove?" I moved closer, one cautious step at a time.

The instant he saw me approach, he stopped, and his gaze darted the room in a flurry. Then, he was gone. He jumped from the bed and ran out the door.

Fuck!

I followed, desperately trying to find the information I'd read and stored away when learning how destructive Cove could be.

I found him in the kitchen, and when he ripped a pairing knife from the block on the counter, I dove forward, disregarding any concern for my own safety.

I hated making him feel confined or frightening him in any way, but I couldn't allow him to hurt himself. From behind, I clamped a firm grip around the wrist with the knife and pinned his second arm to his chest.

"Put it down. I can't let you do this."

"You don't understand," he cried.

He was no longer full of venom, but was dissolving into sobs.

"Then talk to me. Why do you want to hurt yourself?"

"Because I hate it."

His white-knuckled grip on the knife didn't lessen.

"What do you hate?" It took everything to keep the emotion from my voice and remain calm.

"Everything," he blubbered, yanking against my hold. "I'm ugly, and bad, and I hate it." The last statement came out with an edge of anger, so I tightened my grip, fearing him escalating.

"You're not ugly," I whispered against his ear. "You're not bad."

"It's all disgusting and wrong. I hate it all. This body. This skin. I'm so ugly and I'm so, so bad."

"No, you aren't." I hushed him and tried to calm his hysterics. "Please put the knife down. Please. Talk to me, Cove."

He whimpered and sobbed, still clung to the knife like it was a lifeline. An answer to a problem that had plagued him for far too long.

He couldn't let go, so I just held him from behind, closed my eyes, and spoke gentle words into his ear. Even when my arms ached, ensuring he wouldn't break free, and my legs could barely stand any longer, I didn't let go. When he thrashed, I held him. When he sobbed, I held him. When he cursed me, I held him.

His fight lessened, but I still wouldn't let go.

It was well over an hour before a clattering startled me into opening my eyes. The knife lay on the counter and with its release, Cove leaned heavier against my chest.

He'd been silent for a long time, listening to my comforting words and no longer responding. Anticipating he was probably as exhausted as me, I pulled him around and guided him from the room. Like in a trance, he followed without argument. On the couch in the den, I sat and pulled him down into my arms.

He laid his head on my chest and I rubbed his back as I watched the rise and fall of every breath he took.

"I just want to die," he said into the dark room, breaking the lingering silence.

"Why?" His words weighed heavy. All it would take was for Cove to decide one day it was over, and if I wasn't there to stop it...

"Because, then everything will be better. I'm what's wrong. I'm bad and ugly and I can't take it. I hate looking at myself and knowing...knowing..." He stopped and eventually shook his head. "I just hate it."

Remembering Cohen's explanation of how he saw himself as being physically different than the body he occupied, I wondered if Cove struggled the same.

"Can I ask you something?" When he didn't respond, I asked anyhow, "The Cove in the inner world, what does he look like? Is he the man who's ugly and bad?"

"No," he breathed against my chest.

No elaboration followed, so I pressed, "Tell me about him."

He closed his eyes and when he began to speak, his breathing calmed for the first time since he'd appeared.

"I have black hair. It's longer and falls past my chin, but I like it like that. I have a few tattoos, and my tongue and eyebrow are pierced. I have a different complexion. I play guitar and like to write songs sometimes."

His words fell short as his breathing deepened. The heavy weight of his sleeping body sunk more against my chest. I listened to every small sound he made as my own heart thrashed, unable to settle. I'd never been faced with anything more terrifying in my life. Considering I'd gone completely on instinct, I was glad I'd been able to turn the situation around.

That time.

What would happen next time? The entire evening felt like my fault. Even though I knew Oryn had encouraged and been an equal participant in what had been taking place, I should have known better than to proceed. He'd made it clear that intimacy at that capacity wasn't a possibility, so why did we push those limits?

Guilt consumed me and made it impossible to settle. I held Cove to my chest, rubbed his back, and stroked fingers through his hair on occasion as I thought long into the night.

It was near morning when sleep finally found me, but it was far from peaceful, and visions of losing Oryn to a self-destructive Cove haunted my dreams.

Chapter Twenty-One

The following morning arrived too soon when I was woken by someone planting tiny kisses along my jaw.

"Wakey, wakey, sleepyhead." The kisses moved toward my ear where a tongue licked over my earlobe and teeth nibbled. "It's beach day, remember?"

I fought against the leaded weights keeping my eyes sealed shut and squinted into the morning light streaming through the window at the far end of the den. The face above me shone with the most beautiful smile; innocent and bright.

A wretched headache throbbed through my temple. Between having been up half the night and the disturbed amount of sleep I had managed to get, I felt like shit. The ache and hollowness in my chest hadn't left, and I blinked in confusion as I sorted out who faced me.

"You feeling okay, babe? You look a little grey."

Cohen? He was the only person who tended to use pet names. Also, the slight variation in his speech helped confirm my guess.

I rubbed my eyes and tried to shake away the grogginess that seemed determined to cling. My body ached from having slept all night in the same position with Cove on my chest, so when I sat up, I groaned as my body disapproved.

"I'm okay," I assured him. "Rough night."

I studied his face, wondering if Cohen had any knowledge of what I'd been through. Apart from a hint of concern, he was his usual perky self.

"I put coffee on already," he said as he swung his hips and disappeared into the kitchen. "Do you mind if we stop at the mall before we go to the beach?"

The beach.

Shit, in all the excitement the previous evening, I'd forgotten we'd planned that. Hell, it felt like a plan we'd made years ago, not hours.

"Umm, sure. How come?"

Where was Oryn? Why had I woken up with Cohen?

He returned with two steaming mugs and set them on the coffee table before perching a hand on his hip and curling his nose in the dramatic way Cohen often did. He spun and retrieved something from the chair behind him.

"I need to buy a bathing suit. I don't have one, and I'm not wearing these." He held up black swim trunks with matching yellow stripes on both legs. "Eww, right? Not happening."

I scrubbed a hand down my face and stared at the trunks. My processing skills were slugged out and I still hadn't caught up to the fact that we were going to the beach. In my mind, the struggles I'd had with Cove earlier played on repeat. Hours of standing in the kitchen, holding him and waiting for him to feel safe enough to drop the knife from his grasp.

Cohen shook the swim trunks. "Hello? Did you hear me?"

"Yeah, we can hit the mall."

I blinked away the haunting visions and reached for my coffee. If I was going to spend a day under the hot sun, I was going to need a Tylenol as well. Cohen was perky and excited, and when he was in that kind of a mood, he talked a lot. He certainly didn't act like he'd been up half the night, and I wondered if it affected him the same.

"So what about lunch. Are we packing food? Oh, I know, why don't we just grab some snacks. We can eat breakfast here then snack at the beach and later, when we are done, we can just come back for dinner. Does that sound good?"

I nodded as he spoke, not awake enough to have an opinion.

Once we'd finished our coffees, we made a quick breakfast and got ready to leave. I had to stop at my apartment for swim gear and towels, but once we had that in order, we drove to the mall.

The pounding in my head had lessened as Cohen guided me by the hand toward his store of choice.

"What kind of bathing suit are you looking for exactly?"

Cohen grinned as he pulled me into a fashion store I'd never heard of. "Something sexy and more form fitting than baggy old frumpy shorts."

All my mind could envision was the horror on Oryn's face if he knew Cohen was probably shopping for a Speedo. Not that he wouldn't look incredible wearing one, but his self-confidence would never allow for such things.

"Like these," Cohen squealed as he yanked me toward a rack near the back wall.

Exactly what I'd guessed. Tight little spandex Speedo-type suits all hung on display.

Cohen wiggled his brows and pecked me on the lips, lowering his voice, "Tell me I wouldn't look amazing in one of those."

I couldn't fight the smile. "You'd look amazing."

Oryn might not have had the confidence, but Cohen had no shame. He flipped through the hanging suits until one caught his eye and he pulled it out, holding it up for me to see. It was orange and navy blue.

"We have a winner."

I chuckled as he held it in front of himself and pursed his lips in self-satisfaction.

"All right, show-off, let's go."

"You don't want one? You have the perfect body for it."

I laughed out loud at the suggestion. "Not a chance. I happen to like my frumpy shorts."

"Fine." He grinned facetiously and headed to the counter to pay.

Since there were no change rooms or washrooms of any kind where we were heading, Cohen changed in the mall washroom, putting his new suit on under his clothes. I'd done the same at home.

It was nearing eleven in the morning when I pulled into the public beach parking lot. There were a number of people already soaking up the hot sun or swimming. I grabbed our towels from the backseat and we both took a minute to strip down into our swim suits before heading to the sand.

As distracted as I'd been all morning, the moment Cohen stood in front of me wearing only his tight little spandex Speedo, my mind stuttered.

"See," he said, perching his hands on his hips and turning so I could get a full view. "I look amazing, don't I?"

Amazing didn't even cut it. There were no words.

He stopped with his back turned and peered over his shoulder, jutting his ass out further. "How does my butt look?"

"Stunning," I said, unable to take my eyes from him. Instinct would have normally had me reaching for Cohen, maybe running a hand over his ass, touching all that exposed skin, but my gaze caught on the fresh gouges on his arms and my stomach knotted.

A collision of memories pummeled into me. The screaming, the raking nails down his bare arms. The crying. I'd done that. I'd triggered it all just trying to show him love.

And Oryn hadn't come back that morning. What had I done?

"Hey, babe, are you okay?"

Cohen touched my face, drawing me from that nightmare, and I refocused on him. With a slight shake in my hand, I reached out and gently touched his side, tracing his bare skin.

"Yeah, I'm okay. Umm… sunscreen? We should lather up or we'll burn."

Using the distraction, I rooted through the backseat in search of the bottle I knew I'd grabbed as I worked to stay in the present moment.

"Here," I said pulling it out from where it had fallen in the footwell. "Let me help you."

I squirted a generous blob into my palm and coated both my hands. Cohen turned his back and rested his chin to his chest, exposing his neck.

The entire time I applied the lotion, I tried not to register how incredible he felt. When his back was covered and he faced me, I almost shoved the bottle at him to finish on his own, but the warmth and love radiating from his eyes was more than I could take. Unlike Oryn, Cohen carried little inhibition when it came to expressing emotions. Oryn described Cohen as an apparently normal alter. One who had no knowledge or memories of the past, so he carried himself quite differently than some of the others. He was like any ordinary nineteen-year-old in a sense.

And we'd grown close.

The love in his eyes and the fondness he'd grown for me was never tainted by anything. And he did love me. He'd told me so. Hearing it was bittersweet. Cohen had stolen my heart as much as anyone could, and I loved him as wholly and completely as I did Oryn, but it brought an ache to my chest, knowing he may be the only person to return it.

Cohen seemed oblivious to the previous night and all that had transpired. It was hardly fair to treat him with distance because of my own reservations and concerns over what had happened. So, I bit through the trepidation and added more lotion to my hands. That time, as I worked it over his chest and looked deep into his warm gaze, I did my best to let the heavy weight I carried go.

When the sunscreen was mostly worked in, I pulled him to my chest and kissed him deeply. His hands automatically went to my hair, and his fingers twined around the long pieces in the back. I let his closeness calm and ground me. When we broke apart, he smiled.

"All better?"

He read me like a book.

"All better," I confirmed, hoping it was true.

"Let me slick you up now."

He took the sunscreen and proceeded to cover my body as well. Of course, with Cohen, that included taking it further and goofing around.

He smoothed his hands down my chest, coating every inch of my bare skin, but as he reached the waistband of my shorts, he didn't stop and slipped a hand lower.

"Woah." I clamped a hand over his wrist as he took hold of me under my shorts. "What are you doing?" I glanced around the parking lot in a panic, but no one was around.

"I'm making sure everything is nicely coated." He leaned his body against mine and worked his hand over me once, twice, and again. And my dick responded. "Wouldn't want to burn."

"It's not a nude beach. I think we are safe." Another slow stroke. "Oh, God, you have to stop." Only my actions countered my words, and I rested my head on his shoulder, pushing into his hand again.

"You seem really tense today. You aren't yourself. Just let me, I'll watch for people. You enjoy."

"Cohen…"

"Vaughn," he moved to my ear, brushing his lips over my lobe, "relax and let me."

The reasonable part of my brain told me to stop him. I wasn't a young kid trying to prove something, break rules, and have sex in public places. Those days were behind me—weren't they? However, somewhere deep inside, was a tiny thread, a minute, little, squandered piece that had reached exhaustion after having spent months trying to do what was right for our relationship. That part of me just wanted to be taken care of for a change, even if it was a nineteen-year-old man doing the caring. All the times I'd asked to be trusted, in that moment, I needed to trust him.

I closed my eyes and buried my moans into the curve of his neck as his sunscreen slickened hand moved over my hardening dick. The opened car door blocked a large portion of us from potential onlookers, and Cohen's body shielded me on the other side.

He moved his hand slowly at first, drawing long pulls up and down my shaft, twisting his wrist as he reached my tip and lingering to smooth a thumb along my slit.

"Relax," he whispered against my ear. "Does it feel good?"

I nodded into his shoulder. It was euphoric, and my knees trembled as he picked up his pace. I didn't realize how tightly wound I was until that moment. Every tug landed me closer to the finish line, and I dug fingers into his sides when I was unable to supress a moan.

"God, you're so hard. I love it."

His words weakened my resolve, and even though I didn't think I'd been holding back, I thrusted into his hand, encouraging every movement. Faster and firming his grip, Cohen didn't stop. Tingling in anticipation, I sucked in a breath and held it as my muscles tensed and balls drew up. It was about to hit me, and the force was more intense than I anticipated.

On my next thrust forward, I let go, spilling into his hand and burying my cries into his neck as my orgasm nearly brought me to my knees. His pulls didn't stop, and each consecutive one just managed to draw my release further. The intensity was beyond what I'd expected. When my body calmed, Cohen kept his hand down my shorts and slicked his thumb over my sensitive head.

"How's your stress level now?"

I couldn't think straight. My brain wasn't back online, and I gasped and panted as I caught my breath and tried to orient myself again.

"That was intense."

Cohen brought his face around to mine and I managed to find enough strength to lift from his shoulder and kiss him.

"Thank you," I said as my heart rate returned to normal.

"Anytime, babe." He removed his hand from my pants and grinned. "We better hit the water first. You're kinda a mess."

"I blame you."

He smirked and grabbed the blanket we'd brought from the backseat. "Mmm, worth it."

I snapped up the towels and also brought along the bottle of sunscreen since I didn't get fully covered before we'd become distracted.

We wandered along the shore awhile until we found the spot I had talked about that was less crowded. Most beach-goers tended not to wander far from their cars, and the further from the parking area we went, the quieter it became.

We laid out the blanket, kicked off our shoes and headed for the water. It was a sandy shore, which I loved. I'd been to a few different beaches growing up and I hated when you had to walk over razor sharp pebbles and rocks to get into the water.

Cohen reached the water's edge first, gasped and bounced on his feet when the wave splashed his ankles.

"Holy shit, that's cold."

I laughed and raced past him, snagging his arm as I went by. Cold water had never bothered me.

"Come on, don't be a wimp."

As I dragged him along, he squealed and shrieked, but he never let go of my hand. Once we'd run far enough the water sloshed past our knees, I swung an arm around his shoulder and dove, taking us both under.

When we broke the surface again, Cohen was laughing and sputtering.

"Ah fuck, my nuts just crawled inside my body. This is insane." He couldn't stop laughing, and once he caught his breath, he came after me, tackled me, and pulled me back under.

We horsed around and wrestled as we moved into deeper water. The farther out we went, the cooler it got, but Cohen didn't seem to notice any longer.

Once we were out a distance, the fun wrestling simmered, and Cohen swam over and hooked his legs around my waist. Weightless in the water, I held him up as he hung off my neck. Droplets of water dripped off the end of his nose and sparkled in the sunlight across his face. His smile was radiant and one I treasured. It was unique to Cohen and it calmed my heart when I saw it.

The day was perfect, but I couldn't let go of the underlying longing in my heart to know where Oryn was and if he was okay.

Also, my experience with Cove made me ill when I thought about it. He'd literally worked himself into exhaustion last night. But it didn't mean he was okay. He was far from okay.

Cohen's lips found mine unexpectedly and he kissed me, drawing me from my head. It was short, but it got the effect he wanted.

"There you are." He kissed the tip of my nose. "Do you want to talk about it?"

I squeezed him to my chest and kissed him again before responding, "No. I'm okay."

"You keep saying that."

"I really am."

He watched me a moment more before kissing me a final time and getting down. "Race you to shore?"

I pretended to think about it a minute before tearing past him. "Go!" I yelled before diving under and swimming as fast as I could.

By the time we were relaxed on our blanket, I was exhausted. My lack of sleep was catching up with me, and I laid back and closed my eyes as the warm sun dried me. Cohen sprawled on his belly and rested his chin on my chest as he watched a few other people tossing a frisbee nearby.

I played with his hair as it dried, and when I peeked my eyes open, he smiled.

"What are you thinking?" I asked. His joy was nearly palpable.

"That I love you."

My heart clenched, and I brought a hand to his cheek. Cohen's free mind was something I admired. He was the most observant of all the alters and Oryn. Nothing passed him by.

He leaned into my touch and closed his eyes. I copied and drew up the image of himself he'd painted for me months before. I could see him perfectly the way he wanted to be seen.

"You're beautiful," I said without thought. When he didn't respond, I opened my eyes, knowing he was watching me again.

Always ensuring that when I spoke those words, I was seeing the real him.

When our gazes met, he shimmied up and rested his head on my shoulder. We laid for a while, basking in the heat of the day, not saying anything. A short time later, as I called up the image of Cohen again in my mind, a thought struck.

"Can I ask you something?"

"Always," he mumbled sounding half asleep.

"How do you deal with being in a body that isn't yours? One you don't really like."

He chuckled. "I avoid mirrors."

"Oh."

He'd intended it as a joke, and when I didn't laugh, he lifted his head and peered down at me. "You were serious?"

"Yeah. I mean, how do you make yourself okay with it. It can't be easy seeing yourself as one thing and not being that image. Do you get frustrated? How do you handle it?"

Cohen pursed his lips and looked thoughtful before he got comfortable against me again.

"I do things that help me feel more like me. Like, I fix my hair how I prefer it and not how Oryn maybe wants it. I go shopping and buy clothes that are more my style. Like a Speedo. I put music on and dance. But in all seriousness, the mirror is the kicker. I'm okay with it now. I can see past the reflection, but I used to hate looking in the mirror, because it wasn't me."

I rolled these thoughts around and understood exactly what he explained.

"Why?" he asked.

"Just curious."

He saw through that answer, too, but I didn't elaborate, and he let it go. Maybe Cove needed to learn to be comfortable in new skin. Maybe if he could *be* himself, he could love himself more. I was grasping at straws, but with the amount of self-loathing he'd been expressing the previous night, it was worth a shot.

Later that afternoon, after another long swim, Cohen and I packed up and headed for home. The long day was weighing on me and Cohen knew enough at that point to stop asking what was wrong. I couldn't shake my troubled mind and wasn't willing to talk about it.

When I pulled in his driveway, he shifted in his seat and stared at me head on.

"Do you want to come in for dinner? We can cook something together. Maybe you can spend the night." His hand rested on my knee. "You know?"

I stared at the connection. I did know, but my head wasn't there. My concern for Cove and Oryn was trumping all other emotions, and it wouldn't have been fair to Cohen. My head had already tried to ruin a perfectly good day, the last thing he needed was a full evening of that as well. Especially with what he hinted at. If I was going to agree to go in and spend a night with him, it was only fair he have all of me.

"I think I'm gonna pass tonight."

He stilled, and I gradually raised my head to look at him. The hurt on his face crushed me.

"Vaughn, have we done something wrong?"

We.

I blew out a breath and answered with all honesty.

"You've done nothing, Cohen. I had a rough night last night. It's probably best I try and get some sleep tonight."

When his face didn't change, I leaned in and kissed him with a tenderness I knew he loved.

"I love you. Don't worry, okay? I just need some rest."

He nodded and kissed me again. "I love you, too."

He seemed reluctant to get out of the car, but he eventually wandered his way inside. When the front door closed, I scrubbed a hand down my face as my eyes welled with tears. There were days when I felt I was in over my head.

Chapter Twenty-Two

On my drive home, my phone rang. For a moment, I thought it might be Cohen, still worried over how our day had ended. But after a few rings, I remembered he and the other alters provided Oryn enough privacy to not use his phone when they fronted. The ringing stopped and started again. I tipped my phone to glance at the screen, in case by some miracle it was Oryn. If it was, I'd pull over and take the call in a heartbeat. With all that had gone on, I needed to hear his voice.

It was my mother. I ignored it.

Overwhelmed by the past twenty-four hours, running on barely any sleep, and my nerves completely over-exerted, I couldn't stop the flood of tears when they surfaced. Batting at my eyes, so I could at least see to drive home, I cursed my inability to hold it together. What the hell was wrong with me?

When I pulled into my parking spot, my phone rang for the third time.

"Come on, Mom, now? Really?"

I blew out a few breaths and cleared my throat before answering so hopefully I wouldn't sound like I'd been crying.

"Hello?"

"I knew if I let it ring enough you'd answer. That phone is always in your pocket, you can't fool me."

"Ma, I was driving."

"That's not an excuse."

"It is, actually. It's against the law. They'll suspend my license."

She blew out a nonsense burst of air like she didn't believe me. "What are you up to? Why don't you ever call your mother?"

I leaned back on the headrest and closed my eyes. That was the last thing I needed; a guilt trip over not having visited recently.

"I'm sorry, Mom, I've been busy."

"You still seeing that man?"

"Oryn? Yes."

After Christmas dinner, I'd explained Oryn's disorder on a later visit. As suspected—and as it was with a lot of people—my parents were skeptical and only seemed to go along with it because I was so adamant. Even seven months later, I could hear the doubt in her voice when she asked about him. It upset me, because my parents had always been so open and accepting.

"Why don't you bring him for dinner tomorrow night? Do I have to wait for Christmas again to see this man?"

Tomorrow? I wanted to say no for a million reasons. Primarily, I didn't even know if I'd be in contact with Oryn before tomorrow at dinner hour.

"I'll come. I can ask him if he's available, okay?"

There was silence on the other end, and when she spoke, her tone was softer. "Vaughn, why are you so short with your mother?"

I sighed and pinched the bridge of my nose. "Sorry. I'm just a little stressed out right now. I'll talk to Oryn."

"Is it work?"

"Is what work?"

"The reason you're so stressed."

I didn't want to have that conversation with my mother, especially when it dealt so directly with Oryn's alters and his past.

"It's a lot of stuff. I'm okay. I'll see you at dinner tomorrow."

"Are you sure?"

My bottom lip quivered, and I rested my head on the steering wheel as I fought back more tears. Was I that much of an open book that she could see through me based solely on a phone conversation? Swallowing the bubble which threatened to give me away, I tried to answer with confidence and conviction.

"I'm sure. Talk to you later, Mom. Bye."

I hung up before she had time to analyze my response and call me out again. Without getting out of the car, I started it again and threw it in reverse. Fighting back my emotions, I drove across town toward Evan's.

I was barely in one piece when I arrived, but I pulled myself together the best I could before pounding on his door. When he opened it a moment later and our eyes met, I knew based on his reaction, I looked like hell.

"Hey," I said as I shoved my hands in my pockets and rocked on my feet. "You busy?"

"Nah, come in." He held the door wide and I entered. His gaze seared into me as I walked past. "You look like you got dumped."

I shook my head and kept walking straight into his kitchen where I helped myself to a beer from his fridge. Only after I'd cracked it open and drained half did I turn to face him.

"I had a really shitty night and I need to talk. Can you please put comedy and judgment aside for now and just listen?"

He nodded and motioned for me to grab him a beer as well.

We returned to the living room and I sat on the couch and stared at my hands as I tried to figure out where in the mess to begin. Because it was a sensitive topic, I hadn't shared much about mine and Oryn's sex life—or the fact that we still didn't have one. Nor did Evan know for sure that Cohen and I had finally bridged that obstacle back in April.

All he knew was the conversation we'd had months before when I'd been confused about my feelings for Cohen and his persistent desire for us to have sex.

"I'm gonna say some stuff and I want you to keep this shit between us and try to have an open mind, all right?"

"Vaughn, you know I love you, man. What the hell is going on?"

I took a final swig from my beer and put it aside.

"Last night, after we left the restaurant, I stayed at Oryn's." I messed a hand through my hair, knowing the following words would sound strange, especially to Evan. "We haven't had sex yet.

It's something that may not ever happen between us, and I know that. I knew that from the start."

His face shifted to surprise, but he remained quiet, so I continued.

"Oryn really wishes we were able, and sometimes he pushes his own limits. It triggers him. He ends up switching, and half the time I end up facing off with a very pissed off Reed, or Cohen."

"Which one is Cohen?"

"The nineteen-year-old. Cohen and I do have a sexual relationship now which is why it's sometimes him, but that's beside the point. So last night, Oryn pushed himself too far, and in the middle of making out, he switched. Only this time, it was Cove. Cove is extremely unstable. He's inflicted all kinds of harm to Oryn's body. Remember how I told you that the reason Oryn has DID is because of something that happened when he was a kid?"

Evan nodded and waved a hand like he was trying to remember it all. "Yeah, you said long term abuse. Over a lot of years or something."

"Exactly. Well, Cove carries those memories. I think he's the alter who fronted during all that abuse."

"Fuck." Evan seemed to follow where my story was headed.

"Yeah, so as we are being intimate and trying new things, suddenly Cove is there. He snaps. He goes fucking crazy, yelling he's sorry and that he's bad and ugly. He starts tearing his arms to shreds with his nails and eventually bolts to the kitchen where I need to restrain him from cutting or stabbing himself with a damn knife… For hours, Evan. Hours." I swallowed a lump that seemed determined to form in my throat and blinked back the tears that had sprung up again as I spoke.

"Eventually he passed out from exhaustion. I didn't fucking sleep. Couldn't. It haunted me all night, and this morning, Cohen was there and all perky and ready for the beach day we'd planned. He had no idea what had happened. I took him to the beach, tried to keep my shit together, but I don't know what the fuck to do."

My tears fell steady, no longer in my power to stop. I'd gone from organized to rambling to all out blubbering.

"It was the scariest thing I've ever seen. I feel terrible. I caused that. Cove thought he was back in that time, in that place, and he was out of his mind. Evan, what did I do?"

Evan put his beer down and removed mine from my hand.

"Woah. Stop for a minute and take a breath. Just... try to calm down."

I knew too much emotion was hard for Evan to process. He wasn't that kind of guy and it showed when he became awkward.

"I haven't seen Oryn since it happened. I just wish I knew he was okay. We shouldn't have gone that far... Fuck, I shouldn't have left Cohen. What if Cove comes back and what if—"

"Fuck! Just stop for five seconds, Vaughn. Breathe and listen to me."

My body trembled as I forced back my tears and focused on Evan.

"First of all," he said once I was paying attention. "None of this is your fault. What happened to him as a kid; Isn't. Your. Fault. Do you hear me?" Evan bounced off the couch and raked fingers through his hair.

"Fuck! Okay. I'm gonna be a blunt asshole right now, so deal with it. When is the last time you took time for yourself, Vaughn?"

I shook my head, confused. "What do you mean?"

"I mean, ever since you met Oryn, you've thrown yourself into this relationship full-force. Don't get me wrong, that isn't a bad thing and we all do it when something is new and exciting, but look at yourself! You've said a million times, Oryn isn't like other people. From where I stand, I can tell he's a fuck-of-a-lot more complicated."

"He is, but that's not the problem, the problem—"

"Shh, not your turn. The problem is, Oryn isn't *one* guy. He's eight or whatever."

"Six," I corrected.

"Fine, six. Vaughn, you aren't just throwing yourself head first into a relationship with one guy like normal people, you're drowning in a pool of six. You've been so busy maneuvering your way around six different people and making sure that you get to know them all and form relationships with them all that you've left no time for yourself."

I opened my mouth to respond, but he glared, stopping me.

"You're burnt out."

He didn't get it.

"Evan, I just spent the night with a man who was determined to hurt himself because I triggered Oryn while trying to do things *I know* we shouldn't be doing."

Evan heaved a frustrated sigh.

"No, stop blaming yourself. How old is Oryn?"

"Twenty-nine."

"So, can we agree he's probably been navigating these alters and this life for, I don't know, call it ten years?"

I shook my head, uncertain. Oryn hadn't known about his DID for that long, but he *had* spent years undiagnosed with people in his head. "Maybe."

"Even if it was five years. He's been doing this a long time. He's in therapy. He's learned how to manage life the best he can. You aren't responsible for his disorder. You can't stop what happens to him any more than he can. If Oryn wants to get frisky, and then it causes a shitstorm, that's not on you. This other guy…" Evan waved his hand, looking for me to help him out.

"Cove?"

"Yeah. I'm sure his doctors all know of that issue. And it's been going on for longer than you've been around, am I right?"

I nodded.

"Then stop blaming yourself. You know what you need to do?"

"What?" I mumbled.

"Recognize when you've had enough and give yourself a break. You're entitled to a break, Vaughn. It doesn't mean you don't love him. It doesn't mean you can't help him. But you are no good to anyone if you don't take care of yourself. You've run yourself into the ground."

I wiped a tear as it escaped and trailed down my cheek. Evan glared from where he stood with his arms crossed over his chest.

"You're a real jerk sometimes. Do you have to be so harsh?"

Evan cracked a smile and kicked my foot. "It's because I love you, you dick. I just don't love your dick, which is why you have all these man problems. Now relax. I'm getting you another beer and you are gonna explain to me how the fuck this ménage shit works with Oryn and the nineteen-year-old. Now that makes me curious."

Evan ventured to the kitchen, and I laughed for the first time all evening. "You need three people actively present for a ménage."

"Says who? Why can't it be three people who are in an agreed upon sexual relationship."

"Oryn and I don't..." I groaned, dismissing that argument. "We can't all three be in the same bed. It's not possible."

Evan returned from the kitchen and handed me a beer as he wiggled his brows. "Isn't it, though. Think about it."

I shook my head at his nonsense. "Quit complicating my already complicated relationship. It's not a ménage."

Evan chuckled and sunk back on the couch. "Do you agree you need a breather?"

"Maybe. I just can't help worrying about him."

"That's because you love him. Just try not to take onus for everything that happens."

I picked at the label on my bottle and considered. It sounded easier than it was. Whenever Oryn encouraged more intimacy, I wanted desperately to follow him down that road, but the consequences so far had been negative. So, Oryn and I either needed to agree to curb that part of our relationship, or I needed to stop putting responsibility for the results on my own head.

"I'll try," I said, knowing Evan was waiting for an answer.

We drank through our beers in silence, and when I placed my empty on the coffee table and peered over at Evan, he smirked.

"So, you're finally fucking the nineteen-year-old and I'm just learning about this now?"

I groaned and buried my face in my hands. "Do we have to do this?"

"Hey, man, you just brought your problems to my doorstep, I'm entitled to be curious."

Snapping up my empty, I stood and made my way into the kitchen. "Fine, but I'll need to drink more of your beer if I'm explaining."

Evan chuckled. "I'll never understand why talking about sex makes you so uncomfortable."

We spent the rest of the evening talking. As much as I shared about Cohen and our relationship, it was never enough for Evan. But I put my foot down and changed the subject enough times he took the hint I'd said all I planned to say. Conversations turned to Krystina and then sports and eventually my work.

"I thought after you finished that course you'd be trying to get a transfer or something." Evan said. He laid himself across the couch and shoved me to the cushy chair.

"Not sure a transfer will do it anymore. I'm thinking I need something new altogether. I'm bored."

"I knew it! Didn't I say that way back when you mentioned college courses?"

It was true, and I knew it back then as well. I needed a change.

"Yeah, I'll just keep my eyes open and hope something comes up."

Late into the night, I said goodbye and headed for home once again. I was more relaxed and felt better after having spilled my heart to Evan. When I checked my phone after getting home, a twinge of sadness wormed around my heart when there were no messages from Oryn. I hated the idea of being without him for so long.

The following morning was Sunday. I woke late after a restless night and it was after ten before I wandered to the kitchen. I checked my phone as I set the coffee pot to brew. There were still no messages from Oryn, so I typed him out one, not expecting a reply.

Good morning! Please give me a call if you get this. We've been invited for dinner at my parents tonight. No pressure, just gonna call her around noon and confirm if we're going.

I tossed my phone on the counter and waited for the pot to finish. With a full cup of coffee, I made my way into the living room and lounged on the couch as I flipped through the stations on the TV. Sunday morning programing sucked. I left it on some home renovation show and zoned out while I drank my coffee. Everything Evan had said the night before played on repeat in my mind. Oryn was a grown man who had been dealing with his DID for many years. It was me who wasn't used to it. I understood I couldn't be to blame for his past, but triggering him like I had burned a hole right through my heart.

"Stop blaming yourself. It isn't your fault."

I closed my eyes and listened to Evan's words, trying to make myself believe them. Without knowing when, I nodded off and was woken some time later to a knocking on my door. I startled awake and peeled myself off the couch as I yawned. The knocking sounded again; a soft, gentle rapping. I checked my phone as I slugged my way to answer it.

Twenty after twelve. Shit, my day was over half gone and I'd done nothing. I hadn't even called my mother.

I pulled the door open, not sure who I was expecting—Evan maybe—and froze when I saw Oryn on the other side. Or was it?

"Oryn?"

He smiled apologetically and shook his head. "Theo."

My hopes fell, and the disappointment must have registered on my face based on the look of sympathy returned to me.

"Can I come in?" he asked.

Of all Oryn's alters, Theo was the most like him; reserved, soft-spoken, gentle, and kind. The major difference being that Theo tended not to exhibit a great deal of emotion, so all of Oryn's worry and anxiety weren't present. He also held himself with a significant amount more confidence. I was grateful Theo wasn't one to play games, because he could easily fool me if he wanted to.

I backed up a step and allowed him to enter. We hadn't spent a great deal of time together, but I was getting to know Theo better. Ours was a solid friendship, and I knew that was all it would ever be. There was no attraction otherwise, and based on what I'd learned about Theo, there probably wouldn't be.

"Did you want a coffee or something? I can make a fresh pot." The one I'd made when I'd gotten up had long ago shut off.

"Sure, thank you."

I grabbed my cold mugful off the coffee table and returned to the kitchen where I dumped it down the drain. Theo followed and stood quietly as I worked to re-set the pot to brew. The longer the void expanded, the more uncertain I became. Why was he there?

He seemed to read my unvoiced concerns, and once I turned and leaned on the counter to wait for the coffee to brew, he spoke, "Oryn is taking a break. Things are a little chaotic right now in the system."

"Is he co-conscious with you right now?"

"No."

I nodded and ducked my head to stare at the floor. Those feelings of guilt returned, and I couldn't swallow them down.

"I came by so maybe I can help you understand better. Cohen was a little frantic last night, thought you were pulling away and ready to give up on us."

I jerked my head up and was about to defend myself when Theo waved a hand dismissing it.

"Cohen is a spaz sometimes. Ignore it. I calmed him down and filled him in on what he was missing."

I blew out a relieved breath. The last thing I was doing was pulling away. "You guys all have to understand how hard it is being on the outside of all this."

"And you need to understand how hard it is being on the inside of all this."

I couldn't in a lifetime imagine.

"Coffee's done," Theo said, indicating to the pot. "Let's have a seat and I'll try and explain some things."

I automatically made Theo's coffee all wrong, adding two scoops of sugar how Oryn liked it and not taking into account that Theo had his own tastes. Black, no sugar.

We settled on the couch and Theo proceeded to let me into his world as much as was possible.

"Oryn and Cove are at odds. They always have been. Cove desecrates the body and Oryn does everything in his power to keep Cove locked away so he can't. Problem is, the more they fight, the worse Cove is."

"But..." I wasn't sure how to express what I'd seen; what I knew. "I don't think Cove is doing it to be defiant. I think he's hurting a whole lot."

Theo smiled. "Exactly. Dr. Delmar has been trying to work with Oryn to help him understand that. The harder he tries to block Cove from the system, the worse he'll be. If Oryn accepted him and talked to him, Dr. Delmar believes we could get closer to achieving a full system of co-consciousness all the time."

"Isn't that what Oryn wants?"

"Yes."

I threaded fingers through my messy brown hair. "I don't understand. Then why not talk to Cove and work out their differences?"

Theo sipped his coffee and took a moment before continuing. "That's simple. Oryn fears knowing Cove. Cove is the key to his past. A past Oryn doesn't want to remember."

Bile stirred in my stomach and I nodded, looking down into my coffee where it was hugged in my hands.

"I don't think Cove wants to share anyhow, at least from the impression I got."

"He doesn't." When I didn't speak for a few minutes, Theo set his coffee down and shifted. "The reason I'm telling you this, is so you can have a better understanding of Cove. He's hard to reach. If Oryn can form stronger bonds with the system as a whole, he will find a better balance in his life. The sudden triggers will lessen, and he will have more control, but it's all based around good communication and contracts with the system."

"How do you know all this?"

"I listen in therapy. Oryn and I have the strongest bond and closest relationship in the inner world, and it shows in what we are able to do together."

I considered what he explained and asked, "Can he really achieve that with everyone?"

"Absolutely, if he wants to. The system is strong together. The reason he hasn't been able to attain more with the others is because of his poor relations with Cove. Cohen is fiercely protective of Cove and loves him dearly. He hates to see him out-casted. Reed shares a certain comradery with him. They both defend the system. They both have extreme trust issues. But the pair go hand in hand. Without trusting and giving strength to Cove, Oryn will never win Reed."

"And Rain?"

Theo chuckled, and his face lit up like I'd never seen it do before. "He's a child. When the system is whole, he will follow suit. Right now, I ensure he stays away from the problems."

As complex as it all sounded, what Theo explained made sense. My coffee had gone cold as I'd listened, and when I drained the last mouthful, I cringed.

"Is there anything I can do?" Evan's words rang in my head again, reminding me to not take it all on my shoulders, but I loved Oryn and if there was any way at all I could help him settle within his system, I would do it.

"Not really. Encourage Oryn to talk to Cove more. Maybe if it's not just a doctor telling him, he'll listen."

I nodded as Theo stood. "I should probably let you enjoy your Sunday," he said as he made his way to the door.

"Theo," I called, catching up with him. He shoved his feet in his shoes and turned to me. "Can... Can I ask you something?"

"Of course."

"Oryn he... he seems to want things between us that don't seem possible. It's a landslide every time. Should I be discouraging that? Is that hurting him?"

Theo appeared thoughtful for a minute, looking inward as he pursed his lips. "What's hurting Oryn right now is the system's malfunction. I think... if he learns to work with the flow instead of against it, he'll be able to achieve more of the things in life he wants."

As I analyzed his words, Theo opened the door and started down the hall to the elevators. If I understood right...

"Theo," he slowed his pace but didn't turn. "So are you saying it is possible?"

"It is possible." He continued to the end of the hall and I watched him go. When he was about to turn the corner, he paused and peered back. "In time, Vaughn. He can't rush things. Trust is the foundation for everything."

Then he was gone.

When I returned inside my apartment, I flopped on the couch and laid there for over an hour, thinking. When it dawned on me I was supposed to have dinner with my mother, I called and cancelled, explaining it was a bad time and I'd make plans another night when Oryn and I were both free. She was disappointed, but I wasn't sure she'd understand, even if I explained.

Chapter Twenty-Three

I didn't hear from Oryn all week. The constant silence ate at me and made me pace for days. When I'd dropped by his house on Wednesday, I'd been confronted with Theo again. He'd told me to have patience and that Oryn needed a break.

When I'd express that to Evan, he'd thrown his hands up and declared he agreed one-hundred-percent. So, I tried. It didn't mean my brain stopped. I still checked my phone religiously, and at night, I missed him.

I used the extra time to catch up on some reading and to research online for a support network of people who were in relationships with people who had DID. Surprisingly, I found a few. Not only did I read a mountain of information on how to cope when your partner has DID, but the chatrooms were filled with individuals who truly understood my struggles. Not everyone was in the same boat, but there was at least an element of support I'd been missing.

On Friday, we had a big meeting at work to discuss a plan for expansion within the city, and there was discussion over transferring pre-existing team members for a short time to help establish the new facility. It was long, drawn-out, and boring.

When my phone buzzed in my pocket, I dashed a look around and slipped it out to check who was calling. The number came up as Harbor County Hospital Groups. I flinched and was about to re-pocket it as a wrong number when a chill ran through me, and I excused myself as I ran from the room to answer it.

"Hello."

"Hi, is this Vaughn Sinclair?"

"It is." My heart jumped to my throat. "What's this about?" I croaked.

"Hi, Mr. Sinclair, this is Becky Roberts, I'm a nurse at Harbor County Hospital. I have your number listed as an emergency contact for an Oryn Patterson. Is that correct?"

My hand shook, and I had to hold my phone in a tight grasp so I wouldn't drop it. "Yes, that's correct. What happened?"

Only a month before, Oryn had asked if he could add me as an emergency contact in his file. He'd explained he'd never had an alternate contact and they bugged him about it frequently. I'd agreed without thought, not really realizing what it could mean.

"Oryn was brought in for emergency care earlier today. Due to the nature of the injuries, he's been moved to the third floor and admitted to the psychiatric ward for the standard seventy-two-hour observation. I have in his file here that he's under the care of Dr. Delmar for dissociative identity disorder. By the look of it, once he's seen by the doctor, he'll probably be discharged. However, given the later hour, that may not happen until tomorrow."

Injuries? Psychiatric ward? Oh, Oryn. I could only imagine what had taken place.

"Umm... thank you for letting me know. Do you know if he's allowed visitors?"

"The ward allows visitors until eight at night, so yes."

I noted the floor and directions and thanked the nurse again. My meeting was still in progress, but there was no way I was returning after that call. I needed to get to the hospital.

I left my boss a message with his assistant and slipped out into the mid-July heat. As I raced to my car, I shed my tie and unbuttoned my shirt to let the minimal breeze cool my already heated skin.

I cranked the air conditioning and didn't wait for it to kick in before I pulled out of the lot and headed directly for the hospital. Visions of the last time Cove had cut him flashed through my mind. I'd seen him days after it had happened, and although they'd been stitched and partly healed, it had made me ill.

Was that what I was walking into, or would it be worse?

The hospital parking was ridiculous, and I paid to park in the emergency area before racing to the main hospital doors. At the information booth in the lobby, I sought directions from an elderly volunteer who spent far too long explaining how to get to the right set of elevators to reach the secured floor where the psychiatric ward was located.

When I reached the floor in question, the elevator doors opened to a small, sparsely furnished lobby and a large metal door with an intercom system off to the side. As I suspected, the door was locked.

I mashed my finger on the intercom and waited. Within a few seconds, a distant voice came over the speaker.

"How can I help you?"

"Umm... Yes, I'm here to visit Oryn Patterson. I got a phone call saying he was admitted this afternoon."

"I'll send a nurse down to let you in."

"Thank you."

I bounced on my feet as I waited. My heart hadn't stopped pounding since I'd received that call, and despite the cooler air in the building, I was sweaty—probably more from nerves than heat.

There was a buzz and then the large door was pushed open by a young, extremely well-built male nurse. The guy looked more like high security than a caretaker.

Instead of allowing me through, he entered into the small lobby and dropped an empty cardboard box on the ground.

"I need you to empty your pockets; cellphone, wallet, loose change, keys, all of it. Also, you'll need to remove your shoes."

When I paused in confusion, he shrugged. "Policy, sorry. I take it this is your first visit?"

"Yeah," I said, nudging my shoes off and placing them in the box. Next, I emptied my pockets.

When Mr. Macho nurse noticed my belt, he had me add that to his collection as well.

"I'll take you down to the nursing station. You'll need to sign in. Just let us know when you're ready to leave and we'll walk you out with your belongings."

I nodded as I followed him through the metal door. It didn't look any different than the rest of the hospital; same long hallway of rooms with two single beds in each from what I could see. There was a common area with a TV high up on the wall out of reaching distance from the patients. A noticeable difference were the windows. They were all barred with heavy metal grates over top.

At the nursing station, I signed a form and was directed to another common room down further where I was told I'd find Oryn. As I wandered down the hall, I stuck close to the wall, a little unnerved by some of the patients I passed. There was a man yelling at nothing who seemed angry, but no nurse was nearby, so I assumed it was normal behavior for him.

A sketchy looking woman glared as I walked past. She fidgeted with her hands nonstop and seemed to be muttering to herself.

I walked faster.

When I rounded the corner, and a brightly lit room came into view, I breathed a sigh of relief. It was vacant, except for Oryn who sat on the window ledge, leaned against the metal bars as he peered outside.

The entire roof was made up of sky lighting which gave the room a much more comforting vibe. There were tables and plastic chairs all around, and it gave me the sense that it was probably used as their dining hall at meal time.

Before I approached, I observed him from a distance. He wore a tacky hospital ensemble in baby blue; elastic pants and pull-over shirt. It'd been a week, and the moment I saw him—knowing it was really him and not anyone else—tears sprung to the surface. I didn't want to be a mess, so I dried my eyes and worked to keep it together. The last thing he needed was more on his plate.

He was distant and seemed lost in his head. Although he wore a long-sleeved shirt, I could tell by the bulk under one arm that he was heavily bandaged.

I crossed the room silently, and only when I was within a half-dozen feet did I let my presence be known.

"I've missed you," I whispered.

When he turned and I saw the shimmer in his eyes, I couldn't hold back the tears. He was on his feet and in my arms before I could take my next breath, and I crushed him to my chest as though I could somehow root him in place so he wouldn't retreat.

I cried into his shoulder, the impact of my week surfacing and aching through my body.

"I'm sorry." I pulled back and dried my tears. Then I looked him over thoroughly, ensuring there weren't more injuries I might have missed. "How are you?"

He shrugged, the sadness on his face unhidden. "S-same shit, dif-f-ferent day." He sighed. "I feel like eventually, one day, he's j-just gonna end it." Tears welled in his eyes and he shook his head in defeat. "And I'll have no idea. I h-hate him. God, Vaughn, I hate him so m-much."

He collapsed against my chest and buried his face as his own tears fell. Oryn generally said little about Cove. He avoided topics pertaining to him and the havoc Cove reeked on his body at all cost. It was exactly as Theo had described. They weren't friends. By the sound of it, they made better enemies. In an ordinary situation, they might never have chosen to be around each other, except Cove and Oryn shared a space that was more intimate than any other human being could imagine.

That was a problem.

I guided Oryn to a table and slid over a chair so we faced each other. Once he'd pulled himself together, I took his hand.

"What happened? Do you know?"

Defeat returned, and he shook his head. "Not really. I know it was Cove. I'm not stupid. Cohen hasn't hurt me in a long time, but Cove's been so angry lately. Theo called for help, I know, but I didn't have any sense of time until they were stitching me up downstairs." He touched over the bulk under the sleeve of his shirt. "He got me good this time, I guess."

Just then a young man who appeared to be in his early twenties wandered in the room and sat at a nearby table. He rocked, fidgeted, and muttered something I couldn't make out, and his eyes danced all around. Although we were only two tables away, he didn't seem to notice us.

"That's Ethan. He's in and out of here a lot. He's nice, when you can get him to talk. Not sure what's wrong with him."

I watched Ethan as he stared up at the skylights with a look of concentration on his face. From Ethan, my gaze fell to a young woman who walked past and paused to look in the room before continuing on her way.

"Nora," Oryn said, following my gaze. "She's bi-polar."

I shifted back to Oryn with an overwhelming sadness clinging to every part of me. "You know a lot of the people here?"

"I've spent a lot of time here." He pulled up the sleeve on his uninjured arm, revealing the countless scars underneath. "Every time he does this, it earns me an automatic evaluation and up to seventy-two hours of lock-up time. Dr. Delmar will sign for my release tomorrow. You see, I'm not the one who is unstable. Cove is. They already have us on an anti-depressant. Any other treatment plans or drugs they can offer him can't be given, because me and four other people aren't affected by those same problems. The treatments are a lot heavier and would affect the entire system."

He pulled his sleeve back down and rubbed a knuckle against his eye before continuing, "They used to keep me here longer, but it was pointless. So long as I'm here, Cove retreats. When I show no signs of being unstable, they have no reason to keep me. I'm in therapy. I'm on the only drugs I can be on." He shrugged. "I wish he'd just leave us alone."

There were so many things I wanted to say and ask, but it didn't feel like the right time. I knew from Theo that it was essential for Oryn and Cove to learn to co-exist with each other.

According to his therapist, the harder Oryn tried to deny him presence, the worse he would make it for himself. He had to know that. Didn't he believe it?

The bitterness he held toward Cove was thick in that moment—and for good reason—so I changed the subject, hoping to cheer him up.

"Do they at least feed you well?"

Oryn attempted a smile and scanned the mostly vacant room. "Not really. But Theo spoils me, so maybe it's not fair for me to judge."

When he found my face again, I reached over and caressed his cheek. It solidified his smile and my heart calmed with its presence.

"Am I allowed to bring you food? I know they did everything but strip search me coming in here, but maybe I can at least sneak you in a decent breakfast tomorrow morning."

Oryn's brow scrunched as he thought. "I think so. Other people's families have done that before, so it must be allowed. You just can't bring cutlery in here. Anything that can be used as a weapon is a no-no."

"Gotcha. So what do you say I bring you a nice breakfast sandwich and coffee when visiting hours start tomorrow? Save you eating hospital food."

"I'd like that," he said, lowering his gaze to his lap. "I feel bad taking you away from your day like this. I'm really sorry. If you don't want—"

"Shh." I brought his chin up and stopped his words with a kiss. I kept it chaste and quick, unsure how he'd feel about such a display of affection in the middle of the unit. "I'm just happy to see you again. It's been a long week."

He twisted fingers through my hair and wouldn't let me pull too far away as his worry deepened.

"Have I really been gone a week? I don't even know what day it is."

I tried not to let the pain his statement brought show. "Yeah. It's Friday again. We went for dinner with Evan and Krystina last Friday, and that's the last…" I bit back my words, unsure I should draw attention to the incident that had caused his week-long absence.

"I remember," he whispered, bringing his forehead to mine.

Nothing more was said, and we stayed in that closely connected bond, touching each other and absorbing our missed time until the male nurse who'd collected my belongings came in the room.

"Orion, Orion, my man, I'm calling dinner. Just a heads up."

Oryn sat back and smiled at the nurse. "Thanks, Talus."

Nurse Talus winked and wandered back out of the room.

"Orion?" I asked as Oryn shuffled to his feet and took my hand.

"He likes to tease me. When he first started, he was working midnights and I was having a rough night. He found me in my room staring at the stars and sat with me for hours just to talk. He asked me why I was named after a constellation. I had a blond moment and didn't realize he was messing with me and corrected him, telling him my name was Oryn, not Orion. So, it stuck. Now I'm officially Orion to him. I earned the stupid nickname fair and square."

Oryn dragged me from the room and down the hall.

"Why are you escaping dinner?"

He turned into one of the rooms and went to the far bed by the window and sat, pulling me beside him.

"Because it's extremely chaotic at meal times. I don't handle it well and the nurses let me eat after it calms down. Talus initiated that for me, too. He's a really great guy. He looks out for me."

I could only imagine what meal times in a psychiatric ward would look like. Based on the few people I'd passed in the hallway, even my own comfort level was being tested. I was glad Oryn had the support he needed.

"He's a pretty big guy for a nurse. I always imagined nurses to be... I don't know, not as buff."

Oryn laughed and nodded. "I know, right. He's in the right spot actually. Things can get out of hand sometimes, and he's the perfect person to handle it."

I had to agree.

I stayed around through dinner and up until Talus came and found us in Oryn's designated room to announce visiting hours were ending.

"I hate leaving you here," I said as he walked me to the front desk, so I could collect my belongings.

"Don't worry about me. This place isn't scary anymore. I'm used to it."

And what a horrible thing to be used to. I didn't voice my thoughts. Before we arrived at the desk, I pulled him aside and glided fingers down his cheek.

"I'll be back in the morning with breakfast. What time do you think you'll be discharged?"

"Dr. Delmar generally comes in around ten. He sees a number of patients here, but he'll normally squeeze me in first since it's just policy we talk before he signs the papers."

"Okay." I kissed him once before begrudgingly parting from his inviting hold. "I love you. Please take care of yourself."

"I will. I'll see you tomorrow."

Leaving was hard. Driving across town, knowing why he'd been admitted and that it was out of his control, weighed heavy on my heart. Having seen Cove in action, having watched the pain and self-hatred rolling off him that night a week before, I struggled to blame him. As much as I hated the idea of bringing up such a sensitive topic, maybe I needed to share what I'd witnessed. If Oryn could get past his anger, maybe he'd be more willing to work on his relationship with Cove and things could get better for him.

Chapter Twenty-Four

I set my alarm the following morning so I could be showered, out the door, and at the hospital by nine. With Oryn's takeout breakfast and coffee in hand, I rode the elevator to the third floor.

More familiar with the routine that time, I was prepared when a different nurse came through the secured door and asked me to fill the cardboard box with any loose items including shoes, and belt. That time, the nurse also inspected the bag of food I'd brought to ensure I hadn't unknowingly included cutlery. Once I passed inspection, I was granted access and found my way to the front desk to sign in.

Oryn was in his room when I arrived. He was dressed in the same hospital scrubs he'd been wearing the previous day as he laid on his bed and stared at the ceiling. He didn't appear to be sharing the room with anyone. The bed closer to the door was made and there was no indication of a roommate.

The moment I walked in, Oryn's face lit up. It was good to see, especially with his current situation.

"Good morning. I brought food."

He accepted the bag and coffee and peeked inside. "Thank you. I'm so glad. Breakfast today looked sketchy. I probably wouldn't have eaten. And the coffee is terrible."

He placed the baggie with his sandwich aside and cracked his coffee.

"How was your night? Did you sleep?"

He shrugged, taking a careful sip before placing it aside. "Some. These beds aren't exactly comfortable. I'll be glad to get home."

Just as he was about to unwrap his food, a lady nurse with dark, shoulder-length hair came in with a carrier of medical supplies hooked over her arm.

"Hey, Oryn, gonna change your bandage before Dr. Delmar comes, okay."

Oryn dashed a weary glance at me before nodding.

"Do you want me to step out?" I asked.

"Nah, it's okay."

I got the sense he hated me seeing what Cove had done. In all honesty, I had to swallow my nerve as the nurse rolled his sleeve up his arm. Oryn's gaze burned into me, and I looked at him instead as she unwrapped the bandage. I didn't need to see. When he went home, I'd offer to help then, especially considering it was his right arm that time and it would be tricky to care for when Oryn wasn't left-handed.

The nurse worked fast. When Oryn winced, a ripple of sympathy pain webbed through my gut. I hated seeing him like that. Once she finished, she took blood—Oryn explained it was routine—and she left.

"Please eat before your doctor shows up and you miss your chance."

As Oryn picked at his food with less enthusiasm than I'd hoped, I considered the rest of the day—or rather the up-coming days and how they might play out.

"Vaughn?"

"Yeah," I said, refocusing on Oryn. He'd placed his half-eaten sandwich aside and was studying me.

"I've told Dr. Delmar about you. Quite a bit. Do you want to sit in on our talk today? He's mentioned he'd like to meet you."

I'd always considered Oryn's therapy appointments to be extremely private and had never asked about them. Knowing he'd mentioned me to his doctor was a surprise.

"Sure. If you want me there, I'll be there. But I'm happy to wait outside or here while you see him. I know these things are personal and—"

"Vaughn, I included you on my emergency contacts, and we've been dating for seven months, I'm okay with you being present. Really."

Just after ten, an older man in jeans, a brown and white dress shirt, and a white doctor's coat walked in Oryn's room. He had dark, salt and pepper hair that was cut short and combed to the side. The beard he wore was well maintained. At his entrance, Oryn sat up straighter and passed me a comforting smile.

"Good morning..." The doctor tipped his head to the side and studied Oryn's face a moment before continuing, "Oryn. You know I don't like finding out you're in the ward." He had a thick accent I couldn't place, but his tone was good natured and Oryn smiled.

"I know." He touched his bandaged arm almost self-consciously and dashed a look in my direction. "Oh, this is my boyfriend, Vaughn, the man I told you about. If it's okay, I told him he could sit in this morning."

Dr. Delmar shook my hand. "A pleasure." Then he nodded to Oryn as he pulled a chair up and sat down. It looked as though we were meeting right there in Oryn's room. "I think having Vaughn present is a great idea."

I positioned myself beside Oryn on the bed and took his hand.

"Okay," Dr. Delmar said, nodding to Oryn's arm. "Tell me what you know."

"Same old, same old," Oryn mumbled, covering the affected area as though to shield it from view. "We had a rough week. Theo said Cove's been extreme."

"And whose been fronting this week?"

Oryn blew a breath from his nose and pursed his lips. "I think mostly Theo."

"You think? Why aren't you communicating?"

"I am, it's just—"

"It's just you are being selective and not inclusive. Have you talked to Cove? Have you asked him why?"

"No."

"No. Always no. And why not?"

Oryn's nose curled and he brought a hand up to his face. He rubbed at his eye and shook his head ever so slightly. I recognized that action, but so did the doctor.

"Who is talking to you right now?" Dr. Delmar asked.

"Th-Theo."

"You tell Theo, we are having a chat and it's not his turn."

I was shocked at how firm Dr. Delmar was being with Oryn. He was no-nonsense in his approach. For whatever reason, I always assumed he'd be more gentle and understanding.

Oryn lowered his hand and shifted his gaze to his doctor. The expectance on Dr. Delmar's face confused me. Only when Oryn nodded did I understand. He was waiting for confirmation that Oryn had complied with his request.

"Now. Tell me why Cove is angry."

Oryn shrugged like a dejected teenager. "I don't know."

"Is he journaling?"

"Yes."

"What does he write to you?"

"He doesn't write to me. He rants and puts hate all over the pages."

Dr. Delmar narrowed his eyes a moment before crossing his arms over his chest.

"Let me talk to him."

"No!" Oryn snapped, panic crossing his face for the first time. "I-I c-can't... he w-won't listen. He hates me."

It took everything in me not to intervene. What the hell was the doctor doing? I reached for Oryn's hand to calm him, but Dr. Delmar raised a finger up to stop me.

"Oryn. Listen to me." Dr. Delmar leaned in and seared his gaze into Oryn. "He will not go away if you ignore him. He will only become worse the harder you try to restrain or control him. If you want peace in your system, you need to find a balance with Cove. Do you hear me?"

Tears flooded Oryn's eyes and I fought the urge to reach for him again. He nodded, but it was strained and forced.

"The easy communication you have with Theo can be achieved with everyone."

"I know."

"I'm glad you know. Now what are you going to do about it? I'm getting tired of seeing you in here."

Oryn didn't answer, but ducked his head and remained quiet. All that time, I'd walked eggshells around Oryn, treading carefully every day we'd been together. The doctor seemed to have a vastly different approach and didn't allow for any bullshit. It was a surprising, yet eye-opening perspective.

"And how are you managing, Vaughn?"

I startled when the conversation flipped to me. "Umm, I…" Shifting my gaze to Oryn, I paused a moment, but decided to answer honestly. "I had a rough week. This can be a lot to take sometimes."

"Undoubtedly."

Oryn's forehead creased at my confession and his teeth found his lip. That time, when I reached for his hand, I wasn't stopped.

"It's hard not to blame myself."

"Vaughn," Oryn shook his head and the emotion in his voice was thick. "Why would you blame yourself? None of this is your fault."

I cut my eyes to Dr. Delmar and grimaced. It wasn't a conversation I'd planned to have with witnesses.

"It's hard not to," I said to Oryn. "Sometimes, I feel like I trigger the switches, and I never mean it. Then I feel horrible after the fact."

When Oryn went to reply, he was silenced by the same finger that had halted my movement before.

"Being in a relationship with a person who has DID can be extremely taxing. It's easy to get run down while you try to keep up with sudden switches and various personalities day in and day out. What kind of support system do you have in place, Vaughn? Because people in your situation often find they need help, too."

"I just found an online group this week actually. I've chatted with a couple people already who are in the same boat, but have been at it far longer. It's been really insightful."

"That's excellent."

"You are?" Oryn cut in. "I didn't know that."

I squeezed his hand. "I haven't seen you in a week."

"Well, like I tell Oryn, the key to any functioning system—or relationship—is communication." Dr. Delmar slapped his knee, drawing both our attentions and snapping the tension that had grown taut over the past few minutes. "I'm going to sign your discharge. To avoid sounding like a broken record, you tell me what needs to be done from here, Oryn."

"Talk to Cove."

"On Tuesday, bring your journals. I want to hear how it went."

Oryn's discharge took another hour. By the time they gave him back his clothes and I had collected my personal belongings, it was after noon. We drove to his house in relative silence, and when we pulled in the driveway, Oryn shifted and asked, "Will you... do you mind staying?"

I cut the engine and smiled. "If you thought I was dropping you off and running, you're wrong. You're not getting rid of me that easily."

In fact, I'd taken it upon myself to pack an overnight bag and left it in the backseat. Unless Oryn was adamant that I leave, I was spending the night. I needed to be with him, especially with all the worry that had consumed me over the past week.

While he showered, I went through his kitchen cupboards and fridge to find us something to have for lunch. I settled on a large foil tray full of cabbage rolls that I found in the freezer. It was way more than we needed for lunch, but I figured by the time it heated it would be enough food to be a satisfying 'lupper'.

Thank you, Theo.

By the time we ate and cleaned up, it was after four. We settled in on the couch and Oryn snuggled against my side. The contentedness that moment brought was long overdue. Neither of us spoke for a long time, simply enjoying being in each other's company was enough. All the guilt and anxiety the week had carried with it moved into the background.

I combed fingers through his hair and kissed the top of his head. The fresh scent of his shampoo tickled my nose as I breathed him in.

"Am I too much for you?" he asked randomly, tearing me from my thoughts.

"What? No."

He shifted his head over so he could look at me. "You said you had a rough week, and that I'm a lot to take."

"Not you, the situation." I encouraged him to sit up so I could explain. "Last Friday, I spent almost the entire night with an extremely unstable Cove. It was frightening, and I didn't know how to handle it. I managed, but then the following day I wasn't even given a moment to process and Cohen was geared up and ready for the beach."

Oryn's face paled at the mention of Cove's name.

"What did he do?"

I tried to think about the most delicate way to explain. I wasn't so sure I saw Cove in the same light as Oryn any longer. I hoped sharing, as difficult as it was, would help Oryn accept Cove and maybe try what his doctor had suggested.

"I think he was triggered out based on what we were doing. Do you remember?"

Oryn nodded and a flash of sadness crossed his face.

"Oryn, I don't think Cove hates you. He hates himself. Everything I saw, everything I witnessed, showed me a man who is in agony because he carries so much self-loathing he doesn't know how to cope."

Oryn shook his head as tears welled and glistened in his eyes. "No, you're wrong."

It wasn't like I knew his inner world, or could even pretend to understand, but I knew what I'd witnessed. Cove was so broken inside, he could barely function.

"Oryn, he—"

He flew off the couch, batting at the tears slipping down his cheeks. "I'll show you."

He disappeared down the hall and returned a moment later with what I recognized was his journal. He flipped through a few pages and opened it wide, placing it on my lap.

What was drawn on the page was a depiction of pain like I'd never seen before in my life. The words 'die' and 'hate you' were etched in with such force I could feel the grooves under my fingers. There were scribbled, angry lines and holes where the pen had broken through the page. A few coherent passages were intermixed with the destruction. 'I'll never let you in.' 'I'd rather suffer alone.' 'Once bad, always bad.' And so forth and so forth...

I couldn't keep reading. My stomach turned, and rotting bile inched its way up my throat. Shifting the journal back into Oryn's lap, I took a minute to compose myself.

"See," he said. "He wants me to die. He hates me."

I shook my head, understanding how Cove's messages could be misconstrued. "No. Oryn, hear me out. That's not directed at you. That's directed at himself. Cove feels trapped inside a body he hates. Not you. He…" I took Oryn's hand as I was about to tread somewhere we'd never gone before, and I feared where it might land us. "He's been through hell. Cove is the one who was created to withstand the abuse when you were a child, wasn't he?"

It was the first time I'd even suggested that Oryn may have had an abusive past. But I no longer carried doubt. Between my studies on DID and our intimacy barrier, it didn't take a rocket scientist to figure out there was probably a history of abuse.

Oryn froze with widened eyes, but nodded robotically.

"I d-don't know anything about it. Except th-that it happened."

I touched his face, drawing his focus. "And we aren't going to talk about it," I reassured him. "All I'm saying is that Cove underwent a lot of trauma... in this body. The body he now hates and finds ugly. The body he's trapped inside with all the memories that he can't let go of."

Oryn's lip quivered. "B-b-but I don't want him to tell me. I don't want t-t-to know."

I could barely breathe watching the fear pass over my boyfriend's face.

"He doesn't want to tell you. But he's trying desperately to find alternate ways to handle that pain inside. Those feelings of helplessness, ugliness, the self-loathing, he lashes out to make that pain less. Physical pain he can handle. He told me so. So if he inflicts physical pain, the emotional pain doesn't hurt as badly."

Oryn's thoughts turned inward as he considered what I said. He vibrated and shivered, and I brought him against my chest and held him. Maybe I was wrong. But if I was right, then maybe Oryn could make strides in the right direction like his doctor and Theo seemed to think he needed to do.

"What do I do? I don't think we can ever get along. He won't listen to me. He never has."

The following suggestion was a stab in the dark, but when I'd heard Cohen talk the other day, it had dawned on me that it could possibly help Cove as well.

"Maybe encourage him to be himself more. Let him freely express himself like Cohen does. Encourage him to shop for clothes he wants to wear. In the inner world, he told me he liked to play guitar. If he had an outlet and could be Cove on the outside too, maybe it would help."

"He'll probably want to tattoo my body or pierce it or something drastic."

"Set limits. Be willing to discuss those more permanent additions in time."

Oryn flinched. "But I don't want a tattoo."

"But if a small, inconspicuous tattoo helped balance your system and Cove, wouldn't it be worth it?"

Oryn pressed a knuckle in his eye, rubbing at it. When he caught my questioning look, he smiled. "Theo, it seems, agrees with you."

"Perfect. Two against one. Will you try?"

"I'll try," he whispered, sounding less sure than I'd have liked.

Since Oryn refused to allow me to go home, I collected my overnight bag from the car and we got ready for bed. It was getting late when we crawled in since we'd spent all evening chatting about Cove and how he could encourage him to embrace his identity on the outside.

Oryn cuddled against my side and rested a hand on my bare chest, tickling fingers up and down. I tried to ignore the bulky bandage covering his arm and focus on a more positive future. With Cove and Oryn on the same side, there was no telling how much more consciousness he could achieve. It would improve his life a great deal and was his ultimate goal.

Oryn tilted his head and wiggled higher to connect our mouths. I'd missed kissing him and refused to rush when his tongue brushed with mine. We explored and tasted each other for many minutes before Oryn's hand became more brave and explored my chest with a purpose.

Before we could be thrown into a repeat of the previous Friday, I caught his wrist.

"I think we need to go easy for a bit."

His disappointment was visible, even in the low light of the room. "Why? I'm okay."

"But I'm not. Believe me when I tell you I want this more than anything with you, but I'm not willing to rush and risk triggering another episode like last time. It's not fair to me. And if it's not Cove, it's Reed, and you know how that goes."

He sighed and dropped his gaze. "I really want this, Vaughn."

"I know. Me too. And I know how hard you push yourself, but it's not fair to me, or you."

He laid his head back on my shoulder and remained quiet. I hated upsetting him, but if I was going to take care of me, that was one place I could definitely stop the rollercoaster ride.

"Oryn, do you trust me?"

"Yes."

I tilted my head to try and look at him and see if I could see the truth in his eyes, but I was too late and missed whatever reaction had gone with his answer.

"If your doctor is right, then making advances with Cove will help the entire system. As things calm down, I think there will be less resistance holding us back. I don't think it will always be impossible."

He didn't respond, and I succumbed to the fact that I'd probably upset him. I tried not to internalize it and reminded myself I had to look out for me too.

"Vaughn," he said a short while later.

"Yeah."

"I'm going to do my best with Cove. I'll talk to him and see if we can sort this out." He paused for a long time before asking, "Do you think this will ever happen between us? I mean in your heart, do you see it going there?"

"I do," I said without hesitation. "And the day you are ready and able, I'll be here, and we will make love until the sun comes up. I promise you."

I felt him smile against my chest, and I hugged him tighter.

And if that day never comes, I will still be here always.

I didn't voice my thoughts, because I wanted him to hope. For his own sake, I wanted him to believe.

Chapter Twenty-Five

"I'm so nervous. What if they hate me?"

Oryn had been giving me fret-face off and on all day. It was the first weekend in August and I'd officially booked a dinner night with my parents.

"They don't hate you. My mother called you charming."

"No, she called Cohen charming. I'm not charming, I'm sweating." He fanned his shirt front and redirected the air vents in the car so they all aimed at him. "Please tell me your parents have good air-conditioning."

Due to the excessive scars on his arms, and his determination to make a good first/second impression, he'd worn a long-sleeved button-up. The mid-summer temperature, even in the evening, was still well above thirty degrees Celsius.

"You'll be fine. They keep their place really cold. I'm always freezing when I visit."

"Good." He wiped his brow and pulled down the vanity mirror to fix his hair. "Do I look okay?"

"You look amazing. Stop worrying."

He flipped the mirror back in place and sunk back against the seat. "They're gonna hate me. I'm gonna stress out and then Cohen is gonna blast forward and steal the show. They loved him. He's charming," he said with sarcasm and a curled nose.

I laughed at his behavior. "Did you make your deals like Dr. Delmar said?"

"Yes. And they all agreed to let me do this. No interrupting."

"Good."

Oryn had been making an honest effort with Cove over the past couple of weeks. It was still fresh and extremely fragile, but they were talking, which was more than they'd ever done before. It had also allowed Oryn to start making what his therapist called 'contracts' with his alters to ensure rules were followed when he needed them followed. A simple thing like 'let me have dinner with my boyfriend's parents alone' was one of them.

"Then it will all be fine. Mom and Dad both understand about your condition if this goes amuck."

What I hadn't told him, was that my mother had been a non-believer, and I wasn't sure she'd accepted the truth yet or not. Regardless of what she thought to be true, I knew she would never be disrespectful or rude to Oryn in a million years.

We pulled into their driveway at five to six. The sun was still above the horizon and shone sparkling light across the lake in the distance.

"Wow, this is where you grew up? This is beautiful."

"It is. I showed Cohen the beach part of the property last time, but the entire backyard was a mountain of snow. I can show you later if you want."

Oryn nodded as he circled around, taking in the view. Before we could even make our way to the house, the front door flew open and my mother beamed across the front lawn.

"There's my boy."

"Hey, Ma," I said as I approached, holding Oryn's hand.

She smiled kindly at Oryn. "It's good to see you again."

Oryn's teeth immediately found his lip.

"Ma, this is Oryn. You met Cohen at Christmas, remember?"

She clapped a hand over her mouth and looked honestly ashamed for her slip-up.

"I'm so sorry, sweetie. Vaughn did tell me you were coming. It's so nice to meet you."

"It's okay," Oryn said with a smile. "It's an honest mistake. Vaughn's done it a million times."

"Hey," I yanked his arm in fun. "I do not. I have become quite good at sorting you out. The whole lot of you."

And it was true. Although there were a number of times when I'd been oblivious to a switch and hadn't realized they'd taken place until long after. Those times in question had always been moments when I'd been faced with an alter mimicking Oryn and his behaviors. Not intentionally, but because sometimes it was such a natural thing for an alter to take over certain tasks. They often slipped in unnoticed.

My dad appeared behind my mother a few minutes later, squinting over top of his glasses and examining Oryn like he should visibly see a difference in the man I brought from the one he'd met previously. Deducing there weren't any, he greeted Oryn with the same warmth my mother had shown. My father had kind eyes and a distinctive, receding hairline I hoped I never inherited.

"Dad, this is Oryn. Oryn, my dad, Lucien."

They shook hands and Oryn turned to my mother again. "I'm sorry, I didn't catch your name."

"It's Martina, sweetie."

Oryn smiled. "It's really nice to meet you both."

We moved into the living room and sat around as we waited for dinner to finish cooking. The aroma of cooked meat filled the air and rumbled my belly.

"Smells good, Ma. What are you making?"

"Roasted lamb, baby potatoes, and carrots."

"Oh, that sounds amazing."

I'd missed my mother's cooking when I'd moved out. Although I had decent skills and made relatively good meals, it never compared to good old home cooking. Maybe it was the novelty of someone else doing the work.

"Aren't you staying fed? I taught both my boys to cook."

"I am. I just like being spoiled once in a while."

Oryn chuckled. "I knew there was a reason you like staying for dinner all the time."

"Do you cook, Oryn?" my father asked from where he reclined with his feet up in his favorite chair.

"Umm," Oryn dashed a looked between my parents and then answered honestly with a flush in his cheeks. "N-not really, but... Theo does."

With those words, he dropped his gaze and fidgeted.

"Theo?" Of course my mom would ask.

"One of Oryn's alters enjoys cooking. He makes some pretty fantastic food. And yes," I said to Oryn, nudging him to help him feel less embarrassed. "You're on to me. I love Theo's cooking and I'll make any excuse I can to come over and eat. Plus, the company is nice too."

I managed to pull a smile from him which I took for a win. Instead of investigating the opening into Oryn's alters, my mom was respectful enough to change the subject.

"So, Oryn, what do you do for a living?"

Oryn sat up with more confidence. It was a topic he'd been finding pride in recently. "I'm writing a book at the moment, and I'm hoping to have it finished by the end of the year, or early next year. The writing part at least. Editing will take a while. I've also enrolled in college for September. I'll be taking mostly literature and English studies. Not a full course so much as random classes that interest me."

"A book!" My father quirked a brow and fixed his glasses, suddenly more interested in the conversation. He was a lot like Oryn in the sense that he loved to read and learn new things. "What about?"

"Me actually. I'm writing a biography about what it's like to live with dissociative identity disorder. There is a lot of misunderstanding out there, and I hope to give people a better idea of what it's like."

"I bet that would be an interesting read. Wouldn't mind buying a copy for myself when you're finished."

Oryn beamed. "Thank you. I will definitely make sure you get one."

With that, Oryn opened up about his passion for writing and the reasoning behind the specific courses he planned to take in September.

As we gathered around the dining room table for dinner, Oryn had relaxed significantly. His nerves over meeting my parents were long gone. Dinner was fabulous, and we ate as we chatted over random topics.

Once finished, my mother served up coffee and we returned to the living room for more conversation.

"So, I have news," I announced once we'd settled again.

Oryn peered quizzically from where he sat beside me on the couch. I hadn't shared my surprise with him yet and had decided to tell everyone at dinner that night.

"I have an interview at Creatick on Tuesday morning for a position on their creative team. It's an entry level position and the only reason I'm even qualifying for the interview is because Vinny at work has a friend who works there and put a word in for me. But, hey, it's worth a shot."

Creatick was one of the biggest advertising companies in the area. One whose reach spanned all of southwestern Ontario. It may have been a bottom end position, but there was nowhere to go but up if I got in.

Considering my parents didn't know I'd been unhappily plugging away at my job at Oliver Star for over a year, they shared a look of confusion and shock. Oryn, however, jumped with excitement.

"Oh my God, that's so amazing!" Oryn said as he rested a hand on my leg and smiled ear to ear.

"I know. I'm pretty excited. I won't get my hopes up, but who knows."

"What about your accounting position? I didn't know you were looking for work." My mother exclaimed.

"I'm just finding myself restless and in need of something more entertaining than punching numbers at a desk all day. Remember I took that marketing class last year?" My parents both nodded. "Well, I loved it. I was going to keep taking night classes this coming year and expand on it more. If I could get work already, that would be even more amazing."

"Now how would that affect your finances leaving an established position for an entry level one elsewhere?"

I heaved a sigh, hating how my exciting news was instantly being squashed. "It's not always about money, Dad. I can work my way up. I need something that will make me happier."

"That's what's important," Oryn said in a hushed tone.

I smiled and took his hand, silently thanking him for the support. My mother caught my defensive tone and shrugged.

"Sounds exciting. I hope it goes well. You'll need to keep us posted."

"I will," I assured them.

"So," my mother shifted and sipped her coffee as she smiled at Oryn. "Tell us about yourself, Oryn. You and Vaughn have been dating awhile yet he doesn't talk much about you. Where is your family at? Do you have any brothers or sisters?"

Oryn's face instantly drained of any color and the hand in mine squeezed so tight I thought he was going to break my fingers. Of all the things my mother could have asked about. But it was natural when meeting a new partner. I'd heard my parents inquire those things before. It shouldn't have been a surprise, except it was a taboo topic for Oryn. Those were questions even I hadn't asked eight months into our relationship.

"I d-don't know where my f-family is." His breathing changed, and his eyes darted the room like he was wishing for an escape.

"Mom, can we talk about something else?" I glared, trying to impress my thoughts to her silently. Although confused, she took the hint and decided we needed more to drink, escaping to the kitchen.

The conversation shifted to other things and eventually Oryn calmed again. By nine-thirty, we said our goodbyes and headed for home.

The sun had recently set as we walked to the car. Stars had begun to fill the sky.

"I never took you to the water," I realized out loud as Oryn opened the passenger door.

"Another time. I'm kinda tired. Besides," he said with a smirk. "The beach seems to be you and Cohen's thing."

Remembering how much Cohen had enjoyed our day trip, even when I'd been out of sorts, brought a smile to my face.

"You're right. You know, he looks super sexy in a Speedo. Just sayin'."

Oryn's face fell, and his cheeks flamed to such a dark shade of red they glowed in the darkness.

"I don't want to talk about that," he sputtered and got in the car as fast as he could.

I laughed and climbed in beside him. By that reaction, I guessed the skimpy bathing suit had been found.

I'd been spending the night with Oryn a lot more frequently since he'd been discharged from the hospital. The few nights I chose to stay at my apartment were the nights when I allowed myself a break. Often it was times when Reed was fronting and we'd had enough of each other, or if Theo was about. Theo and I got along well, but we'd both learned that it was a good opportunity to have time apart.

Cove had been absent since the hospital. Oryn shared that they spoke regularly, and I could only hope they were making progress together.

As we crawled into bed, our mouths found each other and we shared a deep, passionate half-hour of kissing. We still hadn't revisited anything further, and had come to a balance in the evenings sharing lesser intimate moments.

Once Oryn had curled against my side and we found our comfortable sleeping positions, I played with his hair as I did every night.

"How did you get away?"

I didn't think I needed to elaborate and hoped he took my meaning. After my mother's impromptu questioning earlier, I decided there was no better time to ask. It was something that I'd been curious about a long time, but had been too afraid to voice.

Oryn ran his fingers in circles over my chest. "I'm not entirely sure. It's a part that isn't clear to me. I think Theo did it, but it was before I discovered my DID, so I don't know. Mainly my life is a blur until I was sixteen. I've been on my own since then. Living here. How it came to that is kind of a mystery. I know I struggled to get assisted living back then. Bounced from one doctor to another as they diagnosed me with everything from schizophrenia to bi-polar disorder. I know they tried every medication under the sun to fix me, but other than that, I don't know much. Before sixteen is basically just a dark hole with sporadic moments of clarity intermixed. Not enough for me to really form a proper picture."

I became consciously aware of my breathing and his. Tightness formed in my chest and my heart hurt as I formed my next question.

"Do you know anything about your childhood or is it all… gone?"

He shook his head on my chest and hugged himself tighter to my body. "I have very few memories."

Maybe that was for the best.

Chapter Twenty-Six

"Is the coffee ready?" Cohen called from the bathroom.

"Yes, and I poured you a cup already."

He came bouncing into the kitchen in a tight pair of black underwear with his hair wet and messy from his shower.

"Cream, no sugar?" he asked as he brought the cup to his lips for a sip.

"Shit!" I removed it before he could get a mouthful and upended it in the sink. "Cut me some slack, you guys could at least take your coffees the same."

As I remade his cup, he shimmied up behind me and pressed his almost naked body to my back as he kissed up my neck.

"We like to keep you on your toes."

Since I was only wearing pajama bottoms, when he pressed against my backside, the pressure from his semi-hard dick against my ass was more accentuated.

I replaced his cup on the counter and reached a hand behind me to rub his thigh and pull him closer. He found his way up my neck to my ear and sucked it in his mouth.

"I swear it's impossible to satisfy you," I breathed.

He chuckled against my ear and kissed my temple. "Wanna go again? I have about an hour until class starts. I can be late."

"No." I wormed out from in front of him and went to the fridge to find cream. "You will not be late. This is important to Oryn."

When I turned to add the cream to his coffee, I was rewarded with a curled nose. "You're no fun."

I smirked. "That's not what you said last night."

He stole his coffee and downed a few mouthfuls before replacing it on the counter. He swung his hips, making a display of shaking his ass as he returned down the hall.

"Fine. See what you're missing?"

I couldn't help laughing. Life for Cohen was rarely serious. His light-hearted ways never failed to make me smile.

"I don't know what to wear," he called from the bedroom.

"How is that even possible? You spent an entire day at the mall last week."

I followed him down the hall and leaned on the doorframe to the bedroom as he picked through all the new outfits he'd bought.

Oryn hated them all. But, since they'd decided to share the college experience on a trial basis, he'd submitted to the new wardrobe as well.

There were three outfits laid out on the bed; dark denim skinny jeans, paired with a pale pink knitted cardigan, baby blue skinny jeans with a white button up and baby blue scarf, and black skinny jeans with a red long-sleeved shirt and matching jean jacket.

Oryn's only stipulation was his arms remain covered.

"I vote for the cardigan outfit. It's the most you."

His smile beamed as he picked up the sweater and jeans. "One hundred percent agreed."

He made a display of dressing, ensuring I got an adequate show. As he buttoned his jeans he looked beyond happy. The idea of attending college had been Oryn's. The prospect of taking classes during the daytime when it was a lot busier, however, worried him. When Cohen expressed a craving to be social and how much that aspect appealed to him, they'd made a deal. Up until recently, Theo had been the only alter who Oryn was able to be co-conscious with. In the weeks leading up to the first day of class, he and Cohen had taken that leap as well. So the deal was, as long as Oryn could remain co-conscious with Cohen, then Cohen could be the one to physically attend school. Hence it being a trial situation. They'd made a contract together of how it would all work and agreed on the rules.

It was amazing to see his progress in recent weeks. I think even Oryn was surprised at the barricade that had been created when he'd attempted to control Cove and shut him off from the system.

Once he was dressed, he returned to the bathroom, shaved—much to Oryn's dismay I was sure—and finished getting ready.

Bouncing from the bathroom a short while later he struck a pose and wiggled his brows. "What do you think? Do I look like a sexy college student?"

Too sexy, but how did you tell a nineteen-year-old that?

"You look incredible. Do me a favor, try not to pick up all those younger hotter men while you're there. I get feral when I'm jealous."

He chuckled and grabbed his already organized backpack. "Why would I do that?" He wrapped an arm around my neck and pulled me in for a kiss. It wasn't quick, and it wasn't chaste. His tongue laced with mine and he licked and sucked hungrily. When his backpack hit the ground and his other arm wrapped around my neck, I pulled back on a chuckle.

"No way. Get your ass out that door."

He frowned good naturedly and pecked one more kiss on my pinched lips. "I'm going."

"Let Oryn be there too. You promised."

"I will."

Since learning to be co-conscious with Cohen, the three of us had needed to make a separate deal. Cohen and I had developed a solid relationship which *was* sexual at times and we'd agreed—for the time being anyhow—that Oryn would not be present while those things took place. As much as the connection between the three of us had originally helped eliminate many stresses from Oryn in the beginning, it was becoming a much more separate thing. Oryn and I had discussed moving our intimacy forward, and we both wanted that experience to be personal when it came time.

The unconventional aspects of our relationship didn't even faze me any longer. Outsiders may have found it strange that I had two distinctively separate partners, but it was perfectly normal for us. Based on my online support group, I wasn't alone. Some of the people I'd met carried on four or five separate intimate relationships within their system. Others committed to one. It was personal to each party, and what Oryn and I had developed worked for us.

Since Cohen had adamantly decided I wasn't driving him to the college since he wanted the full experience and planned to take the bus, I saw him out the door. When the snow fell again, he would change his mind.

"Oh," I called after him. "Do me a favor. Remind Reed we have a football date with Evan on Sunday."

Cohen scrunched his nose at the thought. Sports were not his thing. "Yeah, will do."

"Hey," I called one more time before he could get away.

Cohen flipped around, an edge of impatience sneaking onto his face.

"What?"

"I love you."

His feature softened, and he walked back over and kissed me one last time. "I love you, too."

Once he was gone, I found my way back into Oryn's room and dressed for work. I'd succeeded in getting the position at Creatick and had started training the previous week. They'd hired me on a probationary basis, with a contract stating that I'd agreed to keep up with my schooling and work toward a degree in marketing. It was a pay cut, but I didn't think twice about accepting it. I needed the change and eagerly signed up for two night classes right away.

***

After work, I headed back to my apartment for awhile to do laundry, shower, and put together clothes for the evening. I planned to head back over to Oryn's to see how his first day of class had gone. He hadn't texted me, so I could only assume I would be met with Cohen still or someone else.

I needed to encourage Oryn to allow everyone to use his phone. The ambiguity of going to his place and not knowing who I was meeting seemed an unnecessary torture.

With a few belongings packed, I locked up and headed across town. Months back, Oryn had given me a key to his apartment. I hadn't felt it necessary at the time, but since I spent more time there it was nice to have.

I knocked lightly and let myself in. The house was quiet, so I kicked off my shoes and went looking for Oryn. There was a chance he wasn't home yet. He had talked of switching a few of his classes around and needing to make an appointment to do so after class.

I poked my head into the den and found Oryn sitting at the desk in the corner, his open laptop in front of him. There was no question who I faced when I saw he was working on his book. He was deep in thought and hadn't heard me enter. The frown on his face was deep as he stared at the screen. He appeared to be starting a new chapter and the only thing written was the heading, "Cove".

"Writer's block?" I asked, before I got too close and threatened startling him.

He spun in surprise and slammed his laptop. "Hey. Yeah, umm…" He turned to his laptop and considered. "Just trying to figure out how to explain something. Reached a hard part. It's nothing."

Cove. That was a subject I didn't press any longer. If he wanted to share about his progress he would, and he had, but I didn't go digging.

"How was school? Did Cohen follow through?"

Oryn's face tinged pink as he wiped a hand down his face. "He did. It's really weird not being in the driver's seat but seeing it all play out. With Theo, we are alike, so it feels natural kinda, but with Cohen… He talks to everyone. At least he took good notes."

I chuckled. "I'm glad. It will take getting used to, I guess."

"Yeah, for sure."

The goal was for him to be able to do that with everyone. He was a long way off still, but every day was progress.

"I have a meatloaf in the oven and mashed potatoes already done when you're hungry."

My stomach responded with a growl and I sniffed the air, catching hints of the seasoned meat coming from the kitchen. "You cooked?"

He laughed as though I'd said the most ridiculous thing. "Sure, I'll take full credit."

"Tell Theo, thank you."

"He says you're welcome."

We ate and shared more about our day. Oryn explained the course outlines he'd received and what would be on his plate for the up-coming semester, and I told of my work and the new things I was learning.

By evening, we shut down early and took turns in the bathroom before crawling into bed. Oryn lay on his side and smoothed a hand over my skin as I faced him. The desire radiating from his eyes was unmistakable. I could nearly see the thoughts forming in his mind and I waited patiently for him to voice them.

He leaned in and captured my lips, drawing them into his mouth with a small amount of suction before licking and kissing me deeper. His taste was addicting, and I drew him closer as he explored freely and comfortably. Our tongues slid together, lapping and toying, playing in a way that amplified all my senses and drew a moan to my lips.

He pulled back then, and watched me with determination. It'd been a month since I'd put the brakes on. A month of him talking to Cove. A month with visible progress in all areas of his internal system.

"Can we try something?" he asked, his voice barely above a whisper. "Not... a-all of it... umm... just, more?"

My heart responded to his words and jumped to a faster rhythm. Warmth flooded my veins as I studied his grey-blue eyes, looking for hints of uncertainty. I knew there would come a time when we'd try again, but was a month's progress long enough? What *more* was he asking for? In his roundabout way of explaining, I knew he didn't want to explore sex just then. But there was a world of other things he could have been referring to.

"Do you trust me?" I asked, knowing it was key.

His eyes took on a shimmer and he smiled with his heart. "Yes, I trust you."

For the first time in a year, there was no reluctance behind his words and a wave of emotion brought tears to my eyes. I blinked them away and caught his lips again, kissing him with all my heart.

Ignoring my nerves, I let my hands travel over his bare chest as he explored mine in turn. That time when everything had turned ugly, I'd been in the process of discovering something I knew he liked.

I rolled Oryn to his back and straddled his waist, never parting from his mouth. As our kiss heated, I pulled off and peered down into his happy, dreamy eyes.

"Stay with me. I want to explore what I was doing last time, but I don't want to lose you."

He nodded. "Reed is close, but I told him it's okay. I'm okay."

"You only need to ask me to stop and I will."

"I know."

The trust in his words was something that had always been missing. Hearing it, I knew Oryn wouldn't let us go further than he could handle. I only hoped I didn't trigger a mess.

Instead of kissing him again, I brushed my lips along his jaw to his neck. I kissed and sucked him just near his ear where I'd started the time before. His breath came out in a soft moan and I moved down and drew teeth over his collarbone. Planting more kisses in a trail down his chest, I came to a halt at his nipple which had already grown hard with anticipation.

I smoothed a tongue over its pebbled surface and drew it in my mouth, giving him a little suction. He gasped and arched his back the moment I did, and I dashed my eyes to his face to keep watch.

His eyes had fallen closed and his lips were bright pink and parted. He licked at them and moaned as I flicked my tongue over his nipple again. The pleasure crossing his face was the most beautiful thing in the world.

I kept at one side for awhile before dancing kisses across his chest and playing on the other.

"Vaughn," he whispered on an airy moan.

"You need me to stop?"

He shook his head with assurance before lifting his head and peering below. He'd grown hard under my ministrations.

The distinctive rise of his length was apparent under his pajamas, and I drew a hand along his outer thigh, as I watched it. With my next pass over his thigh, I moved my hand to the top of his leg, allowing my thumb to trail closer.

I didn't know how far I could go or how far he wanted me to take it, so I peered up in question, looking for guidance.

The lust and hunger radiating from his eyes was all I received, so I asked, "Can I touch you?"

The nod was barely perceivable, but it was there, and I saw it. He lowered his head and his eyes fell shut again. There weren't any flashing signs of anxiety, so I returned to kiss down his chest, around his navel, and ended at the waistband of his bottoms.

Not wanting to assume the limits of how much touch was okay, I started cautiously, drawing my hand from his leg and caressing it up his inner thigh. On the third pass up, I brushed my thumb over his balls through his pants, and he gasped again, pulling all his muscles taut.

With half an eye on his reactions, I moved my hand up again, and slid over his hard length. The act alone not only brought more pleasured sounds to spill from his mouth, but it made my own body react. Tingling heat coursed over my skin and pooled lower, making my own dick hard and aching to be touched. I ignored it, focusing on Oryn and the new steps forward we were taking.

I stroked him through his pants a few times, Long, slow pulls as I watched the rippling pleasure consume his whole body. Knowing I was the one bringing him that pleasure was a treasure I'd never take for granted. When I knew he was comfortable, I returned to licking and kissing around his navel, tasting his skin and focused on pulling every sound from him I could.

After a few minutes, Oryn began moving in time with my pulls, silently begging for more speed as he rubbed against my hand. I desperately wanted to remove his pants and take him bare in my hand, but I remained cautious.

Keeping a steady rhythm outside his clothes, I moved back up his body and kissed his neck to his lips. When we came together, he ravished my mouth like he'd never done before. I kissed him hard, clacking our teeth and sucking at his tongue as I stroked him again and again. When he was panting and vibrating, unable to kiss or catch his breath, I pulled off and watched him.

I drew my hand up his length and dipped my fingers under the band on his pants. There, I paused.

"Can I?" I asked.

He vibrated against me, his lips red and swollen from our kiss. He was utterly beautiful.

"Yes," he panted.

I slipped my hand under his pants and took his length in hand again. The moment I did, he cried out and buried his face in my neck as I worked him bare. His tip was slick and leaking, adding to the glide with each pass.

I brought my mouth to his ear and drew his lobe in, nibbling and sucking as his body twitched and begged for more.

Each pass brought a steady string of moans. I knew he was close and didn't know how he'd handle an orgasm. Part of me feared it would tip him into hysterics, but I knew there was no turning back.

"Oryn, let go for me. I've got you. It's okay."

He clung with a death grip, digging his fingers into my skin the closer he got. I increased my speed as I continued to whisper words of encouragement, ensuring he knew it was okay and he was safe.

He toppled the edge with a cry, pulsing and spilling into my hand as I worked him through every ounce of his orgasm. Watching and hearing his pleasure was more beautiful than I ever imagined, and I kissed his ear and kept him close as the extreme sensations passed and he came down.

He collapsed on the bed and peered up at me with disbelief in his eyes. He was breathless, and his cheeks were pink.

"Are you okay?" I asked.

"Yeah," he said on a wobbled exhale. "Wow."

I smiled as he stumbled to find words. He radiated with an after-release glow, and I took him all in. "God, you are the most beautiful thing. I love you so much."

He brought a hand to my cheek and pulled me into a lazy kiss he couldn't coordinate. I chuckled at his exhaustion.

"You're so amazing," I said against his lips.

He fixed a piece of my hair from my face and lost himself in my eyes. They shimmered with an over-abundance of emotion I'd never seen before. Tears sprung to their surface, but he blinked them away. They weren't from fear or uncertainty. The only thing he emanated was joy and contentment.

"I love you, Vaughn," he whispered, the words getting caught in his throat. "I know I've never said it before. It-it's hard for me… no one has ever… I mean… you…"

I traced a thumb along his bottom lip, shushing him and taking it all in. I never thought those words would ever cross his lips. Hearing them was breathtaking.

We kissed again, taking our time and relishing the connection. When Oryn pulled back, a look of seriousness filled his eyes.

"Thank you," he said.

"For what?"

"For being so patient with me."

I chuckled and nipped his lips once more before saying, "The best things are worth waiting for."

"I really love you," he said again, taking my face between his hands.

"And I really love you."

His smile was pure, and we became lost in each other for a while longer before he dashed a look below and bit into his lip. "Umm... I'm kind of a mess. I need to go clean up."

I laughed and kissed his nose. "Go do that."

He crawled out of bed as I adjusted the steady ache in my own pants. When he noticed, he paused.

"No. Go clean up. One step at a time. I'll live."

He didn't seem happy with that response, but it was the only one he was getting. I'd take the temporary discomfort over ruining a good night. Oryn had taken a great leap forward and that was what counted. We'd gone places we'd never thought possible, and I knew, with time and patience, we'd explore more.

Chapter Twenty-Seven

September came and went in a rush. With my new job, night classes, and Oryn's schooling, we were busy. Most nights we spent together, treading carefully in what we'd explored. Oryn had been able to reciprocate the experience, but we hadn't gone further.

Slow and safe.

Our days were broken up and shared among alters. The smoother things played out; the better our stress levels. Reed and I dedicated Sundays to football. We went to Evan's for beers and to shoot the shit. Some nights we hit the bar for a game of pool. Cohen stole me on Fridays, and sporadically through the week on the mornings I stayed over. Theo was a man of routine, and if I was around enough, I caught him preparing meals, cleaning, or doing random chores around the house.

Rain was a wild card, showing up at random. His visits weren't as frequent and still tended to be triggered by events that interested him, but we managed. We shared a love for cartoons, and if I tuned them on the television Saturday mornings, I'd end up with his company for awhile.

Cove hadn't made an appearance since our incident a while back. When I asked about him, Oryn assured me things were going well.

On the first Tuesday in October, I checked my phone as I left work. Oryn still attended therapy Tuesdays and I'd often get confirmation when his appointment was over, but my phone had been silent all day. A niggling seed of worry tried to grow in my stomach, but I pushed it aside. It'd been a long time since therapy had triggered Cove to become upset. In recent weeks, Oryn had given permission for everyone—except Rain—to use his phone to message me—provided they identified themselves. The silence was not something I was used to anymore.

I drove to Oryn's, unable to shake the concern, but telling myself he'd probably just gotten busy writing and forgotten to message. When I pulled in the driveway, I hopped out and let myself in the house without knocking, bracing for a problem, but unsure what that problem might be.

As I closed the door behind me, soft music came from somewhere in the house. The gentle plucking of an acoustic guitar. A sad melody that pulled at my heart. I couldn't tell if it was a recording or the TV, nor could I tell where it was coming from, so I kicked off my shoes and followed it.

It stopped once, and then the same few chords and plucked notes resumed with more confidence. It was coming from the bedroom. Once at the door, I stalled, looking and listening to the man before me.

He was dressed all in black and sitting on the floor in the corner, plucking at the Fender across his lap. There was a pack of smokes and a lighter sitting beside a few loose pieces of paper on the ground beside him. Every one of his fingers were dressed with rings of one kind or another, and there were chains around his neck.

He hadn't noticed me, so I pushed the door open further to grab his attention. His gaze came up and found mine.

"Hey." His voice was gruff and raw, exactly how I knew it would be.

"Long time no see," I said, wandering in and sitting on the edge of the bed.

He lowered the guitar and sat it across his lap. It was then when I saw the writing that covered the span of his arm over his scars. A tattoo?!

Ah, fuck. Don't tell me you got a tattoo. Oryn's gonna freak.

I must have looked visibly shocked because he rubbed a hand over the area with a distant look in his eyes.

"Relax. It's Henna. We're trying something."

Trying something?

Was Oryn *considering* a tattoo?

"What does it say?" I asked, craning my neck and trying to read it.

He held up his arm, angling it toward me. The writing was cursive and went from the crook of his arm to his wrist in two lines of words.

Together we are strong.
Together we will survive.

"He liked the quote. We chose the spot together. Now we wear it until the tattoo wears off and decide if we make it permanent." Cove examined the words and smoothed a finger over the lettering.

I shifted to the floor and took his arm, reading it again.

"I think it's really powerful. Did you come up with it?"

"Yeah. And if I put it here," he touched it again, "maybe I won't be so inclined to mess it up, you know?"

"That's smart. What about this arm?" I touched him lightly, tracing fingers over the scars on the opposite arm.

"Still lookin'. Haven't decided yet."

"I can't wait to see what you come up with."

He shrugged, dismissing my comment as he fiddled with the papers around him. On closer inspection, I noticed they were handwritten sheets of music.

"I heard you playing. You're good."

"I'm all right. Got this guitar today. Sweet deal down at Eric's Music Center."

He'd been out and shopping? I was so impressed, I didn't know how to respond. The clothes he wore weren't anything I'd ever seen either, so I suspected he'd done some clothes shopping as well. All of it seemed new; the jewelry, the clothes, and the instrument. He was a whole new person than when we'd last met.

Compared with the Cove I'd faced a few months back, he seemed… well. Although he wasn't over-the-moon happy and still gave off a dark, depressive aura, he wasn't losing his mind and unable to cope with the overwhelming self-hatred that had been eating him alive.

"You've been to the mall, too, haven't you," I said, indicating to his clothes with a smirk. "You look like yourself."

He smoothed a hand down his black shirt and supressed a smile. "Yeah. We decided I could have Tuesdays after therapy to myself. My time. My space. Do my own thing, you know. Like play guitar."

I was blown away by what I was hearing.

"That's really great. I'm sorry, I didn't know you guys had made those plans." I stood from the floor. "I think it's really amazing to have your own time. I don't need to be in your face while you enjoy it. I'm gonna take off."

I gave him a warm smile and moved to the door.

"Vaughn," he called after me.

"Yeah."

"Wanna hear something I wrote?"

The sad eyes staring back at me almost seemed hungry for company. I was shocked at the invitation, but there was no way I would turn him down. If Cove wanted to try and form a friendship, I'd do anything I could to help make that happen.

"Hell yeah."

He adjusted his guitar into position as I moved back to the bed to sit. He plucked a few random strings and slid his fingers over the neck as he thought for a moment.

"Okay, but I'm not done with it yet and it's really rough, so… yeah… whatever, just don't judge me too hard."

I'd never judge you.

"Anything you play will be a million times better than anything I could play, so let's hear it."

He nodded, and took a deep breath before closing his eyes and beginning.

The melody flowed in smooth long sentences as he picked it out and became comfortable with playing for an audience. It was the same gentle tune I'd heard when I'd come in earlier; soft and with an edge of sadness.

It was beautiful.

When he started singing, it took my breath away. I had no idea he was capable. His voice was deep and raspy, much like Cove's normal speaking voice but filled with more emotion than I ever believed possible. He didn't open his eyes, and I almost thought he forgot I was there. Every word scored my heart and his features showed the pain and rawness behind the story he told.

> *Take my hand, guide me along*
> *Be my friend, so we can talk*
> *Fight the demons by my side*
> *In the darkness, we can't hide*
> *The world is changing*
>
> *When the sunlight streams on me*
> *I'll bare my soul for you to see*
> *Break these binds, set me free*
> *Cuz this is who I'm supposed to be*
> *The world is changing*
>
> *No more poison in my mind*
> *No more storms I cannot ride*
> *Don't hold me down, just let me fly*
> *I will get by, I will get by*
> *The world is changing*
> *Our world is changing*

He strummed to a stop and opened his eyes again. When our eyes met, I caught a hint of vulnerability in their depths before he shrugged. "That's all I have so far. Still messin' with it."

Tears rolled down my face, and I wiped them away the minute I noticed my display of emotion was making it hard for Cove to look at me. The intensity behind every word he'd sung gripped my soul and wouldn't let go. Hearing those lyrics spill from his heart was the hope I'd been praying for ever since I'd glimpsed Cove's inner pain months back.

Before me was a man who'd taken great strides forward. He wanted to be better and was working as hard as Oryn to make that happen. I wanted to hug him, but I refrained because our boundaries weren't clearly marked. We were still new to one another.

He placed the guitar on the ground beside him and messed his hair. He fixed the papers he'd been working on into a pile and snapped up his cigarettes and lighter.

"I'm gonna have a smoke."

He removed two from the pack, stuck one behind his ear and the other between his lips before standing. He started down the hall, but I didn't follow. I was still wrapped up in the song and working on putting my emotions back in order.

"You comin'?" he called from the kitchen.

With Cove accepting my company, I didn't want to deny him and followed him outside.

It was a cool October day, but not cold enough to warrant a jacket. A breeze blew and ruffled my hair. Cove leaned against the back fence and lowered his head. He blocked the wind with a hand as he lit his cigarette. I knew Oryn despised him smoking and complained the wretched taste lingered for hours, but I stayed silent. It was as much control over his identity as I'd seen him have, and if he wanted to smoke, I couldn't dispute it.

Besides, it wasn't my place.

He stared at the ground while he puffed on the smoke, seeming lost in his head. I leaned against the house opposite him, unsure what kind of companionship he was looking for. Did he want me to force conversation, or just be there?

After another long draw on his cigarette, he lifted his chin and studied my face. The darkness behind his eyes and the untold misery he carried were still there. He didn't smile.

"Thank you," he mumbled.

"For what?"

He seemed irritated I'd asked, and huffed a breath as he broke our gaze and focused on a spot on the ground. He kicked at the grass, and pursed his lips.

"Cohen said you did this."

"That's only partly true. All I did was express my observations, you guys did the rest."

I knew from previous conversations that Cohen was the only alter who could get close to Cove. They shared their own bond, and as much as it sometimes made Cohen defensive of Cove's behavior, it'd also helped Oryn bridge their differences and form a bond.

Cove's lips firmed, and I thought I saw his face try to crumple, but he shifted and turned his back to me. Chancing rejection, I approached and placed a hand on his shoulder from behind. It vibrated under my touch and a moment later he sniffled and coughed.

"I don't want to live in a prison anymore."

"I have faith that you won't."

He turned, and the self-resistance as he held back tears, made his jaw tense. "You're a good person. We didn't want to believe it. But you really are."

He flicked the butt of his cigarette to the ground and shifted uncomfortably.

"I hope we can be friends, Cove. I only want to help."

He considered those words and then rubbed at his nose as he looked away again. "Do you really love him?"

Him? Him who?

When I didn't respond, he looked back and elaborated, as though having read my thoughts.

"Cohen. Do you really love him?"

Remembering that Cohen and Cove had a close, intimate relationship in the inner world on occasion, I worried I'd overstepped boundaries and maybe caused hurt feelings.

"I do, but Cohen is only one part of a whole, Cove, and you know that. Choosing to come into all your lives meant choosing to love, not one part, but a whole system together."

"But we don't know each other. How can you have made a decision like that without even knowing the whole system?"

I wasn't sure how he'd react, but I reached out and touched his arm. "Because when you love someone, you don't get to just love the good stuff and turn it off when things are difficult. It doesn't work like that. When you fall in love, you are accepting someone wholly and completely."

"Including flaws, you mean. I'm a flaw."

"No." I turned his chin toward me. "You are a unique and intricate part of a whole. You just haven't found your place, but you will. And I'll do anything I can to support you."

He nodded and dashed his gaze to the ground once again.

"Cohen told me to trust you. He said you are for real."

"I hope you can find it in yourself to believe him."

***

"What the fuck! Flip back, you dick, that was mid-play. Wait for a commercial," Evan sneered at Reed.

"It's third and twenty-one, relax. Broncos just scored, I need to know what happened."

I watched Reed hold the remote away from Evan as he tried to grab for it. The two had been bickering since the game started. God forbid their favorite teams play at the exact same time and not against each other. It made for dizzying viewing.

There was no compromise.

Reed had seen Denver's score flash across the bottom of the screen a moment before, and since it had changed since the last time it'd been shown, he couldn't wait to investigate the cause.

"You take up half of my time, I'll take up yours," Evan warned as he shoved a laughing Reed aside.

Turned out Evan and Reed got along really well. It was more or less a love hate relationship. They both adored sports of all kinds, but didn't agree on teams. Sundays were entertaining to say the least.

"Vaughn, tell your boyfriend to turn the channel back."

That earned him a punch on the shoulder. "I'm not his fucking boyfriend."

"And I'm not getting involved," I stated as I dropped my eyes back to the book I'd been reading. It was impossible following either game since they spent more time arguing and flipping channels.

Relenting, Evan pushed off the couch and collected our empties before retreating to the kitchen for another round of beers.

"What are you reading that is more important than football?"

"Stuff," I mumbled, not lifting my gaze.

"Stuff?" Evan handed me a fresh beer and tilted his head to see the cover.

The game had gone to a commercial and Reed accepted a beer from Evan as well as he explained, "He's decided we are a case study that needs dissecting."

"You aren't a case study. I'm learning so I can better know how to deal with your irritating ass."

Reed smirked and sipped his beer, but I didn't miss the flicker of approval that flashed in his eyes. The more time we spent together, the more he saw and understood that I only had their best interest at heart. His trust for me was growing.

We'd become good friends and spent a lot of time together growing that bond.

"More DID shit. You've been studying that for like a year, don't you know it all yet?" Evan asked as he plopped back on the couch beside Reed.

"We are complicated," Reed explained with a laugh. "Vaughn just hasn't figured out yet that those books are all general."

"I know that," I said in defense.

Evan clicked the TV back to his game just as his phone chimed. He snapped it up and grinned like a fool.

"Krystina is on her way over," he exclaimed.

The lovesick look in his eyes was new. They'd been dating for an Evan-record length of time and the longer they were together the more I was certain where it was going.

"Is she bringing her friend?" Reed asked.

"Who, Becca? No, I think she's working."

I ignored the look of disappointment in Reed's eyes. It was probably the biggest bone of contention between us. Even though he abided by Oryn's dating rules, it didn't stop him overtly flirting and expressing his interest in a nice-looking woman. Reed and I had strict 'no touching' boundaries between us, so it wasn't like I could slink up beside him and metaphorically piss on his leg to claim him as my own. For the most part I gritted my teeth and got through it. Reed knew it bothered me, and mostly, I think he did it simply to make me squirm. I'd learned to curb my reactions and not show any signs of irritation. That only made it worse.

"When's the wedding?" I asked Evan instead.

Evan quirked a brow, not taking the bait. "You tell me, lover boy."

I laughed and shook my head, returning to my book. Their game was back on and stole the attention of both men sharing the couch.

Since they flipped in approximate ten-minute intervals between games, it was Reed's turn and Evan proceeded to be a pain in the ass and insult every play the Broncos made, rooting hard for the opposing team. They laughed and bickered until the door buzzer sounded and Evan's attention was stolen away.

The minute I'd observed Krystina becoming more important than football, I knew Evan was done for. Fourth quarter was about to begin, and Detroit was neck and neck with New England, yet Evan lost all interest in his game.

Reed took over the TV and laid across the couch as Evan and Krystina wandered to the kitchen.

A short time later, I felt the heat of Reed's gaze and lifted my eyes from my book.

"What? Why are you staring at me?"

"What are you reading about exactly?"

I held his concentrated stare and dashed a glance to the page again. "It's a chapter about balancing your relationship with alters when being in a relationship with someone who has DID."

I waited for his retort, expecting him to scoff or make fun of my need to study the condition so thoroughly. He didn't.

"You don't need that shit. Trust yourself. You're doing fine."

He turned back to the game. His reassurance meant more to me than he knew. As difficult as it had been forming a bond with Cove, and as distant as Theo sometimes seemed, it was Reed who'd been the least trusting and hardest to break.

He was lost in his game in seconds, and I watched him. Over the past few months, there had been only a rare occasion when he'd triggered forward, and mostly those times weren't because of anything I'd done. When Oryn and I explored more intimacy, Oryn explained Reed was often close, but he listened to Oryn and didn't interrupt.

"Reed?"

"Yeah?" He took a second to turn his head from the game and meet my eyes.

"Do you trust me?"

He seemed taken aback by my sudden question and paused, studying me.

"Yeah. I do."

His words swelled in my heart and I smiled. "Thank you."

He wasn't one for heartfelt moments and he shifted uncomfortably. "Nah, man, thank you. Seriously."

Then, because the moment was more than he could handle, he turned back to his game and feigned interest.

Chapter Twenty-Eight

It was mid-December and I'd tried to convince Oryn to let me drag him to the mall, despite the insane amount of shoppers milling about preparing for Christmas, but I'd lost that battle and was instead in the company of Cohen. I didn't ask if Oryn was knowledgeable of what was going on, deciding that was up to them. They were co-conscious more and more. It'd helped Oryn significantly having less missing chunks of time in his life. But, he also respected Cohen's and my privacy.

"What are we looking for exactly?" Cohen asked as I guided him by the hand through the bustling crowd.

"Christmas stuff. Tree, gifts, decorations, you know."

Cohen ground to a halt, pulling me to a stop. I flipped around to see why. "But we don't celebrate Christmas. We never have."

Part of me knew that, remembering the previous year and being at their house on Christmas day. I wasn't a hugely festive person either, and apart from dinner with my family, I didn't often bother, but that year would be different.

Although we hadn't officially moved in together, my nights at my apartment were fewer and further between. It was something that would need to be brought up soon.

"Is there a reason specifically?"

I had wondered if there might be memories that triggered with the holidays, but after observing and listening to Oryn talk, I'd got the impression it was just something he didn't bother with because he didn't have anyone with whom to celebrate.

"No. Not really. But why now? We don't need to celebrate Christmas." Cohen cocked a hip and rested a hand on top. A gesture that was all him and one that brought a smile to my lips.

"Maybe you and I don't need to celebrate, but there is someone who deserves Christmas and everything that goes with it."

I pulled him along to the toy store at the far end of the mall. As the pieces clicked, Cohen pulled me to a stop again with a crooked smile.

"Rain?"

"Bingo. Now help me out."

We spent the following two hours selecting a few toys we knew Rain would enjoy, a suitable small tree, and a few decorations for the house. Plus, we made sure Rain had a stocking for Santa to fill. I intended on ensuring he had the perfect Christmas experience.

While picking out little tinsel wrapped Santa chocolates for his stocking, a group of men called out.

"Oryn!"

I dashed a look down the aisle and noticed three younger men approaching. One carried a few rolls of wrapping paper, otherwise, the others were empty-handed.

Flipping my gaze to Cohen, unsure how he'd handle the misunderstanding, I was rewarded with a wink and nudge to my side.

"Hey, Daniel, Geo."

I assumed when he didn't acknowledge the third man that he might not know him.

"Holiday shopping?" the man with the wrapping paper asked.

Cohen gave him a duh expression that I'd personally been rewarded with more times than I could count in the past.

"Obviously."

"You get a look at your grades for Mr. Peter's class yet? He just posted the finals this morning online."

"No way." Cohen whipped his phone out and the three men gathered while he tinkered and pulled up his grade.

Just watching the exchange, and seeing Cohen interact with men who were much closer to his age reminded me how young he really was. There were many days I forgot. He slipped into Oryn's roll for school so easily, it made me glad they had decided to share the experience.

Once the men had talked and confirmed grades, Cohen flipped back and beamed.

"Oh, hey, you guys, this is Vaughn, my boyfriend."

I greeted each man respectively, learning the third's name was Jorge, Geo's brother.

"Nice to meet you."

We chatted a bit longer before going our separate ways. Once the men had disappeared, Cohen's interest returned to picking chocolates for Rain.

"Does it bother you when they don't know who you really are?" I asked.

Cohen shrugged. "Nah, not really. I'm as much Oryn as he is me, even though we're different."

"It makes my head spin when you try and explain it. But I get it."

He giggled as only Cohen could and pecked my cheek. "What about a marshmallow snowman chocolate?"

"So long as I don't have to share with him. Toss it in. How'd you do in Mr. Peter's class?"

Cohen raised his chin high with pride. "Ninety-three percent. Boyah!"

"Yeah, not your grade, Oryn's grade. But gloat all you want."

Our shopping trip went on for hours. We went out for lunch and bounced from store to store, spending way too much money, but having a great time together.

I hadn't discussed any of my plans with Oryn, and I hoped he was okay with my decision.

Back at the house, Cohen stuck around and helped me decorate and put up the tree. He turned on some Christmas music station on the TV and danced around, singing along.

I paused while hanging candy canes on the tree as Cohen belted out the lyrics to *Feliz Navidad*. He was horribly off-key, and I cringed.

"Don't laugh, I don't hear you singing."

"Cuz I can't."

It amazed me listening to him. Cove sang with such perfect pitch, his voice utterly different and full of emotion as he paid attention to tone and vibration. Cohen was a hot mess with no skill. Sometimes it shocked me how different alters could be. Oryn had informed me he couldn't play guitar to save his life. Didn't even know how to hold it properly. So, Cove's ability was all his own.

Once we'd finished decorating, Cohen helped me wrap the few presents we'd bought. As I folded the last edge of wrapping paper over the end of a box and held out my finger for tape, Cohen didn't respond. He'd stopped helping and stared into space. Noting and familiar with the response, I peered up, studying him.

"You okay?"

He shook away the haze and smiled sadly as he nodded. "Oryn wants his time back."

I figured as much. Cohen was frequently butt-hurt when asked to retreat. But he also pushed his limits and stole extra time.

"Not yet," I said, leaving the present and grabbing the front of his shirt.

I pulled him toward me until he collided with my chest. Then, I kissed him soundly, dipping my tongue in his mouth and caressing his face as we fell back on the ground with him on top of me. We shared a long moment of tenderness before I pulled back and smiled.

"We have Friday, right? Maybe we can go out and do something. It was good to see you today."

It brought a smile to his face and that was what mattered. "Yeah. I'd like that."

He pecked my lips again and reluctantly got to his feet. Consensual switches had become a more private affair for the system and often they would retreat to the bathroom or another room for them to take place.

Cohen headed down the hall and I watched after him as a tiny twinge of sadness rooted itself inside me. Dividing our time was hard sometimes. As much as I missed Oryn when he wasn't around, I missed Cohen when he was gone as well.

Before he was out of sight, I called out, "Cohen?"

He flipped around in question.

"I love you."

The twinkle in his eyes and soft crease of his smile were all the answer I needed.

❊❊❊

"I can't believe you did all this." Oryn said for the hundredth time, like he couldn't quite absorb the idea that I wanted to give Rain a Christmas.

"He deserves it."

We'd settled down for a dinner of eggplant parmesan—thanks to Theo—in the living room with only the blinking lights on the tree illuminating the room.

"He's been chattering in my head all night, you know. You'll make me crazy before Christmas ever gets here."

I laughed, knowing how Rain could be distracting enough at times, making it hard for Oryn to concentrate.

"You mean more crazy?"

"Ha, ha!" Oryn smacked my arm and laughed.

His schooling had ended for the holidays and wouldn't return until after the new year. I had a few days off over Christmas, but not many seeing as I was a new hire and bottom of the totem pole. We'd planned dinner with my parents again for the following weekend, but otherwise simply planned to enjoy the holidays together in a low-key manner.

We finished eating and watched some TV before bed. As we got ready together in the bathroom, sharing space as we brushed our teeth, I considered bringing up what had been on my mind for a while.

"Can I ask you something?" I said after I spit toothpaste in the sink.

Oryn nodded and watched me expectantly as he continued brushing.

"I think we should move in together."

The brush stilled in his hand and he stared like he hadn't heard me right.

"If you think about it, I'm here all the time anyway. I know there are times we both need space, but we can work it out. I mean, if Cove doesn't want my company, or Theo wants time to himself, I can maybe crash at Evan's or go to my parents'. Reed knows better than to be around when we're in bed already, and—"

Oryn slammed a hand over my mouth and turned to spit in the sink. He rinsed his brush and returned it to the holder before looking back and lowering his hand.

"I think it's a great idea, so stop rambling."

He smiled, and I let out a relieved breath.

"Besides," he continued. "We've already talked about it and I was gonna ask you the same thing."

"You were?"

"Yeah."

"So we can do this?"

Oryn shrugged. "Like you said, we basically already are living together."

So it was settled, we decided in the new year, I would give my notice at my apartment and move my things in to Oryn's townhouse.

That night as we crawled into bed, I was overjoyed at the direction we were heading. We'd come a long way in a year and every day, our relationship was stronger.

Oryn clicked off the bedside light and shuffled around beside me. Then, he crawled closer in the dark. Instead of snuggling up to my side, as was our normal sleeping arrangement, he climbed overtop of me and straddled my hips.

He was naked.

We'd been naked together before, but mostly it was a state we needed to build toward. My hands automatically rested on his hips and I smiled up at him in the dark.

"What are you doing?"

I couldn't make out his face, but I could hear the unevenness of his breathing. "I... Can we try something else?"

My skin prickled with heat and I massaged my hands over his thighs, suddenly extremely aware of his balls resting against my abdomen and my dick growing hard under him.

"What did you have in mind?" I whispered into the dark.

We'd happily remained constant in our intimacy, exchanging hand-jobs, and on a few occasions, had graduated to grinding our dicks together until we'd orgasmed. There had been zero penetration and no oral. They were lines that Oryn needed to decide he was ready to cross on his own, not ones I pushed for.

"I...I w-w..." He was nervous and struggling to express himself. "Umm..." He bent to my ear and whispered, embarrassment thick in his tone. "Will you use your mouth?"

His request made my semi instantly hard, and my insides fluttered, prickling the hairs on my body to stand. Oryn still couldn't use any terminology around sexual terms, and I'd decided it was one of those extreme barriers he couldn't cross, so I didn't ask him to clarify what I knew he was asking.

I'd wanted to taste him for months. Every time I brought him to orgasm and felt his hot release coat my hand, or spill between us, I yearned for more.

I brought a hand between us and took hold of his hardening length, no longer fearful he would react poorly. We'd done those things plenty and he'd grown comfortable with them. He sighed into my ear and adjusted so I'd have more access. I stroked him a few times, exactly as I'd learned he liked it. His breath caught as the sensations bubbled and grew inside him. As vocal as he was, moaning and whimpering his pleasure when I brought him close, he rarely spoke words to encourage me. I'd learned to listen and watch for other clues. He spoke volumes without ever having to say a thing.

With his face buried in my shoulder, I continued, and his body tensed as I drew him closer to release.

"Kiss me," I said into his neck.

He joined our mouths as I tugged him beyond his senses. Our tongues danced and explored together, always seeking more. There was an ardent need growing between us with each passing day. A draw, or pull, to be closer. Like what we shared was never enough. I knew Oryn yearned for more, and in time, I hoped to be able to deliver.

As he grew more confident and thrust back into my hand with every stroke, I broke our kiss and silently encouraged him higher on the bed, intent on having him feed me his pulsing dick.

I always ensured Oryn had the control when we explored new things. Only that time, he shook his head in the dark and didn't move.

"We don't have to," I said, assuming he'd changed his mind.

"No, not that."

He climbed off me and lay on the bed at my side. Then he pulled my arm, encouraging me closer. I let him guide me, unsure of what he wanted, but knowing he couldn't voice his desire. When I understood, I shimmied between his legs and kissed over his navel, licking a trail down further.

I was on fire with anticipation.

He threaded a hand through my hair and guided me lower. My lips skimmed over their destination as I peered up through the dark. As my hot breath coasted across his rigid length, he shuddered and squirmed his hips higher.

He wasn't hesitating at all and seemed confident and sure. I nuzzled my nose around his base and feathered my lips up his shaft to the tip. Salivating at the prospect of what I was about to do, I reminded myself not to rush, or lose myself in the act and forget to be alert for any signs I should stop. The very last thing I needed was Reed to suddenly appear while I had his dick down my throat. Without a doubt, that would be a sure-fire way to end up with a black-eye.

I smoothed both hands up Oryn's inner thighs, spreading his legs slightly and taking a grip of his balls before wrapping my mouth around his tip. When I massaged them in my palm, he gasped, and his grip on my hair tightened.

I licked a circle around his head and was rewarded by a slight spilling of pre-cum. The intense earthy flavor hit my palate and ached right through to my own balls. I glided down his shaft to the base.

Oryn didn't react with anything but pleasure. As I became more confident he was okay, I lost myself in pulling every ounce of pleasure from him I could.

Every movement rewarded me with more moans and whimpers, along with a steady increase of flavor. He gasped for air, and at one point, brought his fingers close to my mouth so he could feel as I took him down my throat.

The entire act barely lasted long enough. I could have sucked him for hours—days—listening to the responses he gave and savoring every second, but Oryn couldn't hold back.

I felt it in his muscles when he grew closer. They became taut and he trembled, no longer able to do anything more than squirm and whimper.

The fist around my hair went painfully tight as he jerked his hips up one last time and filled my mouth with his release. His silent cries rivetted through my body. I found his other hand and linked our fingers as I continued, holding him secure in the moment while he rode the waves of his orgasm through to the end.

As his orgasm died off, I climbed up his body and found his mouth. I kissed him hard and deep, overwhelmed by what we'd shared and unable to express my gratitude that it'd been me he'd chosen to share it with. He hooked his hands around my neck and kept me in place, returning the same passion.

I was in agony, aching with need for release and dripping in my pajama pants. That was by far the most intense moment we'd shared, and I couldn't curb my body's response.

Oryn deftly slinked his hand down my pants and started jerking me as we kissed. His warm, sure touch alone zapped sparks throughout every cell in my body. I couldn't keep kissing and hovered above him as he worked my dick with more confidence than he'd ever displayed.

"Fuck that's good," I whispered through gritted teeth, basking in the growing tingle accumulating in my balls.

He stopped only briefly to lower my pants before continuing. I braced myself above him on trembling arms as the sought-after rush of sensation snuck up on me. Before I knew it, I cried his name and spilled between us, coating his chest with a steady pulsing stream of cum.

As I caught my breath, he slowed and eventually removed his hand.

There was a pause as we peered into each other's sated eyes. He broke the moment first as he glanced between us to where I'd spilled. With a finger, he traced through the mess and brought it between us, considering it as he bit his lip. I thought he wanted to taste me, wanted to nudge himself closer to returning the favor one day, but seemed steadily unsure.

"Do you trust me?" I whispered.

His gaze shifted to me and he nodded without thought. There was no longer doubt.

I took his coated finger and licked it clean. Then, I lowered my face and kissed him deeply, sharing what he'd been too hesitant to try. He didn't resist and lapped at my tongue eagerly, taking all there was to take.

Oh how far we'd gone in a year.

When the kiss naturally ended, I retreated to the washroom to find a warm cloth to clean us up. We lay side by side in the dark, wrapped in each other for a long while without speaking.

"Vaughn?" Oryn whispered some time later.

"Yeah."

"Soon, okay?"

He didn't need to say more for me to understand what he meant. I pulled his head to mine and kissed his forehead.

"No rush. When you're ready."

***

An incessant bouncing on the bed beside me pulled me from dream-land. Oryn and I had been up half the night drinking wine and watching old movies before moving to the bedroom and enjoying other Christmas Eve activities. We hadn't fallen asleep until long past three in the morning.

I cracked my eyes open to slits and squinted at the fuzzy clock on the bedside table in front of me. Without glasses, I could barely make out the numbers and shifted a fraction closer to the edge of the bed to be sure I'd seen it right.

Five thirty-three?

The bouncing continued, and I turned my head in confusion to find out what was going on. If it was Cohen's idea of a pre-dawn joke, I might just smother him with a pillow. The moment I turned over, his face bent until it was barely inches away from mine. He grinned ear to ear—wide and toothy.

Rain! It's Christmas morning, idiot, of course!

"Are you done sweepin', Vaughn-d? Daddy said don't wake you up, but Santa camed."

Daddy? Theo, right!

His voice was a failed attempt at a whisper, and the moment he finished speaking, he resumed bouncing on his knees. I yawned, and my eyes fell closed once again. My head was a ball of cotton and my mouth pasty and thick. Instantly, I regretted our late night and bottle of wine.

"It's kinda early, buddy. Why don't we sleep more."

His fingers pried open one of my eyelids and his exaggerated sad face almost made me laugh—despite my pounding head.

"But dares presents from Santa."

I knew any more rest would be a lost cause, so I rolled to my back and stretched, ensuring my lower body stayed covered in blankets. When I finally opened my eyes, I noticed Rain was wearing a pair of flannel, Batman pajamas. Where on Earth he, or Theo, or whoever, managed to find something like that to fit an adult-sized body was beyond me. It made me chuckle.

"Cool PJs, buddy."

He grinned and dropped his chin to his chest to admire himself. He fisted the shirt and tugged it out to show me. "I'm Batman."

"I love it. Listen, Batman, go hop on the couch and I'll be there in a minute. But don't touch anything before I get there, got it?"

"Yay!"

Rain rolled off the bed and flew down the hall before I could blink. From the den, he sang *Jingle Bells* over and over again as I searched around for the pajama bottoms I'd lost the previous night. It was one thing to be nude around Oryn, or any of the other alters, but Rain was five and my nakedness was incredibly inappropriate.

Once I'd used the washroom and popped a few pain killers for my mild headache, I wandered down to the kitchen.

"I'm gonna make coffee first," I called to him. "Go ahead and grab your stocking, I bet Santa filled that with all kinds of stuff."

After I set the pot to brew and found a mug, I also searched up some orange juice and a small glass from the cupboard for Rain. I chuckled, remembering a time not that long ago when I'd instinctively made him coffee one Saturday morning as we shared a cartoon day and was informed that coffee was 'blecky'.

With a morning drink for us both, I went and found him in the den. He'd already torn through the few stocking items Cohen and I had picked out and was lying on the floor racing a few dinky cars around the tree. Chocolate wrappers were scattered about and smears of the evidence were smudged across his cheeks.

The moment he saw me, he sat up and held his cars to show me. "Vaughn-d look! A Batmobile!"

"Holy crap, buddy. It's like Santa knows you or something."

He nodded with enthusiasm and brought them to the coffee table to drive.

I enjoyed a few mouthfuls of coffee as I watched him. Would there ever come a day when seeing Rain—stuck in a grown-up Oryn's body—wouldn't be accompanied with an underlying sadness? It was one of the more profound reminders I witnessed that showed Oryn's unjust childhood. It wasn't always easy being around Rain and knowing how to act or what to do, but with every day we shared, that uncertainty lessened. Only a few people could possibly understand the dynamic of mine and Oryn's relationship. Mostly, they were other couples whose situations were similar. Some days, I wasn't even sure my parents or Evan could ever properly appreciate it, as much as they tried.

I set my coffee down and shifted to the floor to join him. "Wanna open presents?"

"Yeah!"

Rain clapped his hands and abandoned his cars as he spun to the tree, zeroing in on the biggest box. We hadn't bought many, but enough so Rain would have the Christmas experience he deserved.

We spent the following twenty-minutes opening gifts. Lego Batman playset, Batman coloring book and new crayons, Batman and Joker figurines, and a new Batman fleece throw for his bed.

I gave all the credit to Santa, and beamed as I watched that magical Christmas moment shine in Rain's eyes.

He hugged the Batman Lego to his chest. "I love dis. Can we build it?"

"We sure can, but food first before you eat so much chocolate you spoil your appetite. Then we can play all day. Promise."

While Rain entertained himself with his new gifts—and snuck more chocolate—I searched us up some breakfast. Deciding on scrambled eggs, bacon, and toast, I set to work. I'd found *The Grinch* playing on one of the children's stations on the television and left it running in the background while I was busy. The sounds of Who-voices drifted into the kitchen, along with Rain's elated joy as he pretend-played Batman.

As I plated our food, I kept in mind that Rain didn't like anything touching. He was much pickier than the rest of the alters—much to Theo's disappointment—and often needed encouragement to sit still, eat, and try new things. Oryn and I often ate in the living room, but with Rain, that would only be a disaster.

"Food's on the table, Batman, come eat."

He zoomed into the kitchen and plopped in a chair without argument. It only took a small amount of bribery for him to clear his plate. Promises of more Christmas chocolates and candy canes did the trick.

By the time I cleaned up, Rain had his new Lego set upended all over the floor of the den. Staring down at all the pieces, I was glad for my second cup of coffee and sipped it, seeking the courage and strength to accomplish that daunting Lego task. Then, I joined him on the floor.

It took less than five minutes for me to realize the kit I'd chosen was way over Rain's head. The age recommendation on the box stated ten to sixteen. But it had been the only Batmobile kit that was available.

I kept him engaged, having him sort through and find certain pieces while I worked to follow the instructions and build it for him. I hadn't engaged in anything so complex in many years. Since when was Lego hard? I studied the instructions and fought my way through each step.

Hours later, it was finally done. Rain had long ago given up helping and had curled up on the couch with his new blanket and coloring books. When I peered over my shoulder, he was fast asleep with crayons still clutched in his grasp.

I peeled them from his hand and covered him properly before cleaning up the living room of all the boxes and wrapping paper that had been thrown about.

It was mid-afternoon, my headache had returned, and I was tired. I collapsed in the chair, intent on putting my feet up for a while, when he stirred on the couch and peeked out from his cocoon of blankets.

Only, I recognized the confused look being returned to me as Oryn's. He palmed his temple and scrunched his face as he sat up and scanned the room. If he wasn't co-conscious with his alters, there was always an initial element of confusion that followed when he returned forward. The time gap and orientation messed with him a lot.

He knew and understood Rain had planned to front Christmas morning, but that passage of time was lost on him.

"How'd it go?" he asked as he touched his face and fixed his messy hair.

"He was over the moon. Wore himself out."

Oryn turned back to me and grinned. "Looks like he wore you out."

I pushed myself out of the chair with effort and yawned. "He had me out of bed at five am. I'm going to take a nap."

Oryn bounced off the couch and caught up with me as I wandered down the hall to the bed room.

"A nap? I can make coffee."

I turned and took his face in my hands, kissed him once, and pulled back. "How's your head?" I asked, seeing the mild pain registering on his face.

He flinched. "I have a small switchy headache, but it's no big deal. Why?"

"Because I've had a whooping hangover all day. Someone had me up all night drinking wine, which I'm now convinced was a cruel joke." I brushed a finger over his nose and smiled. "Then, I was up before the birds, barely got two cups of coffee, and spent the last two hours building Lego Batmobiles that I swear are way harder than they look. I'm exhausted."

With one last kiss, I continued my trek to the bedroom.

"Oh," I added, smirking over my shoulder and trailing my gaze over his body. "Cute jammies by the way."

He looked down at himself and his cheeks flamed crimson.

I flopped on the bed and folded myself in the blankets, too tired to even care that I hadn't landed on a pillow. My eyes closed immediately and didn't open when the bed dipped beside me.

"Do you want me to clean up the Christmas stuff? Put it away and make the living room a living room again?"

I reached blindly for his hand. We both understood, keeping out the Christmas decorations meant Rain would probably randomly be present a lot more than usual. Oryn had shared that was another reason he didn't decorate for the season.

"Nah, leave it a day or two. The poor kid fell asleep before I finished his Lego. Let him have his Christmas."

Oryn chuckled and squeezed my hand. "Okay."

"And let me have my nap."

Chapter Twenty-Nine

"Ev, I gotta let you go, I just pulled in the driveway."

"Good luck, man, let me know how it goes."

I fixed my hair in the rear-view mirror for the millionth time and fidgeted with my tie, pulling it loose from its stranglehold around my neck. A bead of sweat rolled down my temple. Even though the April weather was cool and comfortable, my internal temperature was blazing.

"Fuck, I'm freaking out, Ev."

"Don't! You have no reason. Try to enjoy yourself. Send my best to Oryn and tell him I expect a piece of Theo's cake kept aside for me. Extra icing. Do not fucking jip me."

I blew out a breath and glanced to the front window of the townhouse Oryn and I had been sharing since January.

"Okay. I'll keep you posted."

We said our goodbyes and I pocketed my phone as I made my way to the house. It was Oryn's thirtieth birthday, and I'd planned a special evening out for us which included dinner at our favorite restaurant and a walk along the waterfront afterward. We'd decided not to go away that year. I was still fairly new at my job and Oryn had signed up for the spring and summer semester immediately when his other classes had ended.

He and Cohen were determined to get as much under their belt as possible, with a degree in English as their goal. Combined, they hoped to eventually be able to work a real job in the future.

Since Cove and Oryn had found their balance, Oryn's life had become a lot more controlled. He worked with his system and distributed their time equally so no one felt left out. Not only was it less chaotic for him, but for me as well. It didn't mean there weren't surprises on occasion, and spontaneous, unpredictable switches, but they happened with a lot less frequency. His therapist was astounded at the progress he'd made.

I let myself in and kicked off my shoes.

"Hello?" I called.

It was Thursday evening. Although Oryn and I had made plans, it didn't necessarily mean Oryn was the one around at the moment, and I'd learned to expect Theo on occasion when I arrived home.

That day, it was Oryn who flew around the corner with a wide grin plastered to his face.

"Hey! Guess what?" he squealed.

I snagged the front of his shirt and pulled him to me for a quick kiss. "It's your birthday?"

He chuckled and swatted me. "Not that. Come here. I have something to show you."

He dragged me into the den and directly to his laptop where it sat open on the desk in the corner. From beside it, he picked up a thick book and placed it in my hands, nearly bouncing with his excitement.

"It came. Look at it!"

It was his book. Complete and lying in my hands. I knew he'd finished and had had it edited multiple times by a few companies. It was the proof he'd ordered himself before he officially planned to launch it to the world. It was the first I'd been allowed to see it.

Pieces of Me, by Oryn Patterson

There was a picture of a young man on the front that had been given the effect of being broken apart into a puzzle. A few random pieces were not in place and were scattered about, but you could tell they all matched up.

"This copy is for you. I'm not hitting publish until you've read it."

"Wow, so this is it." I was honored, nervous, and excited all at once. Oryn glowed with pride. He'd kept the whole thing a secret and never once let me in on the process.

I thumbed through and paused at the dedication page.

For Vaughn, who never hesitated to love me whole.

I glanced to Oryn and blinked back the tears that prickled the backs of my eyes.

"You're gonna kill me with this, aren't you?"

"Reed wanted me to tell you, this is the only research you'll ever need. So stop with the textbooks."

I chuckled and drew him in for another kiss.

"I'm diving in tonight. I can't wait to read it. I'm so proud of you."

I continued to flip a few pages in awe. The beginning chapters were divided up based on how Oryn had discovered his condition, and the multiple steps he'd gone through to finally get properly diagnosed. It also included the challenges he'd faced being accepted in society.

The last half of the book was dedicated to each individual alter. It spoke of their inner world and the unique way they balanced life. The four men and one child, who I'd come to know well over the past year and a half we'd been together. Each held a special place in my heart separate from Oryn. There had been times when I'd fought with rejection, loneliness, resentment, frustration, and a plethora of other emotions as I'd adjusted to loving someone with DID. It was not always pretty, and the rollercoaster I rode daily was not for everyone. I was a lover, a partner, a comrade, a playmate, a support system, a threat, and even a nuisance some days, but we made it work.

I was blessed to have a man like Oryn in my life.

He kissed my cheek once more and turned to tidy his work station.

"I'm ready to go when you are."

Tearing my eyes from the book, I only then realized he was dressed in a dark pair of jeans and a grey sweater. His hair was perfect, and his stubbled jaw was nicely trimmed.

"I'm gonna hop in a shower. Give me twenty minutes," I said. "Don't forget my dad wants one of these too." I waved the book in his face before heading to our bedroom to find clothes.

"I have him on my list. You first. I need feedback."

***

The restaurant was small and intimate. The perfect location for Oryn's birthday. It offered an array of home-style meals from traditional Italian to American, Greek, Mexican, and Indian. I kept it simple and ordered a roast beef dinner with mashed potatoes and carrots, while Oryn went with chicken enchiladas.

Because it was his birthday, we also celebrated with a couple of glasses of their house wine.

"Oh," I said as I scraped up the last mouthful of food from my plate. "Evan sends birthday wishes and says save him cake."

Oryn smiled and shook his head. "Theo already has a container labeled with his name on it in the fridge. Extra icing."

"Figures."

Theo had everyone's likes and needs when it came to food down to a science—even Evan's.

After dinner, we drove down to the water for a stroll. I parked in our usual spot and grabbed a light jacket from the backseat. The sun had set, and the April air was cool and breezy.

We walked in silence for a long time, hand in hand, enjoying the sights and sounds. The moment we arrived at the harbor, my heart was back to thrashing in my chest as it had been doing on my way home from work and for half the day. I was surprised Oryn hadn't commented on my sweaty palms and jumpy nerves.

As we rounded the path and were deciding whether to head into the forested area to continue, I pressed Oryn against the railing.

He chuckled and peered at me in question. "Why are we stopping?"

To give myself a moment to compose, I kissed him long and deep, brushing our tongues together and reveling in his taste and the feel of his warm body against mine.

In the beginning, I could never have moved in on him so abruptly, but time had worked wonders. Oryn's trust was solid, and he no longer startled as easily.

"Because it's your birthday, and I have something for you."

He smiled shyly and rubbed his hands down my arms. "You didn't have to get me anything. I don't actually want to be thirty, so I'd have been happy if we just pretended it didn't happen."

I chuckled and brushed a thumb along his bottom lip. "Too bad. Getting old sucks, but we all have to do it."

I shoved my other hand in my pocket and clung to the item I'd had stowed away all evening. With my other hand, I cupped his cheek and brought my forehead to his.

"You know I love you, Oryn. Since the day I met you, I was drawn in by the unique person you are. The more I got to know you, the more amazing you became. I am in awe of the man you are and feel profoundly grateful to be part of your life. We've come so far, and I only want to keep going."

His eyes glistened and he dashed a look about before returning his gaze to my face. Worry painted his brow, and I lifted my face to kiss it away.

I pulled the small box from my pocket and folded it in his hand. He didn't move, and his eyes never left mine.

"It was really hard to know how to do this and not leave anyone out, so Theo, Reed, and Cove already know what's in this box, and I can only hope Cohen is close enough to hear what I'm about to ask."

I stroked a single finger over his temple, wishing I could draw Cohen to the front if he wasn't there already.

Oryn's Adam's apple bobbed, and a single tear escaped and tracked down his cheek. I caught it with my thumb and brushed it aside.

"I want to spend the rest of my life with you," I whispered. "All of you. Will you marry me?"

His lips parted, and another tear unleashed as he dropped his gaze to the box I'd placed in his hand. Wordlessly, he opened it.

Choosing the perfect band had been a challenge. I knew what I wanted in my mind, but hadn't been successful in finding the perfect match. So, I'd had it specially designed. A unique ring for my unique man.

I'd chosen white gold—since Cove preferred wearing a lot of stainless steel jewelry. I figured it would match and cause him less anxiety. When we'd discussed it, he'd appreciated the gesture.

Imbedded in the band were seven small diamonds. The cut of the one in the middle was slightly different then the others. It was intended that way.

"Each diamond represents someone. I'm the different one in the middle. Beside me are you and Cohen, because the three of us are the most intimately connected. After, are Reed and Cove because the bonding friendships we have are distinctly powerful. Then, Theo and Rain. Father and son. The two elements that make us a family. All together, we are complete."

Oryn remained quiet as his tears silently fell. He turned the ring around in his fingers and brushed over the diamonds. At one point his hand went to the side of his head and he chuckled through a sniffle.

"What's going on?"

"Cohen is going crazy. He's so excited right now."

I smiled and kissed his head again, directly over the place he'd touched, trying to connect with Cohen on a different level. "And what do you guys think?"

Oryn met my eyes and brushed away more tears before nodding. "Yes. From both of us, yes."

My heart swelled, and I took the ring and worked it on his finger. Then I kissed him soundly, the nervous shake I'd been carrying still quaking through my body. The warmth of our happiness dispelled the cold air surrounding us.

"I hope this works as an adequate birthday present. You never did tell me what you wanted."

Oryn examined the ring on his finger with a contented smile before looking up. "This is perfect. I didn't tell you, because I wanted to surprise you."

I quirked a brow. "Aren't I supposed to be the one surprising you? It's your birthday."

He held up his hand, wiggling the ring. "You did. I didn't see this coming."

"But…" I prompted.

He looked around and across the water before shrugging with a mischievous smile. "Let's go home."

"Oryn…"

He snagged my hand and dragged me back toward the car without a word.

Even as we removed our shoes, his curious smile hadn't dissipated. Its intensity had grown, along with my suspicions.

Before he could walk away, I grabbed his hand and pulled him against me. "Talk."

He studied my face, and a hint of nerves replaced the smile. He opened his mouth to speak, but closed it again when no words followed. Licking at his lips, he tried again. "Umm… I…"

He cut his gaze to the ground and bit his lip at another failed attempt. I caught his chin and pulled his face back up. I had a pretty good idea what he couldn't voice, but needed to see his face to be sure.

"What do you want, Oryn?"

He took in a shuddering breath. "All of it. I'm… I'm ready, Vaughn. That's what I want for my birthday."

I could hardly remember how to breathe in that moment. The air had been knocked from my lungs and my heart raced. Since the day I'd understood Oryn's struggles, I'd taken all he could give and never expected or pushed for more. There were a million other ways to express love, and I'd spent a year and a half showing him. The idea almost felt surreal.

"Are you sure?"

Oryn came forward and brushed his lips to mine. "More than sure."

He took my hand and guided me down the hall to the bedroom. Once inside, he turned to face me, eyes roaming my body. I could see his wheels turning and wondered how close everyone was and how elevated his nerves were. Stepping forward, he took hold of the hem on my shirt and slowly drew it over my head. When it hit the floor, I copied the action, discarding his sweater with mine.

His hands roamed my chest, as though exploring for the first time. A look of awe and contentment settled on his face. He seemed calm.

Exploring his body, I traced my hands up his arms, letting my fingers skid over the lines of words he'd had tattooed over his scars in February. A reminder for both Oryn and Cove that being united worked better than being at odds.

Together we are strong. Together we will survive, was written in cursive script over one arm. While, *I won't fade into darkness. I will be heard,* covered the other. Not once had Cove felt the need to hurt the body since July. Nine months without incident. Nine months of a new-found peace in Oryn's system.

And that night, Oryn had decided himself prepared and trusting enough to take that final step together.

I had questions I wasn't sure he'd considered. As he unbuttoned my pants and slid them over my hips, I brushed my lips along his neck to his ear. I expected with such a huge step that he'd want full control—but he'd proven me wrong in the past.

"Do you want me to bottom?" I whispered. I was comfortable either way and had never had issues flipping in the past.

A barely perceptible shake of his head followed. *No?* I lifted my face as his hands roamed across my back, slipping over my backside and grazing the roundness of my ass.

"No?" I asked, confirming.

"Cohen said you were gentle, I can't… I don't…I don't really know what I'm doing, I trust you, Vaughn. I feel safe with you."

"You are safe with me," I assured him. "Always."

Our lips came together, and we kissed, wet, sloppy, tongue-knotting kisses as we rid ourselves of the rest of our clothes. I backed him to the bed, and we fell together, never parting, doing all we could to be closer.

The profoundness of what we were about to do had me trembling with nerves. I'd never believed it possible, even when hope was dangled in front of us months back. His skin was warm and smooth under my wandering hands, and I couldn't stop touching him. The kindled fire we shared smoldered to life and burned with intensity.

He lifted his hips and ground his stiff length to mine. His new comfort level was astounding. The contact buzzed through me, my skin prickled alive with the sensation.

Our shared kisses turned hungry and desperate in no time. Our glide together intensified. Warmth slid through my veins. Oryn broke our kiss and stared up with swollen lips, his need radiating from behind blue-grey irises.

"Please, Vaughn."

Heart thrashing, I located a few supplies and watched him close as I coated a few fingers with lube. There were places we hadn't explored, and where I was headed was one of them. I kept our foreheads together as I drew his legs up and delicately smoothed a finger toward its destination.

There was more lust than fear, but I wanted reassurance I wasn't going too far. Oryn may have been determined, but it had backfired in the past, and I wanted to be sure he stayed with me.

As I ran a lube-slickened finger over his entrance, his lips parted, but he didn't take his eyes off me. Slowly, as I pressed a single digit inside his warmth, I spoke assurances and calm words.

Because he tensed at the initial intrusion, I took more time. When he adjusted, I worked in another as I claimed his mouth.

Over time, he relaxed and accepted my fingers with ease, moaning when I purposefully hit his prostate a few times.

"Vaughn," he begged into my mouth.

He didn't need to explain, I knew he was ready. Suited, I pressed his legs up, and leaned over him to continue my invasion of his mouth. I'd never tire of tasting him and kissing him. When I slid my length over his hole, he pulled back and cupped my face in his hands. Studying him, bracing myself on an arm by his head, I took him all in.

"Are you ready," I asked, barely croaking out the words.

"Yes."

I rested my forehead to his, and with as much self-control as I could muster, I pressed inside. Fear was a permanent fixture in the back of my mind. I never knew how much he could handle and crossed each new line with extreme caution. The determination and desire remained in his eyes. When he needed a minute, I waited, but each inch more only escalated his lust.

When I was fully inside, we kissed again without moving. A surge of triumph seeped from my heart seeing how far Oryn had come.

The tight pull of him around me was intense. My body was on fire and needed to move. When he gave me the okay, I didn't hold back.

It was like nothing I'd ever known before. Sharing that connection with Oryn was every bit the definition of perfection and life changing.

From that moment on, we were one. Moving together and sharing in an intimacy we didn't know would ever be possible.

The build was slow, and as it grew and bloomed through my body, I never wanted it to end. Kissing became impossible as we neared that invisible ledge. Oryn may not have been openly vocal in bed, but his slight gasps and the way his eyes called to me, I knew he was close. His lower lip quivered with need in the most heart stopping way, and I nipped at it as I continued to thrust deep into his body.

I guided his hand between us, encouraging him to touch himself. It was a boundary he fought, something that made him extremely uncomfortable, but we'd slowly grown past those uncertainties over time. As I picked up my speed, rocking into him and angling myself so I'd hit that sweet spot with every motion, he didn't hold back. His eyes fluttered closed as he allowed the wave to pour over him. When he gasped, and his head fell back on the bed, warmth spilled between us. At the same moment, his ass clamped around me. I was almost knocked over the edge as well.

Within a few short thrusts, I was there. I held him securely in my arms and didn't let go, keeping our bodies as close as was possible through all of it.

Our erratic breathing was the only sound for a long time as we came down. I ensured I removed myself soon after we'd finished, eliminating any post-sex fears that might arise. Ones that may have been dampened while the adrenaline was so high.

I cleaned us both up with a warm towel and pulled him against me, squeezing him to my chest.

"That was amazing," he whispered. The awe was thick in his voice.

"It was. I'm a little speechless."

"And out of breath still," he teased.

Chuckling, I kissed his head. "Yeah, yeah, we can't all be thirty."

Silence returned as we lay together in the dark. I'd never been more content in my life.

"Are we really getting married?" he asked.

I could feel his smile rise against my bare chest, and I rubbed a hand up his back and weaved my fingers through his hair.

"Yeah, we are."

"I love you, Vaughn. Thank you… for everything."

"I love you. All of you."

Epilogue

"Ma, leave it, for crying out loud, it's fine."

Nothing would dissuade her determined attempts at straightening my shirt, bowtie, cuffs, hair, anything she could possibly find to fiddle with.

"Do you really want to get married a wrinkled, crooked mess?"

I bit back my next argument, reminding myself if I could get through that day, Oryn and I would be on a plane to Tahiti by the following morning and out of reach of my mother for a good two weeks.

"Mom, leave him alone for God's sake. It's not even my wedding and you're making me crazy."

I passed my brother, Lucas, a look of thanks when my mother finally relented and focused her attention on the flower arrangement she would be carrying during the ceremony.

Oryn had selected combination bouquets for the small wedding party that consisted of gorgeous yellow roses and elegant lilies tied with bows of silky white, sculpted ribbons. Leave it to my mother to fuss over something that couldn't be more perfect.

As per Oryn's request, we'd dressed and readied ourselves separately with the intent of seeing each other for the first time when we both entered the church at the beginning of the ceremony. I'd left Oryn in Evan's and Krystina's care. My sister-in-law, Ally, was bouncing rooms and ensuring I had an update as needed. She'd been absent for almost a half an hour and I checked the time again, wondering where she was at. She'd been my only connection to Oryn since we'd parted ways that morning.

It was twenty to three and the ceremony was supposed to begin on the hour. I tried not to pace or obsessively check myself in the mirror. My mother would pick up on that and assume I needed fixing and start fussing again.

As I was about to ask Lucas to go find his wife, the door to the small room where we waited flew open and a frantic Evan, dressed to the nines in a black suit, burst through.

When his gaze found mine, my stomach turned over.

"Yeah, all this 'we can't see each other before the wedding bullshit' ends right now. You get your ass next door, because I don't know what switchy is, but according to Oryn, it's bad and he feels it."

Shit!

I'd feared the day's stress may overwhelm him. Somewhere deep inside, I'd anticipated it. My mother went pale and Lucas mouthed '*switchy?*' looking clearly confused.

I didn't hesitate and ignored my mother's calls as I followed Evan out the door and to the other side of the church and the room where Oryn had been getting ready.

When I entered, he was huddled in a corner with two hands pressed to the sides of his head and his eyes were squeezed closed. Krystina and Ally were awkwardly squatting beside him in their dresses, looking confused and uncomfortable.

"Ev, can you guys," I nicked my chin to the door, subtly asking them to leave.

He hopped forward and took the two women with him. With the commotion, Oryn opened his eyes and looked around in a panic.

When he caught sight of me in the doorway, he shook his head frantically. "No, we can't…" His hands went to his head again before he could finish his sentence.

I knelt in front of him, and forced his hands down, lifting his chin.

"Never mind the whole tradition thing. It's hocus pocus and means nothing. Talk to me. What's going on?"

He shook his head like he was trying to shake something off and pressed a knuckle in his eye.

"I'm all switchy. Everyone is… they are all here." He indicated to the space around his head in frustration.

"It's all chattery and nonstop," he tried to explain. "No one is listening."

"Oryn, look at me." He worked to focus on my face, but his distraction by all the voices was apparent. "We talked about this. If someone else has to come forward, it's okay. It won't change what happens here today, and you can still be a part of it."

He nodded, and rested his head against the wall at his back. "It's so distracting and chaotic. I'm sorry."

I knelt in front of him, knowing my mother would shoot me if she was in the room, and encouraged him into my arms. He sunk against my chest and closed his eyes. In the two and a half years we'd been together, I'd learned Oryn inside and out. The book he'd written about his life was a beautiful window into his world, and like Reed had said, I didn't need any other books to help me understand the man I was marrying. I only needed to listen and keep my eyes open.

"Is this too much today?" I asked into his ear as I stroked a hand over his back.

He nodded, knowing the truth between us worked best when sorting out complex moments. As far as Oryn had come, social situations were still extremely overwhelming. In our everyday life, going to work and venturing outside the home was mainly left up to Cohen. Oryn had taken comfort knowing he didn't need to struggle with that any longer. The ability to be co-conscious with most of his alters had changed his life.

Our wedding was something he'd been determined to do on his own. Through the entire planning process—even when our guest list grew in numbers—he'd wanted to be the one to hold my hands in front of everyone and share vows. The reality was, some things were still beyond his reach.

I kissed his temple and breathed in the skin tingling scent of his cologne.

"I know you won't be far. It's okay."

He pressed a palm into his eyes again. "I'm sorry," he mumbled.

I knew the moment Cohen slipped in. The way he leaned against me, the way he held himself, and even the way he breathed was different. All minute little clues I'd come to learn.

He remained in my arms and enjoyed the embrace for a long time. A small rap on the door drew us apart and Evan poked his head in.

"You two have five minutes. Everything okay?"

"Yeah," I assured him, waving for him to leave.

The door clicked as it closed, and I turned back to Cohen. He was scanning me with a smirk.

"You look really good," he said, reaching out to adjust my bowtie. It had been knocked askew during our hug.

"You look pretty good yourself."

He smoothed a hand down his cummerbund and started buttoning his jacket. "I still say the rose accents would have been better. I don't hate navy, but come on, pink would have been hot."

I offered him a hand and he stood, fixing the rest of his suit in place before meeting my gaze.

"Are you disappointed?" he asked.

"No." I didn't hesitate.

For months I'd been torn over who I wanted to stand before me as we took that leap into married life. Oryn owned every piece of my heart, but Cohen and I had something special on its own. In the end, it didn't matter. At the end of the day, I was marrying the whole Oryn package. I was saying I do to spending my life with him and the five alters who shared his world. It meant accepting the complexities, the unconventional ways we did things, and the random moments that were unpredictable—like the one in front of me.

I took his chin and kissed his lips softly. "I love you whole. Who stands beside me today makes no difference."

The ceremony began shortly thereafter. My mother and father walked down the aisle, followed by Lucas and Ally, then Evan and Krystina. As had been Oryn's choosing, we were both to meet at the top of the aisle and walk down together as well, the only variation was, I met Cohen instead.

Upfront, the focus drew in on us and the love we shared and the joy that had brought us together. When asked to face each other and hold hands, I peered deep into the familiar blue-grey eyes across from me. Even if Oryn couldn't be forward, I knew he was there. I knew he was taking part the only way he could.

When vows were spoken, there was a rolling chuckle when Cohen promptly corrected the minister and insisted on saying "I, Cohen, take this man" and not using Oryn's name. I'd personalized my own to reflect the love I carried for not one person, but six, and ensured they were all included.

More words were spoken, and when the minister proclaimed, "you may now seal your marriage with a kiss", I took Cohen's face, with every intent of crushing my mouth to his, when I caught him glancing to the gathered guests all sitting in pews watching. A tiny ribbon of fret marred his forehead before he turned back. I paused, frozen in observation. A small smile curved my mouth.

"Oryn?" I whispered against his lips.

His nod was nearly imperceptible. But when his hands came up and clung a death grip to my sides, I almost laughed.

"Would you k-kiss me already before I pass out."

I didn't need any more encouragement. Stealing his next breath, I brought us together in an unbreakable bond. One that sealed our love for all of eternity. With that kiss we were whole. We were one. We were complete.

Just as we would be from that day forward.

THE END

Other Titles by Nicky James

Standalone Contemporary
Trusting Tanner

Twinkle Star

Love Me Whole

Healing Hearts Series
No Regrets (also available in audio)

New Beginnings: Abel's Journey

The Escape: Soren's Saga

Lost Soul: AJ's Burden

Historical
Until the End of Time

Co-Written
Once Upon a Prince: A New Age Fairy Tale

(Written with Jaclyn Osborn)

Tales from Edovia Series
Something from Nothing

Buried Truths

Secrets Best Untold

Printed in Great Britain
by Amazon